AS THE MOON WAS RISING . . .

"You're much too beautiful tonight, Phina." Whitley's voice was husky. "Much too tempting." He cupped her cheek with his palm and leaned very close to her. "Go while I'll allow it," he whispered.

Phina didn't want to go. Desire and expectation rippled down her back and settled in the pit of her stomach. She wouldn't let him send her away now.

Their eyes met. "You shouldn't be alone tonight," she said, not knowing where the words she spoke were coming from but knowing they felt right.

"How is a desperate man to take that statement, Phina?"

Now was the time to back down or go forward and leave regret behind. Desire for this man overpowered her modesty, her innocence, her duty.

"As an invitation."

Glory Nights

Charla Cameron

PINNACLE BOOKS
WINDSOR PUBLISHING CORP.

Prologue

"I didn't steal the horse, you dirty rotten bastard!" the boy shouted as the bearded man tightened the ropes which held the youngster's hands behind his back.

"Hanging'll shut your mouth for good, boy, but until then I think this'll do."

The man's fist connected with Whitley's jaw, shooting spirals of pain up Whitley's cheek, snapping his head backward and sending him flying to the ground. Whitley tried to catch himself with his palms, but the force of his weight landed on one hand and separated his arm from his shoulder. He cried out in pain as he dug the heels of his dusty boots into the sun-parched dirt, trying to lift himself off his arm.

Grabbed by the front of his shirt, Whitley waved his good arm wildly and cried out again when suddenly he was yanked upright and slapped across the face.

"That'll teach you to cuss me, boy," the stockily-built, bearded man said, rubbing his skinned knuckles. He turned to his partner who was throwing the hang-

5

man's noose over the limb of a white oak. "You got that ready, Potter?"

Whitley tried to focus on the man but one eye was swollen shut and vision in the other blurred. His bottom lip bled from the beating the two men had given him when they first saw him walking the horse toward town.

Whitley didn't want to cry. He didn't want to feel the unbearable pain in his shoulder and on his face. He didn't want to beg for his life, but he didn't want to die either.

The thinner man with rotted front teeth caught the rope and pulled it tight, before looking at his partner. "I'm not sure we're doing the right thing, Dozer." He took off his sweat-stained hat and scratched the back of his head as he glanced toward Whitley. "Mr. Stevens never told us the horse was stole."

"I 'spect Mr. Stevens will be glad we took care of this here problem for him." He spit a spew of brown juice out of his mouth, then wiped his lips with the back of his hand. "We'll tell him we caught the horse thief and hung him. He won't care."

Through his blurred vision Whitley watched the two men. He was trembling. He was scared. He hadn't stolen the damn horse. Over the years he'd swiped breeches and shirts, and he snatched food on a regular basis, but he'd never stolen a horse. What'd he need a horse for? He had no place to go.

Whitley's shoulder ached with burning pain as he listened to the two men. He tried to suppress the low moans that escaped his lips. He had to do something fast. These men meant to hang him without even talking to the sheriff. He shook his head, trying to clear his eyes but only succeeded in making his long brown hair fall in his face.

The man called Potter tested the rope again. Whitley's mouth felt dry and his tongue thick, but he had to try again. "I didn't steal the horse. I found him down by the pond." Even to his own ears his voice sounded weak, frail, and afraid. He couldn't seem to stop shaking.

"You're harping like an old woman, boy, and ain't nobody listening to you."

The moment of life and death had arrived, Whitley realized. He wasn't going to talk his way out of this one. These men would only laugh if he tried to use the "poor little boy" act that had saved his skin on a number of occasions. The trouble was he wasn't little anymore. He had awakened one morning to find that he was taller, fuller, older.

Whitley had a decision to make. He'd already tried to make them believe him. Now he could fight and force the men to beat him until he was senseless, then hang him, or he could remain quiet and die like a man. His heart raced at the thought of dying. He couldn't stop his lips from trembling. He'd told himself and others many times he was tough and wasn't afraid to die. But now that it was actually going to happen he was afraid. He didn't want to swing from the end of that rope.

Tears collected in his eyes. He tried to blink them away. Whitley didn't try to stop the men from helping him mount the horse they accused him of stealing. The pain in his shoulder intensified as his seat settled into the saddle. Heat from the sun burned the top of his hatless head. He felt the horse's warmth beneath him. Whitley clenched his eyes, his teeth, his hands.

7

The stockier man slung the noose around his neck and tightened it. The rope was heavy, rough against his bare skin, chafing it almost immediately. Every muscle in his body was taut, waiting for the jerk that would lift him out of the saddle to dangle from the tree.

"I didn't steal the damn horse," he mumbled when the man called Potter met his gaze.

"Well, son, you gonna hang for being caught with the horse in your possession."

His tone was so matter of fact, Whitley knew further words were useless. He cleared his mind of every thought except the one telling him the pain wouldn't last long. If he were lucky death would come quickly.

The sound of a rifle shot cracking through the air made Whitley flinch and the horse shifted beneath him. For a moment he stopped breathing, thinking he'd been hanged. He heard a man's loud voice and quickly opened his eyes. He wasn't dangling from the tree with his neck broken. Whitley felt faint. The roaring in his ears kept him from hearing what the stranger was saying to his two accusers. He couldn't pass out now. He'd fall out of the saddle and hang himself for sure. Taking deep breaths he calmed himself.

Whitley swallowed hard. The horse shifted beneath him again. He was confused. The stranger forced the men who beat him to get on their horses and ride away. His savior came closer, but the sun was too bright for Whitley to see him clearly. Maybe he wasn't a man. Maybe he was an angel. Whitley'd spent enough winter days hiding out in churches to hear preachers talk about angels appearing out of nowhere to aid believers. Whitley had never thought he was a believer—until now.

8

"I didn't steal the horse," he whispered as the rope was removed from his neck. "I didn't steal the horse," he mumbled again, hoping the tears that fell from his eyes wouldn't show on his face.

"It's all right, son. Calm down. Nobody's going to hang you today."

The angel sounded like a man. When Whitley focused he saw that the angel looked like a man. He cried out suddenly when the rope was removed from his hands and his dislocated arm fell limply to his side.

"Hellfire! They made one hell of a mess out of you, didn't they?"

With care the angel/man helped him off the horse and settled him on the dirt, then gave the horse a quick slap on the rump. Whitley was in so much pain he couldn't enjoy the relief of seeing that damning horse hightailing it for the two men who were now mere dots on the horizon.

"You got any reason to lie to me about stealing that horse?" the angel/man asked.

"No sir," Whitley said, shaking his head. "You gonna let those men hang me?" he asked, not quite ready to believe his tormenters were gone for good.

He knelt beside Whitley. "No. You won't see those jokers again. What's your name, son?"

"Whitley," he answered, wiping tears and strands of hair out of his eyes with his good arm.

"Where do you live?"

"All over. No place special."

"How old are you? Fourteen? Fifteen?"

Dazed from the beating and pain, Whitley thought about the question. "I—I don't know." The angel/man's dark brown eyes peered into Whitley's. He

9

didn't want him to think he was lying. "Nobody never told me."

"How long you been on your own?"

"Forever, I guess. I can't remember a time when I wasn't hiding in barns and stealing bread. I know my name is Whitley." He winced as a sharp pain stole up his arm and wrapped around his back.

"You seem like a brave lad to me."

"Yes sir," he answered, hoping the angel/man hadn't seen how frightened he was while sitting on that horse with the rope around his neck.

"They did a good job of beating you up. I hope you got in a few licks."

"Yes sir," he said again.

"You sure you don't have a ma or pa waiting at home for you?"

"I think I had a pa once. I ain't sure," Whitley said again, feeling faint from the pain, from the shock, from the relief.

The angel/man rubbed his clean-shaven chin and studied Whitley for what seemed like a long time. "You don't have a home, and I don't have a son. I'll make a deal with you, Whitley. If you swear to me you're not a horse thief, I'll take you with me and give you a home."

He was right. The man was an angel and he was going to take Whitley home with him. Relief choked in his throat and made his chest tight. Still a little afraid the man might change his mind, Whitley slowly shook his head and said, "I swear I ain't no horse thief."

"You can call me Anchor. We best get started, lad." He rose from his bent knee. "We won't make good time riding double. Those jokers might decide to come looking for us and we don't want to be found."

Anchor muttered something to himself and looked down at Whitley. "I'll teach you all there is to know about managing a plantation and a horde of slaves. If you prove yourself worthy, I'll see you have a home for the rest of your life."

Trembling, Whitley could only answer, "Yes sir."

"We better take care of that arm first."

Without further words Anchor placed a booted foot on Whitley's thigh, then reached down and firmly grabbed his bony wrist in one hand and elbow in the other, rotating the boy's arm as he lifted upward.

Whitley screamed.

Chapter One

Lower Georgia: 1842

It was his. All of it. Carillon Plantation with its sixty thousand acres, seventy-three slaves, and two sawmills. And the most beautiful young lady in the county was to be his bride.

Whitley stood on the platform he'd built for the musicians at the far end of the ballroom and looked out over the crowded room. Handsomely dressed men twirled splendidly gowned women around the brightly-lit room. Whitley felt a pride he'd never felt before. All the people before him were his friends. They'd all come to Carillon to enjoy his food and drink, dance, and to hear him announce his engagement to Flannery Matheson.

He'd kept his promise to Anchor. He'd done well with his book learning and had finished at the top of his class. He'd earned the respect of the slaves. He knew the plantation. Every inch of it. He knew how to manage it, how to make it work for him, how to respect it, and how to love it.

The music stopped and Whitley saw Flannery making her way to the front of the room, her mother and father by her side. Ellison, his overseer and best friend since arriving at Carillon fifteen years ago, made his way toward the platform, too.

Flannery smiled up at him as he moved to the center of the small stage, ready to make his announcement. As he waited for the guests to quieten, Whitley looked down at the golden-haired Flannery and smiled. No man had ever been as lucky. He was sure of that. Fifteen years ago he had nothing to call his own, not even his life. At this moment, he had everything he could want. The only thing that could have made the evening any better was if Anchor had been standing beside him.

The door knocker sounded but, thinking it was the arrival of a late guest, Whitley didn't let it stop him from beginning his speech. "Ladies and gentlemen, friends. Welcome. I'm pleased you could join me at Carillon tonight. It's truly a night for celebration."

Hearing loud voices coming from the front of the house, Whitley paused. It was unlike Lon to let a disturbance occur with guests in the house. He saw Spiker, his manservant heading toward the voices and, certain the two slaves could take care of the problem, Whitley continued.

After a quick smile to Flannery, he started again. "As most of you know, I have a special reason for asking all of you here tonight."

The voices grew louder. Instead of a late guest, Whitley decided someone in the crowd must have had too much to drink. "You all know I wanted Anchor to be here—"

"Get your hands off me!" a woman's disquieted

13

voice rang above him. "How dare you presume to touch me."

Whitley tensed. What in the hell was going on out there? He looked at Ellison and nodded for him to go and take care of the problem.

"I'll have the sheriff throw you in jail if you touch me again." The woman disrupting the party swept into the ballroom, stopping short of the crowd. Her long sable-colored hair fanned out behind her in a shimmering mass against her red cloak. Her honey-colored dress was a startling contrast to the wrinkled cape draping her shoulders, indicating she'd been traveling for an extended length of time. Even though she stood a far distance from him Whitley saw that the young woman was lovely. Her round expressive eyes were as dark as her hair. Defiance showed in the tilt of her chin and the lift to her shoulders. But behind her beauty and her aggression he saw something else, too. The young woman was frightened.

He had never seen her before. He was sure of that. In the past fifteen years he'd gotten to know everyone in Decatur county and most of the people in the surrounding counties.

The woman's gaze darted fearfully around the room, reminding Whitley of a deer caught in a bramble bush. "I want to see Anchor McCabe," she demanded in a breathlessly whispered voice.

The hushed crowd parted as the woman started forward. She'd obviously decided that since Whitley was the one on the dais, he was the one she needed to talk to.

Ellison flanked her on one side and Spiker the other as she continued to move down front.

"I'm sorry, Mr. Whitley," Lon said, shaking his

head where he stood at the end of the room. "She jest got louder when I tried ta keep her out."

"It's all right, Lon," he told the old man who'd been letting people in and out of the doors of Carillon for more than twenty-five years. He turned his attention back to the intruder.

"I want to see Anchor McCabe," she stated again, stronger this time.

"Who's asking to see him?" Whitley demanded, irritated that his engagement party had been interrupted by someone he didn't know. He was especially unhappy she was demanding to see Anchor.

The woman looked from Whitley to the two men guarding her. She lifted her chin and stated, "I'm his daughter. I've come to live with him."

A collective gasp echoed around the ballroom. Every eye in the room deserted the interloper and looked at Whitley. Stunned, Whitley simply stared at her for a moment, then denial sprang from within him. "You lie."

Whispers and murmuring spread among the startled guests. Whitley fought to get control of his emotions. He had to keep control of the crowd. And he had to get this woman out of the ballroom. Collecting himself, he said, "I'll be happy to speak with you, Miss—"

"Phina. My name is Phina." Her voice was softer this time but she hadn't lost that frightened expression from those deep brown eyes.

"Ellison, Spiker, show Phina to my office and give her refreshment. I'll join you momentarily."

Murmurings in the crowded ballroom grew louder. Whitley was taut with anger and, he realized, fear. He swallowed hard as he glanced at Flannery. She looked confused. He had to get to the bottom of this woman's

15

alarming claim, but first he had to take care of his guests.

"Ladies, gentlemen, if I could have your attention," he said, and waited a moment. When the crowd continued with their mutterings he repeated his statement again before the guests quieted enough to hear him. "There's no need to stop the party. Drink your champagne and dance." He turned to the musicians and in an irritated voice said, "Play. Loud." Ignoring the murmuring, he jumped off the stage and hurried to Flannery.

"Whitley, who is she? What does she want?" Flannery asked, her blue-eyed gaze darting between Whitley and her father.

He took her hands in his. The dark pink gown she wore emphasized the pink now splattered on her cheeks. "I don't know. I've never seen her before." He kissed her hand. "Don't worry. I'm sure this is some ploy to get money from me or a bed for the night." He looked at her father, the stalwart owner of The Pines, a wealthy plantation in its own right. "I'm sorry this happened."

"I suppose it's not unheard of to have this sort of thing happen. Have you had others like her show up?" the tall broad-shouldered man asked.

"No," Whitley answered emphatically. "There's no cause for alarm because there's no truth in what she claims," he said but inside he *was* alarmed. He was angry too. The music was loud, but no one was dancing. Everyone stood around in little groups talking, each giving their own interpretation of the events. Whitley fumed. How dare the black-haired woman spoil this special night.

16

"Whitley, you'll get rid of her, won't you?" Flannery asked, her blue eyes batting dark lashes at him.

He smiled at her and kissed her hand again. "Of course I will." He turned to her mother, a soft-looking woman, almost as beautiful as her daughter. "Mrs. Matheson, I know this is upsetting for both of you. Why don't you take Flannery to the table and get her something to drink? I'll have this taken care of before you know it, then be back to make our announcement."

"I'll go with you," George Matheson said, giving his glass of champagne to his wife.

Whitley held up his hand. "No. I'd rather handle this by myself. Just take care of Flannery." He lightly squeezed her hand and hurried away.

Several well-meaning guests tried to stop him on his way to his office to offer their advice but Whitley shunned them all. He wouldn't be sidetracked. He was hell-bent on getting to that young woman and finding out just what in the devil she thought she meant by her bold-faced lie.

Whitley went out the back door and down the steps. The March night air was chilling but didn't cool his temper. He strode around to the side of the house and entered his office by the French doors off the flagstone patio. He could remember only one other time in his life that he'd had this feeling. That time he'd been sitting on a horse with a noose around his neck. There was no reason for him to feel so threatened now, but he did.

He burst through the doors, opening them with a clamor and shutting them with a bang. His gaze immediately lighted on the pale woman standing in front of the fireplace. A scowl formed on his face. He stood,

17

legs apart, ready to do battle. "Who the hell are you and what do you want?"

She flinched from his brusque manner, but tried to calm herself by untying the ribbons at her throat that held her cloak on her shoulders. "I told you. My name is Phina and I'm Anchor McCabe's daughter."

Whitley scoffed and looked around the room. Spiker stood in front of the flat-topped Louis XIV desk. Ellison leaned against it in a lazy fashion, looking bored with the whole situation. The two men were wise not to speak.

Phina laid her cape over her arm and stared at Whitley. She was young, he thought. Not yet twenty he was sure. She was slight of build, yet her manner and carriage spoke of good breeding. Her skin tone was naturally pale, a stunning complement to her dark hair and eyes. But what respectable woman wore her hair spread seductively over her shoulders in public? As he looked her over he calmed. Why was he letting this wisp of a girl put him in such a temper? No one had a right to Carillon save himself. Why had he reacted to her threat? He should have simply dismissed her outright as a fortune hunter. It probably pleased her to see that she'd struck a nerve with him.

"Your little plan won't work. Anchor doesn't have a daughter and never has." He kept his cold gaze trained on her face.

Undaunted by his show of outrage, she took a step toward him. "What you say means nothing to me. I didn't come all this way to speak to you. I know this is Anchor McCabe's house. I insist you tell him I'm here."

If he wasn't so angry Whitley would be amused by her assertiveness. Only her eyes gave away the fact that

18

she was frightened. "You are in no position to insist on anything. Now tell me who you are."

"I told you. My name is Phina." She held her ground. "I came all the way from New Orleans to see Anchor, not you."

Relaxing a bit, Whitley said, "You have to settle for me."

"No, I don't," she said firmly, taking another step toward him. "I have proof I'm his daughter. I demand you tell me where he is so I may speak to him."

Her words sent a chill up Whitley's spine. She seemed so sure of herself. No. She couldn't be Anchor's daughter.

"What proof do you have?" A menacing edge laced his voice.

"Do you think I'm going to tell the man who's keeping me from my father?" She leaned forward and jerked her hands to her waist. "Tell me where he is."

Whitley walked toward her and didn't stop until their noses were almost touching. "Anchor is dead," he said tightly. "He died suddenly just over three months ago."

Her dark eyes rounded as did her full lips. "No!" Phina whispered. "It can't be. I've come too far. I had so many things to say to him—so many things to ask him." She looked around the room, glancing at the two other men before letting her gaze settle on Whitley again. "You're lying to me. I know you are." Her voice was husky. "He can't be dead."

"He's not lying," Ellison said, walking over to the ornate side table. He took the top off a heavy crystal brandy decanter. "Anchor started having pains in his chest and arm early one morning. He was gone before lunch." He poured a small amount of brandy into a

19

glass and held it out for Whitley. When Whitley shook his head, Ellison added more liquor to the glass, then drank from it.

"Who are you?" she demanded of him.

"Ellison Hartly. I'm Whitley's best friend, or better known to some," he said a little sarcastically, "as the overseer of this grand plantation."

"And you," she asked, swinging around to face the well-dressed, muscular darkie. "Who are you?"

"Spiker, Miss Phina. I look after Mr. Whitley."

She turned and faced Whitley, but spoke to Spiker, "Is that because he can't look after himself?"

"No, Miss Phina, Mr. Whitley, he—"

"Spiker," Whitley said his name calmly. Nothing Spiker could say would erase the meaning of her words. He would only make it worse.

"And who are you?" she asked.

Whitley stiffened, surprised she didn't know who he was. "I'm Anchor's son and *only* heir. My name is Whitley."

A soft moan escaped Phina's lips. She had expected Anchor to have other children—sons and daughters, but she hadn't expected him to be dead. She might have been able to soften Anchor toward her and be given an allowance so she could take care of her mother, but now what could she do? Anchor's son would have no reason to be merciful to his father's bastard child.

A picture of her mother's pale face flashed across her mind. She remembered the long nights of endless coughing, labored breathing and high fevers. No she couldn't give up that easily. Anchor McCabe had wronged her mother nineteen years ago, and she never asked for one penny from him. Even though he was

20

dead, Phina couldn't give up her plans. Not when her mother needed medications and care. If it were just for herself she'd wouldn't even be here, but now that her mother was ill and couldn't work they needed help.

Phina took a deep breath, lifting her chin, her shoulders and her spirit. "I'm his daughter, and as his daughter I'm entitled to all the privileges that go with my parentage," she said with renewed strength. She dug into her drawstring purse and brought out two letters. "This is proof of what I say."

Whitley looked at Ellison before taking the yellowed paper from her hands. The first letter he read quickly. It was a man's writing, showing bold strokes of a pen. The contents stated that in the spring of 1824 while Anchor McCabe was visiting New Orleans he lodged in the Groutas house. Diana Groutas was a young woman at the time. Mr. McCabe spent many nights in Diana's bed. Eight months after he left she gave birth to a daughter she named Phina. The letter was signed by a doctor.

Without lifting his head Whitley opened the other letter and read. The writing was smaller, softer and not as legible, but told the same story and was signed by Diana Groutas.

"You have nothing here but paper," Whitley said thrusting the letters back to her. "Am I to believe this when Anchor never mentioned you or your mother?"

She took the letters and held them tightly in her hands. "He never knew about me. Mama knew he was a married man and she didn't want to upset his life. She didn't need his money because she had a generous allowance left to her after her parents death."

"So you want me to believe you've come to claim

21

what your mother didn't want—a part of Anchor's fortune. Spiker, send her on her way."

Spiker reached for her but she whirled away. "I've told you not to touch me," she reminded the slave. She looked at Whitley, her eyes sparkling with anger, determination, and desperation. "These letters speak the truth. Look at me. Mama says I have Anchor's dark hair and eyes and his features, too."

"Any of a thousand men could have given you those things," Whitley countered.

"I demand you take me seriously!" She moved closer to him. This time she was the one who brought their faces so close together they felt each other's breath.

"You can demand nothing. You have no legal claim to any of Anchor's estate."

"Whitley." Ellison took hold of his arm. "This obviously can't be settled tonight. Go back to your guests. You can take this up with the sheriff tomorrow. He'll settle this for you."

Lowering his gaze to the hand on his arm, Whitley agreed he was letting the conversation get too heated. He wasn't about to get into a shouting match with this woman. "Yes, of course you're right, Ellison." Whitley moved away from Phina and straightened his evening jacket. He could see by the redness in Ellison's eyes that he'd had too much to drink, yet he was the one who realized that Whitley was getting nowhere with Phina. But the thought of anyone other than himself laying claim to Carillon shook him to the core.

Whitley turned to his manservant. "Spiker, get one of the house girls to take Phina to a guest room upstairs and prepare her a tray."

"And water."

Whitley cut his eyes around to her.

"I've been traveling on a stagecoach for three days. I'd like a tub of water to wash."

"See to it," he said to Spiker.

"Yes sir." The Negro buck nodded to Phina, then left by the French doors.

Turning back to Phina, Whitley said, "I'll give you food, a bath and a bed for the night. But come tomorrow morning we visit the sheriff. Then I want you out of this house."

Chapter Two

The muscles in Whitley's neck tightened as he made his way back into the ballroom. Candlelight from the chandeliers threw sparkles and glimmers onto the gilt wood decorated room. The musicians still played heartily but no one danced. The guests had remained in their intimate little groups. Raised voices reduced to hushed whispers as Whitley strode into the room.

"Whitley, do tell us what is going on."

He clapped the planter on the shoulder and assured him, "Everything's taken care of," without slowing his pace.

"Everyone knows neither of Anchor's wives had a child," an older woman said as Whitley passed.

"You're right," he told her.

"Where did the girl come from?" another woman asked.

"New Orleans, I think," Whitley responded and kept walking.

"What did she say her name was?" a statesman asked when he came near.

"Phina, Senator—that's all I know."

"Is she Anchor's daughter, Whitley?"

"Whitley, a moment of your time."

"What did she have to say for herself?"

Bypassing all the well-meaning questions and comments as he waded his way through the ballroom, Whitley kept one purpose in mind. He wanted to find Flannery and reassure her he had everything under control.

At last he saw her by the patio doors surrounded by friends with worried-looking faces. She caught sight of him, pushed the girls aside and hurried toward him, her dark-pink gown swirling around her.

"Did you get rid of that dreadful girl?" she asked in a hopeful manner, her beautifully shaped lips forming a slight pout.

He shook his head. "Not yet. Flannery, I'm—afraid we're going to have to put off the announcement of our engagement." Her eyes widened and she gasped. "It's for the best," he soothed as her father came up beside her. He looked at George Matheson. "I'm sure you'll agree with me, sir, that the appearance of this woman has taken the focus off our reason for the party. With your approval I suggest we have another party in a month or two and announce our engagement at that time rather than compete with the show that has already transpired tonight."

"Well—ah—" Mr. Matheson stumbled over his words, clearly not knowing how to respond to Whitley's astonishing suggestion.

"I was going to suggest the same thing, Papa," Flannery offered, taking the heat off both men. "Perhaps we shouldn't have agreed to hold this party without a proper mourning time for Mr. McCabe even though he insisted we go ahead with the plans before he died. There's no way we'd get the attention we

25

deserve tonight if we went ahead and announced." She looked around the room. "Everyone is too busy talking about that woman who sashayed in here a few minutes ago interrupting the announcement and taking over the party. When news of our engagement is released I want the whole county talking about *us,* not some crazy woman's rantings."

"All right," George said, clamping his lips together solidly for a moment. "We'll wait."

"I think it will be best if you take Flannery home now."

George Matheson nodded. "I agree. I suppose we'll see you for Sunday dinner as usual?"

"I'll be there. Do you mind, sir, if Flannery and I have a few moments on the porch while you and Mrs. Matheson say your goodbyes?"

Flannery remained silent.

Mr. Matheson seemed to study the question a moment, then said, "All right. For a minute or two." He patted Flannery's arm. "Wait on the porch for us, dear, we'll be right out."

Whitley took hold of Flannery's elbow and ushered her out the front door into the crisp night air of early spring. The sky was sprinkled with twinkling stars and a half moon. Other couples, more interested in each other than Whitley's concerns, had found their way out onto the porch so Whitley led Flannery down the steps to the darkness of the front lawn.

"Whitley, I'm not happy you've taken me so far away from the house," she complained as they stopped beside a row of shrubbery.

"I'll have you back on the porch by the time your father arrives." He took her hands. "Is it wrong for me to want a minute alone with you?"

26

She tried to slip her hands out of his but Whitley wouldn't let go. Finally she accepted his hold on her and looked up at him. "No. But I'm not supposed to allow it. I have my reputation to worry about and so should you."

"I know," Whitley said on a whispered sigh that didn't hide his irritation. Sometimes he wanted to damn the rules of society and Flannery for obeying them.

"You have exactly one minute, then we must go back on the porch like Papa said."

"All right," he reluctantly agreed. "I wanted to tell you how sorry I am that things turned out the way they have tonight."

She smiled up at him and Whitley was struck once again by how beautiful she was with her blue eyes, blonde hair, and generous lips. What man wouldn't want to take her to bed and love her all night?

"No need to fret, Whitley," she said in an unconcerned voice. "A month or two in our marriage date won't matter. We'll have the rest of our lives together."

It mattered to him, he thought as he squeezed her hands and led her back to the porch. Since he'd proposed, he'd promised himself that he wouldn't go to another woman to satisfy his needs. That was three months ago when Flannery turned eighteen. She'd already insisted on a six-month engagement, indicating that a year would be better. Whitley knew he couldn't wait a year. They had considered postponing the formal announcement of the engagement when Anchor died, but Anchor didn't want it delayed so they'd continued with the plans.

He'd never met a young woman who stuck to the

rules as closely as Flannery. He'd courted her for over a year and in all that time he'd managed to get four kisses on her cheek and one on her lips. That one was allowed the night he asked her to marry him. And she'd made it clear no other would be allowed until they were officially engaged. A mere understanding wasn't enough to allow him liberties. Whitley wasn't happy that Flannery dictated to him when he could kiss her and when he couldn't, but he'd wanted a wife who was above reproach.

Whitley knew all the reasons he wanted Flannery for his wife and love didn't have anything to do with any of them. He wanted the most beautiful wife, the most sought after, the most prim and proper wife, the most dowered wife the South had to offer. Marrying the perfect lady and having sons was just one of the many ways he had intended to repay Anchor for all that he'd done for him.

Damn, it still hurt when he thought about Anchor, about what tonight was to have meant to both of them. Fifteen years ago Anchor had saved his life and given him the opportunity to be his heir and master of this vast plantation. Anchor had not only saved his life, he'd given him the very best of everything. That's why Whitley had to have the best possible woman for his wife. And dammit, if the best wives were cold unresponsive wives, then he'd accept it. He wouldn't settle for less than the best.

Whitley had gone from having nothing—to possessing it all. He'd never let anyone take Carillon from him. He owed Anchor that much.

* * *

Easing the door shut behind her, Phina leaned against it and breathed heavily. She closed her eyes for a few seconds and calmed herself. Only for her mother would she have put herself through what happened tonight. She cared nothing for the money of a man who she'd never known.

When she opened her eyes and looked around her, Phina was in the loveliest bedroom she'd ever seen. She pushed away from the door and walked around the room, aware of the woolen rug beneath her feet, touching the fine wood of the furniture, feeling the luxuriousness of the fabrics. The walls were painted a light shade of lavender and the draperies and bedcover were made from a floral print of dark and light pinks, shades of lavender, and a deep purple. The American field bed had an arched tester frame with a canopy made from a pink chiffon material that fell in soft folds to the floor. The lowboy and wardrobe had the same tapered legs as the bed with a rich mahogany coloring and patina.

Impressed by it all, Phina noticed the way the furniture was placed in the room, the way everything matched. All the furniture was built by the same maker. The richly-colored fabrics, prints and solids, matched and complemented each other, unlike the three small rooms she shared with her mother in the house where they lived and worked.

Anger and resentment welled up inside Phina. Blast Whitley! Anchor McCabe's son lived in this glorious house while she and her mother lived on the third floor of a small, drab boardinghouse, working into the night making dresses for the wealthy women of New Orleans. She was Anchor's daughter as surely as Whitley was his son, and she would prove it to the sheriff

29

tomorrow. Phina slipped her fingers under the neck-line of her dress and brought out the small silver bell that hung around her neck. She lightly caressed the warm metal. No one would force her to give up until she'd received her rightful inheritance.

She had to do this for her mother, she kept telling herself with every footstep. She didn't want any part of Carillon for herself but she had to make Whitley think she did. He'd never agree to give his father's former mistress one penny, but in time, he might be persuaded or forced to be generous to his father's daughter.

It had taken Phina several weeks to save up enough money to buy a stagecoach ticket and have a few coins left over in case she didn't find Carillon right away. She didn't know what she would do if she were not able to convince the sheriff that she was Anchor McCabe's daughter.

Phina walked over to the brocade-covered slipper chair and sat down to unlace her shoes. She couldn't allow anger to take control. She had to remain calm and controlled if she were going to best Whitley. In truth, she'd never minded her work too much. Sewing wasn't difficult or dirty work. At least she didn't have to clean up after strangers or empty chamber pots as her friend Irene had to do. Irene and her mother Sally cooked and cleaned for the boarders.

According to Phina's mother, Diana, they had been in good shape when her parents died, but through the years the money had been depleted. Five years ago when Phina was thirteen, Diana had to sell their house in town and find work to supplement their dwindling money. They had taken three rooms at the Elms Boardinghouse.

Diana made the dresses, then Phina added buttons,

bows, lace, ribbons or whatever finery was needed to complete the dress. Many had been the times she'd had to take off the trimming and start over because a fussy woman had changed her mind.

Sewing for the wealthy had some advantages. Phina had learned more about how to walk and talk correctly from the women who came in to be fitted for their dresses. Her mother saw to it that she had enough reading and writing to write down the ladies' measurements, special instructions, and dates they wanted their dresses finished. She discovered she enjoyed reading and working with numbers. And she'd never been more glad that she'd learned so much than when she was talking to refined Whitley McCabe.

She slipped her feet out of her shoes and wiggled her toes. It felt wonderful to be out of those over-the-ankle burdens. Shoes were fine for walking outside but inside the house, feet should be free. Rising from the chair she walked over to the window and looked out into the darkness. In the shadowed moonlight she saw Whitley talking to a blond-haired woman in a gorgeous pink gown. She was beautiful with her hair the color of a goddess. Phina had always wanted to have light-colored hair and eyes. But Phina took after her mother and father with hair as dark as midnight and eyes as brown as a roasted chestnut.

Her gaze drifted back to Whitley. He was probably a handsome man when he wasn't scowling, she thought. He was tall and lean, yet broad through the shoulders. He'd impressed her as a man with little patience. She saw none of the good qualities in him that her mother had praised Anchor for having.

Too jittery to watch the couple any longer, Phina turned away from the window and walked over to the dresser. She had to prepare herself for the arguments Whitley and the sheriff were sure to throw at her tomorrow. She pulled out the padded stool and sat down in front of the mirror. Her long black hair draped her shoulders like a cape. One by one she'd lost the four combs she was wearing when she left New Orleans three days ago. Her pale cheeks were flushed from an attack of nerves and her dress looked limp and wrinkled. She winced. No wonder Whitley didn't want to believe anything she had to say. He was probably appalled she'd entered his house looking so disreputable, so unpresentable with her thick hair spilling over her shoulders and down her back.

Without thinking she opened the top drawer to the dresser, hoping to find some combs, ribbons or pins to tie her hair. Surely someone must have left a hairpin or two behind. But to her dismay all the drawers were empty. She had to find some pins. No respectable woman went around in public with her hair down. She made a fist with her hand and brought it down hard on the dresser, rattling the top on a powder jar.

The bedroom door opened and Phina jumped. An older darkie girl walked in carrying a tray covered with a large white cloth. Phina was embarrassed by her little display of temper and hoped the girl hadn't heard her hit the dresser.

"I was tole ta bring dis up ta ya. If it ain't enough, I's get ya some mo'."

Phina noticed the proud way the girl carried herself. She wasn't slothful and although her words weren't pronounced correctly Phina understood her. She had an air of self-confidence Phina wished she felt right now. The girl wasn't very tall, and she guessed her age to be about thirteen or fourteen.

32

Like the darkie Whitley had called Spiker, the girl was clean and her clothes well cared for. Her hair was covered with a black scarf. Most of the Negroes she'd seen on the streets in New Orleans were dirty, their clothes ragged and their speech unintelligible. Whitley obviously took very good care of his slaves. That gave her hope that he was a decent man at heart and would in time do what was right by her and her mother.

"Thank you," Phina said softly and walked over to the lowboy where the girl set the tray. Her mouth watered as the smells of the food reached her. She'd left New Orleans with four dresses and two loaves of bread. She didn't know if it was the thought of real food or what she had facing her tomorrow that made her stomach muscles tighten.

The girl slid a tapestry-covered side chair over to the chest, then looked at Phina with expressive black eyes. "Sits here and eats yore dinah. I'm Tasma. Mr. Whitley said he wants me ta look after you tonight."

"Thank you," Phina said again, in a stronger voice this time. "But I can take care of myself." She had since they sold their house and let their housekeeper go. Irene and her mother were too busy running the boardinghouse to fetch and carry for Phina and Diana.

The plate was heaped with boiled potatoes, chunks of beef, greens and a large chunk of bread. In separate small bowls there were spoonfuls of butter, spiced apples, and two tea cakes. It was a feast. Phina wiped her lips with her tongue. Well, she wasn't going to let one mouthful go to waste. She'd eat it all. She might never see this much food on a single tray again. She sat down and picked up the three-pronged fork and speared the smallest potato, putting the whole thing into her

33

mouth. It was delicious. Next she cut off a large piece of the meat. While she was eating she noticed that Tasma picked up her satchel and laid it on the bed.

"Dis all you brought?"

"Yes," Phina answered, wiping her mouth with the napkin. "But you don't have to worry about that. I can unpack later. It won't take long."

"Unpacking dis is my job."

"No, really I can do it. I'm not used to anyone doing things for me," Phina argued as she dipped her fork into the apples.

Tasma waved a hand at Phina. "You finish yore dinah, Miss Pennie. I gots to do what Mr. Whitley tells me ta do."

Phina looked down at her plate and realized there was no way she could eat all the food. Anger surged inside her again, sapping her appetite. How could she eat so much when she knew her mother would have only skimpy meals that were prepared at the boarding-house and carried to her room by Irene? Silently she renewed her vow to obtain an allowance so she could buy her mother's medicine and provide a better life for them.

She laid her fork aside and took a deep breath. "Tell me, does Whitley have any brothers or sisters?" Phina asked, thinking there might be someone in the family easier to deal with than Whitley.

"No, he all Mr. Anchor had. Been here since befo' I's born."

If she wasn't so tired Phina might have laughed. It wasn't hard to figure out that Whitley was at least fifteen years older than Tasma and had surely been born before her. Well, at least she didn't have to worry about convincing any other brothers or sisters to accept her claim.

"Finish yore dinah. I gots hot water and a tub coming up so yous can wash. Den, I'm gone tuck you in de bed."

Phina twisted her lips into a pucker. She hadn't been tucked in bed for years. It was silly to have someone do these things for her when she was fully capable. "I'm not a child. I'm almost nineteen years old. I can see to myself."

"Not as long as I's here, Miss Pennie. Now finish yore meal afore it gets cold."

Looking into the trusting dark eyes of the pleasant girl, Phina knew she would have to allow Tasma to do her work. Besides, she was too tired to argue any longer about it. In fact, she wanted nothing more than to have her bath and lay down on the bed. Three days on the stage had left a crick in her neck and shoulders and an ache in her back. She longed to stretch out on the bed and let her mind and her body relax, if only for a short time. For as sure as it was nighttime, she wouldn't completely relax until the matter of her inheritance was settled.

Tomorrow she would tell Whitley she didn't need a servant. Tonight she would let the slave girl do whatever she wished. She leaned back in the chair and watched Tasma take her dresses out and shake them before hanging them in the wardrobe.

In the quietness she realized the music had stopped downstairs. In its place she heard the clinking and clanking of carriages, people talking and an occasional burst of laughter. It appeared the party guests were leaving.

She'd had no way of knowing a party was going on

when she decided to hire a carriage and make the two-hour journey from the town of Bainbridge to Carillon. Anyway, if it were true that Anchor McCabe had recently died why was his son holding a party without waiting for a proper mourning time? What kind of son was he?

She thought of her own mother. There were days Diana didn't want to get out of bed. During the winter she had developed lung fever and a bad cough with periodic fever she couldn't seem to shake for more than a day or two at the time. At one particular bad time, thinking she was going to die, Diana had decided to tell her daughter the truth about her father. She wanted Phina to go to him if she died. Diana insisted Anchor McCabe was a kind man with a good heart and would welcome her. The weather turned warmer and the fever went away. The coughing had gotten better, but Diana hadn't fully recovered. She was still weak and listless most of the time.

Later, Diana didn't want Phina to make the trip, but Phina insisted she had to find her father and ask him for financial help. But of course, Phina didn't tell her mother she wanted to do it for her. Diana would have never agreed to that.

And Phina knew she could always go back to New Orleans and agree to marry Mr. Braxton, one of the boarders. He'd been asking her for close to a year now. He was a nice man and did very well for himself with his bookkeeping job down at the docks. But Mr. Braxton was almost fifty years old, and Phina couldn't bring herself to say yes.

Now she was here, but Anchor was dead. It looked as if she was going to have to fight Whitley McCabe and the sheriff for an allowance from her father's plantation. She didn't want to think about what would happen if the sheriff wouldn't recognize her claim. Because of her mother's health she had to succeed.

"Dis all de dresses you brought, Miss Pennie?" Tasma asked, looking over her shoulder to Phina.

"Yes." Phina nodded, then said, "My name is Phina. Fe-na."

"Phina," Tasma pronounced, a big grin stretching across her dark brown face making her eyes shine with the feeling of accomplishment. "Miss Phina."

"That's right." Phina smiled.

A knock sounded on the door and Phina jumped.

Tasma waved her hand toward Phina and started for the door. "That'll be yore wash water and it's jest in time."

Phina rose and stretched her arms over her head, then kneaded the knotted muscles in her neck. She liked Tasma. She liked this room. She fingered the silver bell hanging around her neck. So far, she liked this place called Carillon. But all those feelings had to be put aside for now. She had to be ready to do battle with Whitley McCabe at the sheriff's office tomorrow.

Smiling, Tasma gently closed the door of Phina's bedroom. She'd done all she could for the new white woman. She was a strange one. Tasma shook her head. Most white girls wanted to be waited on hand and foot, including having the sheet tucked around them after they laid down. Miss Phina sure was different, Tasma thought. She wouldn't even let her help with her washing.

Tasma leaned back against the door. She had been smiling since Spiker had hurried into the cook house

37

calling her name over an hour ago. She'd been watching him for several months now and had tried on a number of occasions to get him to notice her when she passed him in the hallways of the big house. Most days though, he wouldn't even look her way. It had set her heart to thumping to have him call her by name.

She'd turned fourteen a few months ago and Rubra, her mother had told her it was time for her to start looking for a man to give her children of her own. Tasma started looking and discovered the only man she wanted was the only one who wasn't showing any interest in her—Spiker.

Standing outside Phina's door, Tasma closed her eyes and folded her hands across her chest. She wasn't in a hurry to go back to the cook house or downstairs to clean up after those white folks. They sure knew how to make a mess. She thought most of them had left. She'd heard carriages leaving for over an hour now. The arrival of Miss Phina had caused quite a stir among the guests, and Tasma couldn't help but wonder what all the fuss was about.

"What are you doing?"

Caught unaware, Tasma jumped.

"What are you doing standing outside that door?" Spiker asked as he came walking down the dimly lit hallway toward her.

Tasma's heart pounded. She'd never seen a more handsome man than Spiker. He had slim hips, a wide chest and powerful looking arms. Unlike most of the other slaves at Carillon, he kept his hair cut close to his head. And he was the only one brave enough to wear a closely-cropped, thin mustache above his upper lip. Tasma smiled again. He sure had looked fine tonight all dressed up like a white man in those fancy clothes.

She knew Spiker had a wife a few years ago who'd died during childbirth. He hadn't looked at another woman since that time as far as Tasma knew. If there'd been talk, she'd have heard it.

Finding her voice, Tasma said, "I'm looking afta Miss Phina jest like you said to. What you think?"

"How are you looking after her from this side of her door?" he asked, stopping a few inches from her.

Feeling safe in her position as a house girl, and the fact that she was Rubra's daughter Tasma said, "Why you think you run dis house? Dat's my mama's job. Not yores."

Spiker gave her a cold look. "I do what Mr. Whitley tells me to do same as you and *your* mama." He cut his eyes around to the door. "What is she doing?"

"She say she tired and gone ta bed." Tasma felt as hot as tallow melting in a fire. No man could hold a candle to Spiker. But how was she going to get him to notice her as a woman? She wanted nothing more than for Spiker to put his arms around her and kiss her. That would be better than a lazy afternoon with nothing to do.

"What you want ta know fo'?" she asked, looking up at him with dreamy eyes.

His gaze didn't waver. "I don't. Mr. Whitley wants to know."

Tasma moved closer to him and lowered her voice. "Yous can tell him she ate her dinah, washed and she's already in de bed."

"You look after her until Mr. Whitley says otherwise. He wants her ready to leave first thing tomorrow morning."

Spiker turned to leave, but Tasma called to him.

"Spiker, why you don't come callin' on me some-time?"

"What?" he asked, clearly shocked by her question. "What are you talking about? You're nothing but a girl."

"I's courting age now. I's fourteen. I's ready for a man. Mama said I was."

She reached out to touch him but Spiker stepped back. "Your mama just wants to find you a husband so she won't have to worry about you. But it's not going to be me." He pivoted and hurried down the hallway, then down the stairs.

Tasma wasn't happy. Other men in the slave quarters had been giving her the eye for nearly a year, just waiting for Rubra to give the signal that she was ready to have them come calling in the evening.

After Mr. Anchor died, Mr. Whitley told them that he would let them lead their own lives as long as they did their work during the day. That meant they didn't have to get his permission to court. All the slaves liked him because he wasn't as hard or demanding as Mr. Anchor had been. And everyone knew Spiker had been Mr. Whitley's favorite slave since Mr. Anchor had him whipped a few years ago for running away. Tasma was young at the time but remembered watching and thinking that Spiker must be the strongest man in the world because he didn't scream when the leather strap hit his bare back. Ten lashes and Spiker never said more than a grunt or two.

Tasma smiled. Spiker was a fine man.

He stood in front of the window in the parlor, a glass of whiskey in his hand, wearing nothing under his

40

robe. Ellison found that he slept less and drank more now that Anchor had died. Anchor had been good to him but never generous the way he always was to Whitley. By most standards Ellison couldn't complain. Anchor had given him a large house, five acres of land, and an older darkie named Samson to look after him. But on nights like this one it seemed like little compensation for the years of work he and his papa had put in at Carillon.

When Ellison's father died four years ago, Anchor made him the new overseer. Ellison had his own office at the north end of the west sawmill. Some of his time was spent planning what the slaves would be doing during the week. The rest of the day was spent checking on them and making sure their chores were getting finished. Once a week he'd take his paperwork to Whitley for him to look over and they'd decide which field would be planted in cotton and which for corn, or if any of the farming or sawmill equipment needed to be replaced. One thing he'd learned early was that Anchor and Whitley always had final say.

Ellison finished off his drink and wiped his lips with the back of his hand. He should have been the one giving the grand party tonight. He should have the rights to Carillon. Not Whitley. Anchor had always favored Ellison from the time he was six years old until the day he brought Whitley home with him.

Pushing the drapery panel aside he looked down the narrow dark road. She'd had time to come to him. It crossed his mind that maybe Samson hadn't gone for her, but then he knew better. Samson wouldn't disobey him. Ellison dropped the curtain and walked back over to the highly polished side table and poured himself another jigger of whiskey.

He'd heard talk and knew that some of the other slave owners in the county had their pick of the women. Just because Anchor and Whitley were too high and mighty to call the pretty ones to their beds was no reason for him to suffer when he wanted a woman. He chuckled to himself. The hell of it was that he really didn't like darkies. He didn't like to be around them, except for the one who kept catching his eye. Chatalene.

Restless, Ellison looked around the room. If Anchor hadn't brought Whitley home with him fifteen years ago Carillon would be his now.

A faint knock sounded on the front door. Ellison smiled and set his glass on the table and headed for the door. He couldn't hide the anticipation he was feeling. He'd been watching Chatalene for months.

With eager hands he opened the door. She stood there in a shapeless smoke-colored shift, a black scarf wound securely over her hair. Although she had a frightened expression on her face tonight, Chatalene was a beautiful Negress with skin the color of lightly creamed coffee. She had big expressive eyes. Her lips were full, tempting and intimidating. He opened the door wider for her to come in. Samson stood behind her.

The darkie started to follow her, but Ellison put his arm out and stopped him. "Go find something to do, old man," he said and closed the door.

Chapter Three

Trepidation descended upon Phina as she walked down the stairs the next morning, cape over her arm and bonnet in her hand. She'd been so tired from her journey she'd fallen asleep as soon as she lay down and was still sleeping when Tasma came in and opened her drapes, flooding the room with sunshine.

Phina had chosen her sage-colored dress to wear today because she felt it looked best with her dark hair and eyes. While she'd breakfasted on tea and hot buttered biscuits filled with cooked berries Tasma had pressed the wrinkles from her skirt with a hot iron. All of her dresses were simply made with long-sleeves, round necklines, fitted bodices and full skirts. Phina knew her clothes weren't fancy but they'd been made from some of the best fabrics available. Sometimes she and her mother would be allowed to keep leftover material and occasionally there would be enough to make a dress or at least enough for a new skirt. And no one could put a garment together better than her mother.

Knowing that her hair was clean and her dress pressed gave Phina a little more confidence than she had last night after arriving tired and dirty from three days on a bumpy stagecoach. Tasma hadn't been able to find any combs for her hair, but she'd managed to make a respectable chignon at the back of her nape by using the hairpins and a ribbon the girl had brought her.

Tasma had told her that Whitley wanted to see her as soon as she was dressed and that he would be waiting for her in his office. Her stomach knotted at the thought of another verbal battle with him. Phina wanted nothing from a man who never knew she'd been born. But she believed with all her heart that Anchor McCabe owed her mother. She'd never give up until she had enough money for her mother to live comfortably for the rest of her life.

She had no trouble finding the office. It was the same room she'd been taken to last night, but at the time she'd been too frightened to remember much of anything about it. Phina stood in front of the door for a few moments, shoring up her strength and courage. She didn't know much about men and it frightened her to have to talk to Whitley again. But not wanting to keep him waiting longer, she knocked on the door and waited for his call to enter.

After taking a deep breath she turned the knob, opened the door and walked inside. Deciding it was best not to show any of the weakness she was feeling she said, "I'm ready to go see the sheriff whenever you are."

The leather chair creaked as Whitley rose from his desk. A commanding figure of a man, he was handsome with light brown hair that fell just below his collar and bluish-green eyes so hard they seemed to look through her. He was dressed in a white shirt and

44

black-striped cravat with a black jacket and trousers.

"I'm glad to see you want to get right to the point. No pleasantries like good morning or how are you today needed between us." He leaned a hip against the desk and looked into her eyes. "Why don't we stop this nonsense right now, Phina? I'm willing to forget about the interruption you caused last night and allow you to go your way, if you tell me who put you up to this scheme and why."

The fine hairs on the back of her neck bristled. The nerve of him. "This is no scheme. Like it or not, Anchor McCabe is my father and nothing you can do or say will change that fact."

Whitley moved away from the desk and looked at her sternly, then said, "I am Anchor's only heir. The carriage is waiting out front. It's a long ride to the sheriff's office in Bainbridge. Are you sure you're ready?"

"Most assuredly." Phina lifted her green bonnet and placed it on her head, tying a bow underneath her chin.

Stiffly, they walked side by side out of the house and down the front steps. Even though the evenings were still cool, the bright spring sunshine made the days warm.

Lon, one of the darkies who'd tried to force her to leave last night stood in front of the covered carriage, batting a fly away from his face. While Whitley spoke to the slave Phina took the time to look around. It had been too dark for her to see much of anything when she arrived.

The circular drive crested in front of the stately home, a mansion with six large Ionic columns supporting a semicircular roof which towered over the Palladian-styled porch. The balcony extended across the entire front of the house and was supported by twelve smaller Corinthian columns. Front double doors were bracketed by glass panels. A spacious green lawn spread out from the house and down a lane shaded with white oaks. On the left side of the lawn a gazebo stood surrounded by colorful flowers. From the middle of the ceiling hung a silver bell. Phina gasped, and slipped a hand underneath the neckline of her dress and caressed the tiny silver bell that matched the one hanging in the gazebo.

Whitley took hold of her arm to help her into the carriage. Phina flinched and snapped her head around to look at him.

"You do want me to help you up, don't you?" he asked, the scowl still etched in his face.

"Of course," she managed to say, but wondered why she'd felt so—odd when he touched her. It was almost like a tingle ran up her arm and settled in her stomach. Phina sat down and gathered her skirts around her legs as Whitley climbed in beside her, careful not to touch her. The darkie cracked the whip and the horse took off at a trot.

Phina remained rigid, hugging the side of the carriage, trying not to touch him as they started down the drive. She couldn't help but feel a touch of resentment that Whitley had so much when she and her mother had so little. The carriage hit a hole, knocking her head against the cab. It was going to be a long ride into town.

Ten minutes into the ride Whitley wanted to kick himself for not having Cass, the stable boy saddle a horse for him. The carriage was stuffy and hot and the ride bumpy. When he looked over at Phina she looked

46

unbearably cool. And why not? She was dressed in a simple dress with, he noticed, a minimum of petticoats underneath, and he was stuffed tight in a cravat and jacket. He took off his hat and fanned himself. This was all her fault, he thought. She had him so tied in knots he hadn't slept an hour last night. It had never crossed his mind that anyone might challenge him for Carillon, especially a snip of a woman, a stranger.

One of the carriage wheels hit another hole, throwing Whitley against Phina. The back of his palm glanced against her soft breast and he quickly moved away, but not before his stomach and groin muscles tightened. Her gaze flew to his.

"Sorry," he mumbled as Phina crouched farther into her corner of the carriage. What he wanted to say was dammit. This was going to be one long ride into town.

Two hours later Lon stopped the carriage in front of the Decatur County Sheriff's Office. Whitley jumped down and took hold of Phina's arm to help her. He was glad she avoided his eyes. She appeared too close to him when he looked into her dark eyes and that made him uncomfortable.

"Lon, while you're waiting for us, go over to the mercantile and check for mail."

"Yes sir, Mr. Whitley," the old man said as he wrapped the reins around the brake handle.

A quick glance told Phina there wasn't much to the town. Rickety buildings lined each side of the dirt road. The tavern and mercantile were easy to spot because of the large signs hanging over the doorways.

There were no boardwalks along the streets in front of the buildings, Phina noticed as they walked up to the sheriff's office. Once inside she found the room

47

smaller than she expected. The wooden walls were unpainted and the smell of stale coffee permeated the room.

"I've been expecting you, Whitley," the short rotund sheriff said as they made their way inside. The two men shook hands. "I heard what happened last night."

Whitley was sure that he had and probably from more than one person. "Good to see you, Abe," Whitley greeted, making no reference to his comment. "This is Phina—?" He turned to look at her.

"Just Phina," she said in a soft voice.

With the force of a well-planted fist Phina's words hit him, reminding him of a time long ago when he was known only as Whitley. He remembered how proud he was the first time he was referred to as Anchor McCabe's son. Phina stood erect with her hands clasped in front of her. Her drawstring purse with fringe decorating the bottom dangled from her wrist. She looked so fragile he thought a good puff of wind might blow her away, but she carried with her the strength to destroy his life.

Whitley shook off the ill-effects of her words and continued. "Phina, this is Abe Pelham, sheriff of Decatur County."

"I'm pleased to meet you, Sheriff," she said.

He nodded and said, "Miss Phina," then looked back to Whitley. "What can I do for you?"

Keeping her gaze on the sheriff Phina spoke up. "I have proof I'm Anchor McCabe's daughter, thereby entitling me to assistance from his estate."

"Do you now." The sheriff's gaze shifted from Phina to Whitley. He hooked his fingers around his suspenders just above his waistband. "Far as we all

48

know, Anchor didn't have no daughter, Miss Phina. What kind of proof do you have?" he asked.

Opening her reticule she brought out the two letters. Whitley hadn't seemed impressed by them but maybe the sheriff would be. She handed him the letters.

"Phina showed up at Carillon last night and insisted that she is Anchor's long lost daughter," Whitley said. "But as you said no one has ever heard any mention of Anchor having a daughter."

Phina didn't like his snide insinuation. "I wasn't lost," she said, throwing an irritated glance toward Whitley. "Anchor didn't know about me. If he had I'm sure he would have brought me to live with him. My mother knew Anchor was married and never told him she was pregnant. It's all there in the letters."

"In any case she believes—"

"If you don't mind," Phina said, interrupting Whitley. "I'd like to tell my own story."

"Excuse me." Whitley bowed mockingly. "By all means. Tell your own story. I fear I couldn't do it justice anyway. I'm not adept at lying, and how do you achieve that frightened expression?"

Phina had known Whitley wasn't going to make this easy for her. She had to remember she was doing this for her mother so she clamped her teeth down on her tongue to keep from giving Anchor's arrogant son a piece of her mind. She had to face reality. Even if the sheriff agreed the letters were proof, Phina would still be at Whitley's mercy for the amount of the allowance.

Ignoring Whitley's comments Phina turned back to Sheriff Pelham. She tried to appear confident on the outside, but inside she was a wreck. What would she do if the sheriff put no more stock in those letters than Whitley had?

49

She cleared her throat and repeated her explanation of the night before to the sheriff. "Both letters state that I was the child of their union," she finished.

"I see." Sheriff Pelham took the letters and looked at them.

Phina remained still and quiet while he read the papers. Whitley paced back and forth in the small room. First rubbing the back of his neck, then his shoulder, and later his chin.

Finally the sheriff looked up, glancing from one to the other. "Well, the letters say exactly what you say they do. The trouble is that I don't know whether or not that makes them true."

"Perhaps this will help." Phina reached around her neck and unfastened the chain that held the small silver bell. Palm up, she handed it to the sheriff. "My father sent this to my mother shortly after his stay with her." A quick glance at Whitley's face told her he recognized the bell. From the pocket of her skirt she pulled the note Anchor had written Diana. "He sent this along with the bell." Phina read from the paper:

> The time I spent with you last month made me a happy man, but as we discussed, my marriage prevents us from being together. Since there can be no place for you at Carillon, please accept the enclosed bell and remember I wish things could have been different for us.
>
> Truly,
> Anchor

"Let me see that." Whitley's face was red with anger as he snapped the paper from her hand.

50

"Does that look like Anchor's handwriting?" the sheriff asked Whitley.

"A little." He looked down at Phina, a hard expression on his face. "But that doesn't mean it is."

"It's Anchor's," she said calmly. "And the bell matches the one I saw this morning hanging in the gazebo on the front lawn."

The sheriff scratched the back of his head. "It appears to me that this is a matter for the court and Judge Rogers to decide. He won't be back in town for about six weeks."

Whitley muttered an oath. "This is ridiculous, Abe. You and everybody in this county knows she's not Anchor's daughter."

"I am," Phina spoke up firmly. "You've no right to deny me."

"This is a scheme you've come up with to get something from his estate. Anyone could have made up this story and those letters, including having that bell made."

"That's not true," she argued. "Check the dates against Anchor's business ledgers. That will prove he was in New Orleans at the right time."

"It doesn't prove he slept with your mother," he countered angrily.

"Calm down, both of you," the sheriff said, pushing against Whitley's chest and stepping between the two. Abe hooked his thumbs around his suspenders again. "Whitley, you know it's my duty to check this out, and I plan to. If we find she's not telling the truth we'll send her back where she came from, but I have to look into her story. She does have those big round eyes like Anchor's, and everyone in town knows he gave both his wives a bell when they married."

51

"Abe—" Whitley complained as he started pacing again, putting his hands in the pockets of his breeches, then pulling them out again. "Whose side are you on?"

"Unlike you, he's trying to be fair," Phina inserted into the conversation.

The sheriff laughed, his rotund belly shaking. "Looks to me like you two may end up being sister and brother. You're sure fighting like it. So that's exactly what I suggest you do. Go back to Carillon and live together as brother and sister until the judge gets back. You may even find that you like each other."

Phina gasped at the thought of liking this arrogant man.

"That will be a cold day in hell," Whitley muttered under his breath.

Phina had to do something and she had to do it quick. She needed money immediately to help her mother. With neither of them working she had to send her mother money for her medication and expenses. "Sheriff?" Phina asked, "I understand your need to check my story, but I was wondering if I might request that you ask Whitley to give me an allowance of twenty dollars a month until the judge arrives."

"What? That's outrageous," Whitley said coming to stand beside them. "Surely you don't intend to even consider this preposterous proposal."

"Sheriff, I've had to leave my job as a seamstress in order to come here. A woman needs personal things." She ventured a quick glance at Whitley. That's all she needed to tell her how angry he was. "If I could just have a small allowance, I'm sure I'll manage until the judge comes back to town."

The sheriff gave her a kind look. "Seems reasonable to me. I don't think it'll hurt you or Carillon to give her a few dollars to see her through. That way she won't have to be coming to you for every little thing she needs. In the meantime, while we wait on Judge Rogers, I'll send a couple of letters to New Orleans and check out her story myself. Will that make you feel better?"

"Yes," Whitley said tightly, his anger barely kept in check.

"What's the name of this boardinghouse where you and your mother live?"

"The Elms. Diana Groutus is my mother's name. We've nothing to hide."

Whitley walked over to the door and jerked it open. "Send word, if you hear anything," he said tightly.

"I'll keep you posted," the sheriff said to Whitley, then nodded to Phina. "It was nice to meet you, Miss."

Phina smiled. "Please let me know if you need anything, Sheriff. I'll be at Carillon." Not bothering to look at Whitley, Phina swept past him and out the door.

Whitley followed and shut the door with a bang behind them. He grabbed Phina's wrist and swung her around to face him. He took hold of her upper arms and brought her face up close to his.

She winced from the pain his strength caused. His eyes sparkled with anger, and she felt his body tremble with fury. "Let me tell you something." His words were hissed. "I will see you in hell before I'll share the plantation with you."

Furious that he'd touched her, Phina jerked away from him, rubbing her arm where he'd held her so tightly. "I plan to take my rightful place here at Carillon. Your boorish behavior won't frighten me away."

Chapter Four

If Whitley thought the trip into town was long and
disturbing the journey back to Carillon was hell. He
vowed to never be caught in the confines of a small
carriage with Phina again. Not only was he unhappy
with himself about the close quarters, he was furious
that the snip of a woman tried to lay claim to Carillon.
She had the gall to ask for an allowance, telling the
sheriff she had need of personal things. And Abe had
the lack of good judgment to tell him to give it to her.
Whitley had fully expected Abe to treat her as the
nuisance she was and send her on her way.

Hell, he knew what the *personal* things were she
needed, he thought, as the carriage bumped and jarred
its way toward Carillon. She wanted new clothes and
bonnets and probably jewelry, too.

He chanced a glance in her direction. The dress she
had on was expensive material and had been well
made, but it was simple in design. No doubt fabric and
trimming for fancy dresses and bonnets would be the
first things she'd buy. Remembrance of how she'd
looked last night as she swept into the ballroom with
her velvety black hair streaming down her back

flashed across his mind and caused a knot to form in his stomach. He made a tight fist and clenched his teeth. He didn't want to find her attractive. He didn't want to look at her as a woman. She was a manipulative fortune hunter, and he intended to treat her as such.

Phina turned around and caught him staring at her. Their eyes met before Whitley shifted in his seat and looked out at the slowly passing landscape. She didn't appear as self-satisfied with herself as she should be, he thought, considering she'd just finagled herself a few weeks lodging at Carillon and a tidy sum of money in her pocket as well.

He could strangle Abe for deciding to wait until Judge Rogers came back to town to throw her off Carillon. He'd always thought Sheriff Pelham was slow to take a stand on important issues and this proved his ineffectiveness to Whitley. Abe should have immediately told her the letters were not proof she was Anchor's daughter and have been done with it.

What would he do if Rogers believed her story? Whitley sighed and rubbed his forehead as self-doubt set in. She had more than mere letters. She had sworn statements claiming her allegation was true. What if the judge wanted to see his papers? He had nothing in writing. His only proof lay in the community knowledge that Anchor *intended* to make him his legal heir. Would that stand up in a court of law against a sworn statement made by a doctor and the mother?

How many people knew Anchor hadn't signed that will making Whitley his legal heir before he died? Whitley thought back. He was quite sure Ellison and Anchor's lawyer, Robert Higgins were the only ones. When it came right down to it he supposed anyone could lay claim to Carillon. But Whitley had to keep in mind that he was the one who had control of the bank accounts, the slaves, the house, and the property. And that was the way it was going to stay.

He had already spoken with Robert about the will. Anchor had planned to sign the papers on the night of the party and announce to everyone that Whitley was to be his legal son and heir, and then announce that Whitley would be marrying Flannery. Robert had assured him that because Anchor had no other known living relative there would be no problem with him becoming full owner of Carillon. But what would happen now that there was someone who could challenge him? He was sure Robert would testify that Anchor had him draw up the documents but had never made it official by signing those damned papers. Where was that going to leave him in a court of law? Whitley didn't know, but he intended to talk to Robert and find out. And he intended to prove Phina was lying.

The carriage hit a hole and Phina bumped up against Whitley's shoulder. "Sorry," she mumbled as Whitley scrunched farther into the corner of the cab of the carriage. That tight feeling attacked his stomach again. Dammit, there was no need for him to react that way. She was just a woman. It was probably because he was hot and tired of riding in the carriage so close to her. Silently he vowed to never get this close to her again.

No need to wait for Abe to get around to checking out Phina's story either, Whitley thought. He'd send someone to New Orleans himself. He didn't trust the sheriff not to go soft on him just because Phina batted her eyelashes at him. He'd send Ellison to find out her real identity.

Thoughts of Ellison brought his conversation with Rubra earlier that morning to mind. Maybe it would do his friend good to get away from Carillon. Ellison was drinking too much. He knew it and Ellison did too.

Ellison was good with the books. Whitley had never caught him cheating him or the people they did business with. But none of that would matter if he didn't stay away from too much liquor.

Whitley sighed silently as he remembered something Anchor told him years ago. "Ellison is a good boy. He's smart, too. But he's always hungry. It doesn't matter what you do for him he always wants more. You remember that."

And Whitley had, but he'd never really understood what Anchor meant until now. Ellison wanted more than his small house and five acres of land. Whitley knew he wanted Carillon.

Yes, he'd send him to New Orleans. There were plenty of women there he could bed. Maybe he'd be better when he returned.

Phina was hot, tired, and a bundle of jumbled nerves by the time they arrived at Carillon. Whitley hadn't even spoken to her on the long trip home. Once or twice their arms had brushed and he'd jerked away from her as if she had a plague. He had done the gentlemanly thing and helped her down from the carriage as soon as it stopped, but she could tell that he did so grudgingly.

After they entered the house he turned to her and said gruffly, "I have several things to say to you, but we'll discuss them later tonight. Right now, I'm tired

57

and I need to see to some business. Dinner should b
ready by the time you've changed." He pulled hi
watch out of the pocket of his waistcoat. "I'll see yo
in an hour." He turned to go, but quickly pivoted bacl
to face her and said, "We dress for dinner and meet i
the parlor."

Stunned and hurt that he'd been so abrupt, so un
friendly all day, she watched Whitley walk down th
hallway and disappear into his office. Standing in th
middle of the spacious foyer Phina had never felt mor
alone in her life than she did at this moment. Wa
dealing with this arrogant man worth the money sh
needed for her mother? Slowly, she looked around a
the grandness of the house with its fine furniture, gil
covered moldings and expensive draperies. Whitle
McCabe had everything he could ever want. An
much more than he needed. Yes, for her mother, i
would be worth putting up with him.

While she was standing there deciding she had th
courage to continue this fight, a tall stoutly-buil
woman walked out of a small room off the galler
toward Phina. She wore a faded black dress with
clean shepherd's apron over it. A red scarf adorned he
head. She carried a stack of folded clothes in he
hands.

"Did I heah Mr. Whitley calling fo' me?" th
woman asked as she drew near to Phina.

"I don't believe so," she answered. "I don't believ
we've met. I'm—"

"Oh yes, I knows you." The woman laughed husk
ily, causing her dark brown eyes to sparkle. "You th
woman what upset Mr. Whitley's party."

"Ah—well—" Affronted by the darkie's accusation

58

Phina stuttered for a moment. "I'm not sure that I did," she finally said in defense of herself.

"Yes'um, yous did all right. Mr. Whitley don't say much but I seen it in his eyes. He shore 'nuff mad." Another low chuckle rumbled in her chest. "Oh yes. I 'spect everybody in dis county knows you by now."

Phina had a hard time getting upset with the woman. She sounded like she was making fun of her, but Phina could see the woman wasn't being malicious with what she was saying or her laughter. She was simply amused.

"Whitley didn't have to break up the party last night just because I arrived. In fact, I assumed he hurried me out of the ballroom so the party could continue."

The woman shifted the clothes from one arm to the other. Her amused expression turned to one of disapproval. "He weren't gone 'nounce his wedding plans afta yous came running in here like ya did."

Phina cringed as the slave's words registered. No wonder Whitley was so hostile toward her. Not only was she insisting she was his half sister, she had interrupted his engagement party. Her gaze scanned down the hallway to his office. It wasn't too late for an apology—but she'd best wait and do it tonight when they met for dinner, rather than disturb him right now.

She glanced back to the woman. "I'm sorry, I didn't get your name."

"Rubra. I take care of Mr. Whitley and his house fo' him."

"I see," Phina said as she untied her bonnet and took it off. But she really didn't see. Last night she was told Spiker took care of him. She couldn't help but

59

wonder why Whitley needed so many people to take care of him.

"My girl Tasma," Rubra continued, "she de one lookin' afta you."

Phina smiled for the first time since leaving New Orleans. "I like Tasma. She's a very sweet girl."

A prideful grin spread across Rubra's face as she tucked the clothes between her arm and ample hip. Phina was sure those well-chosen words had just earned her a much needed friend.

"I guess you've been at Carillon for a long time."

"Yes, 'um, I have. Mr. Anchor's daddy bought me jest befo' he died."

"So you knew Anchor's wife?" she asked, trying hard not to sound as if she were prying.

"Sho I did. Knowed both of 'em."

"Sheriff Pelham mentioned that Anchor was married twice. Which one of his wives was Whitley's mother?"

Rubra laughed so hard she almost dropped the clothes she was holding. "Weren't none of dem women his mama. No sir. Mr. Whitley don't have no mama."

Phina walked closer to her. "I don't understand. Of course he has a mother."

As quickly as Rubra had started laughing, she became bored with the subject and started up the stairs. "If'n he did, I ain't never heard 'bout her. Mr. Anchor jest went away one day afta his second missus died. When he came back he had Mr. Whitley with him."

"Wait," she called to the darkie who was at the top of the stairs. Phina's heart hammered. "Are you sure Whitley was not the son of either of Anchor's wives?"

Rubra turned back around and looked down on

60

Phina. "Course I'm sho'. I've been in dis house mo'n thirty years. Now I's got work ta do."

Fury descended upon Phina the way darkness descends upon a forest. Slowly but surely. She picked up her skirts and whipped around, heading for Whitley's office. Forgetting that she had decided to be nice to Whitley she barged into his office. Stomping past Spiker, she marched up to Whitley's desk and asked, "How many bastard children does Anchor McCabe have?"

Whitley rose, anger lighting in his face. "What the hell are you talking about?"

"Rubra just told me you don't belong to either of Anchor's wives. That he went away one day and came back with you. I assume you are the illegitimate child he knew about."

"Anchor has no bastards."

Filled with the injustice of his words, Phina struck back at him. "I am his bastard daughter!" With one sweep of her hand Phina swiped the papers, ink jar and pen from Whitley's desk, splattering the dark, thick liquid on the rug. Spiker grabbed her arms but she fought him and managed to get away.

"Spiker, leave her alone!" she heard Whitley shout. She turned on the slave with deadly calm and said, "It doesn't matter to me whether I fight Whitley or you, but I'm warning you. If you touch me again, I'll do my best to scratch your eyes out."

"Yes, Miss Phina." His response was just as calm.

"Spiker." Whitley moved away from his desk. "Go tell Rubra to send someone to clean up this mess, then tell Ellison I want to see him before dinner."

"Yes, sir." Spiker glanced at Phina as if to make

sure she wasn't going to attack him or Whitley then turned away.

Phina kept her gaze on the slave until he left the room. Her breathing was ragged as she looked at the dark ink staining the rug and Whitley's papers. Phina winced. How could she have been so destructive? She didn't realize how angry she'd become. Now that she'd settled down she was ashamed of her behavior. Ashamed of what she said to Spiker. She'd already been told his job was to take care of Whitley and he took his job seriously.

She moistened her lips. "I'm sorry about the rug. I didn't mean to lose control like that."

Whitley took off his jacket and threw it over a chair. "Forget the rug. For your information, Phina, I am not Anchor's bastard son, I'm his adopted son."

Her eyes widened. "Adopted?" She'd made a fool of herself. She should have calmly asked him to explain, but instead she'd barged into his office ranting like a demented fool.

"That's right." He untied his cravat and pulled it from around his neck and threw it on top of the discarded jacket.

She avoided his eyes. "I—I didn't think—about that possibility—"

"Oh, holy saints." Rubra hurried into the room. "How'd dat ink get on dis rug?" She brushed Phina aside and bent over the mess. "Mercy!" She looked up at Phina. "Gets on outta heah befo' you gets the tail of yore dress in dis. You too, Mr. Whitley, gets outta here so I's can clean dis up."

Phina glanced over at Whitley. A frown marred his handsome features. "I'll see you at dinner, Phina," he said tight-lipped.

62

Deciding to get away while she could, Phina fled to her room.

"Spiker said you wanted to see me?"

Whitley looked up from his paperwork and saw Ellison standing in the doorway of his office. "Yes, come in."

He pushed away from his desk and rubbed the back of his neck. That long carriage ride and the argument with Phina had left him ill-tempered and his muscles tied in knots. Rubra had made quick work of getting the rug out of his office. The rug was ruined but the ink hadn't soaked through to the wood floor.

"What did Abe have to say?"

"That's what I want to talk to you about," he answered, getting immediately to the problem at hand. "Sit down." Whitley saw Ellison's gaze stray to the sideboard where the liquor sat on a silver tray. Whitley was pleased when Ellison decided against the drink and took a seat in the chair.

Whitley cleared his throat and said, "Against my strong protests Abe agreed that Phina could stay on at Carillon until Judge Rogers returned to town. He assured me he would check into Phina's story, but the truth is, I don't trust him to do a thorough job. I want you to do it for me."

Holding out empty hands Ellison said, "How?"

Whitley kept a poker face. "Go to New Orleans."

Ellison's eyebrows shot upward, but Whitley continued. "It's a job I'd rather do myself, but it's for those same reasons I can't leave Carillon right now."

"So you need to stay here and keep an eye on Phina. And you want me to go to New Orleans to check out

63

her story?" Ellison rubbed his clean-shaven chin thoughtfully.

"Exactly. I want to know if this boardinghouse she talks about is actually there. Check out the doctor, and see if you can find out anything about her mother." He extended a sheet of paper toward Ellison. "I wrote down all the pertinent information for you. After you've looked it over let me know if you have any questions."

Ellison nodded as he took the paper and scanned the information.

"Think you can handle a city like New Orleans?" Whitley asked, hoping to quell the eagerness inside him.

Ellison laughed as he folded the paper and put it in the pocket of his jacket. "I can try."

"Good. I'm counting on you to find out who Phina really is."

"I may have to visit *every* house in New Orleans," he said, grinning.

"Whatever it takes."

Ellison's gaze met Whitley's blue eyes. "You're really worried about her, aren't you?"

"No." Whitley lied easily, to himself and to Ellison. And both of them knew it. "But I'd be a fool not to go before Judge Rogers with all the information I can get on her. Like I said, I'd go myself, but I don't want to leave her at Carillon unattended."

"When do you want me to leave?" Ellison said as he rose from the chair, glancing again at the sideboard.

"Monday morning sound good?"

Ellison nodded.

Whitley rose and picked up an envelope containing two hundred dollars. He expected Ellison to visit a couple of whorehouses and play a few games of cards while there.

"It may take me a couple of weeks." He put the money in his pocket along with the information.

Whitley didn't mind as long as he brought back proof as to who Phina really was. "Whatever it takes," he repeated.

Chapter Five

Tasma watched Miss Phina walk into the parlor to meet Mr. Whitley for dinner, then picked up the skirt of her mushroom-colored dress and hurried out the front door. She wanted to spend some time with Spiker before she had to be back in Miss Phina's room to help her undress. Everyone on the plantation was talking about how Mr. Whitley and Miss Phina didn't like each other, and she didn't expect them to sit across from each other at the dinner table for long.

She knew Spiker usually had his meal while Mr. Whitley had his dinner, so he'd be free in case Mr. Whitley needed him for anything before he went to bed.

Spiker lived in a small one room house on the edge of the slave quarters with two other men. They were both field hands and Tasma would never look twice at a plowboy.

Twilight was fading fast as she scampered around the house. Tasma liked daylight and she liked night, but she didn't like dusk. She just didn't feel right about that time of day when the sun had already set but the stars hadn't come out. Maybe the sky would be dark and the stars shining brightly by the time she started back to the big house.

"Where you going in such a hurry?"

Tasma spun around and saw Cush coming out of the cook house. For just a moment, she wrinkled her eyes and nose into an irritated expression. The last thing she wanted right now was to be hindered by anyone. Cush was tall and so thin he didn't look like he had a muscle on him anywhere. The rope holding up his breeches wasn't any longer than a baby snake. Not only wasn't he broad-shouldered, and thick-muscled like Spiker, Cush worked in the canning garden. And while working in the vegetable garden wasn't as low a job as a field hand, Tasma still had no interest in Cush.

"I can't talk now, Cush," she said as he stopped beside her. "I's gots to eat so I can be back at de big house ta see ta Miss Phina afta she has her dinah."

"I won't keep ya none," Cush said as he looked down at the ground, too shy to look into her eyes while he posed the all important question. "I's hoping I could come calling on you dis evenin'."

"I-I don't know." Tasma hedged, still holding tightly to the folds of her skirt. She was hoping to talk Spiker into calling on her.

Cush raised his head and blinked several times, looking as if he were unsure as to what to say next. "I already asked yore mama. She say it all right fo' me ta come by tonight. She don't care none."

Thinking the easiest and quickest way to get away from Cush was to agree so Tasma said, "All right, but I won't be home till late."

A big silly smile stretched across his face. "Dat's all right. I'll be waiting on de steps fo' ya."

67

Tasma nodded to him before continuing down the path through the pine trees to the slaves' quarters. She bypassed their cook house and the food that would be waiting for her to hurry the extra distance to Spiker's house. When she approached the small house she slowed down. The front door was shut and the house looked deserted. She wiped her lips with the back of her hand and slowed her ragged breathing.

Not knowing exactly what she wanted to do, Tasma approached the door cautiously. She stood there a moment and bolstered her courage before knocking on the door. No one answered. She called Spiker's name, then opened the door and looked inside, calling his name again.

She peeked around the doorjamb and into the room. It was dark and shadowed, but she could see a crudely built wooden table standing in the middle of the room with a candlestick on it. Three chairs sat around it. A rocker with a torn cane seat stood in front of the fireplace. Each of the three walls had a cot pushed against it and a tall chest with a shaving plate and small mirror on top of it stood in front of the only window.

Tasma climbed the three steps and tip-toed into the cabin. Shirts and breeches of varying sizes hung on the walls. She walked over to the shaving stand and picked up the lye soap that rested in a small tin bowl. Putting the soap under her nose she sniffed it. A tingling feeling attacked her stomach. It smelled just like Spiker. She held it in her hand and breathed in deeply and imagined it was Spiker's cheek so close to her nose.

"What are you doing in here?"

Surprised by the loud voice Tasma dropped the chunk of hard soap on her toe. "Ow!" she squealed and bent to rub her injured foot. "What you doing hollering at me for? I ain't out in a field somewhere. I's right in front of ya." She expected to see blood on her toe and was a little bit disappointed when she didn't.

"What are you doing in here?" Spiker asked again.

Forgetting about her foot, Tasma rose and looked at him. He set a plate filled with a generous amount of beans, two pieces of bread and three strips of bacon with scrambled eggs on top of them onto the table.

"What's wrong wid me comin' in heah?" she asked. "I didn't mess with nothin'." As she said this she realized she had been holding his shaving soap in her hand when she heard him behind her.

"This is *my* house and it's off limits to you. Now get." He turned his back to her and stuck a dipper down into a pail and filled a tin cup with water.

"You still here?" he asked when he turned around and pulled out a chair.

"I ain't hurtin' nothin' jest standin' here, am I?"

"Yeah," he said roughly. "My supper's getting cold." He took hold of her arm and ushered her toward the door.

Tasma tried to stop him by dragging her feet across the floor, but he was too strong for her. "I's hopin' you gone come callin' on me," she managed to say.

"I told you last night I'm not interested." He slid an arm around her waist and pressed her to his hip as he lifted her off the ground and carried her down the three steps.

"How you know you not interested if 'in ya don't come ta see me?" Tasma asked.

"You're too young for me," he snapped.

"I'm a woman now. Mama said I was." She protested his accusation and his treatment of her.

69

"And I told you I don't listen to your mama or nobody else." He deposited her on her feet.

Pouting, Tasma jerked her hands to her waist and said, "Cush asked if he could come calling on me. And I tole him he could."

"Good. He'll make you a fine man."

That wasn't what she wanted to hear. "I don't wants him ta come callin', I's want you, Spiker," she complained in a softer, womanly voice.

Spiker sighed. "Go home, Tasma. I'm too old for you." He went back inside and shut the door behind him.

Tasma was disappointed he wouldn't agree to come calling but that didn't keep her from smiling. She hugged herself with her arms as she started for the cook house. She was warm all over from having Spiker's hands on her. Her legs felt as watery as a tub of warm jelly. No one could make her name sound as sweet as Spiker could.

After thoroughly rebuking herself for her display of temper earlier that afternoon, Phina walked into the parlor wearing her red dress. It was by no means a formal dress like she knew Whitley expected her to wear to dinner, but it was the newest dress she had. Tasma had found her a length of red ribbon and had styled her hair into a loose chignon at her nape. She'd tied the rest of the ribbon in a pretty bow and pinned it to the neckline of her dress.

Whitley stood with his back to her pouring himself a drink from a crystal decanter. A beautiful Empire sofa covered in dark green velvet with two matching side chairs sat in the middle of the room. On the back

70

wall hung a floor to ceiling mirror framed by ornately carved gilt wood. It was through the mirror that Whitley noticed her standing just inside the doorway. She watched his gaze sweep the length of her. For an instant she thought she saw appreciation in his eyes but it was gone so quickly she realized she must have imagined it. His reproachful expression returned.

At times it was difficult for her to resent his attitude. She could understand his reluctance to accept a half sister he never knew he had and share a portion of his inheritance with her. But she couldn't worry overly-much about his feelings. She had to keep her mother's welfare uppermost in her mind.

"Good evening," she finally said and walked farther into the room, her petticoats making the full skirt of her dress swish around her legs.

He nodded. "You're right on time. What would you like to drink?" he asked, still looking at her through the mirror. "Lemonade or something stronger?"

Phina had never tasted anything stronger than tea and she wasn't fond of the bittersweet taste of lemonade. "Nothing, thank you. I'm fine right now. I feel I should apologize again for my outburst this afternoon."

Whitley put his drink to his lips and took a generous swallow before facing her. "You've apologized twice now, Phina. That's enough."

She was surprised he cared so little about the ruined rug and if he didn't want it mentioned again she'd comply to his wishes.

"Why don't we go on in to dinner." He set his glass on the sideboard and motioned with the sweep of his arm for her to proceed him through the archway and into the dining room.

71

She felt rebuffed. He should have offered her his arm or at least walked by her side. She guessed it was his way of reminding her she was an intruder.

Breathtaking elegance showed in every detail of the dining room. From the heavily ornate cornices above the draperies to moldings on the ceiling. Quickly, Phina scanned the room. She had never seen so much crystal. Bowls, glasses, vases, candlesticks and candelabras lined built-in shelves, side tables and open cabinets. A mahogany pedestal table with Chippendale chairs centered the room, and a massive Empire sideboard with two candlesticks on each side graced one wall. Two Ionic columns supported the mantel.

Phina tried not to be impressed as she sat down in the chair Whitley held out for her, but how could she not be. The McCabe wealth was evidenced in every feature of the house and its contents.

Whitley poured a small amount of red wine into their glasses before taking his place at the head of the table. As soon as he was seated a young woman came out of the warming room carrying a tureen of piping hot soup and emptied a ladleful into each bowl.

The squash bisque was delicious so Phina ate all of it, but noticed that Whitley hadn't finished. After the bowls were taken away Chatalene, the woman serving them, brought out two plates of beautifully-prepared, equally-proportioned amounts of cooked onions, green peas, roasted potatoes and two thick slices of beef. Phina realized how out of place she was in the house. At home, bowls of food were set on the table and passed around. Everyone helped themselves. And while Whitley hadn't said a word since they sat down, the boardinghouse table was always lively with conversation as the boarders shared their experiences of the day with everyone else in the house.

She'd eaten about half the food on her plate when she decided she couldn't stand eating in silence any longer. Maybe Whitley was used to being so properly quiet, but she wasn't.

"Exactly how large is Carillon?" she asked.

He seemed surprised at first that she'd spoken but laid down his fork. "Why do you ask?"

His question sounded accusing, but Phina decided not to let his tone bother her. She was entitled to know a few things about her father's plantation. "Well, since it's to be my home for the next few weeks I'd like to know a little more about it."

"Your mother didn't tell you about it?"

Phina dabbed at the corners of her mouth with the lace-edged napkin. "She's never been here, you know. She only knew Anchor for the few weeks he stayed in her home."

He picked up his wine and sipped it. "What *did* she tell you about Carillon?"

"Not much. Only that it was a large plantation on the western banks of the Chattahoochee River. How long has Carillon been here?"

"I suppose there's no harm in telling you the history of the plantation. Anyone around here could tell you as much." Whitley sat back in his chair and picked up his glass of wine. "Anchor's father started Carillon back in 1790 with less than ten thousand acres and seven slaves. The land was actually better for farming up in North Georgia but the Cherokees had already claimed a great section of it at that time, so Anchor's father settled here along the southern banks of the Chattahoochee River. Anchor was his only surviving

73

child and inherited full title to Carillon back in 1805. By that time another twenty-five thousand acres had been added and the slaves had multiplied to over thirty. Over the years, Anchor added the rest of the land which put us over sixty thousand acres about five years ago. This house was started in 1801 but not completely finished until just a few months before Anchor's father died."

"And how many slaves does Carillon have now?" she asked.

"Over seventy, but we haven't bought a slave in ten years. Those we have manage to give us three or four each year."

"You mean by having children."

"Yes."

Phina pushed her plate away. "I really don't know anything about owning slaves. But somehow it doesn't seem right to me."

Whitley smiled and Phina felt a catch in her throat. It was the first genuine smile he'd given her and it affected her greatly. What was she doing being attracted to this man? The very thought of it was an outrage. She couldn't allow her feelings toward him to soften. He was going to do everything in his power to keep her from getting an allowance, and she had to have that money for her mother's medicine and care.

"I'm sure you've heard some of the same horror stories I've heard about how poorly slaves are treated. And in some cases I'm sure that's true. But not on Carillon. We treat our slaves as human beings. There are certain rules they must obey, but basically they are free to live their own lives. They work, marry and have children just like the rest of us. In fact, they have their own little village a half a mile away."

74

"A village?" she questioned.

"Yes. We call it the slaves' quarters. The darkies have their own cook house and vegetable garden and a meetinghouse where they can gather in the evenings to visit or play some of their games. Everyone has a job. By the age of five or six we can usually tell what work the child will be best suited to and we start training them for that job. For instance, some girls will learn to sew, some clean and others cook. As for the boys they will either work in the fields, the sawmills, stables or gardens. And everyone has Sundays off unless there's work to do that can't wait."

Phina wasn't surprised by the pride she saw in Whitley's features and heard in his voice. He loved the plantation and it was no wonder he didn't want to share it. And Phina had to agree that it didn't sound like the slaves on Carillon had such a hard life.

"I guess the only difference between slaves and employees is they aren't free to leave," she said.

He seemed to study her intently for a moment. Phina noticed that his eyes were more blue than green tonight. "There's more to it than that. Employees are not given their clothes, food, medicines and a place to live. Unless, of course, their wages reflect it. If the slaves need it, we supply it."

She hadn't thought about it that way. She was eager to learn more about the plantation and while she had Whitley talking she was going to ask more questions. "Tell me, what's an example of the kind of work that couldn't wait until Monday to be done?"

He moved restlessly in his chair. "If there hasn't been any rain for three weeks and the corn is drying in the fields no one takes the day off. Everyone works to pull it."

"Including you?" she tested him, her eyes looking into his for any hint that he might stray from the truth.

Chatalene came out and removed the plates and he continued. "I've been known to spend my days in a corn field, a cotton field or carry bags of grain to the gristmill. I've spent many days at the sawmill." His eyes narrowed. "There's no work on this plantation that I haven't done, Phina. Anchor insisted I know everything about Carillon. Until Anchor died I often spent my days cutting down trees, chopping cotton stalks or pulling corn. Now I have to spend too much time in the office keeping up with the records and accounts."

She believed him when he said he'd labored. He did look fit. Not like some of the overweight dandies who roamed the streets of New Orleans leading their pampered lives. Chatalene placed small dishes of sweet bread with sugar and cinnamon sprinkled over it in front of them.

Phina tasted the sugary treat. It was wonderful. "Earlier you said you had something you'd like to discuss with me. What did you have in mind?"

"A few things. Since the sheriff saw fit to give you permission to stay here until Judge Rogers comes back to town, I have a few rules I want you to obey."

She prickled with umbrage at the word obey. He might be her adopted brother but surely he didn't expect her to obey him. "Rules?" she questioned, her gaze immediately locking on to his.

"Yes." He pushed aside the dessert and sipped his wine again. "I'll not expect to see you for breakfast nor for a noonday meal should you decide to have one, but I'll expect you for dinner each night at seven. Tasma, the young woman who's been taking care of

76

you, will continue to be your personal servant. Should you need to go into town just ask me, and I'll arrange for someone to take you. You're free to roam about the house, the gardens and grounds."

"I don't need a servant," she spoke up, bristling at the tone of his voice and the orders he was issuing as if she were a prisoner at Carillon. "Unlike you, I'm perfectly capable of taking care of myself. In fact, I'm used to it."

He looked at her strangely for a moment. She believed it to be surprise she saw in his expression. But she didn't know if it was because she didn't want the servant or because she had the nerve to refuse him.

"But in this house," he said calmly, "we do things right."

Phina pondered his words, then decided not to fight with him about this. There would be many things they would cross swords over during the next few weeks and she shouldn't waste a jab over the ones that she could easily live with. She would accept Tasma as her personal maid.

"Is there more?" she asked, a little tight-lipped.

"That covers it for now."

"Very well," she pushed her chair away from the table and swung her legs around to the side. "Before I excuse myself from the table there is one other thing I'd like to apologize for. Rubra explained to me that I burst in on your engagement party last night, and I want you to know that I'm sorry about that."

He gave her a rueful look. "I have no idea how you did it but your timing couldn't have been worse. You arrived just in time to stop the formal announcement."

Her gaze held fast to his. "I'm sorry," and she was,

and that was the last time she would apologize for that.

"Don't play with me, Phina," he said in a coolly controlled voice. "You timed your entrance so everyone would know you were laying claim to Carillon."

Phina almost rose out of her chair. She was furious. "How could I have known such a thing?"

"Anyone within sixty miles could have told you about the party."

"The stage dropped me in town and I didn't ask anything except directions to Carillon. How dare you suggest otherwise."

Whitley threw his napkin to the table. "How dare you presume to come into my house and demand that you have rights to it. After your grand entrance last night I believe you capable of anything."

She moved to the edge of her chair. "I only want what's mine by legal right. An acceptable allowance from my father's estate."

"You do know that even if the judge should say you are Anchor's daughter, I will still have control over the plantation."

"Yes, but I'll be allowed to share in its prosperity."

"Carillon is mine." Whitley's eyes turned cold. "I won't share it with you. I think it very convenient that three months after Anchor died you show up at the door claiming to be his long lost daughter."

"I was never lost!" Her voice rose and her hands clenched. "How many times do I have to tell you that? Anchor didn't know he had a daughter. He thought he had only you."

"You know, we could bypass all of this and get right to the reason you're here, if you'd tell me who sent you."

"No one sent me. I came on my own. Anchor McCabe owes me *and* my mother. I'm not going away."

Whitley rose. "Your mother? So somehow your mother found out that Anchor died and sent you here to try to extort money."

"No!" She sprang out of the chair and stood before him. "My mother didn't want me to come. I left without her blessing."

"Then why are you here?" he demanded, his eyes cold and unrelenting.

"I intend to see that Anchor pays for what he did. He slept with my mother while he was married and like it or not I'm your half sister. He was an unfaithful—"

"Don't say it!" Whitley grabbed hold of her upper arms and brought her face dangerously close to his. "You may say all the vile things you want about me. Most of them will be true, but don't ever say anything bad about Anchor. Never. You didn't know him."

"That's not my fault."

"You came only to get his money."

"Money I deserve." She yanked her arms out of his grasp.

"No! You don't." He pointed a finger at her. "You can't barge in here and think you're going to take a part of Carillon because your mother couldn't keep her skirts down and got pregnant."

Without thinking, Phina raised her arm and struck Whitley, a hard, open-palm, resounding slap. He grabbed her wrist and jerked her against him. Her skin twisted beneath his fingers and she cried out. She tried to strike him again and he shoved her back against the table, knocking over the wineglasses. He held her so tight against the table the edge penetrated her layers of

79

petticoats and pressed into her buttocks. She struggled against him, trying to force his body away from hers. She freed one arm and thrashed wildly only for it to be caught a moment later.

His eyes glowed with anger as he bent over her. "Don't ever do that again, Phina. I'll hurt you." His words were low and gravelly.

Seeing how angry he was and knowing that he could easily hurt her she nodded her understanding. Phina realized too late that Whitley not only loved Anchor McCabe, he'd worshiped him.

Whitley straightened. Neither took their gaze off the other as he pulled a velvet bag from his jacket pocket and laid it on the table beside the wine-stained tablecloth.

"Here is your allowance for three months. This should keep you happy until the judge returns. Enjoy it, Phina. It will be all that you get."

Chapter Six

Whitley dismounted in front of the gracious four-pillared home of George and Bertha Matheson. He'd spent every Sunday afternoon for the past year visiting with Flannery and her parents in their parlor at The Pines.

He handed the reins and his gloves to the darkie who came running to meet him.

"Good afta'noon, Mr. Whitley."

"Hello, Hirsh."

"Looks like we gone have rain afore dis day's over."

Whitley looked up at the graying sky and shook his head. They'd had an unusually dry winter so spring rains would be welcomed. "Maybe I'll get home before it starts."

Every time he'd come over recently he wished there was some way he could get out of coming the next Sunday. The afternoon routine had never changed, he thought as he climbed the six steps to the veranda that stretched around both sides of the large house.

Moses met him at the door, took his hat and asked him to wait in the gallery while he went to tell the Mathesons Whitley had arrived. They were expecting him, had prepared for him, but he wasn't allowed into the parlor until he'd been properly announced.

Whitley found it even harder than usual to bide his time today while Moses performed his duty. On the hour's ride over to The Pines he'd chastised himself for the way he'd treated Phina last night. He hadn't wanted to be so rough with her, but no one had hit him since Anchor saved his life. In a wild moment his survival instincts took over and he'd rushed her. She had already angered him with her comments about Anchor and the slap put him over the edge. He didn't like to lose control like that. If by some chance Phina was Anchor's true daughter, Anchor must have slept with her mother while he was married to his second wife. He swore under his breath. What was he doing thinking like a school boy? Anchor was a good man, but Whitley had no proof he was a saint.

Most of the night he'd damned himself for thinking of Phina as a beautiful woman he'd like to take to bed. He'd pressed too close to her when he'd hemmed her up against the table. His roughness had caused her hair to fall out of its loose chignon and its dark richness had tumbled down her back and pooled on the white tablecloth. Her black hair and brown eyes against her pale skin made her very beautiful and desirable. Whitley shook his head to clear her from his mind. There was no doubt about it. When he went into town to see Robert, he planned to visit the upper floor of the Branchwater Tavern. He just might stay all night. Anchor had told him to never mess with a girl of good breeding, but to take his pleasure with the women in town. Whitley had always followed that rule.

Moses came back and Whitley followed him into

the parlor. He shook hands with George and greeted him. Bertha smiled at him from her usual place on the settee and held out her hand. "How nice to see you again," he said and lightly pressed a kiss to the back of her palm.

"You know we're delighted to have you, Whitley."

"Yes, ma'am," he said and turned his attention to Flannery. She was lovely in her apricot-colored dress trimmed with matching lace, bows and short bulbous sleeves. Her golden-colored hair piled high with curls shone in the sunlit room.

"Flannery," he said softly, wishing he could want her more than he did. "I've been waiting all week to see you." As Whitley said the words he knew they were a lie, but he also knew they were expected.

"Shh—" she whispered, "before Mama hears you."

"What will you have, Whitley?" George asked.

"Scotch," Whitley said and to himself added Scotch dammit! He'd had Scotch every Sunday for the past year and George still asked him what he wanted. Bertha always had a sip of sherry and Flannery a lemonade. But George would never presume Whitley wanted Scotch.

"Did you hear about the renegades attacking Gregory Plantation north of here?"

"No," Whitley answered as he settled in the wing back chair opposite Flannery. "I thought all the Indian problems were settled when Jackson had them moved out West a couple of years ago."

"So did everybody else, but there's talk that a few of the wild ones have banded together and left the reservation. It appears they've come back seeking revenge on all white men."

"It wasn't the planters who forced the Indians to

83

move out West. It was the government," Whitley said, even though he knew some settlers had pushed for their removal.

George laughed as he handed Whitley his drink. "Try explaining that to a bunch of illiterate renegades and see how far you get."

Whitley didn't laugh. He didn't have anything against the red man. In fact, Anchor learned some of the farming procedures they used at Carillon from the Indians who'd farmed the fertile lands along the upper banks of the Chattahoochee River. He glanced over at Flannery who was intently looking at her father. "How bad was it?" he asked.

"Burned the orchards and three of their barns, so I hear. No lives lost. Yet," he added dryly.

"We're not in any danger are we, Papa?" Flannery asked, her big blue eyes shining with concern.

George handed her the lemonade and patted her cheek affectionately. "Not in the least. They're two hundred miles away, dear. However, rest assured, Flannery, if I hear of them coming any closer I'll take the proper means to ensure your safety."

After a few more minutes of talking about the Indians George finally got around to asking the question Whitley had been expecting since he sat down. "How did it go with the sheriff yesterday?"

Whitley sipped from his drink before answering. He wasn't unprepared. "It appears we're going to have to wait and let Judge Rogers settle this. Abe is afraid to make a decision on this one. He expects the judge to be back in town in about six weeks."

Bertha gasped. Whitley kept his eyes on George, knowing that he'd see in Flannery's face what he heard from her mother. Silently he cursed Phina for putting

84

him in this predicament. When you go from having nothing to having it all it was hard to give up even the little things and it was damn hard to give up the really important things like Flannery and the respectability and social standing she brought with her.

"Should I speak to him?" George offered.

"I feel certain he'll insist it's a matter for the courts, but please do if you think it will help."

George nodded.

Whitley shifted in his seat and sipped his drink again before saying, "I'm afraid this affront to Anchor's name can't be cleared up as quickly as I hoped. For now, the sheriff has agreed Phina can live at Carillon and that I should give her an allowance." Whitley paused and took the time to look at the faces before him. There was no doubt in his mind that this had been discussed between the three of them earlier. He was sure he saw relief shadow Bertha's expression. The Mathesons stayed away from anything that might hint at a scandal. Whitley continued. "I suggest we postpone the formal announcement of our engagement until such time as I can devote my time to Flannery and give our engagement the attention it deserves."

"This woman is serious about her claim?" George asked.

"It appears so. I'm sending Ellison to New Orleans tomorrow to find out more about her. If she insists on staying until the judge returns, I'll be ready for her."

"Good idea. She's sure to be found out." George turned toward his wife. "Bertha?"

She waved her delicately-stitched handkerchief across her chest. "Oh, whatever you feel is best."

"Flannery?" George faced his daughter and asked.

"Oh, I agree with Whitley, Papa. We can't an-

85

nounce our engagement now. We don't know what will develop from this woman's accusations, and I don't want to be a part of it. It would ruin my chances of another marriage proposal."

Her statement brought Whitley to the edge of his seat. What in the hell was she doing worrying about another marriage proposal? She was going to marry him. This was just a postponement of the announcement.

"That's right," Bertha agreed. "We have Flannery's reputation to consider. It could be ruined by this."

"That's the way I felt about it," George said. "We'll accept your postponement of the announcement, however, we'll give you an adequate amount of time to get this problem straightened out. After that we'll allow other gentlemen to court Flannery."

"How does that sound?" he asked, looking at his wife.

"More than fair," she answered.

George turned to Whitley.

He looked at the woman he wanted to marry, not because he loved her or because he was dying to get her into bed. No, he wanted to marry her because of what she represented to his life and the fact that Anchor wanted him to marry her. Even in death, he didn't want to let Anchor down. Putting aside his true feelings once again, Whitley smiled at Flannery and her mother.

"More than fair," he agreed.

Phina stood at her bedroom window overlooking the east garden with its rose-covered arbor and the spacious front lawn. It was the last week in March and

86

colorful flowers bloomed all over the yard. She would love to go out and walk around the well-tended grounds, sniff the lovely flowers and swing in the gazebo underneath the bell, but **she** had something more important to do inside the house.

Tasma had told her that Whitley spent every Sunday at The Pines with the Mathesons, and she was waiting for him to leave. As soon as she saw him ride away she was going downstairs to begin her search. She decided the library was a good place to start looking for old journals or business ledgers that would prove Anchor McCabe was in New Orleans at the time she was conceived. If she didn't find what she wanted there, she would search the attic, and if she still didn't find what she was looking for, she would go into Whitley's office and his bedroom to plunder through his belongings. She believed Anchor had documented his visit to New Orleans nineteen years ago, and she intended to find the written proof before Whitley destroyed it.

She'd known he would fight her every step of the way but last night when he grabbed her she realized just what a dangerous position she was in. She'd wished a thousand times she hadn't struck him. She'd never slapped a man in her life. Surely Mr. Braxton had never given her reason to behave in such a manner. But how could she have allowed Whitley to say such things about her mother without striking him? By the same rule, she realized he couldn't let her talk about his father without getting angry.

A visit into town was on her list of things she had to do, too. She needed to send the money Whitley had given her last night to her mother. She wondered if Whitley knew he had been so generous to her. The little velvet bag he'd thrown on the table for her had contained as much money as it'd take her four months to earn. She'd send it all to her mother, except for a small amount she needed to buy some ribbon and lace for her dresses and combs for her hair.

With her arms folded across her chest, Phina drummed her fingers nervously back and forth. She had to believe the judge would rule in her favor and bestow a permanent allowance on her.

From the corner of her eye, she saw Whitley on a powerful-looking horse riding down the long avenue of white oaks interspersed with flowering shrubs, the horse's hooves kicking up dust as he went. She'd wait until he passed under the arched gateway before she headed downstairs. She knew she had to have a plan if the judge ruled against her. Her mother was taking more of the medication and not working at all. Right now the only thing she could think of that would help them would be to marry Mr. Braxton. She knew he would help her take care of her mother. He'd made that clear.

As soon as Whitley passed under the archway Phina turned away from the window and headed for the library. She wondered why the house was so quiet as she walked down the wide staircase, then remembered Whitley telling her the darkies had Sundays off. It was just as well they did, she thought, considering that Tasma had told her Whitley had been going to The Pines for close to a year.

The library was at the back of the great house, opposite Whitley's office. One wall was taken up with tall French windows and the other three walls were covered with darkstained shelves filled with books of

88

all different colors and sizes. For a moment the task seemed too large.

It would be so easy to hide old ledgers or journals among all these books. There must be several thousand. She would have to take it a row at a time. She would have loved to have the afternoon free to roam about the house, to look at and touch all the beautiful things in each room. But there wouldn't be too many days that she would have the house all to herself so she had to work steady and fast.

Phina pulled the first book down and looked it over. It wasn't a ledger, but a copy of poetry. She carefully turned the pages and glanced at it before returning it to the shelf, reminding herself that she couldn't take the time to look inside each book if it were clear by the cover it wasn't a journal. She picked up the next book. She'd continue on the bottom shelf and work her way up to the top of each case until all three walls had been searched.

Phina didn't think she'd been in the library very long when from behind her she heard a man clear his throat. Startled, she swung around and saw the man who had been with Whitley the first night she arrived, Ellison.

"I thought I heard a noise in here," he said in a friendly voice, a smile on his lips. "How are you doing?"

After calming her breathing, Phina said, "I'm settling in very nicely, thank you."

She didn't know why she felt so nervous. No one could possibly know the real reason she was looking through the books in the library. She put the book she was holding back in its place on the shelf and faced him directly.

"I was hoping to catch Whitley before he left for The Pines. Have you seen him?"

"Yes, you missed him," she said, folding her hands in front of her. "I watched him ride away only a few minutes ago."

"No matter." Smiling, he walked closer to her. "I'll see him tomorrow."

Phina thought Ellison splendidly dressed in his white shirt, striped waistcoat with matching brown trousers and jacket. He appeared to be as tall as Whitley but a bit heavier Phina felt sure. His hair was a shade of dark brown with premature graying showing along the temples.

"Are you looking for anything in particular?" he asked. "Maybe I can help you. You could say I've grown up in this house."

"Oh, no, really," she insisted and moved away from the bookshelf. "I thought I'd look for something to read in the evenings. This afternoon I'm going to look around the house to get familiar with everything. The place is so big it really takes a while to go through it."

"That's true. There's six bedrooms, the ballroom, two parlors, plus all the other rooms." Ellison walked over to a small rosewood table trimmed with a brass inlay and poured himself a drink from the crystal decanter. He looked back at her. "I was just thinking that any man who owns a house like this should have at least a dozen children to fill it."

Phina smiled. She had thought the same thing earlier in the day. "At least."

Ellison chuckled and leaned against one of the wing chairs that flanked the table. Phina felt herself more at ease with Ellison than she ever had with Whitley. With Whitley she had her guard up at all times.

90

"It's a big house for one man to live in to be sure." He waved his hand around the room. "But how else is a planter to show his wealth if not by glorious white pillared mansions."

Phina remained quiet and looked closer at Ellison's eyes. They were green, but had none of the blue she saw in Whitley's eyes. She was certain she heard a trace of jealousy or bitterness in his voice, but he cleverly kept it from showing on his face. His smile remained friendly.

"So you know how to read," he said. "That's quite an accomplishment for a young lady."

"In my profession I have to know how to read," she said. Even though she was enjoying the conversation she hoped he wasn't going to get too comfortable with that drink and the chair. She had a lot of books to look through.

"And what profession is that, Phina?"

"I'm a seamstress. I had to learn how to read and write so I could write down directions when our customers describe how they want their dresses made. Mama and I could never remember all the trimmings and colors they'd want."

"And where do you work in New Orleans?"

"At the boardinghouse where I live." Phina was certain Ellison was obtaining this information so he could tell Whitley, but she didn't mind. She would have been happy to tell Whitley McCabe anything he wanted to know about her or her mother. They had nothing to hide. All he had to do was ask, rather than assume she was lying about everything.

"My mother sold her family home a few years back. We're comfortably settled in a boardinghouse. A woman named Sally and her daughter Irene take care of it and the five boarders. Mama and I live and work on the third floor."

Ellison nodded. "And your mother's name is Diana Groutas."

"Yes. Is there anything else you'd like to know?" she asked, thinking she didn't approve of Whitley letting someone else do his dirty work.

Ellison chuckled again. "I see I didn't fool you with my leading questions."

"Not for a moment."

"In that case, I'll go and leave you to your—ah reading." He set the empty glass back down on the silver tray and started to walk away but had second thoughts. "I guess you know Whitley is sending me to New Orleans to check out your story."

She didn't try to hide her surprise. "No, I didn't, but now that you mention it I don't know why I didn't expect him to send someone. I guess I assumed he'd let the sheriff take care of that." Suddenly a thought struck her. "Do you plan to visit my mother?" she asked, taking another step toward him.

"I'm afraid I'll have to question her. After all, she's the one claiming Anchor was your father."

Phina cleared her throat. Her mother hadn't wanted her to make this trip. What would she do if her mother decided to go back on her word and renounce Anchor as being her father? No, her mother wouldn't do that to her.

"Ellison, if I were to write my mother a letter and send a small package would it be too much trouble for you to deliver it for me?"

He shrugged. "I don't see why not since I'm going anyway. Sure, I'll do it for you. But—"

92

"Oh, if it's too much trouble or if you think Whitley would mind, I understand."

He chuckled. "That's not it at all. I'm simply surprised you trust me to deliver it."

He had a point. Maybe she shouldn't trust him. She looked at him, smiling so friendly at her. Surely, if he wasn't to be trusted he wouldn't have pointed it out. "I'm sure if Whitley trusts you to oversee this plantation, and go to New Orleans to check on my story, I can trust you to deliver my letter and package to an ailing woman."

"You can count on me, Phina."

"Thank you. It'll only take me a minute to run upstairs and get it ready."

"Take your time. I'll pour myself a drink while I wait for you," he said as he took the top off the heavy decanter.

Whitley was in an ill temper as he walked through the front door of Carillon. He'd ridden the last twenty minutes home in a drizzling rain that soaked him to the skin. Whitley hated to get wet, and besides that, the corn they'd started planting two weeks ago needed a day of rain to soak through the hardened top soil and get to the roots.

He'd beat the lingering water off his hat and taken his boots and soggy socks off and left them on the porch to dry. He was about to run up the stairs, strip off the wet clothes and fall onto the bed when he glanced down the hallway and noticed a light coming from the library. Thinking Rubra must have left a lamp burning and knowing how dangerous that could be he headed for the library.

As he rounded the door, he saw Phina curled up in one of the chairs. Her shoes were on the floor in front of her and her feet were tucked underneath her. Thick black hair fell over her shoulder and down her chest. Light from the low burning lamp cast shimmers and sparkles on her hair. A small fire burned in the fireplace, warming the room, warming Whitley. She raised her head and looked at him with those beautiful dark eyes. He was struck by her loveliness and how oblivious she seemed to be to her appeal.

He was outraged with himself for finding her so attractive. Damn it, he'd just left the woman he was supposed to find more desirable than any other. The only thing he knew to do was to counter his unwanted feelings with anger.

"What are you doing in here?" he asked in a challenging tone, and immediately knew it was a stupid thing to ask. It would be clear to a simpleton that she was reading. And, he had told her she was free to roam about the house.

"Reading." Her eyes sparked defiantly for a brief moment. "Do you plan to ban me from the library now that you know I can read?"

A trickle of rainwater left his hair and ran down the side of his cheek. He had to settle down and calm himself before she thought him an idiot. He ran a hand over his wet hair and slicked it back from his face. "Of course not. I only meant that I'm surprised to see you in here this late." He continued to wipe water from his face and neck.

Phina uncurled her legs and slipped her stockinged feet back into her lace-up shoes. "You're wet."

"Now who's stating the obvious?" he asked, his tone softening.

Whitley thought he saw Phina give him a hint of a smile and his stomach muscles tightened. She pulled a dainty handkerchief from underneath her sleeve and extended it toward him. Whitley looked at the piece of white cloth and couldn't help but think of it as a peace offering. Their eyes met and he saw only softness and gentleness in hers. He took the handkerchief.

"You look like you could use a cup of warm milk." She laid her book in the chair. "Why don't you go upstairs and get out of those damp clothes. I'll go out to the cook house, stoke the fire and warm you some milk. You don't want to catch cold."

"That sounds very nice," Whitley said before he caught himself. What was he saying? He couldn't have her warming him milk. "But I think I'll pass. I don't want you to go to all that trouble."

She gazed up at him and smiled. "It's no trouble."

It was on the tip of his tongue to agree to her gentle persuasion, but he knew he had to decline her friendly overture. "No, I need to go on up."

A strange inner warmth covered him. Phina was dangerous. She'd made him feel so at ease in his own home that he was immensely drawn to her kindness. He wanted to wrap her in his arms and hold her close. Dammit, he'd liked the fact that the light was on to welcome him when he got home. He liked the fact there was a fire to warm him and a beautiful woman to offer him milk. He'd never had a woman do those kind of things for him and he found Phina's offer comforting and her presence appealing. In the years he'd been traveling to Flannery's house each Sunday he'd never felt as welcomed or as cared for as he did at this moment.

"In that case, I won't keep you, but before you go,

I'd like to ask if I might have use of a carriage to take me into town one day this week."

Her words reminded him of why she was at Carillon. He couldn't afford to start thinking of Phina as a sister or a lover. He had to force her out of Carillon, out of his life and marry Flannery. No doubt she wanted to go and spend the money he'd given her. That edgy feeling he'd had when he first came home returned. He didn't try to keep disapproval out of his voice. "Of course. I'll send Spiker in with you."

Phina's surprised gaze flew to his. "Spiker? I assumed Lon would take me."

Too late, Whitley remembered that Phina and Spiker didn't seem to get along. But after hearing that renegade Indians were in the northern part of the state causing trouble he was reluctant to send Lon. Whitley didn't expect the Indians to get this far south because the Cherokee's land had been farther north, but no use in taking chances on a trip that far away from Carillon.

He didn't want to tell Phina there'd been trouble with Indians. That would probably scare her more than going with Spiker. Besides, he knew Spiker would never hurt Phina. Spiker just had a bad habit of over-protecting him.

"You'll be safe with him. Take Tasma with you if it'll make you feel better. Just tell me what day you want to go and I'll tell them to be ready."

Phina sighed with relief when Whitley turned and left the room. Yes, she would take Tasma with her. He might trust that large darkie with the closely-shaved hair and thin mustache, but she didn't.

Thank goodness Whitley hadn't questioned her about the book she was reading. She'd found one of

Anchor's journals. A brief scan of the book had let her know that the entries had been written about five years after her birth. And while she was fairly sure she'd find no mention of her mother in this one, it proved her theory that Anchor had indeed kept a record of his life, and she could quite possibly find one written about his trip to New Orleans and his stay with her mother—if Whitley hadn't destroyed it.

She picked up the worn black book. In the meantime, she'd read this journal. She firmly believed Anchor was her father. Her mother wouldn't lie about a thing like that. By reading the journal maybe she would find out what kind of man her father was.

Tasma didn't know how much longer she could stand to sit beside Cush. She wasn't exactly sure what she'd expected him to do when he said he wanted to come calling but she knew it was something more than just sitting on the front steps of her house listening to him talk about how he hoped to be in charge of the grounds one day and be closer to the big house. He didn't plan to work in the canning garden all his life.

When he'd first arrived he asked if she wanted to walk down to the pond and sit on the rocks, or over to the meetinghouse to see if anything was going on there, or did she just want to sit outside and talk?

She couldn't imagine Spiker asking her what she wanted to do. No, he was so strong and commanding he'd just tell her what they were going to do.

"You's mighty quiet, Tasma," Cush said after they'd been silent for a few minutes.

"What you wants me ta say?" she asked, looking

out into the darkness. "I don't have nothin' ta say lessen you ask me somethin'."

Tasma raised her arms above her head and stretched out of boredom. She looked up into the darkness. The black velvet sky was sprinkled with tiny little stars, calling to her, twinkling at her. They reminded her of Spiker's eyes. His eyes sparkled every time he looked at her and warmed her all over.

"I's thinking maybe I should ask yore mama if'in we could talk ta Mr. Whitley 'bout a house of our own. What do ya say ta dat?"

Startled by his statement, Tasma jumped off the steps, jerking her hands to her waist. "You crazier than a howling dog, dats what. Dis is only da second time you come calling on me. I ain't ready ta set up house wid you. I gots to court mo' men than you."

"I's not talking 'bout right now, Tasma, but I knows you de one I wants fo' my woman." His voice had a sense of urgency.

"Well, I ain't ready. I's got ta have more'n one man come callin' on me fo' I settle down to chilens."

Cush unfolded his lanky frame and stood in front of her. He grabbed the waistband of his sagging breeches and pulled them farther up his bony torso. The clear white of his eyes shone against the darkness. "I hears talk yous interested in Spiker."

"Where yous hear dat?" She challenged him.

"It's all over dis place, Tasma. Everybody talkin' 'bout it. Deys all seen you making moon eyes at him over in de big house, followin' him around everywhere. He ain't interested in no woman but his dead wife. And you best remember dat, Miss Tasma. Besides he's nearin' twenty-year older'n you."

Tasma had known that sooner or later everyone

would know she loved Spiker. That was fine with her. Now no one would be surprised when she married him.

"I 'spect you better lets me handle my business, Cush. Now you gets home. I's tired and ready ta go ta bed. I's gots ta be up early ta look afta Miss Phina."

He stood there for a moment. "Can I's have a little kiss first?" he asked as he looked down at his feet.

It was on the tip of her tongue to say no when she realized she needed to know how to kiss. Spiker had been married before. He might not want a woman who didn't even know how to kiss him. She'd best let Cush show her how to do it.

"All right," she agreed. "Jest a little one."

Ellison lay in his bed and looked out at the night from his open window. He couldn't sleep. He wasn't excited about the trip to New Orleans, but he did want to keep Whitley happy. And he couldn't help but wonder what Phina had put in the tightly wrapped package for her mother. He just might decide to take a look before he gave it to the woman.

He needed Chatalene, he thought as he sipped the drink that was always beside his bed. Although he wanted her like hell, it wouldn't be smart to send for her too often. So far it didn't appear that his indiscretion had reached Whitley, and he'd just as soon keep it that way. He didn't want any holy sermons from Whitley on the rights of slaves. They had no rights. Why else were they deemed slaves if not to serve the white man? When he took over the job as overseer after his father died three years ago he told the darkies

99

he wouldn't always do things the way his father had. This was just one way of proving that.

There was a woman in town named Beverly he was considering courting. She'd probably do all right as his wife and give him sons, but he'd already decided he wouldn't give up Chatalene. He closed his eyes and remembered the feel of her breasts underneath his hand, the way he fit so tightly inside her. He smiled. No, he'd never give her up.

Ellison opened his eyes but instead of Beverly coming to his mind it was Phina he saw before him, smiling prettily. Now there was a woman he wouldn't mind taking to his bed. Her skin wasn't dark like Chatalene's but she had beautiful black hair. He laughed. Why not have both women?

An idea took root in his mind. Ellison threw his hands behind his head and sank down on his pillows. Why not court Phina? One woman was just as good as another as far as marrying and having babies were concerned, and when it came to the thought of bedding them, Phina was definitely more desirable than the light-haired Beverly.

He needed to give this idea some thought. What if Phina's story was true? If she was Anchor's daughter Whitley would at the very least be forced to bestow a handsome allowance on her. Ellison wouldn't mind that at all. Then there was the bit of information Whitley had failed to tell anyone. The unsigned papers making Whitley Anchor's son and heir. Ellison sat upright in bed. Was there a possibility the judge would give Phina the whole goddammed plantation if he knew the papers were never signed? He licked his lips and wiped the taste of the expensive whiskey from the edges of his mouth. He slammed his fist into the bed-covers beside him. By god, it could happen!

Ellison suddenly changed his mind about not want-ing to go to New Orleans. He wanted to go and get proof that Phina *was* Anchor McCabe's daughter. There was no chance Whitley would be interested in Phina with the way he'd stayed true to Flannery the past year. Whitley's only chance would be to bribe the judge. Ellison laughed to himself. Whitley try to bribe a judge? Never. He was too damn honest. He'd rather lose Carillon than to do something so unscrupulous. But what would Whitley do if Ellison courted Phina and asked for her hand in marriage?

Thoughts of getting his hands on Phina and Caril-lon made Ellison hot and hard. He reached above his bed and pulled on the cord that rang a bell in Samson's room. How could he deny himself Chatalene tonight? To hell with what Whitley thought. He needed the dark-skinned beauty in his bed.

Laughing, he fell back against the pillows.

Chapter Seven

"I was wondering how long it was going to take to hear from you," Robert said, as Whitley walked into his office early Wednesday morning.

"No doubt you've heard about my houseguest," Whitley said dryly.

Robert sniffed and leaned back in his chair. His large frame making the chair creak beneath his weight and his rotund stomach forcing the buttonholes on his waistcoat to spread and gape. Robert had a fondness for rich foods and it showed prominently in his jowls and his fat, stubby fingers.

"Whitley, please." He motioned to a chair. "She interrupted your engagement party. By now the whole state knows a young woman is claiming to be Anchor's daughter. I only hate that I was under the weather and unable to attend myself. Surely it was a sight when she came bursting through the door, pushing Ellison and Spiker aside as if they were nothing more than balls of cotton." He chuckled. "Yes, I wish I could have seen it."

Whitley wasn't happy that the incident had been embellished, but he knew there was no use in trying to set the story right. Instead, he went straight to the heart of the matter. "You said it well, Robert. She *claims* to be his daughter."

Too restless to sit, Whitley refused the offer of a chair, preferring to walk over to the window and look out at the quiet street. "I sent Ellison to New Orleans to find out who she really is. He left first thing Monday morning. We should know something in a couple of weeks."

Robert tapped his forefinger against his lips. "Keep in mind that Anchor spent a great deal of time in New Orleans in his younger years. There's always the possibility—"

"No!" Whitley spun around. "No, she's not Anchor's daughter. If Anchor had thought there was any chance he had a son or daughter he would have never taken me into his home and promised me Carillon."

"You said it well." Robert mimicked Whitley's words as he placed his hands on his stomach and laced his stubby fingers together. "If Anchor had known he had a child he would have given you no more than he gave Ellison."

Whitley swallowed hard. He knew what a precarious situation he was in. Dammit, he knew!

"You drew up the papers making me his legal son and leaving me Carillon in his will." Whitley pointed his finger at Robert.

The man didn't flinch. "But they were never signed."

"That doesn't alter his intention," Whitley shot back tersely. "You told me after he died that the courts always look at intent as well as the facts."

"True, Whitley. It was Anchor's intention to make

103

you his heir—" he paused. "Because he didn't think he had an heir from his own blood."

Taut with the fear of losing Carillon Whitley's body ached from the strain. "What are you saying? Anchor loved me like a son."

"I'm saying that *if* this woman can prove she's Anchor's daughter you don't have a hope in hell of getting one penny from Carillon. Phina will get it all."

"She can't prove Anchor was her father."

"How do you know?"

"Because it's not true."

"I've heard she has his coloring, his hair and a resemblance in her features."

"Dammit! Robert, I'm Anchor's only heir. And I'd like to think my lawyer was on my side."

Robert sighed audibly and shifted in his chair. "I'll testify that Anchor wanted you to have Carillon. But if the judge believes she's Anchor's daughter it won't matter what Anchor's intent was when he died."

"Don't play with me, Robert. I'm in no mood for it." Whitley's voice was dangerously low. To think that last night he was feeling kindly toward Phina. He was pleased she'd asked to warm him some milk. He couldn't allow himself to be taken in by her, to be fooled by her beauty or the womanly kindness he yearned to accept.

"When Anchor took that rope from around my neck and saved my life he told me if I worked hard and proved myself Carillon would be mine one day. I loved him as a father and he loved me as a son. I've always honored him. I won't let anyone take his plantation away from me."

Robert's disturbed gaze met Whitley's. "It's not your decision to make, Whitley."

"Anchor made the decision fifteen years ago."

"She ain't never been ta town, Miss Phina," Rubra said as she stood on the front porch wringing the tail of her apron, waiting for Phina to climb onto the carriage that would take them into Bainbridge. "You best not let her outta yo sight. No tellin' what dat girl get into. You too, Spiker. It's yore job ta take care of dis Miss Phina and my girl. Don't you let nothin' happen to 'um."

Phina noticed that Spiker remained surly and paid no attention to the chattering woman as he continued to check the horses's harness.

"Don't worry about us, Rubra," Phina said, trying to calm Rubra's fears. "Nothing will happen to either of us."

Phina glanced up at the sky. It was a beautiful shade of blue, not a cloud in sight. She looked around the lawn outlined with neatly trimmed shrubs and colorful flowers. Her gaze lighted on the gazebo with the bell hanging from its ceiling, and she automatically reached up and touched the bell that hung around her neck. It was no wonder Whitley didn't want to give up even a small portion of Carillon.

The front door swung open and Tasma came running out, a picnic basket hanging over one arm. "I's gots our food rights heah, Miss Phina. Yous get thirsty jest let me know."

Rubra brought Tasma up short by grabbing hold of her skirt as she flew past. The woman pointed her forefinger at Tasma and gave her a stern look. "Don't

105

yous give Miss Phina no trouble," she warned. "She don't have time ta be lookin' afta you and gets her business done, too."

Tasma's dark eyes widened. She nodded. "Yes, Mama. I'll be so good won't no one even knows I's been in dat town."

"Get on up then," Rubra ordered. "Spiker, don't jest stand dere. Help Miss Phina in de carriage."

Phina's eyes met Spiker's. His gaze was hard, penetrating, unyielding. It appeared he remembered her promise if he should ever touch her again. "Would you mind?" she asked in a soft tone, knowing it would be difficult to climb up by herself.

Spiker hesitated, then walked over and took hold of her elbow and helped her into the carriage. From the other side of the carriage Tasma climbed up onto the driver's seat and plopped down, placing her basket of food at her feet. With a quick jump Spiker joined her and picked up the reins. He slapped the strips of leather to the horse's rump and the carriage bolted away from the house. Phina could hear Rubra shouting last minute instructions to Tasma and Spiker but couldn't make out the words.

Three minutes into the ride Phina wished she was up on the driver's seat where Tasma and Spiker sat. She couldn't see very much of the landscape from the back of the carriage. She watched the white oaks as the carriage passed and tried to count them but Spiker had the horses going at a quick pace. She knew when they'd passed under the arched gateway that read CARILLON.

As the carriage bumped along she tried to sit up and look out the side but the position put a crick in her neck so she gave it up and sat back.

106

Without realizing she was doing it, she started noticing Tasma slowly easing herself closer to Spiker. Occasionally she would look over at him, but Spiker kept his eyes on the road ahead of him and his attention on the job at hand.

When Tasma was close enough that his elbow hit her arm a couple of times he turned to her and said, "What are you doing so close to me? Move over. I don't have room to work the reins."

"I ain't too close to—" Tasma's words were cut off as the carriage hit a hole and Spiker's elbow whacked her under the chin. Her eyes widened in alarm.

"See, I told you," he said, speaking sharply to her. "Now move over and give me some room."

Silently cupping her chin, Tasma scooted away, but a few minutes later a smile appeared on Phina's face when she saw the girl slowly inching her way back toward Spiker.

Tasma was in love with Spiker. Phina knew the signs. She had acted the same way a few years ago when she and her mother first moved into the boardinghouse. There was a young man named Billy Swanson living there. Phina wanted to be near him every minute he was there, but he always treated her like a bothersome little girl. He moved away a few months later and she never saw him again. She'd almost forgotten about him. Now Mr. Braxton was showing an interest in her.

Phina leaned back against the cab. Why couldn't Mr. Braxton be as young and handsome as Whitley? Why couldn't he—Phina put a stop to her thoughts. Whitley was trying to keep her from what was rightly hers. She had to remember that and not dwell on the things that she liked about him.

107

When they arrived in town almost two hours later Phina was happy to be out of the stifling carriage. Spiker had errands to do for Whitley so Phina allowed Tasma to go with her to the mercantile.

Tasma gasped loudly when she first walked into the shop. "Look at all dis stuff, Miss Phina. Ooo, ahhh. Has you ever seen de likes of dis befo'? I's never seen so many different things in one room."

Phina smiled. It had been a long time since she'd been impressed by a mercantile. "Enjoy looking, Tasma, but don't touch anything," Phina told her.

"I won't tech a thing."

Smiling to the middle-aged woman behind the counter as she passed, Phina walked by the foodstuffs and gardening supplies and headed for the fabrics and trimmings. A quick assessment of the table told her she would be very limited in how she could fancy her dresses with the small selection of ribbons and lace to choose from. What materials and accessories that were available had all been thrown onto a large table. She was used to neatly stacked bolts of cloth and perfectly lined rows of lace in the shops in New Orleans.

She would just have to take the time and sort through all the rubble on the table. She took off her gloves and pulled her reticule from around her wrist and handed them to Tasma. "Hold these for me. I've got to dig underneath all this and see what I can find."

Half an hour later Phina was satisfied she'd found enough trimming to beautify her red dress and her honey-colored one. Under a bolt of calico she found a good-sized piece of tulle. She would use that to make a scalloped overskirt that could be worn with either dress. A wide band of white velvet ribbon would work as a sash that would look good with both dresses too.

108

She found enough colors of ribbons, lace, buttons and satin to remake the dresses and make them presentable for dinner. She also found enough lace to make a detachable white collar and cuffs that she could use with either dress and a length of black velvet, too. If she were careful she could make the two dresses look like she had several by making everything detachable.

When she was confident there wasn't another piece of trim she could use she found herself wandering over the store looking at all the variety of things available while Tasma talked nonstop. Phina didn't mind, though. She knew the girl was excited about her first trip into town.

As the day passed, Phina took time to smell each different bottle of scented water. She touched all the beautiful powder jars, and she fingered each little hand carved wooden animal. When she finally took her purchases up to the counter to pay for them she noticed four lovely ivory hair combs on a shelf behind the woman.

"Could I please see the combs?" she asked pointing to them. She desperately needed a pair.

The woman took them down and placed them on the counter in front of Phina.

"Oh, Miss Phina dis is so purty," Tasma said, lightly touching one of the combs.

"Yes, they are," she answered. The ivory had been beautifully carved into the shape of butterfly wings. She looked up at the owner. "These are lovely."

"You must be the young woman who's staying at Carillon."

Phina smiled. "Yes, I'm Anchor McCabe's daughter."

"Never told us about you, he didn't," the woman

said in a matter-of-fact tone. Her masculine features were set in a firm expression.

Undaunted, Phina said, "I know, but that's because my mother never told him about me. How much are they?" she asked, giving the combs back to the woman.

"Eight dollars," the owner said. "That's mighty fancy workmanship on those combs."

Phina's heart sank. They were the most exquisite combs she'd ever seen. She needed the trimmings for her dresses and couldn't buy both. She would have to continue to use the hairpins. They easily fell out of her hair and didn't hold it in place very well, but they'd have to do.

"Yes, I can see that, but I'm afraid they're more than I can afford right now. Maybe later."

"I can put them on Whitley's account for you. The rest of this stuff, too."

"Oh, no," Phina said quickly. "I'll pay for this myself. And I'll come back for the combs later. When I can pay for them."

The merchant shrugged. "I hope they're still here when you get the money. This color was made for hair as black as yours."

Phina paid for her purchases and she and Tasma walked back to the carriage where Spiker was waiting for them. Spiker reached for her elbow to help her into the carriage but she pulled away and said, "Spiker, I believe I want to ride up front with you. Put Tasma in the back."

Startled, Spiker stepped back.

"Dat ain't proper, Miss Phina," Tasma said quickly, moving to stand between the two of them.

"She was talking to me," Spiker said, pointing a thumb at his chest.

Tasma swung around to Phina. "What's yous wants ta ride 'side Spiker fo'?" she said with a pout on her lips.

"I can assure you it's not that I want to ride beside Spiker." She cut her eyes around to him. "It's that I want to see the land as we go back to Carillon."

"But it ain't proper," Tasma complained again.

Phina could see Tasma getting the upper hand of this conversation if she didn't take immediate control. "I don't care what is proper at this point, Tasma. I want to see what lies between here and the plantation and I can't do that from the back of the carriage."

Tasma jerked her hands to her hips, jutting out her bottom lip. "My mama said fo' me—"

"Nobody cares what your mama says. I've already told you that," Spiker said as he grabbed hold of Tasma's arm. "Your mama don't run this plantation. Now get in the carriage and shut up so we can get going."

"Yous gone lets him talk ta me dat way, Miss Phina?" Tasma asked as she struggled against Spiker's hold.

It was clear Tasma was used to her mother taking up for her. It was also clear that Spiker had a habit of taking hold of people. "Let her go, Spiker. You don't have to grab someone to make them do what you want them to." He cut his eyes around to Phina. It was clear he didn't like her.

Tasma gave Spiker a smug look.

"Tasma, I know you have my welfare at heart. I appreciate it, but I can take care of myself." She glanced up at Spiker again. "Second, I have very little

111

knowledge of slaves and how to manage them. However, I do know you are supposed to do what I tell you to do without talking back to me." She paused. "Now get in the back of that carriage and don't let me hear another word out of you or I'll be the one talking to Rubra and Whitley."

Tasma blew her breath out of her nose like a bull and stomped onto the carriage.

The ride back to Carillon was beautiful. After Spiker and Phina got over their initial shyness of being so close, Phina started asking questions and Spiker relented and answered, even though he didn't appear happy about her inquisitive attitude. They ate bread and cheese as they traveled, not taking the time to stop. Spiker showed her where the Flint and the Chattahoochee Rivers met and how they became the Apalachicola River a few miles farther down stream. He told her about some caves with springs on the west bank of the Chattahoochee and other caverns that were farther south on the Chipola River. He pointed out where Carillon began. He drove by corn fields where the stalks were just breaking above the ground. He also took her by one of the sawmills which stood on the upper banks of the river. One thing she was acutely aware of as she rode around the plantation with Tasma mumbling insistently in the back was that Carillon Plantation was big. And it was beautiful.

Phina fingered the silver bell that hung around her neck. A picture of her mother's pale face, graying hair and trembling hands crossed her mind. Why couldn't she think about the possibility of moving her mother to Carillon? She knew Diana would get stronger if she could get out of the stuffy old boardinghouse and sit in the sunshine, smell the flowers, and listen to the

112

birds chirping. Having the undivided attention of someone like Tasma, Rubra or Chatalene would help her mother regain her strength and health in no time at all.

Yes, it was definitely worth thinking about.

Chapter Eight

Whitley mounted his horse and headed toward home. Rather than hire a replacement for Ellison for the two or three weeks he'd be gone to New Orleans, Whitley had decided to do the work himself. He could catch up on his book work when Ellison returned. Right now he had thirty field hands plowing from sunup to sundown. With the corn in the ground they had to get the ground ready for the peanut and cotton-seed that would be planted in the coming weeks.

Plowing was slow going because the ground was so hard. There had been a few light sprinklings of rain over the past couple of weeks but not enough to soak into the soil and moisten the deep layers of earth. When the wind blew, dust from the plowed fields filled the air, making it hazy as particles of dirt were left hanging in the dry air.

Whitley had been so tired the past few nights from being in the saddle for the first time in months that he'd only eaten a light supper in the kitchen and fallen into bed. Now he was getting used to the long and hard workdays, and he didn't feel so tired. He'd sent word to Rubra that he would be eating in the dining room tonight and for her to ask Phina to join him. He liked the idea that she was there to have dinner with him. He found comfort in knowing he didn't have to spend the whole evening alone.

Dusty from his day in the fields, Whitley had decided to wash in the river before going to the house. He had sent Spiker for clean clothes while he swam in the chilly water of the Chattahoochee. It was odd the way he hadn't been able to get Phina off his mind. His constant thinking of her the past few days had yielded one positive thought. He'd decided that he should spend more time with her and get to know her. Surely if she became comfortable with him he would be able to question her without arousing her suspicions. Eventually she would say something he could use against her. He was sure of it.

A few minutes later Whitley was in the parlor sipping Scotch, waiting for Phina to join him. He heard her coming down the stairs and rose from the chair. She entered the parlor, and, no matter how hard he tried to deny it, he was attracted to Phina the way a man was attracted to a woman he wanted to take to bed.

Phina was a beautiful woman, but he knew the attraction came from more than that. Whitley knew many beautiful women including his fiancé. He hadn't been able to put his finger on just what it was about Phina that caused that tightening of his chest, that stirring in the lower part of his body. It couldn't be her self-confidence. Flannery was full of that and it hadn't attracted him to her. It could be that Phina was sensitive. She'd shown that the night he'd come home wet. By her clothing and manners he knew her to be conservative, too. Maybe it was that built-in desire to

115

conquer and control that which challenged him. Certainly she challenged him with her claim. Or was it simply that womanly presence in his house.

Their eyes met as she swept into the room and Whitley knew that whatever it was that made him want her was going to be a damn hard thing to fight.

"Good evening," she said softly. "I trust you're feeling better."

He tilted his head and grinned a little. His gaze left her face and scanned the length of her. "Were you told I was ill?"

She smiled and brushed a strand of loose hair back with her hand. "Oh no, not ill, just very tired. Rubra told me you were working in the fields this week and only taking a light supper in your room."

"Yes. I've been trying to do both my job and Ellison's while he's away. Now I'm getting used to the saddle again and it was a bit easier today." Whitley wished he hadn't noticed that Phina looked damn good in red. At first glance, he thought the dress was new but soon realized that it was the same one she'd worn before only now she'd added the white lace collar and cuffs and a wide velvet sash at the waist. She'd done an excellent job of making the old dress look new and different. He wished she'd braid her hair and pull it into a tight bun at the back of her head the way Flannery did some times so those wayward strands of hair wouldn't fall so becomingly around her face.

He'd been so certain, at first, that his sexual attraction to her had been because he hadn't been with a woman in a while. But he'd taken care of that earlier in the week when he'd gone into town to see Robert. He'd had quite a good time with one of the upstairs girls in the tavern. But looking at Phina now, it was

116

apparent he was going to have to visit the place more frequently. He was too easily aroused by Phina.

"Would you like something to drink?" he asked, knowing he had to get those kind of thoughts off his mind.

"No. Thank you. I'm fine, but before we go into dinner, I was wondering if I might ask something of you."

"I don't see why not. It will give me time to finish my drink. Sit down." He pointed to the green velvet settee for her, and he took the brocade-stitched wing back facing her.

"I was hoping I might be able to spend some time with you tomorrow."

He tried not to show his surprise at her statement as he asked, "I'm not sure I know what you mean by spending time with me."

"It's quite simple." She folded her hands in the lap of her red dress. "I'd like to know more about this plantation. I want to know exactly what it does and how it works."

Memories flooded Whitley's mind. He'd felt the same way when Anchor first brought him to Carillon to live when he was a gangly young man. Whitley never knew his age for sure, but Anchor had told him he looked to be about fifteen so on the day he arrived at Carillon, the eleventh of October, Anchor had declared it Whitley's birthday.

The whole concept of a self-sustained house and land that took care of so many people intrigued him and he wanted to know everything about Carillon. Like Phina, he thought he could learn it all in one day. In truth, he was excited about the prospect of sharing his knowledge of the plantation with someone else the

117

way Anchor had shared it with him. But he quickly reminded himself that Phina was not the one to share that information with. She could take it away from him. He would have to wait until he and Flannery had a son. Then he would teach him everything he knew.

Fighting his growing attraction to Phina the way he had in the past, Whitley said, "You won't be around long enough for it to matter."

Phina's back stiffened and her eyes blinked rapidly. "That's a matter of opinion. I believe I will."

His words stung her. Whitley saw it in her eyes. He didn't want to hurt her, but he didn't want her to think anything had changed between them. It hadn't. In a way, he easily identified with her because like her, he had no father to call his own until Anchor took him in and promised him Carillon. He felt sorry for her, too. But she chose the wrong man to claim as her father.

"I promise not to make a nuisance of myself," she said when he remained quiet. "I want to know more about this plantation."

"Why?" he asked abruptly. "So you can impress the judge with how much you know about Carillon."

"No, because Anchor was my father," she answered just as quickly. Phina moved to the edge of her seat and leaned forward to give emphasis to her words. "You may never believe Anchor is my father, but I will always believe it. My mother wouldn't have lied about something like this." Her hand went to her throat. "Besides, I have the bell as proof."

"You know what I think about that bell," he said cautiously.

Looking into her eyes, Whitley saw she truly believed that Anchor was her father. He could deny it all he wanted, but that wasn't going to make her change

118

her mind. Her mother had spoken and for Phina, that made it so. For the first time since her arrival, Whitley understood there was no use in arguing with Phina about any of this. All he had to do was convince the judge there was reasonable doubt as to whether or not Anchor was her father. Robert should be able to do that. If Diana Groutas allowed one man in her bed chances were she allowed others.

Whitley finished his drink and set the glass on the small table beside him. With that settled he could allow himself the pleasure of the things he could enjoy about Phina. Like the way it pleased him to look at her, banter her, challenge her. Yes, there was no reason why he shouldn't enjoy Phina's womanly presence in his house.

Understanding all this softened Whitley and he asked, "What kind of things do you want to know about Carillon?"

"Everything."

He laughed. That answer showed how ambitious she was and how little she knew. "Everything? I don't think you have any idea how much there is to learn about a place this size. Why don't we start by you telling me what you already know about Carillon."

Phina brushed at her errant hair again and settled more comfortably on the settee. "I believe you told me *we* have sixty thousand acres of land and over seventy slaves. Yesterday, on the way back from town, Spiker told me *we* own forty horses, twelve carts, and thirty plows. Things like timber wheels, hoes, spades, and axes are too numerous to accurately count. One of the reasons for this is because the slaves take them to the fields and lose them, *we* buy more, then they find the lost ones."

Whitley gave her an amused smile. "No *we,* Phina. Carillon owns those things. And *I* own Carillon."

Pleased with herself, she continued as if he hadn't spoken. "Spiker also showed me where the Chattahoochee and Flint Rivers meet and form the Apalachicola River. He drove the carriage past the sawmill on the west bank near our docks where we ship our corn, cotton, and lumber down the river to the Gulf of Mexico."

"Are you sure Spiker told you all this? He's a man of few words. And the two of you haven't been getting along very well."

"I think he answered because he felt he had to. Once I managed to get him to talking he opened up and answered every question. I found out we spend an average of twelve hundred dollars a year on horses and oxen, about three hundred on plows, carts, scythes and all the other things needed to farm the land. Oh, and he told me about five hundred dollars are spent—"

Whitley held up his hand. "Enough. I can see that Spiker left nothing out. I knew he was smart, but I didn't realize he'd learned so much from me over the years."

"He's also devoted to you, you know."

Her voice was soft, her expression was gentle. "Did he tell you why?"

She shook her head and another wisp of hair fell from her chignon. "I assume it's because you are his master. I know he's fiercely protective of you as are all the slaves."

Whitley nodded. For a fleeting moment he felt the need to tell her why Spiker was so devoted to him, but something held him back. Sharing that part of his life with Phina could make them closer, and he needed to avoid that at all cost. Whitley knew he was vulnerable. He hadn't been around a lot of women in his lifetime and never had he lived with one. He couldn't allow himself to become attached to Phina. He had Flannery waiting for him.

"You told me how when you were younger Anchor made you work in the field pulling corn, picking cotton and working in the sawmill."

"That's true. He wanted me to learn every aspect of the plantation because he knew I would one day own Carillon." He rose from the chair. "I think you know as much about Carillon as you need to because, Phina, when the judge gets back into town, you'll have to leave."

Her gaze flew to his. Again, he knew his words had hurt her but they had to be said. He would be nice to her, enjoy her, but he couldn't let her think he had changed his mind about her claim on Carillon.

Phina lifted her chin. "Whitley, I fully expect the judge to side with me. Unless you decide to do something unlawful."

He looked down at her. "Unlawful? What are you talking about?"

"I suppose you could bribe the judge to see things your way?"

His eyebrows drew together in a frown. He would never do anything to dishonor Anchor's name but he wasn't sure he wanted her to know that. "I'm Anchor's son and only heir. The judge will see it that way because that's the truth."

She rose. "No, it's not. I'm his daughter."

They faced each other. Whitley liked the fact that she didn't cower before him. And nothing he'd said had daunted her. He liked that fact too. "Since you seem to be in want of something to do while we wait on the judge, I'll turn over the managing the house workers to your care. I'll tell Rubra and the others to report to you. Do you think you can handle that?"

"Of course I can. What I don't know, I'll learn."

"Also, you should feel free to ask Rubra to get Samella to help you make your new dresses. She's excellent with a needle."

Phina opened her mouth to speak but hesitated. Finally she said, "I don't believe I'll be making any new dresses for a while."

He looked at her curiously. "I thought you went into town to buy fabrics for new dresses. I thought that's why you wanted an allowance."

"No."

That frightened look she had the first night she arrived returned to her eyes. "I don't understand."

"I—I might as well tell you the truth. I sent most of the money to my mother. She's been ill and can't work. She needed that money to pay for her room and board and for medication."

"And you'd do anything to get it for her, right?" His words didn't hide his annoyance.

She stiffened, drew herself up straighter. "I didn't lie if that's what you're indicating."

"And you don't believe she lied to you about Anchor?"

"I'd stake my life on it."

Whitley heard the earnestness in her voice. Suddenly things seemed clearer to Whitley. Phina wasn't here because she wanted anything from Anchor's estate. She was here because of her mother. He admired her for that. He admired her strength and her courage to travel two hundred miles and demand recompense. But that didn't mean he'd let her win.

"I'm sorry if my dresses still aren't suitable for your dinner table. I did my best to make them presentable. I'll be happy to have dinner in my room."

Her apology touched him warmly. She was giving him leave to excuse her if he thought her inappropriately dressed. "No, Phina. You are more than presentable. You are in fact a very beautiful woman, beautifully gowned. And it's admirable of you to be so concerned for your mother's welfare. Will the money I gave you be enough for her until you return?"

Phina's shoulders relaxed. "Yes," she whispered.

He nodded. "Let's go into dinner."

Later that night Phina lay on her bed propped against the pillows reading the last pages in Anchor's journal. Now she wasn't so sure that reading the journal telling about his life had been a good idea. After only a few pages she knew that Anchor McCabe was a good man. The journal proved he was a just man too. He treated all men fairly. He took good care of his slaves and he gave money to the church in town.

Phina closed the book and leaned her head against the bed frame. She couldn't help but wonder if she would be different today if she'd grown up in a house like this. One thing was sure. She wouldn't have to consider the possibility of marrying a man she didn't love in order to have enough money to take care of her mother.

She thought of Mr. Braxton. He wasn't an unpleasant man. But she'd always expected more, wanted more of those unexplained feelings of tingles, goose bumps and butterflies when she looked at the man she planned to marry.

A light knock sounded on the door and her eyes popped open. Tasma must have forgotten to tell her something. She threw back the sheet and scrambled barefoot to the door and opened it. Whitley stood in front of her. They looked into each others eyes for a moment and Phina felt something intangible pass between them. Her heartbeat sped up.

"Oh," she said grabbing the front of her cotton nightgown and holding the drawstrings together. "I thought you were Tasma. Just a minute." Shaking, Phina ran back to the bed and threw on her worn satin robe.

Whitley stepped just inside her room. "I'm sorry to disturb you so late but I noticed your light on when I came up so I went back downstairs and got this for you to study." He held out a sheet of paper.

Her robe securely tied about her waist, Phina took the paper and looked at it. In the shadowed lamplight she saw that it was a copy of the plot plan for Carillon. She looked up at him and for the first time saw softness and gentleness in his eyes and on his expression. It made her breath quicken.

"It's a drawing of Carillon." He stood so close to her Phina felt his warmth. She felt butterflies in her stomach, tingles up her back and goose bumps on her arms.

Whitley leaned over her and pointed to the tree-lined drive at the bottom of the paper. His arm brushed her shoulder. It surprised Phina how a simple touch from him tightened her stomach muscles.

"You see here the arched gateway and the lane up to the main house where we are. The carriage house is off to the left side here and the *garconniere* is to the right. The kitchen is directly behind the main house here and the smokehouse behind it. To the left here is the formal garden and over here the vegetable garden. This area here is the slaves' quarters and beyond that the docks and the river. All the surrounding land is fields or woodland. The legend will help you."

He looked down at her and she looked up at him. Phina didn't know what it was, she only knew something was drawing her to him. She swallowed hard. "Thank you," she whispered.

"After you study this scale and know where everything is you'll be better prepared to understand how a plantation works."

"Yes, I can see that." She moistened her lips. "What made you decide to show me this?"

The way he looked at her caused a flicker of hope light inside her.

"I don't want you to get lost should you go out for a walk. And—because I finally realized you have the right to believe your mother."

"But you don't believe her."

He shook his head, then turned away.

Chapter Nine

Phina stood in the library looking over the last wall of bookshelves. Two walls had already been searched yielding three different journals where Anchor had written about different times in his life. One of them had an entry of a trip to New Orleans, but it was dated three years before Phina was born. She concluded that at one time the journals were probably shelved together. Dusting and cleaning the shelves and books over the years must have separated them.

She'd come to look forward to having the house to herself on Sunday afternoons and evenings over the past month. Tasma would usually pop in a couple of times to see if she wanted dinner but other than that she was left alone.

Since that night a couple of weeks ago when Whitley had given her the plot plan to Carillon there had been no harsh words between them. What he'd said to her made sense and it was good advice for her to use in settling her feelings about him. She appreciated the fact that he agreed she had the right to believe her mother and by the same rule she had to agree that he had the right to believe that Anchor was not her father. He was wrong, of course, and in time she hoped to prove it to him. One way she could do that was to find a journal that proved Anchor was in New Orleans nine months before her birth.

Early in the evening with four shelves to go, Phina decided to take a break. Earlier Tasma had brought her in a plate of buttered bread, a dish of cooked peaches and a pot of steaming tea. She checked and there was tea left in the China pot so she poured it in her cup and sat down to rest. If Whitley stayed at the Mathesons as long as he usually did she could rest a few minutes and still be finished before he returned.

Phina unlaced her shoes, took them off and settled back against the settee to enjoy the tea and think back over the past two weeks. It hadn't taken her long to fall into a routine at Carillon. She had immediately found favor with the slaves who worked around the house. Hetty was in charge of the cooking and Chatalene did the serving of the meals as well as other chores in the house. Samella was the seamstress. She discovered the slaves actually liked for her to question them about their job. They were eager to tell her what they did for Carillon and Whitley and seemed to be quite proud of themselves.

Tasma stayed at Phina's side each day ready to fetch or carry anything she might need. After several days of watching Tasma around Spiker, Phina was convinced that she was in love with him. And it was clear that Spiker considered her a child who kept getting in his way. Rubra, she noticed, liked to boss all the slaves, but had no trouble taking orders from her. Phina was sure Whitley must have told her that Phina was to manage the house.

Although Rubra had kept the house running

smoothly and in good condition, Phina had found that the formal garden had been neglected. She hadn't had much experience with flowers, shrubs or trees but knew she could work with one of the slaves on the garden and make it the showplace it should be.

The past three days she'd been busy helping Samella make new clothes for the slaves. A task that she was not only good at but thoroughly enjoyed. Each of the men and boys were getting three collarless shirts with full long sleeves and a pair of dark brown breeches for Sundays. All of the women were getting two new work dresses made of a coarse cotton fabric in a faded shade of black. But their Sunday dresses were being made from a shade of blue that matched the sky on the clearest of summer days.

As she finished her tea, her thoughts turned to Whitley. She seldom saw him during the day, but they came together in the evenings for dinner. He always answered her questions about the plantation and on one occasion he'd agreed to let her go with him to the stables when a new horse was being delivered. The next night she asked him if it would be all right for her to be taught to ride once she finished helping with the slaves' clothing. Whitley agreed that Cass could teach her in the late afternoons.

Phina closed her eyes and leaned her head back against the sofa. Whitley. She was sure he didn't like her any better than he had the night she arrived, but sometimes she caught him looking at her in a way that made her breath grow short and her stomach muscles tighten. There were times when she wanted to just reach out and touch him, but then she'd remember that he was going to do his best to throw her off Carillon and the moment would pass.

Phina set the empty cup on the tray and went back to work. The third book she took off the shelf was a journal. When she opened it she smelled the aged mustiness of the coarse, yellowed paper. The first entry was dated in January of the year she was born. Her fingers trembled and her stomach lurched with anticipation. Trepidation forced her to simply hold the book for a few moments. This book could contain the last bit of information she needed. She had her father's coloring, hair and his features, she had his signed note and the bell, now if this journal could prove he was in New Orleans at the right time of year, how could the judge or Whitley not believe she was Anchor's daughter.

While summoning the courage to look through the book, Phina heard the front door open. Her heart rose in her throat. Whitley had returned early! What if he asked about the journal she was holding? She pressed the book to her chest and held it tightly. No, she was having a streak of guilty conscience. There was no way he could know she had been looking for proof of Anchor's visit to New Orleans. Still clutching the book to her chest she stepped out into the hallway and called, "Hello?"

"Phina, it's Ellison. I'm in the foyer."

She fell back against the door frame and breathed a sigh of relief. She'd almost scared herself to death. She slipped her feet back into her shoes and headed down the hallway. Ellison was placing his hat on the hat stand by the door.

"Have you just returned?" she asked.

He turned to her smiling broadly. "This very minute. I haven't even been home." His gaze swept down her face. "You're looking lovely as usual."

129

"Welcome back." Phina returned his smile. His flattery pleased her even though she knew it wasn't true. She was tired, her hair was falling from her bun and dust was smeared across the bodice of her dress.

"Thank you." He took a step closer. "It's been almost twenty years since a woman lived here. It's nice to have a beautiful woman welcome me back to Carillon."

She noticed the skin underneath his eyes sagged with dark circles and his lids looked puffy. It didn't appear he'd slept well while he was gone. "It's a long stage ride from New Orleans. I know you must be tired."

"A little. I feel better now that I've seen you."

Phina didn't know how to respond to his statement. He was certainly going overboard with his flattery.

"I tried to time my arrival when I was sure Whitley would still be at the Mathesons. He is gone, isn't he?" Ellison asked.

"Yes," she said, wondering why he wanted Whitley to be gone. Surely Whitley should be the first person he'd want to see so he could report his findings. "He left at his usual time so he should return in an hour or so."

"Good. That gives us a few minutes alone." His smile widened again. "I have something for you, and I didn't want to give it to you with Whitley around." Ellison slipped his hand into his coat pocket and pulled out an envelope. He extended it toward her. His eyes sparkled with satisfaction. "A letter from your mother."

"Oh, how wonderful!" Phina dropped the book on a side table and squealed with delight as she took the letter from him. "I haven't heard a word from her since I left a month ago."

Her fingers shook as she tore open the envelope. She scanned the letter quickly, knowing she'd read every word many times in the coming weeks. "She says that the coughing is completely gone now, and she's feeling a little stronger. She misses me, and she appreciates the package I sent her." Phina looked up at Ellison, a sincere smile on her face. "I can't thank you enough for doing this for me. I don't know how I'll ever repay you."

His expression turned serious. "Maybe I can think of something. Someday."

He smiled again and suddenly Phina felt uncomfortable. His words seemed to indicate more than they actually said. "You saw my mother?" she asked, pushing the disturbing feelings aside. "How did she look?"

"I'll tell you everything, but why don't we go into the parlor so I can fix myself a drink. It's been a long hot day for me."

"Of course it has." She admonished herself for not offering him refreshment immediately. Phina stuffed her mother's letter into the pocket of her skirt. "I'll get you a drink. What would you like?" she asked, as they walked into the parlor.

"I'll have a whiskey." Ellison settled himself onto the settee, throwing one arm over the top.

Phina walked over to the side table where the crystal decanters sat on a silver tray. There were five different containers on the tray. Three of them held amber colored liquids and two of them were clear. She had no idea which one held the whiskey he wanted.

"The one with the square top," Ellison said, after she'd stood there for a moment.

"I know Whitley has a drink most evenings before dinner, but I've never noticed which decanter he pours from."

Ellison chuckled. "Whitley would drink Scotch and it's in the one with the ball top."

Phina took the top off the container. The strong smell was almost offensive. If it tasted as bad as it smelled she didn't know how anyone could stand to drink it. She poured a generous amount into the glass and handed it to Ellison.

He patted the cushion beside him. "Join me."

There was something about the look on his face that concerned her. She wasn't at all sure it was proper for her to sit so close to him with no one else in the house. But not wanting to appear disagreeable, she sat down beside him. She wondered if Ellison knew he was disconcerting her. She wanted to hear about her mother, but Ellison's behavior was a little too familiar.

He sipped his drink. "I'm going to be honest with you, Phina. Your mother doesn't look good. She's very thin, pale and weak. When I was talking to her there were times she could hardly hold her eyes open."

Phina moaned softly. Her hands tightened into fists. What was she going to do? She looked up at him imploringly. "In her letter she told me she was feeling better. I read it to you."

"I'm sure she didn't want to worry you. In fact, she asked me not to tell you how poorly she was feeling, but I felt you needed to know."

"Yes, of course, you were right to tell me. I should have never left her." Phina rose from the settee. "I'll make plans to return to her right away."

"No!" he said almost too loudly as he sprung from his seat. "No, Phina," he said more calmly the second time. "Your mother is in good hands. Irene and her mother are taking very good care of her. And with the money you sent her—"

Phina's gaze flew to his.

He cleared his throat. "Ah—she asked me to open the package for her and read your letter to her. I didn't mind. I was happy to do it for her. She was very pleased you were able to send money to her. Phina, I don't think you need to go to your mother right now. You can do more for her by remaining here and establishing yourself as Anchor's daughter. What Diana wants you to do is stay here and fight for your inheritance. And I believe she's right."

"M-my inheritance?" Could it be that Ellison really believed her? And if Ellison did, wouldn't that open the way for others to believe her?

He stepped closer and picked up one of her hands and squeezed it with his fingers. "That's right."

"But I—I don't understand. My mother didn't want me to make this trip."

"I believe your letter of how well you were doing helped change her mind. And, Phina, I found no evidence you lied about anything you said."

Ellison was acting very strange. She didn't know what to make of him. She would have thought he wouldn't have wanted to tell her anything until he'd spoken to Whitley. But no matter what he said, she still wasn't sure that she shouldn't leave immediately to go to her mother.

Phina watched him take a generous swallow of the liquor, then pour more into the glass before turning back around to face her. "Oh, lest I forget, Irene wanted me to tell you that a young man named Pete has come calling on her twice. And one of the other

133

boarders, a gentleman by the name of Charles Braxton asked about you. I told him the same thing I told your mother. That you were splendidly happy living in one of the most beautiful mansions in all of the South. That you have your own personal slave to care for your every wish. And—"

The front door opened and Ellison stopped. An irritated expression clouded his face. "Damn! That must be Whitley," he whispered and looked at the glass in his hand.

"Ellison," Whitley called from the foyer.

"In here, Whitley," Ellison answered.

Whitley's stomach tightened when he walked into the parlor and saw Ellison standing so close to Phina. It was about time he made it back, but he wondered what in the hell he was doing talking to Phina.

"Good evening, Whitley," Phina said as he walked into the room.

He nodded to her and quickly gave his attention back to Ellison. He didn't like the strange feeling that attacked his insides when he saw the two of them together.

"When did you get back?"

"All of ten minutes ago." Ellison held up his glass. "I was washing down some of the dust. Care to join me?"

"No thanks." Whitley could see that Ellison had already been back long enough to be into the drink. Whitley looked over at Phina.

"Well, I have my letter from my mother and a book to read. If you'll excuse me, I'll go upstairs. Good night, Ellison, Whitley."

"Good night, Phina. And as I told you. Don't worry about your mother. She's getting good care."

134

Whitley stood stiffly and watched Phina smile sweetly at Ellison, then hurry from the room. He didn't speak until he heard her bedroom door shut. "What in the hell are you doing talking to her?" he asked.

Ellison's green eyes narrowed and his hand tightened around the glass. "I just came back from seeing her mother. Diana's not a well woman. It's only natural Phina would want to know how she's doing. Besides, her mother gave me a letter for her. I was delivering it. It that a crime?"

"No, of course not." Whitley was ashamed of his attitude. There was no reason to think anything was going on between the two of them. He was in a foul mood and knew it. He was tired of the two hour ride over to the Mathesons and back every Sunday. About halfway home he'd promised himself he'd find a reason that he couldn't make it next week. He didn't think he could face another staid Sunday at their house.

"How's Flannery?" Ellison asked.

"She's fine. Now tell me what you found out."

Whitley didn't bother to sit down but motioned to Ellison. He chose to stand, too. Their eyes met.

"It's doesn't look good."

"For me or for Phina?"

"You."

Whitley forced himself not to change his facial expression. "In what way?"

"Her story checks out."

"Details, Ellison," he said in an irritated voice.

"I spoke with the doctor and he confirmed everything he wrote in his letter."

"I'm not worried about him."

135

"Two of Diana's neighbors that I spoke with confirmed she has lived in the same neighborhood all her life. She's never been married. She came from a well-respected family, but a few years ago she sold the family home and moved into the boardinghouse with Phina. The only hint of scandal that ever came from the Groutas house was when Diana became pregnant nineteen years ago—shortly after an extended visit from a traveler."

"Damn!" Whitley rubbed his chin. "What did you think about her mother?"

Ellison sighed deeply, then finished off his drink. "Diana is sick. I don't know what's wrong with her. She's weak—listless, I think would be a more accurate term. She had a hard time keeping her mind on our conversation, but—"

"Go on."

"She convinced me Phina is Anchor's daughter."

Whitley couldn't move. He was too stiff with anger. "A listless woman who couldn't keep her mind on the conversation? How?"

Ellison loosened his cravat. "She talked freely about her time with Anchor. She might not know much of anything that goes on around here today, but she remembers the past as if it were yesterday. She knew some things that only Anchor could have told her. For instance, she knew that his first wife was given a gold bell, the one that belonged to Anchor's mother, and that he'd had a silver bell with a diamond in the middle of it made for his second wife. She of course was given the plain silver bell that Phina wears."

"Everyone in the county knows about those bells, Ellison." He ran a hand through his hair.

"Does everyone know that the reason he had a different bell made for his second wife was so he could keep the gold bell for his firstborn? I sure as hell didn't know that. I thought he buried her with it."

Whitley folded his arms across his chest. "I knew it. Anchor gave me the bell the night he told me he was having Robert draw up the papers making me his son." He noticed that bit of information seemed to bother Ellison.

"All right so she didn't lie about meeting Anchor and maybe she didn't lie about sharing his bed, either. It still doesn't prove that Phina is his daughter. If she let one man in her bed she could have let another. If that woman had known Anchor at all she would have known that he wouldn't want his daughter growing up a bastard."

Ellison's eyes rounded in surprise. "Whitley, Anchor wasn't the saint you try to make him. There's no way he would have brought that woman or her child to this plantation and shamed his wife."

"You're wrong," Whitley said firmly. "He wanted a child so badly he picked me up off the streets and offered me his home."

"Only after his second wife died leaving him childless. And I think that you forget sometimes that Anchor treated *me* like a son until he found you. I've always thought the reason he took you in was because he knew I had a father and you didn't."

"I'm not arguing that point, Ellison. I know he would have gone to Phina's mother if he'd known she was pregnant with his child."

"And done what?" Ellison's voice rose in pitch. "Anchor was married to a young woman of social standing. Do you think he would have brought Phina or her mother into this house and shamed her."

137

Whitley calmed. "No, of course not. But he would have claimed her when his second wife died and failed to give him a child. He wouldn't have brought me home with him if he'd known about Phina."

"I agree. He wouldn't." Ellison set his glass down. "I'm afraid you're going to have to face the facts. I think Phina is Anchor's daughter, and you should start preparing for the judge to believe the same thing."

Anger welled in Whitley. "Don't give me advice I don't ask for."

Ellison shrugged his shoulders. "I'm tired. If there's nothing else I want to go to bed."

"Go ahead."

When the door shut behind Ellison, Whitley swore harshly. What was he going to do when even his best friend believed Phina? Everyone could believe Phina, but he never would. And he'd never give up control of Carillon.

Tasma lay on her cot looking at the darkness and listening to her mother snore. She'd heard talk that Spiker went down to the river and swam every night. Cush and some of the other slaves were making fun of him for doing it. They said he did it to wash and that only white boys liked to wash. They teased Spiker about acting like he was white.

She eased out of bed, wondering if she could slip in and out of the house without waking Rubra. It was a long way down to the river, but there were a lot of stars out to brighten the night. Besides if she made it to Spiker's house soon enough she could follow him down to the water.

The iron bedframe didn't creak when she rose from the cot. Shadowed moonlight filtered in from the thin curtain covered window. She saw her boots on the floor beside her feet. She decided not to put them on and risk the noise waking Rubra. If she could get out the door without waking her she'd have it made. She tiptoed to the door, hardly daring to breathe. With the greatest of care she opened the door. A small creak sounded as loud as a rifle shot in the stillness. Her mother mumbled something in her sleep but didn't stir enough to wake up. Tasma stood still a moment before stepping outside and quietly pulled the door shut behind her.

As soon as her bare feet hit the cold earth she took off running. She stomped on pebbles, twigs and leaves but didn't slow her pace in her headlong dash past the other houses, the meetinghouse and the cook house. Her heartbeat hammered in tune with her feet. Her arms worked by her sides, pumping her forward through the trees and into the darkness. Tasma didn't slow down until she saw Spiker's cabin in the clearing. She flattened back against the side of his house and gasped for breath. Her heartbeat slowed and a smile stretched across her face. She'd made it. A fine film of sweat dotted her forehead. Victory was sweet.

Tasma leaned around the corner of the house and watched Spiker's front door. She felt damp. She was sweating as much from fear of being caught as the heat from running. Stars twinkled down upon her as she waited for his cabin door to open.

It didn't take long for Tasma's bare feet to feel the chill of the April night and her damp dress clung chillingly to her skin. She put one foot on top of the other trying to add warmth to their stiffness. Just as she was beginning to believe that Spiker had already left for the river and she would have to go down alone the door opened and he stepped out. Her heartbeat sped up again. A clean shirt and pair of breeches were thrown over his shoulder. Tasma shivered as she pushed away from the safety of the house and into the clearing to follow Spiker.

Spiker walked fast, easily eating up the ground to the river. Tasma found herself almost running to keep up with him.

In a narrow section of the path she stepped on something sharp and pain shot up her leg. She grabbed her mouth to keep from making a sound. She didn't have time to look at her foot but it hurt each time she put her weight on it.

When she heard Spiker humming she slowed down and walked very carefully. It wouldn't do for him to hear her. She caught sight of him pulling off his shirt and ducked behind a large bush. She scoured every vantage point from the leafy bush until she found a hole in the leaves big enough to watch Spiker.

He laid his shirt on a large rock near the edge of the water. Tasma sighed softly. His skin shone a dark coffee brown in the moonlight. The muscles in his chest and arms rippled and flexed as he stripped away his breeches. For a few seconds he stood naked in all his glory in front of her. Tasma wouldn't let her eyes blink. She didn't want to miss one second of seeing him. He was a magnificent-looking man.

Spiker turned around and headed for the water, and she was presented with a powerful looking back, tight buttocks and thick thighs. A closer inspection of his back showed crisscrossed scars slashed across his skin. Tasma remembered the beating he'd received a few

140

years ago. To her, they only added to his handsomeness. He was the first man she'd ever seen completely nude, and she was sure he had to be the finest looking man the Lord ever made. How could she think about marrying Cush?

Her legs were weak by the time he dove into the water and swam out of her sight. She sank back onto her heels and breathed in deeply. Her hands and feet were cold from the crisp spring night, but she'd never felt more contented in all her life.

Spiker hummed and sang a few words as he splashed around in the water. If she'd known how to swim she would have joined him.

A few minutes later, he was stepping into his breeches when she felt something cold and wet crawl across her foot. Thinking it was a snake, she squealed and hollered. Jumping out from behind the bush she ran and threw herself into Spiker's arms, almost knocking both of them to the ground.

"What the devil! Tasma, why are you screaming? What's after you?" he asked, trying to pry her arms from around his neck. "What are you doing out here?"

"S—somethin' wet and cold ran 'cross my feet." Tasma explained, trying to hold on to Spiker. Not only did she like the feel of his damp skin underneath the palm of her hands, she wasn't in a hurry to be planted on the cold ground again. Without thinking she reached up and placed her lips against his and kissed him.

Spiker let go of her hands and took hold of the side of her face and pushed her away from him. "Don't ever do that again, you little fool."

Tasma looked up at him with her big dark eyes. "I jest wanted ta know what it felt like ta kiss ya."

He eyed her warily as he grabbed his shirt and pulled it on. His eyebrows drew together and his eyes narrowed. "You followed me down here so you could spy on me while I was in the water, didn't you?"

Tasma didn't answer. She just looked at him and pretended to be hurt by his rough tone. She couldn't understand why he seemed to always be mad with her.

He moved his face close to hers. "If you ever follow me again, I'm going to turn you over my knee and whip your little ass."

That promise got Tasma's attention. "I didn't do nothin' wrong."

"Do you believe me?" he asked harshly.

She nodded.

"Good. Cause I mean it. You should know better than to follow a man down to the river. You could get in big trouble for doing that. Now, come on, I'm taking you home."

Spiker grabbed her arm and forced her to keep up with his longer stride as they moved along the path. Her foot started hurting again, and Tasma wanted to cry out for him to slow down that her feet hurt and branches were slapping her in the face, but she remained quiet. Spiker seemed angry enough to go ahead and give her a whipping if she said anything else.

A few minutes later they came into the clearing by his cabin and met two older boys and Jasper on their way to the river. The boys snickered and pointed at them.

"Damn it all," Spiker said as he let go of her. "It'll be all over the quarters tomorrow that we were out together tonight." Spiker clamped his teeth shut tightly for a moment and looked around as if he expected someone else to show up. "Get on home before I change my mind and give you that whipping for getting me in trouble."

"You won't gets in no trouble, Spiker."

"The hell I won't. Does your mama know you're out here spying on me?"

Tasma shook her head.

"That's what I thought. Now get on home before somebody else shows up and I have to knock their heads."

He was upset, but she felt wonderful. Everyone was going to assume she was Spiker's woman. Nothing would make her happier. She lifted her shoulders a little higher and smiled up at him. "I'll see ya tomorrow, Spiker."

Tasma thought she saw a wisp of a smile from him just before she turned and fled.

Chapter Ten

"You're sure, Rubra?" Whitley asked as he sat on the veranda on the east side of the house, waiting for Chatalene to serve his breakfast.

"Yessir," she said pointedly.

"How do you know this?"

"Chatalene done tole me 'bout it. Dis ain't de first time it happened. She say Samson came to her house and tole her Mr. Ellison had ta see her so she had ta go. She been tole she has ta do what Mr. Ellison says do. She didn't know he gone keep sendin' fo' her."

He looked up at the large woman and pushed his chair away from the table. "Since when do those of you who work in the house answer to Ellison?"

Her eyes widened. "He de overseer, ain't he? Mr. Anchor made him de overseer when Mr. Ellison's papa died three years ago. If'in de rules changed ain't no one tole us."

"He only oversees the fields and the field hands. The house girls are to listen to you or Phina. I thought I'd made that clear."

"Well, it is now," Rubra said, throwing her shoulders back and brushing a hand down her spotless apron.

"Do you have any reason to doubt her?" he asked.

Rubra shook her head slowly. "Oh, no sir. She's telling de truth. Chatalene got no reason to lie 'bout a thing like dis. She don't want ta cause no trouble. She's 'fraid Jasper gone get mighty mad if'in he hear 'bout dis. He's hopin' ta make her his woman fo' too long. He don't want no white man messing wid his woman."

The thought of Ellison forcing Chatalene to come to him not only made Whitley angry, it disappointed him. He'd expected more from Ellison. His excessive drinking was no doubt the cause of this violation of Chatalene. "Has he hurt her?" Whitley asked.

"No, sir." Rubra picked up the tail of her apron and wiped the corner of her mouth. "You done saw her dis morning. She ain't hurt. But she don't like it. How you'd like it if'in I made you crawl in de bed wid me?"

Whitley gave her a reprimanding look. "Don't try to be funny, Rubra. I'm in no mood for it."

She walked over to the serving table and picked up the coffeepot. "I's wasn't trying ta be funny. She ain't happy bout dis."

"I'm not either." Whitley swore under his breath. He pushed the cup of black coffee away from him and looked out over the lawn. Early morning sun was just topping the trees, throwing sunshine on the veranda. He had dressed in a lightweight cotton shirt for working in the office today. With Ellison back he wouldn't have to go to the fields with the slaves.

Ellison. He'd changed since Anchor had died. One thing was sure. Ellison was drinking too much. He was caustic and sarcastic at times, too. Whitley had a feel-

145

ing the whiskey was at the root of his problem. But whatever the cause—it had to be stopped. The slaves had to feel safe in their homes. Ellison would either follow the rules or he'd have to leave.

The door opened and Chatalene came out carrying two plates. One was filled with fluffy scrambled eggs and a piece of fried ham. The other held three golden crested biscuits and a small bowl of cooked figs. Rubra stepped aside and Chatalene carefully placed the plates in front of him.

Whitley had never really taken the time to look at Chatalene. He knew her name, her age, and her position in the house. According to Anchor that was all he was supposed to know. He knew all the slaves names, their ages and whether or not they were born on Carillon or were bought from another owner.

One of the first things Anchor had taught him was to know his own people, but not to befriend them. "You can't get too close to them, Whitley," Anchor had told him. "If you become friendly with them, you'll end up getting mixed up in their lives and that leads to trouble because they start expecting you to treat them differently from the rest of the slaves."

The only time Whitley had gone against that rule was the night he watched Spiker whipped. He'd cut the ropes that held Spiker to the post and had taken him to his cabin and cared for him. And he'd never regretted it, although, Anchor's words had been proven true many times. All the slaves assumed he favored Spiker.

Whitley watched Chatalene pick up his coffee cup and move away from the table. She wore a red scarf over her hair. All the women who worked in the house had to wear a scarf. Anchor had been adamant about that and Whitley had seen no reason to change the rule, but there were others he knew needed changing.

Chatalene's dress was clean and pressed which was also a requirement for working in the house. She was tall for a woman, but not big-framed like Rubra. She kept her head lowered so he couldn't see her face as she walked over to the sideboard to get him fresh coffee, not knowing Rubra had just warmed it.

Her hands looked soft and her nails well-cared for, he noticed as she poured hot coffee into a clean cup.

"Chatalene," he spoke her name gently. She looked up at him. Her big brown eyes were clear and expressive. Her cheek bones were high and her lips fully shaped. Her nose was smaller than most of the slaves and her complexion was smooth, soft looking. Once he put all the parts of her face together he saw a very pretty woman, a gentle woman. It was no wonder Ellison was attracted to her, but he was wrong to give into his desires.

"Yessir?"

Her voice was soft but throaty, and he saw hope in her eyes. "You tell Samson that—"

"Samson won't listen ta her!" Rubra broke into Whitley's sentence indignantly. She stomped over to stand beside Chatalene. "He belong to Mr. Ellison. He don't belong ta you. Told me so many times."

"You're right of course, Rubra." He turned back to the young slave. "If Samson comes for you again you're not to go. Instead, I want you to go to Rubra immediately and tell her."

"Mr. Ellison won't like dat," Chatalene answered softly.

"I don't intend for him to." He swung around in his chair. "Rubra, when Chatalene comes to you, you're to tell Spiker to come let me know. Don't wait until morning. Do you understand?"

"Yessir, I do. You aim to stop Mr. Ellison from playing round wid our women-folk."

Whitley nodded and swung his feet back under the table. He wasn't very hungry, but he hated to see the food they'd prepared for him go to waste. He picked up his fork and dipped into the eggs.

Later that morning Whitley was in his office working hard at catching up on his bookwork of the last three weeks. He'd actually enjoyed his time in the fields with the slaves, but he quickly realized he couldn't do the job of overseeing the field work and manage the entire plantation. Both were full-time jobs.

He worried that they might lose all the corn crop as a food product if it didn't rain soon. It wouldn't be a total loss because dried corn could be ground and made into cornmeal and feed for horses and livestock. But it would definitely bring more money if it was beautiful sweet corn for the vegetable markets up North.

The cotton wasn't planted yet, but Whitley was already worrying about the peanut seed they were putting in the ground the past two weeks. It needed rain.

And if the corn and peanuts weren't enough to worry about he had Phina and Ellison dogging his thoughts, too.

A knock sounded on his office door and he looked up to see Lon standing in the doorway. "Mr. Whitley, Mr. Robert is here ta see you."

"Robert? Send him in." Whitley pushed away from his desk. It was unusual for Robert to ride all the way to Carillon during the week. Something had to have come up. That caused a knot of fear in Whitley's

148

stomach. Robert liked to come out to Carillon on Friday so he could stay the weekend and enjoy the good food and rest.

"Come in, Robert and sit down." Whitley motioned to the chair for him as he rose. "What would you like to drink?"

Robert eased his bulky body into the velvet covered wing back in front of Whitley's desk. His jacket spread open, revealing a waistcoat with fancy brass buttons and a watch chain dangling from his pocket. "Whew!" He took out his handkerchief and wiped his face and neck. "Water, please, Lon. Later I'll have a cup of hot tea and maybe a little something sweet to go with it."

"Yessir. What can I get for you, Mr. Whitley?" Lon asked.

"Nothing for me right now." Whitley leaned against his desk and crossed his ankles. "I'm a little surprised to see you, Robert."

He folded his handkerchief and put it away. "I've good news for you."

"I could use some good news. The fields are so dry I'm afraid to put cottonseed in the ground." Whitley hoped he sounded calm. He didn't want Robert to know that his sudden visit had his muscles in knots.

"Yes, I noticed it looked like a dust storm out here when I rode up. The air is so heavy with dirt I had to put my handkerchief over my nose the last few miles. Had I known it was this bad, I'd have sent for you to come into town. But no, I thought I'd enjoy a pleasant ride for a change." He brushed his coat and dust flew into the air only to settle upon him again.

Whitley decided they'd had enough small talk. "So tell me this good news."

Robert looked up at Whitley. "Abe received word

149

yesterday that Judge Rogers is due back in town on Thursday."

"He's returning early?" A shudder of apprehension flew up Whitley's back. His anger at Phina was renewed. Because of her he had to fight for what was his. With the drought and Ellison's behavior he didn't have time to fight Phina, too.

"Apparently so." Robert pulled his waistcoat down over his round belly. "I suggest you and Phina come in on Friday and speak to him. The sooner you get this over with the better for all of you."

Whitley moved away from the desk and stood in front of the window. He looked out in the formal garden and saw Phina down on her hands and knees digging in a flower bed. How could he stay angry with a woman who liked to work in the flower garden? His anger disappeared and a wisp of a smile touched his lips. Phina had told him the formal garden had been neglected and that she was going to give it some much needed attention. He'd expected her to tell one of the slaves what she wanted done. Not do the work herself.

He turned away from the window. Day after tomorrow it wouldn't matter anyway. Flannery would have to see to the restoration of the formal garden. Because come Friday, Phina would be out of Carillon, out of his thoughts and out of his mind, he tried to convince himself.

Walking back to his desk, Whitley asked the lawyer, "You'll go with me?"

"Absolutely."

Lon came in with the water and Robert drank thirstily, emptying the glass before bringing it down from his mouth. He sighed gratefully and set the glass on the tray the slave held out to him. "Very good, Lon, thank you."

"I'll let you know when we're ready for tea."

"Yessir," Lon paused. "Should I tell Rubra Mr. Robert will be staying for dinah?"

"No, no," Robert spoke up. "As much as I appreciate the fine hospitality and food at Carillon I have to return to town today."

"That will be all for now, Lon."

The old man nodded and excused himself. Whitley rubbed his chin with the palm of his hand and studied Robert for a minute. In all honesty, he didn't like what he was going to have to do to Phina. After he'd realized she had the right to believe her mother, he'd actually liked having her around. He'd even found himself wanting to test that physical desire that had rose up between them on a couple of occasions. But, he was promised to Flannery. And he couldn't let Phina have any part of Carillon.

"I've been thinking since our last meeting."

"I'm sure you have." Robert laid his hands on his ample stomach and laced his fingers together. "The question is, what have you been thinking about?"

Hesitating briefly, Whitley said, "I believe there are ways you can present our case to the judge without telling him that the will and adoption papers were never signed."

"Surely, I can." His eyes narrowed and he drummed his fingers.

"And the judge would have no reason to doubt your word about any of this, would he?"

"None whatsoever—"

Whitley leaned back against his desk again and stared at Robert. "I hear a *but* in there."

"But what's in it for me?" Robert gestured outwardly with his hands.

Of course, Whitely didn't expect him to do this without compensation. And he reminded himself that he wasn't asking Robert to lie, only for him to avoid telling the whole truth. "You'll get your usual fee, plus a handsome bonus when the judge sends Phina packing."

Whitley didn't like being this underhanded. Anchor had taught him to be honest above all else. And in a way he was. He had no doubts that this was the right thing to do. It was. Anchor would approve, he was sure. He just wasn't convinced he was going to be happy with himself when it was over. With any luck, Rogers would see through Phina's ruse and dismiss her claim as false without asking to see Anchor's will or Whitley's adoption papers.

"For my own information, Whitley, tell me, do you believe her story? Do you believe she's Anchor's daughter?"

"No." He said without hesitation. If he ever started believing that, he'd have to give her Carillon. Whitley would never do that.

"Good. Your conviction will help our case." Robert pulled on the hem of his waistcoat again. "We won't deny the possibility that Anchor stayed at Diana Groutas's house or that she was intimate with him. However, we'll assume that if she let him into her bed, she could have let others, therefore any number of men could have been Phina's father and given her the dark hair and eyes."

A twinge of guilt hit Whitley but he brushed it aside. He was doing what Anchor would have wanted.

"If Judge Rogers decides a hearing is needed I'll simply agree to give her an allowance."

"You can, but be prepared for her to be back next year, and the next, wanting more money each time." Leaning heavily on the arms of the chair Robert rose. "I think I'd like to freshen up before I have that cup of tea."

"Phina, my God! What are you doing down on your hands and knees in that garden."

Glancing up from her weeding, Phina saw Ellison striding toward her, looking as if he thought her dress on fire.

"Oh, good afternoon, Ellison." She took off her gardening gloves and brushed the back of her palm across her forehead as she rose to meet him.

"Why are you doing this? Cush, Deke, Jasper or one of the other slaves should be doing this for you."

She smiled pleasantly and brushed the dirt from her skirt. "I'm working in the flowers because I want to." She gazed out over the overgrown garden, knowing it must have been glorious years ago when it had the mark of a woman's touch. The arbor that stood in the middle of the grounds hadn't been painted in years and weeds and vines tangled with the pretty pink roses that fought for their space. Phina didn't know much about flowers but she did know they needed consistent care.

Ellison's expression changed abruptly. "By all means, Phina, if it makes you happy to dig among the flowers, then do so. But I have to tell you. You are the prettiest flower in this garden."

Surprised by Ellison's flattery, she responded the

153

only way that seemed appropriate and said, "Thank you. It's nice of you to say so."

"It's true, Phina. With your dark hair and eyes, you're quite beautiful."

"Well," she said tucking wayward strands of hair underneath her bonnet, feeling a little uncomfortable. "You certainly know how to make a woman's day seem brighter." She didn't know what to make of Ellison's extreme flattery. He seemed to gush with it every time she saw him recently.

Ellison moved a little closer. "Phina, while we have a moment or two alone I want to speak to you about something."

"Of course."

"I'm quite taken with you. I've tried not to show my feelings, of course, because of Whitley. I don't think he would be happy to know that his overseer is interested in a woman who is trying to take the plantation away from him."

Caught off guard by his statement, Phina gasped. "I'm not trying to take Carillon from him. I only want what should be rightfully mine. An allowance is all I'm seeking."

"Yes, that's what I meant." He smiled, but it didn't reach his eyes, she noticed. "What I wanted to ask you is if I might have permission to come calling on you."

She was momentarily speechless. "Calling on me?" she finally asked. Ellison was filled with surprises today. Phina shook her head. "I'm very sorry, Ellison. I couldn't possibly agree to that for a number of reasons."

"And what may I ask would keep you from allowing me to court you?" He grinned almost boyishly.

She was baffled by his interest in her. It was best she

let him know right now that she had no interest in him. Trying to be gentle she said, "Ellison, you are a very handsome and charming man, but I have too many things going on in my life to even consider the possibility of courting you or anyone for that matter. Not only do I have my fight with Whitley, but I have my mother and my life in New Orleans to consider as well."

He smiled again. "I didn't expect you to agree immediately. But get used to the idea, Phina. I don't plan to give up so easily."

Ellison reached over and touched her cheek. Phina's first impulse was to draw away from him, but before she could, she heard footsteps approaching and turned to see Whitley walking toward them. Phina berated herself under her breath. The last thing she wanted was to be caught in a compromising position with Ellison.

"I hope I'm not interrupting anything too cozy," Whitley said tightly as he stopped in front of them.

"Not at all, Whitley," Ellison said calmly. "I was just telling Phina that we have slaves to do this kind of work." He turned back to Phina. "I didn't get all the dirt off your cheek, but it's better."

Phina's hand flew to her cheek as she looked at Whitley. The glare on his face told her he didn't believe Ellison. She didn't usually see Whitley or Ellison during the day. Why was she suddenly seeing both of them on the same day? She brushed her skirt. "I know I must look a mess."

"I suppose one can't work in a garden and not get dirty."

Phina was sure there was a hidden meaning in his words, but he immediately turned to Ellison and asked, "How are we doing on getting seed in the ground?"

"We're working on the east fields closest to the river."

"I want you to stop planting and start hauling water to the seed we've already put in the ground. When it rains, we'll start planting again." Whitley's voice had an edge.

Ellison placed his hat on his head with slow deliberate movements as if he meant to irritate Whitley. "We'll start first thing tomorrow morning."

"Have a couple of the men check on the corn to see how it's doing. If it can't be salvaged for market. Maybe we'll use some of it for feed."

"I'll see to it. Anything else?"

Whitley shook his head.

Ellison turned to Phina and tipped his hat. "It was nice talking to you."

"Good day, Ellison."

Whitley's gaze met hers. "I wouldn't suggest getting too friendly with Ellison," Whitley said, annoyance showing in his tone.

It wasn't hard to figure out that something was going on between the two men, and Phina wasn't going to let it have anything to do with her. She lifted her chin defiantly, deciding she wouldn't respond to his innuendo.

She caught herself staring at Whitley. He was a handsome, well-built man. She liked the way his hair fell around his collar. She liked the strength she saw in his features. And for a crazy moment she wished that it was Whitley showing an interest in her.

"I only came to tell you that I just received news the

156

judge is due back in town the end of the week. We'll go in to see him on Friday."

Phina's chest grew tight with tension. She was assaulted by a sick feeling in her stomach. In a matter of days it would all be over. In a way it was a relief knowing the time had been set, but still in another way the news was unwelcome and offensive. With all the proof she'd collected, the judge could deny her claim.

Fighting the true feelings inside her Phina kept her expression straight as she said, "I'll be ready by seven o'clock Friday morning."

"And Phina, getting close to Ellison won't get you any closer to getting Carillon." He spun on his heel and walked away.

Tasma walked down between the rows of waist-high corn. The stalks with their long, limber leaves rustled against her arms as she moved through the field. Warm sunshine beat upon her head and the back of her neck. Dirt caked around her ankles as her shuffling feet kicked up dust from the dry earth. Heat from the sun and dirt were the two main reasons Tasma was glad that she was a house slave. She didn't like to be hot or dirty.

When she came into a clearing at the end of the cornfield she saw Cush and two other men kneeling in the tomato patch, staking the plants. Cush was a hard worker and she knew he loved her, but she still had her heart set on Spiker. Tasma looked around the large vegetable garden that produced enough food for the main house and all the slaves. It was all neatly laid out with peas, beans, corn, tomatoes, squash and other plants she didn't recognize because they were too young to bloom. "Cush," she called to him. When he looked up she waved for him to come to her.

He smiled and waved back at her. He rose and spoke to Jasper the older man beside him, then started running toward her. A few moments later he stood in front of her breathless, his white teeth shining against his dark face. His shirt was dirty and stained with sweat. "It sho' good ta see ya in de middle of de day, Tasma. What you doin' heah?"

"I's done come heah fo' Miss Phina. She need some gardening tools. A spade or hoe or somethin' like dat. I tole her I don't know nothin' 'bout dem thins' but you'd know what she needs."

"What Miss Phina want wid a spade and hoe?"

"She done started weedin' de flower garden. Down on her hands and knees pullin' dem weeds."

"What!" He rubbed sweat from his upper lip with the back of his hand, then wiped it on his breeches. "She ain't suppose ta do dat."

"I knows. I tried ta tell her, but she won't listen ta me." Tasma touched her forehead with her fingers. "It's too hot out heah."

Cush touched her elbow and said, "Come over heah under dis tree and cool off."

Tasma allowed Cush to lead her to the cooling shade of a nearby tree. "I's don't knows how you work out in dis heat."

Cush laughed as he swatted at a fly that buzzed around his head. "I'd rather be heah dan shet up in dat house all day."

She leaned against the trunk of the tree and looked up at Cush. "I's got ta rest befo' I's go back ta Miss Phina."

"I'll take her dem tools if'in ye wants me to," he offered.

Tasma yawned and stretched her hands up and over her head. "I guess it'll be all right if'in you walks over dere wid me," she said, feeling lazy and content to rest under the tree with Cush's attention on her.

"You sho' do look perty ta day, Miss Tasma." Cush placed a hand on the tree beside her shoulder and leaned toward her. "I'd like ta kiss dem perty lips."

She started to say no, then remembered she was letting Cush teach her how to kiss so that when Spiker kissed her she'd know how to do it properly. Tasma reached up and placed her arms around Cush's neck. Sighing he pressed his lips to hers, his body against hers. His hand slipped down her rib cage and rested at her waist.

Tasma allowed her hands the freedom to roam over Cush's back as his lips meshed with hers. Much to her disappointment Cush's back felt thin and bony, not firm, not full, not complete like Spiker's. She wondered how much longer she was going to continue to let Cush court her when it was Spiker she wanted. She gave him a gentle shove and he backed away.

"Yous set me on fire," he said breathlessly. "Dem kisses makes me wants ta marry ya tanight."

"Hurrumph," she said, straightening her dress, thinking one day she'd say thank you to him for teaching her how to kiss. "I's ain't marryin' and I done tole ya dat. We'd better gets dem tools fo' Miss Phina comes lookin' for us."

Chapter Eleven

Phina sat with her back straight as the carriage bumped and jarred its way into town. Around her neck hung the silver bell Anchor had given her mother nineteen years ago. On her wrist swung her reticule which contained her letters. In her hands she held the journal which proved Anchor's business took him to New Orleans during the time she'd been conceived. With all her heart she prayed it would be enough for the judge to consider her plea and give her a permanent allowance. If the judge approved that, she had been thinking about the possibility of asking Whitley to allow her and her mother to live at Carillon.

The past three weeks she'd discovered that Carillon was a wealthy plantation, but that wasn't all that made her want to be a part of it. She'd found peace and comfort at Carillon. She'd found favor with the slaves and she liked each one of them, including Spiker, even though he had a bad habit of wanting to protect Whitley from her.

Whitley was obviously doing a tremendous job with the farming aspect of the plantation, but she'd discovered that a lot of work needed to be done to the gardens and the mansion. The garden she'd already started on. And at a glance, the house looked to be in perfect order and immaculately cared for. But a closer inspection, Phina found that all of the furniture in the house could use a good rubdown with wax, the draperies in every room needed to be dusted, and the walk area of the hardwood floors needed to be reshined. Smoke from the fireplaces had settled on some of the walls and made them dingy.

How she would love to stay at Carillon and make the improvements in the house and gardens. If she were allowed to stay, she would move her mother to the plantation. It was so beautiful there in the early mornings with its warm sunshine and the late afternoons with their gentle breezes. Tasma could wait on her the way she had for Phina. Diana was bound to get better. Surely if she prayed hard enough the good Lord would honor her plea for her mother's life and soften the hearts of the judge and Whitley so that she and her mother would be given an allowance and permission to live at Carillon. But as Phina thought along those lines, a beautiful blonde woman in a dark pink dress flashed across her mind.

She'd discovered that the woman was Whitley's fiancé. Flannery was her name. And as much as Phina might want it to be so, she had a feeling that Flannery wouldn't want Anchor's bastard child and former mistress in residence at Carillon.

Looking out of the carriage past Spiker's broad shoulder, Phina saw Whitley riding a little ahead of the carriage. He rode tall in the saddle, posting easily, fluidly to the horse's gait. The tail of his coat flared behind him. His trousers pulled tight over his thigh and she saw the muscles working in his leg. She'd noticed before what a handsome man he was. She'd also noticed that her breath grew short and her breast tightened whenever she was near him.

Phina had to admire Whitley's strength even though it worked to her disadvantage. He fought hard for what he believed in and she'd seen no indication that he was trying to do anything underhanded. If she'd met Whitley under different circumstances she would have given in to the attraction she felt for him. And for a time, she was beginning to think his feelings for her were softening, but now it appeared he couldn't wait to get her out of his house and out of his life.

The carriage rolled to a stop in front of the sheriff's office. Resolve forced Phina to stiffen her features and muscles. She wondered if Whitley knew how important this meeting was to her. He was thinking she only wanted an allowance. Now she wanted more. She wanted Carillon to be her home. A heavy feeling settled along the plane of her chest. Her legs didn't want to move properly as she stepped down from the carriage. She trembled. She was frightened but tried desperately not to let it show. Phina was determined to be strong, firm and unwavering in her belief that she was Anchor's daughter.

Phina stood by the carriage and looked around the town, hoping to shore up her courage before facing the judge. The main street of town showed little activity. From where she stood she saw three horses tied to a hitching rail on the other side of the road. A wagon loaded with wooden crates passed in front of her. Everything seemed peaceful except the raging emotions warring inside her.

Whitley waited in front of the sheriff's door for her, his hat held in his hands. He stood there, tall, confident. She wished their relationship could be different.

Somehow, on weak legs she made it over to Whitley, her breathing so hard her chest hurt. Maybe it was useless to try to appear calm when the quality of her and her mother's life was at stake. She wondered if she was asking too much of herself. Could she stand up before the judge and label herself as Anchor McCabe's bastard? She thought of her mother so frail and sickly. Yes, she could do it.

As she stood before him, Whitley looked down at her with compelling eyes and for a moment she thought she saw remorse in his features. With nervous fingers he played with his hat. He said her name so softly it might have been a sigh, but she heard it.

"I want you to know this isn't personal. I would do the same thing no matter who wanted a share of Carillon."

She answered quietly but firmly, "I've known that right from the beginning."

He waited a moment longer as if he wanted to say more. He even opened his mouth as if to speak, but in the end changed his mind. Instead, he opened the door to the sheriff's office and motioned for her to precede him.

The sheriff and another portly-looking man stood huddled together in the far corner of the room. They broke apart when she stepped inside, and the heavy-set man walked forward in a rush. "We've bad news," he said.

"What?" Whitley asked as he came up behind Phina.

"It's simply unbelievable." His voice was excited, his eyes wide with alarm. "The stagecoach Judge Rogers was travelling in was attacked and burned by

163

Indians about a hundred miles north of here. All the passengers were killed."

"Oh, no!" Phina gasped, holding tightly to her journal. "That's horrible."

"My God! Robert, Abe, are you certain of this?"

"I'm sure all right," Abe said, pulling his breeches up higher on his waist as he came toward them. "Got the news just a few minutes ago. The best the marshals up North can figure out is that we've got two different renegade bands of about ten or twelve each. Creeks and Cherokee mostly, they think. Just about has to be two groups of them. Maybe three because they've hit in different areas on the same day." He shook his head and seemed to ponder the situation a moment.

"What's making them do this?" Whitley asked. "The Cherokees have always been peaceful Indians."

"Most of them still are as far as we know. The man I talked with this morning said it appears a small group of them got together and decided they'd come back to Georgia and punish the white man for taking their land and forcing them to the other side of the Mississippi. A survivor from one of the attacks remembers hearing one of the Indians say, "Remember the trail where we cried.""

"There's a government posse out looking for them as we speak." The heavy-set man Whitley had called Robert spoke up again. "Because their number is so small it's easy for them to hide in the timberland and the swamps. They're a crafty lot. It was fairly easy to round them up when there were whole villages, thousands of them. But it's not so easy this time."

"And they can live on almost nothing, you know," the sheriff added. "They're used to eating wild berries, leaves and such. Never thought they'd get this close to

164

us, though. We didn't take none of their land when the government drove them like cattle out West three years ago."

"Quite frankly, after what I've heard about the things they were forced to endure during their removal and how many died, I'm not surprised some of them are trying to get even. I'm sure they consider all white men to be alike." Robert offered his opinion in a matter-of-fact tone.

"No," Whitley defended. "Davy Crockett, John Ross, Daniel Webster and a host of white men spoke in favor of the Cherokees. They all fought hard to help them keep their part of Georgia. When the final treaty was given to the Senate it only passed by one vote."

Phina listened intently to the conversations going on around her. She wasn't well versed on the removal of the Indians from Georgia to the wilderness beyond the Mississippi, but she'd heard that thousands of them had died on the trip. As Phina listened she realized she had something in common with the Cherokees. She would have to be forced out of Carillon. She wouldn't give it up willingly. She would fight to claim her heritage.

When she gave her attention back to the conversation in the room they were discussing the judge's family, and she was touched by a stab of sorrow. She knew his family would miss him. She listened a few minutes longer, then stepped forward.

"But what are we going to do?" All eyes in the room turned toward Phina. She laid her purse and the journal on the small desk beside her. "What are we going to do without a judge to make a decision."

Robert brushed Abe aside and stopped in front of

Phina. "I don't believe we've met. I'm Robert Higgens. So pleased to meet you."

"I'm Phina. And I'm sorry about the judge and the Indians plight too, but I'm most anxious to have my fate resolved today."

"She's right, Abe," Whitley said. "What do we do now?"

All eyes shifted from Phina to Abe. He threw up his hands and answered, "We'll have to wait until a new judge can be appointed."

"No!" Whitley, Robert and Phina said in unison.

"We need to get on with our lives, Abe." Whitley's tone of voice was firm.

Phina knew Whitley was talking about his fiance and his marriage and for a moment she felt something akin to jealousy. "I'm Anchor McCabe's daughter and I deserve a permanent allowance."

Whitley glowered at her. "You're a fortune hunter out to get something that doesn't belong to you."

"How dare you say that! Nothing could be further from the truth. Besides, nobody cares what you think about me."

"Do you want the truth of what I think, Phina? I think you and your mother are tired of working for a living and you're trying to find an easy life by mooching off a man your mother slept with."

Rage erupted inside her. It was bad enough he'd say such things about her. She wouldn't let him speak so vilely of her mother. "You take that back!"

"It's the truth!"

"Whitley! Phina!" Robert shouted to be heard. "Nothing can be settled this way. Calm down the both of you."

Abe scratched his nose with the back of his hand,

looking as if he wished he were somewhere other than the middle of this argument. "I've already explained that this is a matter for the courts. I can't settle this. My job is to uphold the law. The way I see it, neither one of you is breaking the law. The only thing I can tell you to do is keep going like you are now until a new judge can be appointed."

"And how long will that take?" Whitley demanded.

"How should I know. I don't expect them government people to be worrying about us when they got damn savages burning and killing all across the state."

"Why can't you just send her packing?"

Phina shook with rage. How dare he start that again! "I'm Anchor's daughter and you know I am. I have rights."

His eyes turned mean. Muscles in his neck worked furiously. "If I thought for one moment you were Anchor's daughter I would gladly welcome you into Carillon. But I think this is a ploy you've come up with to get money for you and your mother because she's used up her inheritance."

Phina's hand flew out and struck him across the face. Whitley grabbed her wrists and shoved her up against the wall, knocking her head against the plaster. She winced and struggled to free herself from the strength of his body and his arms. "I told you I'd hurt you if you ever did that again." His words were forced from between clenched teeth.

Out of the corner of her eye Phina saw Abe and Robert pulling on Whitley's arms and coat, trying to free her from his stronghold. She heard their pleas and demands for him to let her go, but Whitley ignored them. She was so angry she wanted Abe and Robert to go away and let her fight it out with him. "How dare

167

you speak of my mother that way! Anchor did a poor job of teaching you manners!"

Shaking off his friends constraining hands, he spoke with breathless rage. "Don't bring Anchor into this. I have a mind to slap you, Phina to show you what it feels like."

"Go ahead! Your hands could never hurt me as much as your words do." Her words were a hiss.

"You force me to say those things by your lying!"

"I'm not lying!" She struggled against him, intent on freeing herself and slapping him again. When she managed to free one hand, she struck out at him but her hand fell on Robert's cheek instead of Whitley's. He grunted and moved away. Whitley had forced her hands above her head when the sound of a gunshot stilled them both. Fragments from the ceiling fell to the floor.

Phina gasped for breath. Whitley too, as he kept his body pressed close to hers. Their gaze met and held. She watched as the look in his blue-green eyes changed from rage to passion and for a delirious moment Phina thought he was going to kiss her. Abruptly, he let her go and backed away.

"That's better," Abe said, placing the butt of the rifle on the floor. "I've had enough of this shouting and name calling. Now get along home and act like respectable people. If I hear tell of this kind of fighting going on again, I'm going to throw you both in my new jail for disturbing the peace."

Whitley and Phina looked at him stunned. "You don't mean to let them go back to Carillon together after what we witnessed, do you?" Robert asked, wiping his face with his handkerchief.

"Sure I do. Brothers and sisters fight like that all the

168

time. Husbands and wives, too." He paused. "Just don't let me hear tell of it again."

Phina looked at Whitley. He stared at Robert while he stuffed his shirt back underneath the waistband of his trousers and straightened his jacket.

"Whitley, I don't know what to do," Robert said, putting away his handkerchief. "I suppose we could go to the governor and see—"

"No," he said with deadly calm.

"Well, we're not getting any satisfaction here."

"I said no." He pushed his hair away from his forehead with both hands. "Phina and I will go back to Carillon and as the sheriff suggested, we'll act like civilized people until a new judge can be appointed." He picked up his hat and put it back on his head and walked out the door.

Whitley didn't want to ride beside the carriage on the way back to Carillon. He wanted to ride hard and fast and work off some of the anger he'd directed at Phina. Now that the debacle was over he was thoroughly ashamed of himself. He kept hearing Phina say, "Your hands could never hurt me as much as your words do." And dammit, he knew it to be true. He'd wanted to hurt her because she wanted Carillon, because she was so desirable he was forgetting about Flannery.

He strode over to his horse and pulled his rifle out of its holster on his saddle. As if he sensed his master's turmoil, Spiker met him beside the horse. Whitley shoved the gun into Spiker's arms and the darkie's eyes rounded in shock.

"Mr. Whitley—"

"Shut up, Spiker and listen to me." Whitley rummaged through his saddlebags for extra shells. In a way he could understand the Indians' anger. He felt the same way about Phina wanting to take a part of Carillon away from him. He could just give her an allowance and send her on her way but Robert was right, he'd never feel safe if he did that. She'd return one day and want more and more money until she had him back in front of a judge wanting to take the entire plantation away from him. No he had to fight her now and get it settled.

"Keep this rifle between your legs all the way back to Carillon, and don't waste any time getting home. The Indians they were having trouble with up North are closer than we thought. I don't think they'll come this far south, but it's best you stay alert, just in case."

"Yes sir."

"Don't let Phina dawdle in there. Go get her and get home."

Spiker's thick eyebrows arched upward. "I don't think Miss Phina likes for me to tell her what to do, and I know she doesn't like for me to touch her, Mr. Whitley."

"Do it anyway. If she slaps you, it won't sting for long." Whitley swung into the saddle. He looked down at Spiker. "Get going."

After another long look, Spiker turned and headed for the sheriff's door.

Ellison sat in a large chair in his parlor and listened to thunder rumbling in the distance. A glass and a bottle of his favorite whiskey sat on the table beside him. Light from a low-burning lamp made shadows play on the wall in front of him.

He'd been waiting at Carillon for Whitley when he'd

arrived back shortly after noon. The bastard had been short-tempered when he tried to question him about the hearing before the judge. The only thing Ellison had gotten out of him was that the judge had been killed by some Indians. Renegade Indians in southern Georgia was unheard of the past few years.

A flash of lightning lit the room brightly for a split second. Ellison picked up his glass and sipped the liquor. He remembered when the stuff used to sting his tongue. Not any more. It went down smooth and easy. He sipped it again. It was time he brought Whitley down a peg or two. And he had just the information to do it. Whitley would rue the day he confided in him that Anchor had never signed the will or the legal adoption papers making Whitley his son.

Ellison chuckled as the thunder rumbled. If he courted Phina and got her to agree to marry him, he would tell her that Whitley's claim to Carillon was shaky at best, and she had a good chance of the judge awarding her everything. At least she had some written proof. All Whitley had was the past fifteen years of living in Anchor's shadow. He'd play it safe, though. No use in upsetting Whitley until it was necessary.

He smiled. Damn it, if he played his cards right he could have Phina, Carillon and Chatalene.

"Chatalene." Her name drifted from his parted lips as softly as the rustle of angel wings. She had a beautiful body. He had inspected it thoroughly before he touched her the first time. He hadn't kissed her yet. He wasn't sure he wanted to. In a way she was intimidating, although he'd never let her know that. He closed his eyes and remembered back to the last time he'd been with her.

She'd lost that wild-eyed frightened look she had the

171

first time he called her to him, although she was still timid when she undressed for him. That first time she didn't know what he'd planned for her. Now, she knew he wasn't going to hurt her. The things he did to her were enjoyable.

With a will of its own his hand slid down his stomach and caressed the bulge between his legs. In his mind's eye he saw a beautiful brown body with firm breasts, indented waist and rounded hips. Yes, he enjoyed touching her. Ellison closed his eyes and laid his head against the chair back and replayed her last visit in his mind.

She'd stepped inside and he had closed the door behind her. Knowing what he'd wanted she'd gone straight to the bedroom and stood at the end of the bed. A lamp burned on the lowboy, giving the room a soft glow.

"Take off your dress," he said.

Wordlessly she obeyed.

His gaze fell on her breasts, to her stomach, then lower and back to her breasts again. There was something immeasurably pleasurable about looking at the naked dark woman. He nodded and she raked the pillows to the floor and threw the coverlet to the foot of the bed. He grew hard as he watched each movement of her toned body, her softly defined shoulders, the small of her back, slightly rounded hips swaying as she performed the task of preparing the bed for them. When she was finished she crawled up on the bed and lay down. She remembered what he'd had her do the first time. He liked that.

Ellison parted his robe.

A loud clap of thunder jerked Ellison from his daydream. He shook his head to clear his thoughts and found that he'd exposed himself. What the hell was he doing? He closed his robe and poured himself another drink. He could have Chatalene if he wanted her. Why sit here in the chair playing with himself when he could send for her. Lightning flashed again. And he'd better do it now. A storm was brewing.

Chapter Twelve

Whitley paced back and forth in front of the window in his office. It had been thundering and lightning for over an hour but not a drop of rain had fallen. Heat lightning wasn't uncommon in the area, but it usually happened in the hottest part of summer, not the end of April.

But even if he hadn't been waiting for rain, he wouldn't be able to sleep tonight. Phina was on his mind. She'd sent word by Tasma that she had a headache and wouldn't be joining him for dinner. That had been fine with him. The truth was that he wasn't up to seeing Phina yet. He knew that whenever he did see her he would have to apologize for his behavior at the sheriff's office. And apologizing had never come easy for him.

He stopped in front of the window and looked out as he waited impatiently for the rain to start. The corn and peanuts needed a good drenching. And if the ground was soaked with a hard rain they could start planting the cottonseed by the end of the week. A flash of light brightened the gazebo which housed Carillon's bell—the bell Anchor's father had presented to his new bride after she told him she wanted their house named Carillon because she loved to hear the ringing of bells.

Rubbing his eyes Whitley moved away from the window and resumed pacing. Not only did he have the crops to worry about, he had to make some decisions concerning Phina. Abe's suggestion to live as if they were sister and brother would never work. He was sure of that. He didn't feel brotherly toward Phina. A tightening flexed his groin. No, he felt a lot of things when he looked at Phina but brotherly love wasn't one of them. Phina was beautiful, headstrong and courageous. She had adapted to Carillon with no problems, and according to Rubra she got along very well with all the slaves. She saw a need to restore the formal garden and had gotten right to the job, even doing some of the work herself. Phina was also very loyal. He saw evidence of that by the way she stood by and stood up for her mother.

Another thing he liked about Phina was that she wasn't predictable. In any given situation he knew how Flannery would behave. All he had to know was the rules of society to predict Flannery's action or reaction. But she was the kind of wife Anchor said he needed. And Whitley had never disobeyed Anchor. He couldn't see Phina reprimanding him as if he'd been a naughty boy for wanting a few kisses. In truth, the only problem he had with Phina was that she wanted a part of Carillon.

The sound of the back door opening caused Whitley to tense. He wouldn't have given the noise a second thought if it hadn't been for what he'd heard in town about the Indians. Apparently, they were killing and burning fields and homes without conscience. He didn't like the fact they were so close to Carillon. He glanced up at the ornate brass trimmed clock on the mantel and in the dim lamp light saw that it was almost midnight. It was too late for any of the slaves to be coming inside the house.

He quickly moved over to his desk and opened the top drawer on the right, exposing the pistol that always lay ready to fire. He slipped his hand around the pearl handle while keeping his gaze on the doorway. Under the circumstances, he couldn't be too careful.

Lightning flashed as Spiker appeared in the doorway. Relief washed over Whitley and he let go of the gun. If the authorities didn't catch the renegades soon, or if he heard they'd moved farther south he'd have to consider giving weapons to the slaves. He wasn't sure he wanted to do that. One of Anchor's hard and fast rules was, never give a slave a weapon. "If you do, he'll turn against you," he'd said. Whitley wasn't so sure he believed that now that he was older. He'd had no problem trusting Spiker with the rifle today.

"What is it?"

"Ellison," Spiker said calmly. "He sent Samson to get Chatalene."

"Dammit!" What was Ellison trying to prove? Why couldn't he keep his hands off Chatalene? The only thing Whitley could figure out was that Ellison was testing him. He wanted to know if he was going to remain as firm and strong as Anchor did on such things. Obviously, the time had come to show him that the rules hadn't changed when Anchor died. Whitley intended to keep the integrity of Carillon the same.

"Are you sure about this?" He couldn't believe he'd ask anyone to venture out tonight. There's a storm brewing.

"It's true. I've got Lon holding Samson so he can't go back and tell Ellison she's not coming."

Whitley gently closed the desk drawer. "Lon is older than Samson. How can he keep Samson from leaving?"

"He's holding that rifle you gave me this afternoon on him. He won't go anywhere while he's looking down the barrel of that gun."

"Good thinking." Whitley walked from behind the desk and grabbed his hat and jacket off the hat tree. "Has it been long?" he asked as they walked down the hallway toward the back door.

"I don't think so, sir. I came as soon as Tasma showed up at my door."

"Tasma?"

Spiker nodded once. "Her mama sent her to get me just like you said."

As they stepped out into the darkness Whitley saw that a sprinkling of rain had started falling. By the low rumble of thunder in the distance he knew the current storm had passed but had a feeling another was right behind it. A solid hour of hard rain would do more for the crops than a light drizzle most of the night.

Whitley lifted the collar of his jacket to keep the rain off the back of his neck as they hurried down the steps. He and Spiker walked briskly in the rain toward the stables on the eastern side of the main house where the riding horses were kept. The work horses were stabled farther away in the barn down by the slaves' quarters.

"How did it go on the trip home today?" Whitley asked. "Did Phina say anything?"

"No sir. After you rode away, I went inside and told her you said it was time to go. I helped her into the carriage and we took off. You said not to waste any

177

time getting home so I didn't. I didn't want to have to stop and fight Indians along the way. She tried to get me to slow down a couple of times, said all the jarring was giving her a headache, but I kept the horses running fast."

A smile lifted the corners of Whitley's mouth. He could see Phina tapping Spiker on the shoulder and telling him to slow down. She probably hadn't been lying when she said she had a headache. A fast carriage ride could make you feel like you'd been beaten. He chuckled. "I guess you decided you'd rather fight Phina than Indians?"

Spiker took the teasing good-naturedly. "No sir. I don't want to have to fight either one of them."

Together they opened the heavy door of the stables and Whitley grabbed the lantern while Spiker backed Whitley's stallion, Drake, out of the stall. "Which horse do you want me to ride?" Spiker asked as he threw the blanket over the stallion's back.

"You're not going," Whitley said as fire started at the base of the wick and flared to life, sending a yellow glow of light throughout the stable.

Spiker lifted the saddle and slung it on top of the blanket. "I don't think you should go alone. Ellison's changed. He's not like he used to be."

"You know, I think Phina's right." Whitley hung the lantern on a nail and came up beside Spiker. "You try too hard to take care of me."

"That's my job. I'm supposed to take care of you."

Whitley pulled an oiled poncho out of his saddle-bags and slipped it on over his head, then resettled his hat down low on his forehead.

"I'm not worried about Ellison."

"I am." Spiker tightened the cinch. "A few of the

178

men are complaining about him. I'm not the only one who's seen the changes."

"Ellison's having a hard time adjusting to Anchor's death. He's drinking too much right now, but I think that will pass." It had to, Whitley thought to himself, or he'd have to get rid of him. "I want you to go take that rifle away from Lon before he gets shaky and pulls the trigger by mistake. Then I want you to go back and stay in the house until I get back. I don't want Phina left alone."

"Because of the Indians?" Spiker asked. He moved away from the horse and Whitley mounted.

"They're still more than a hundred miles away as far as the sheriff can tell. What worries me is that he said there were two or three bands of them. You never know when one of them might decide to come this far south." Spiker handed him the reins. "I'll feel better once I know they've been caught. I'll be back as soon as I can."

Whitley pressed the horses' flanks with his knees urging him forward. As soon as they cleared the doorway he dug his heels into Drake's sides and took off. Clouds had covered the moon and the stars, but lightning every few seconds lit his way. His poncho fell below his knees but the driving rain and wind soon had the oilcloth cover whipped back behind him, leaving his legs exposed. The rain fell harder and it was a welcome sight. He wasn't happy he had to ride in it to Ellison's house, but he was damn proud to see it coming down. From all he could tell a fierce storm was on the way. Whitley couldn't help but hope the worst of it would hold off until he made it back to the house.

A lamp burned in Ellison's front window as Whitley rode toward the house. He wished they didn't have to have this conversation. It never should have come to this. Whitley had given Ellison the opportunity to clear up the matter and he had failed to do it. Now Whitley didn't have a choice. He had to speak to him.

The rain came harder and the wind grew fierce as Whitley dismounted and walked up on the porch. He knocked on Ellison's door, then took his hat off and beat it against his leg. While he waited for Ellison, he lifted the poncho and dried his face with his shirt sleeve. Damn, he hated being wet.

Ellison opened the door and his eyes rounded in shock. "Whitley, what are you doing here this time of night?" He stepped aside. "Come in. Is something wrong?"

Whitley shook his head, the expression on the over-seer's face told him he knew why Whitley was at his door in the middle of the night. "I'm dripping so I'll stay out here. Besides, I won't be long."

"Suit yourself." Ellison pulled the sash of his robe tighter. "What can I do for you."

Whitley looked directly into Ellison's eyes as the sound of driving rain beat down around them. "I know about Chatalene." He didn't like what Ellison had done and he wasn't going to pretend it was accept-able. "I'm not going to embarrass either of us by talk-ing about the specifics. I'm here to tell you that it will stop. Don't send after Chatalene or any of the other women again."

Ellison chuckled nervously. "Whitley, listen. Don't make a big issue out of this. It's nothing really." He fumbled with the front of his robe. "I don't know what you've been told, but I'm not forcing Chatalene to come to me. Ask her if I've ever hurt her. Ask her." He defended his actions.

"I wouldn't care if you came home and found her naked in your bed." Whitley didn't let his hard expression change. "I'd expect you to throw her out. You're not to touch her."

The jovial expression left Ellison's face. "Why? It's acceptable at most plantations for the master, his sons, or his overseer to have their pick of the women darkies. I don't know why Anchor always shied away from it. Surely, there wouldn't be so many doing it, if there was anything wrong with it. Hell, the women want it."

His words angered Whitley. He didn't believe for a moment that Chatalene or any other woman wanted to be forced into a man's bed. But he understood why Chatalene thought she had to come when Ellison called.

"You're the overseer of the plantation, Ellison. She thought she had to obey you." Whitley had spent enough time in the streets to know about obeying people of authority. He wasn't going to allow Ellison or anyone else to abuse his slaves.

Ellison stepped out on the porch with Whitley. The wind whipped his dark brown hair into his face and flattened his robe against his chest. "Listen, we've been friends too long to let something as unimportant as this come between us."

Whitley took a menacing step forward. "I wouldn't have come out in this storm if this wasn't important."

"All right!" Ellison backed away. "The honest truth is that I didn't want this to happen. In fact, I've been fighting it for months. Damn, Whitley, haven't you ever been attracted to someone you didn't want to be attracted to? Hell, she's a darkie." He clutched the front of his robe again. "Do you think I like myself afterward? Don't you think I tell myself every time it

181

happens that it will be the last time I send for her. But then I remember how she makes me feel. She's so—" He sought the right word,"—Unresponsive that it makes me want her twice as bad."

"Ellison." Whitley held up his hand to stop him from continuing. He hadn't heard much of what Ellison said past his question, "Haven't you ever been attracted to someone you didn't want to be attracted to?" Right now he was having a hell of a time with his attraction to Phina.

"No, Whitley. I've got to make you understand."

"I don't want to hear this. Damn it! We're not nineteen any more. We grew up and we don't talk about things like that now."

"Then why in the hell are we having this conversation? My God! It's not like this is a big thing. She lays down on the bed, I poke her and it's over. I've never even kissed her. I don't want to, but when she's underneath me I—"

Thunder crashed loudly followed by a jagged streak of white lightning. Both men ducked as if they expected the roof to fall on top of them.

"Don't say any more, Ellison. Just give me your word that you won't touch any of the slaves. There are plenty of women in town willing to give you the entire night for a few dollars."

"Dammit, she'll tell you I haven't hurt her."

Whitley took a deep breath and held firm. "That's not the point. If you send for her again, you'll have to leave Carillon. I'm that serious about this. If one of us follows the rules. We all have to. Just because Anchor died doesn't mean the rules changed." Whitley placed his hat back on his head. "Have I made myself clear?"

"Perfectly." Ellison said with a sneer.

After pulling the poncho back into place, Whitley turned around, walked back into the rain and mounted his horse.

Ellison stood on the porch and watched Whitley ride away. He was more determined than ever to see that Phina took Carillon away from the high and mighty Whitley. He had to be careful, though. There was a lot at stake. He didn't want to completely ruin his relationship with Whitley until he had Phina where he wanted her. He had to give her a little more time to get to know him and trust him. That way she wouldn't be so shocked when he told her Whitley's secret about those adoption papers and asked her to marry him.

He'd make a habit of dropping by to see her every Sunday evening after Whitley left for The Pines. She'd already let him know she couldn't be rushed. The dead judge gave him the time he needed to court her.

Thunder pealed again. Ellison shivered. If he took his time and worked things right he could have Carillon, Phina and Chatalene.

Chuckling to himself, Ellison went inside and poured himself a drink.

Phina awoke to the sound of crashing thunder. Her eyes popped open and lightning brightened her room as if it were daytime. An eerie scratching noise came from outside her window. She lay motionless in bed, trying to determine the source of the noise. At last, she cleared her head enough to remember the large tree outside her bedroom and knew that the wind must be pushing a limb against the pane.

She lay in bed a short time longer, then decided to get up and look outside. Between the thunder and the

183

scratching she couldn't sleep anyway. Looking out the window confirmed that the wind and rain blew fiercely. Now that she was fully awake she realized she was hungry, having skipped dinner. Spiker's wild ride home had left her head aching and her stomach in an upheaval. Maybe Tasma had thought to leave some bread or cheese in the warming room for her. She decided to go downstairs and see. She lit a candle, then put on her robe and belted it. She decided against tying back her hair. It never stayed in the hairpins for long anyway. The wood floor was cool to the bottom of her feet as she stepped off the rug.

Holding the candle in one hand and the skirt of her robe in the other she eased down the stairs, careful not to make any noise. When she started down the hallway she noticed that a light was on in Whitley's office. Obviously the storm was keeping him awake, too. At first she was delighted to think that he couldn't sleep well. It served him right for the way he'd treated her at the sheriff's office. But as soon as she thought that she knew it was wrong. She and Whitley were going to have to live together for an indefinite period of time. For her sake and her mother's, it would be best to make amends and start over.

She padded barefoot down the hallway to the office. But instead of seeing Whitley when she rounded the corner she saw Spiker sitting in one of the wing backs, his eyes closed. Her gasp made his eyes pop open. He jumped out of the chair, and she jumped back.

"Spiker, you frightened me. What are you doing in here this time of night?"

"You scared me too, Miss Phina. I'm in here to guard—I'm in here waiting for Mr. Whitley to get back to the house."

"What?" Forgetting she was angry with him for his hellish handling of the carriage earlier that day, she walked farther into the room and set the candle on the desk. "Are you saying that Whitley has gone out in this storm?"

Spiker looked around the room as if he expected someone else to answer for him. Finally he said, "Yes, Miss Phina. He went out a little while ago."

"But where? What could be so important he'd go out in this downpour?"

"I best not tell you about Mr. Whitley's business, Miss Phina."

She pursed her lips. "All right. Do you expect him back tonight?"

Spiker nodded.

"Then he'll be wet as a beaver building a dam. I'll go get some towels for him to dry with and you go out to the cook house and see if there's any milk. If there is put it in a coffeepot and bring it here. We'll heat it over a candle. It should be warm by the time he returns."

"Yes, ma'am." He paused. "Are you sure, Mr. Whitley is going to want warm milk?"

"Of course. Everyone likes warm milk. Now hurry."

Phina picked up the candle and walked out of the office behind Spiker who was shaking his head. The slave headed for the back door, and she headed for the stairs. Lightning and thundering continued to split through the air and shake the windows. At the top of the stairs Phina opened a small closet and took out two large pieces of soft cloth. She started to go immediately back down the stairs but on second thought, decided to go into Whitley's room for his robe. The

185

sooner he got out of his wet clothes the better. If she had everything waiting downstairs for him he could change in the warming room while he drank his milk.

She knew which room belonged to Whitley, although she'd never been in there. The door was shut. She hesitated only a second, then sticking the towels under her arm she opened the door and went inside. The candle didn't afford her much light as she looked around the room. She saw that he had a tall wardrobe, a highboy and a lowboy in the large room. Over by one of the windows was a grouping of two chairs and a round table. The bed sat in the middle of the room. Curtains made from a heavy dark green material hung from the canopy. They were pulled away from the sides and tied at the rounded posts.

Phina walked over to the bed. Whitley's robe and nightshirt lay on the foot. The robe was a dark burgundy satin and his nightshirt a white cotton. The green coverlet had been turned down, making the bed ready for sleep. White sheets glowed softly against the darkness of the room. His pillows were fluffy. Phina walked up to the head of the bed and reached out and touched the pillow where Whitley would lay. The sheets were cold, the material soft beneath her palm. She envisioned Whitley dressed in the purple-red robe lying on the bed, propped up on his elbow. He beckoned her with a smile she found so desirable she wanted to fall on to the bed and snuggle against him.

A noise from downstairs caught her attention, a door opening and closing. Either Spiker had come in with the milk or Whitley had returned. She took a last glance at the bed. Whitley's image was gone. Reprimanding herself for foolish notions, she grabbed the robe and hurried out of his room.

Phina found Spiker in the warming room setting the pot of milk on a wire stand. He lit the candle underneath it with a matchstick. Raindrops glistened in his hair. His shirt and breeches were soaked from having run from the house to the cook house to get the milk. When he turned and faced her they just looked at each other. Slowly Phina handed him one of the towels. Spiker hesitated before taking it.

"You can go on home, Spiker, I'll wait for Whitley."

"No, Miss Phina," he said, wiping his face and neck with the towel. "Mr. Whitley is expecting me to stay in the house until he returns. You go on to bed. I'll take care of him."

"Yes, I know. But I don't think you need to be in those wet clothes for very long. You could catch lung fever. My mother had it this past winter and still hasn't fully recovered from it."

"No, ma'am. I'll be fine." Thunder rent the air again and lightning continued to flash. "It's mighty bad out there. I hope Mr. Whitley gets back soon."

"Did he go far?"

"No, ma'am."

"What took him out in this storm?" she asked casually, hoping to catch him off guard.

"He went to see Mr. Ellison about—" He stopped and his eyes widened a little. "About the crops."

The back door burst open and Spiker and Phina rushed to the doorway and looked down the hall. Whitley swore and stomped around as he tried to pull the dripping poncho over his head. Somehow it had caught on his collar, and he was having a devil of a time getting it off.

Spiker and Phina ran to his aid.

187

"Here, let me see what the problem is," Phina said, reaching up on her tiptoes to pull the oilcloth away. In a matter of seconds they had the poncho off. Spiker opened the door and threw it back on the porch. Whitley looked stunned when he saw Phina standing in front of him.

"What are you doing up?" he asked as he brushed wet hair away from his face.

"I couldn't sleep. What are you doing out in the rain at this time of night?"

Whitley's gaze caressed her face for a brief time. "Taking care of business," he answered, and brushed past both of them and hurried into the warming room. He leaned against the wall and took off a soggy boot and sock.

"When I couldn't sleep I came downstairs to see if there was a bite of something to eat in the warming room and found Spiker waiting for you. I knew you'd be wet when you came in so I sent him to get some milk to warm for you, and I went upstairs for your dry clothes." She turned to Spiker as she opened a cabinet and took out a canning jar, seal and lid. "You best go on home and get out of those wet clothes." She poured some of the heated milk into the jar and capped it tightly. "It may not be very hot by the time you get home but it'll be better than having nothing warm inside you."

Spiker looked at Whitley. He nodded for him to take the jar. "Phina's right, Spiker. You hurry home and get into some dry clothes. I'll talk to you tomorrow."

"What about your horse?"

"I took the saddle off and threw a blanket over him. He should be fine."

"Yes, sir. Good night, Miss Phina."

"Good night, Spiker."

Whitley let his other boot and sock drop to the floor as Spiker made his way out of the room.

"You and Spiker seemed to be nice to each other. That's a change."

Phina ignored his comment about Spiker and turned her back to Whitley and busied herself at the counter. "Your robe is lying there on the chair for you. Get out of those wet clothes while I pour your milk."

"Milk." She heard him chuckle along with the sounds of his changing. "Phina, I've never had warm milk in my life."

"Well, there's always a first time." She heard his breeches hit the floor. She was nervous and she wasn't sure why. She poured herself a cup of milk, too. It wasn't like solid food but it would take the edge off her hunger. She tasted the milk while she waited for him to finish dressing and realized it tasted strongly of coffee. Maybe it hadn't been a good idea to warm the milk in a coffeepot.

"I guess the rain will be good for the crops," she said as the sound of clothes rustling continued behind her.

"I don't think we can save the corn but it'll help the peanuts and soften the ground enough so we can get the cottonseed down."

"That's wonderful."

"You can turn around now, Phina. I'm covered."

She took a deep breath, picked up his cup and turned around to face him. His wet hair was slicked back from his face and forehead making him more desirable than he'd ever been to her. She was reminded of the way she envisioned him when she was in his

189

bedroom. She wondered if he'd ever thought about her the way she had been thinking about him tonight.

Whitley took the cup from her and sipped the liquid without taking his gaze off her. He squinted his eyes and drew his mouth into the shape of a tight bud. She knew from the horrible expression that he didn't like the warm milk.

"This needs a little something more. Follow me."

They were both barefoot as they walked down the hallway and into the parlor. He took her cup and added a generous amount of liquor into both cups. When he handed it back to her she said, "I've never drank spirits before."

"After a night like this, I think a little brandy is in order." He lifted his cup in salute. "Take my word, it won't hurt you." He took a sip. "Mmm—Much better. Maybe there's something to this warm milk after all." He sat down on the small settee and stretched his legs out in front of him. His robe parted, showing most of one leg from the knee down. A light coating of golden blond hair covered his skin down to his ankles. There was something intimately charging about looking at his leg, about being alone with him. Phina wasn't sure it was proper to be in the presence of Whitley with both of them dressed in their robes.

"Go on, taste it."

She did as she was told and sipped the mixture. She held it on her tongue for a little while and found that it was slightly sweet, with a bit of sting. He was right. It was actually good. She sipped it again, then twice more. It tasted of heavily creamed coffee with a hint of sugar in it.

"Sit down, Phina, I want to talk to you."

She took a seat on the edge of the settee beside him

190

but didn't let her back touch the carved back panel. The atmosphere around them was different. Was it the storm outside or the storm that had been building between them for weeks now?

"All afternoon I've wanted to apologize for what happened earlier today at the sheriff's office."

"So have I," she added quickly. "I sometimes find it difficult to hold my temper in check when I'm with you."

"I find the same thing true. I've realized that one of the reasons for this is that I'm attracted to you, Phina, and I don't want to be." His eyes never left hers. They held her captive.

Phina's breathing came faster as she searched his face. His nearness overwhelming her. He had nice eyes when they weren't scowling at her. They were perfectly shaped and clear. He was seductive, dangerous. "I find that to be true for me, too," she answered honestly.

With the admissions out, they both drank from their cups again as they continued to watch each other. Phina's face and neck grew warm, her fingertips tingled.

"All right. We both have the problem," he said, his lips wet with drink. "What are we going to do about it?"

Her neck and cheeks flamed hotter. She moistened her lips with her tongue as she looked at his tempting lips. "Nothing," she whispered.

"Nothing, Phina." His voice was soft, alluring. "That's impossible. You're a beautiful woman. You're a desirable woman." He set his cup on the small table in front of them. He ran a hand down the length of her hair as he gazed into her eyes. "I want to kiss you, Phina. Right now. Just once."

His words, his expression were so seductive the power of her womanly feelings burst forth. Yes, she wanted him to kiss her but should she admit it? "I—I don't think that's proper," she whispered huskily, trying to fight the stirrings inside her body.

"I agree it's not. But right now, Phina, I don't care." He took the cup from her hands and reached over and placed his lips against hers and applied a small amount of pressure. Phina remained stiff. It felt strange. Her breath quickened. He moved away just a fraction and tasted her lips with his tongue. Heat flared inside her and Phina let go of her control. A young man had kissed her a couple of times when she was sixteen and Mr. Braxton had kissed her a few times, too, but neither of them had caused this burning desire deep inside her. She felt like she wanted to consume Whitley.

"Do you like it, Phina?" he whispered against her lips.

"Yes," she answered breathlessly. "Kiss me again."

He slid his arms around her back and pulled her up to his chest. He was warm. She felt his strength. His lips moved back and forth across hers, teaching her how to kiss. With a will of their own her hands snaked around his back and she felt firm muscles beneath the soft satiny material of his robe.

Whitley placed his hands on either side of her face and cupped her cheeks. His thumbs drew a lazy pattern on her skin. From her face, he let his hands glide down her neck, playing with the lobes of her ears as his fingers passed them. Phina felt every touch, every caress. When his hands made it to her shoulders they rested, then moved down her arms and back up again. His lips left hers and moved to her cheek, over her jawbone and down the column of her throat. At the

192

MORE PASSION AND ADVENTURE AWAIT... YOUR TRIP TO A BIG ADVENTUROUS WORLD BEGINS WHEN YOU ACCEPT YOUR FIRST 4 NOVELS ABSOLUTELY *FREE* (AN $18.00 VALUE)

Accept your Free gift and start to experience more of the passion and adventure you like in a historical romance novel. Each Zebra novel is filled with proud men, spirited women and tempestuous love that you'll remember long after you turn the last page.

Zebra Historical Romances are the finest novels of their kind. They are written by authors who really know how to weave tales of romance and adventure in the historical settings you love. You'll feel like you've actually gone back in time with the thrilling stories that each Zebra novel offers.

GET YOUR FREE GIFT WITH THE START OF YOUR HOME SUBSCRIPTION

Our readers tell us that these books sell out very fast in book stores and often they miss the newest titles. So Zebra has made arrangements for you to receive the four newest novels published each month.

You'll be guaranteed that you'll never miss a title, and home delivery is so convenient. And to show you just how easy it is to get Zebra Historical Romances, we'll send you your first 4 books absolutely FREE! Our gift to you just for trying our home subscription service.

BIG SAVINGS AND FREE HOME DELIVERY

Each month, you'll receive the four newest titles as soon as they are published. You'll probably receive them even before the bookstores do. What's more, you may preview these exciting novels free for 10 days. If you like them as much as we think you will, just pay the low preferred subscriber's price of just $3.75 each. *You'll save $3.00 each month off the publisher's price.* AND, your savings are even greater because there are never any shipping, handling or other hidden charges—FREE Home Delivery. Of course you can return any shipment within 10 days for full credit, no questions asked. There is no minimum number of books you must buy.

4 FREE BOOKS

TO GET YOUR 4 FREE BOOKS WORTH $18.00 —MAIL IN THE FREE BOOK CERTIFICATE T O D A Y

Fill in the Free Book Certificate below, and we'll send your FREE BOOKS to you as soon as we receive it.

If the certificate is missing below, write to: Zebra Home Subscription Service, Inc., P.O. Box 5214, 120 Brighton Road, Clifton, New Jersey 07015-5214.

FREE BOOK CERTIFICATE

4 FREE BOOKS

ZEBRA HOME SUBSCRIPTION SERVICE, INC.

YES! Please start my subscription to Zebra Historical Romances and send me my first 4 books absolutely FREE. I understand that each month I may preview four new Zebra Historical Romances free for 10 days. If I'm not satisfied with them, I may return the four books within 10 days and owe nothing. Otherwise, I will pay the low preferred subscriber's price of just $3.75 each; a total of $15.00, *a savings off the publisher's price of $3.00.* I may return any shipment and I may cancel this subscription at any time. There is no obligation to buy any shipment and there are no shipping, handling or other hidden charges. Regardless of what I decide, the four free books are mine to keep.

NAME _____

ADDRESS _____ APT _____

CITY _____ STATE _____ ZIP _____

TELEPHONE ( ) _____

SIGNATURE _____ (if under 18, parent or guardian must sign)

Terms, offer and prices subject to change without notice. Subscription subject to acceptance by Zebra Books. Zebra Books reserves the right to reject any order or cancel any subscription.

ZB0693

GET
FOUR
FREE
BOOKS
(AN $18.00 VALUE)

neckline of her robe he stopped and buried his face in the crook of her neck and shoulder and held her, while his tongue explored her soft skin.

When she could stand the chills of desire no longer she cupped his face with her hands and brought his lips back to hers. The kiss deepened, hardened with hunger for more. Whitley slipped his hand into the opening of her robe and caressed her breast. Phina moaned softly.

"I don't know what would be worse, Phina," he whispered against her lips. "Fighting you or making love to you."

His words brought her back to reality. She pushed away from him and scooted off the settee. She brushed her hair away from her face and straightened her robe.

"I think we're letting the storm get to us. We're saying crazy things—doing crazy things." She ran a nervous hand down the front of her robe.

Whitley picked up his cup and finished off his drink. "You're right. It must be the storm."

She nodded. "Good night, Whitley." She turned and fled up the stairs.

The taste of milk, coffee and brandy had been washed from her lips and mouth by Whitley. The taste of Whitley stayed with her way into the night.

Chapter Thirteen

Tasma huddled under the eaves of Spiker's house and waited for him to return. Rain puddled at her feet and splattered mud on her legs. The wind blew a fine mist onto her face and plastered her dress against her skin, but still she waited.

After Rubra had gone to sleep, Tasma had sneaked out of the house and ran back to Spiker's cabin. When she left she didn't know it was going to start raining so hard. She'd surely be drenched good if she tried to make it back to her house before the storm let up. Besides, she wanted to talk to Spiker. She wanted to know what was going on. The only thing she knew was that Chatalene showed up at their door an hour or so ago looking like a scared rabbit. Rubra had told Tasma to go to Spiker and tell him to go tell Mr. Whitley that Mr. Ellison had sent for Chatalene again.

Her mother wouldn't tell her any more than that, but Tasma knew why Mr. Ellison had sent for Chatalene. There wasn't but one reason a white man would send for a slave in the middle of the night. What she didn't know was what Mr. Whitley planned to do about it. That's why she wanted to talk to Spiker.

After Tasma had given Spiker the message, he took off running toward the big house. She didn't have time to question him. By the time she made it back to her house Chatalene had gone home and Rubra was already back in bed. Tasma didn't know how anyone could sleep with so much going on.

In the distance she heard running and splashing of feet in water. She leaned forward and sure enough a band of lightning showed Spiker heading her way. When he came upon her, she rushed out into the drizzling rain to meet him.

The rain and darkness obscured Tasma's vision and she misjudged her distance from Spiker. She ran into him. All of a sudden, she was thrown against the side of the house. Her head and back hit the boards hard and she groaned from shock as much as from pain. Before she could get out a word, Spiker's forearm pressed into her throat, cutting off her air. Frantic, she clawed at his arm and tried to scream. He grabbed her hair and jerked her head back, knocking it against the wood again. A flash of lightning lit the sky and for an instant Spiker's and Tasma's gaze met.

"Damn!"

Spiker jumped away from Tasma as if she'd been a hot poker. "Damn it, girl, what are you doing jumping me in the dark? I could have killed you."

Tasma held her throat and coughed, trying to catch her breath. She shook from fear, from being wet. Taking deep breaths, she leaned against the side of the house out of the rain. Her head hurt where Spiker had thrown her up against the house.

"Who's out there?" someone called from inside the house.

"It's me, Spiker. Go back to sleep."

"Yous all right?" the man asked.

"I'm fine, Cass. Go back to bed."

"Why's you attack me likes dat, Spiker?" she asked in a hoarse whisper, still holding her throat.

Spiker moved under the eaves with her, putting his nose in front of hers, flattening her against the wall again.

"You silly goose. How was I to know it was you rushing out to meet me. You could've been an Indian."

"An Indian?" Her eyes widened as she struggled to see his features in the darkness. He pressed closer to her and Tasma felt something hard from his belly pressing into her chest, but she ignored it. She liked him being so close. She didn't want him to move away from her. "They's ain't no Indians 'round heah. What's yous talking crazy fo'."

Lightning flashed and Tasma got a good look at his face. Spiker was angry. Rain had collected in his closely cropped hair and drizzled down his face and neck. Seeing him reminded Tasma of her own uncomfortable wet feeling.

He leaned closer. "What are you doing here?" His words were almost a growl. "You been spying on me again, haven't you?"

She had to talk fast. "I's wanted ta come see what Mr. Whitley did 'bout dat Mr. Ellison sending fo' Chatalene."

"That isn't any of your business. Does your mama know you're here?"

Pouting her lips, Tasma said, "Course not! She sleeping like a babe when I's left."

"Then get on home before she finds you missing."

Tasma knew he was getting ready to go inside and

leave her. She slipped her arms around his neck and pressed close to his warm body. "I wants ta be your woman, Spiker."

He tried to remove her arms but she locked her hands together behind his neck. They struggled and ended with him holding her hands above her head, the length of his body pressed into hers. Something hard and unmoving inside his shirt bore down upon her chest bone. She cried out. "What's ya gots in ya shirt. It's killin' me."

Spiker let her go and pulled a jar of milk out of his shirt.

"What's yous doin' wid dat jar in yore shirt? You stealin' from de big house?"

"Of course not. Miss Phina gave this to me."

"Why?"

"Nothing you need to know." He wiped water out of his eyes with the back of his hand. Looking back to Tasma he said, "I'm telling you this for the last time. I don't want a woman, Tasma. I had one woman and she was the only one I wanted. Now you find yourself another man."

"I don't wants no other man, Spiker," she answered earnestly in a childlike voice. She slipped her arms around his neck again.

Spiker threw her hands down, grabbed her by the upper arms and shoved her into the rain. "Go home! You're a spoiled little girl. You think you're supposed to have anything you want because you and your mama work in the big house. Well, you're not getting me. Go find yourself another man." He turned and fled into his cabin.

Tasma stood in the rain, trembling, tears running down her face and mixing with the rain. What could

197

she do to make Spiker love her? She sniffled and cried harder. She could get another man if she wanted to. Maybe she should show Spiker that.

Lightning flashed and thunder rumbled loudly. Tasma took off running. Rain beat against her but she didn't stop until she found herself at Cush's cabin. She beat on the door and called his name.

Within seconds, Cush opened the door. "What's de matter!" he exclaimed as he dragged her inside. He yanked a shirt off a nail and started drying her face.

"Jest hold me, Cush." She fell into his arms weeping pitifully. Cush held her close and stroked her back comfortingly.

When her heaving turned to mere sniffles and she'd settled down and stopped trembling, Tasma realized how warm Cush's body was against her wet clothes and cold body. They stood in the middle of the one room cabin, her dress dripping on the floor, holding each other.

"You sure you's okay, Tasma?" he asked. "Did anybody hurts ya?"

She snuggled her nose into the warmth of his neck. "I's jest don't wants ta go home yet."

"Don't have ta," he said. "Jasper ain't heah tanight. He's staying wid Chatalene." He kissed her forehead and spoke softly to her. "Ya can stay as long as ya wants."

When he lifted her chin and brushed his lips against hers Tasma closed her eyes and pretended it was Spiker who held her so close and touched her so lovingly.

His kiss deepened, his hands caressed parts of her body no one had ever touched. Cush picked her up and laid her on his cot. Tasma kept her eyes shut tightly as he pushed her dress up and pulled her drawers down.

Thunder rumbled in the darkness.

Chapter Fourteen

Whitley worried. For the first time in Carillon's history the Chattahoochee River was in danger of flooding its banks. He stood on the east bank of the river and watched the rushing water flow downstream. Over the past three days the turbulence caused by the wind and rain had turned the usually beautiful dark blue water the color of lightly creamed coffee. He'd given up on trying to stay dry. His hat and oilskin poncho were little barriers to the sometimes fierce wind and driving rain. The wet clothing sticking to his skin made him feel damp and uncomfortable. His horse wasn't taking to standing in the rain any better. He snorted and sniffed restlessly behind Whitley.

Since early morning he'd ridden down to the river several times. Yesterday he'd stopped worrying about the young peanut plants that were just breaking through the ground. The deluge of rain had already washed half of the tender plants away. He had a bigger problem.

The lowest point of the river in a twenty mile stretch was directly in front of the slaves' houses and the pecan and peach orchards. A mile and a half down river where the docks were located the water was two feet lower. He wasn't as worried about the trees, but the houses could be flooded or destroyed if the Flint River continued to rise upriver and dump its overflow into the Chattahoochee. The rain hadn't stopped for long at a time since it started, and by the looks of the sky it wasn't going to stop any time soon.

He turned to Ellison who stood beside him gazing at the rushing water. "Do you think it will help?"

"What? Filling sacks with dirt and lining the banks?" Ellison shook his head. "Personally, I don't think it's worth the effort."

Whitley bristled. It was clear Ellison was still in a temper about their conversation concerning Chatalene. "You don't think it's worth the effort to try and save the slaves' homes?"

Ellison settled his hat lower over his eyes. "Most of them are one-room cabins. It won't be a great loss. Even if the Chattahoochee and the Flint overflowed their banks the water would never reach the mansion so I wouldn't worry about it."

Whitley's hands tightened on his horses reins. His damp skin chilled. He shivered as he watched his friend's unconcerned features through the fog and drizzling rain. He wished he knew what had caused the drastic change in Ellison since Anchor's death. Whitley knew that Ellison had loved Anchor like a father.

But recently, Ellison seemed more interested in himself and what he wanted rather than what was best for Carillon. He seemed to have forgotten that the slaves were an important part of the plantation. It was because of the slaves' hard work that Carillon had prospered. Whitley had to take care of them. And while it was true that most of their houses were small they had their own possessions in them, and Whitley knew they wouldn't want to lose their homes.

"It's too late to tell me not to worry," he said sharply. Whitley swung himself into the saddle. "I want you to call everyone into the meetinghouse." Ellison looked up at him complacently and it angered Whitley even more. "I want every man, woman, and child who's old enough to work to meet me there in thirty minutes." He pulled back on the reins and dug his heels into the horse's flanks and took off toward the mansion, rain splattering his face. He needed everyone who could work and that included the five women who took care of the house.

Phina stood in the warming room with Rubra when Whitley walked in a few minutes later. If possible she was even more beautiful to him now than before he'd kissed her. Every time he saw her he wanted to pull her into his arms and kiss her again and again. He enjoyed having her in his house. She was extremely appealing and very desirable. He liked little things about her like the way fine strands of hair fell from her chignon and framed her face. His gaze connected with hers. He saw concern in her face and it pleased him that she cared enough about Carillon to worry.

He nodded to Phina, then looked directly at Rubra who handed him a cup of steaming coffee. The warmth of the cup, the coffee and Phina's presence made him feel better. He took time to sip the coffee.

"Rubra, I want you to send everyone here in the house down to the meetinghouse immediately. They'll receive instructions about what to do down at the river. I want you to stay here and cook a big pot of soup. Enough for everyone."

"Me? Cook?" Rubra pointed to her bosom with her

thumb. "Ah—I can't cook. Dat ain't my job, Mr.—"

"Then learn," he interrupted her. "You're lucky I'm not sending you down to the barn to fill bags. Now go round up all the girls in the house and get them down to the meetinghouse." He shifted the cup to his other hand, liking the way the heat warmed him.

"Yessir," Rubra said and hurried out of the room, mumbling to herself about not wanting to cook.

"What can I do to help?" Phina asked, moving closer to him.

Whitley's poncho dripped water onto the floor. He shook his head. "Nothing. Unless you want to help Rubra with the food."

"Why do you need all of the slaves at the meetinghouse?"

"The river is threatening the bank near the slaves' quarters. We're going to fill burlap bags with dirt and make a barrier to try to keep it from overflowing and flooding their houses."

"I'll come too," she said, removing the apron she'd donned while helping Rubra polish a writing table she'd found in the attic and wanted in her room.

"That's not necessary, Phina. In fact, I don't want you out in this rain. Rubra could use your help in the cook house. She'll have to cook for the slaves. They'll be cold, wet and hungry by the time this is over. Besides, filling bags is hard and dirty work."

She looked into his eyes. "I'm not afraid of hard work."

Whitley believed her. "I can see that. But I think you'll be more useful here. I've got to go."

"Shouldn't you put on dry clothes before you go out again?"

Whitley needed to take Phina in his arms and hold

203

her, but knew the folly in doing that. One of the things he liked about her was that she seemed to care about him. Wanting to warm milk for him or see that he had on dry clothes. Maybe it meant so much to him because he never had a mother to do those things for him. Surely that was the reason he was so drawn to Phina.

"I've already changed twice today. It doesn't do any good. I'll just get drenched again." He put his cup down and walked out.

Phina heard Rubra giving orders to Chatalene, Tasma and the other two house girls. They were complaining to her that they didn't want to go out into the rain and get wet. Without thinking twice, Phina walked into the dining room where the five had gathered.

Tasma leaned casually against one of the chairs but straightened when Phina walked into the room. "Miss Phina, I's so glad you heah. Mama wants me ta go down to da meetinghouse in dis rain. I's told her I had ta stay heah and looks afta you. I ain't going out in dat bad weather."

The other three girls looked at Phina with their dark brown eyes gleaming and mumbled their agreement.

"I's told 'em Mr. Whitley wants 'em now," Rubra immediately defended.

Tasma's vocal disagreement and attitude didn't surprise Phina. She'd been surly all morning. She was usually jovial and easy to get along with. She guessed the rain had everyone in a temper. "Rubra's right, Tasma. You'll go down to the meetinghouse and you'll go immediately. The river is rising rapidly. There's danger of it flooding its banks and threatening

204

your homes. We've got to try to save them. Now take off. All of you."

"But, Miss Phina—"

"No buts, Tasma." Phina remained firm. "Get going."

The other three girls hurried out but Tasma sulked and scuffed her feet as she reluctantly moved through the doorway. Phina looked down at her dress. There was no way she could be of much help to Whitley in her heavy skirts and petticoats. Not only would they be cumbersome, once they got wet she wouldn't be able to carry their weight, let alone do any work. She needed a plain shift like Tasma, Chatalene and the other women wore. Or, she thought, breeches like Whitley's would be better.

She looked at Rubra who was watching Tasma shuffle out the door. "Rubra." Phina waited for the woman to look at her. "I'd like an old pair of Whitley's trousers, a shirt and a pair of suspenders."

"Whats you want all dem clothes fo'?"

"I'm going to wear them."

"What!" Rubra shook her head. "You can't wears his clothes," she grumbled.

"Of course I can. I'll cut off the legs to the right length and use the suspenders to hold them up."

Rubra arched her back, ready to defy Phina. "I can't lets you cut up Mr. Whitley's clothes. He won't like it."

Phina gave her a stern look. "Whitley needs every hand he can get. I intend to help him save your homes. Now, you're wasting time. Get the things I asked for and meet me in my room. Oh, and I'll need one of those hats with the wide brim. Hurry," Phina called as she picked up her skirts and ran out of the room.

A few minutes later Phina walked out of the house not recognizing herself. The long-sleeved shirt, the cut-off breeches and hat made her look like a young boy. She didn't know exactly what would be going on down at the river but she wanted to be a part of it. This had been her father's home, and might one day be her mother's home. She didn't want anything to happen to it. If anything threatened the plantation, man or nature, she was ready to fight.

The rain was a steady downpour as she made her way down to the meetinghouse. The sky was a thunderous shade of gray, offering no hope of the sun shining through. Within a couple of minutes she was soaked to the skin. Her feet squashed in her boots and water ran down her back. At least the wide brimmed hat kept the rain out of her eyes. She thanked God it wasn't cold.

Recalling the detailed plot plan Whitley had given her Phina knew exactly where everything on the plantation was located. She hurried toward the meetinghouse nestled in the center of the slaves' quarters. She was relieved to see the darkies still inside the large one-room building. Phina opened the door and stepped inside. The room was packed so she leaned against the back wall and wiped water off her face and neck with her hands. She heard Whitley speaking so she listened.

"Now that I've told you what the problem is, I'm going to tell you how we're going to fix it. We're going to build a levee. We'll pack the lowest section of the bank with sacks of dirt. Some of you will go into the barns and fill the bags. Others of you will tie the sacks and bring them to the river where we'll stack them on the bank. Don't worry about digging holes in the floor of the barn. They can be refilled later. Right now we need dry dirt and the barn floors are the only places on Carillon that are dry."

Phina couldn't see Whitley but she heard him clearly. Already she was planning how she could help. She wouldn't be any good at scooping dirt into the bags or carrying full sacks to the river, but she had a lot of strength and dexterity in her hands from years of sewing. She was used to tying knots and breaking off threads. She could make herself useful by securing the sacks with the roping.

"There's been no change in the weather the past three days. With the rain as heavy as it has been at times we can't wait around until the last minute to see if the skies clear. We've got to work fast. We only have about five hours of daylight left. Some of you men come with me to the river to start clearing the ground for the sacks. The rest of you divide yourselves among the barns. Ellison, I want you to keep the wagon moving. As soon as it's loaded get it to the river. Let's get that levee built."

Phina ducked her head and hurried out the door with the crowd. She didn't want Whitley to recognize her. She was afraid he would send her home, and she didn't want to go. There was no doubt in her mind that she could be of use to him and Carillon.

She looked for Tasma or Chatalene but in the sixty or so slaves hurrying out the door, she couldn't find either of them. Finally, she followed the group that was heading for the main barn where the work horses were kept. It was the closest barn to the river.

As soon as she entered the barn Phina saw that someone needed to take charge and tell everyone what to do. Phina took the job and easily put Whitley's plan into place. She told the children to hold the bags open while some of the men and women shoveled dirt into them and packed it down tight. She had two women cutting lengths of rope and the strongest man was to carry the filled bags to the door and put them on the wagon when it arrived. Phina gave herself the job of securing the top of the sacks with roping she tied into a square knot.

Lanterns gave off a yellow light and showed dust from the flying dirt hanging in the air. After only a few minutes the room became hot and stuffy.

By the time Phina's clothes started drying from the rain they were getting wet again from sweat. With little more than an hour's work behind her Phina's hands burned with pain. By the end of the third hour the flesh of her fingers and palms were red and swollen from working with the rope. She looked around the dimly lit barn. The youngsters, faces smudged with dirt and sweat, complained from fatigue. The other slaves, sweat staining their clothes, dirt shading their skin, worked hard shoveling dirt, tying sacks and talking in soft whispers to each other. No one took a break. Outside the rain continued to fall, hard at times. Once in the afternoon she heard thunder and saw lightning as a fierce storm passed by. She worried about Whitley and the others being down by the river and deep inside herself she knew she wanted to go and be with Whitley.

Ellison came in a couple of times during the afternoon and shouted for them to work faster. She kept her head down and her hands hidden so he wouldn't recognize her. At one point she looked up from her task and saw him grab Chatalene by the arm and jerk her aside and talk sharply to her. She started to say

208

something to him about the rough treatment but remembered it was his job to oversee the slaves, so Phina kept quiet, thinking that maybe he'd caught Chatalene resting.

As the day grew late Phina's work slowed. Her fingers swelled so fat she could hardly move them, and they bled in several places. Dirt coated her hands and arms, her chest hurt from breathing in the dusty air. If she didn't take a break and get some fresh air she was going to faint. She was no longer being effective. It was time to turn her duty over to another. Thinking maybe there would be something she could do down at the bank she turned her job over to another woman and headed for the river.

The rain fell steadily and thunder rumbled in the distance as she made her way to the banks. She was wet, tired and her hands throbbed and ached. She tried holding them under her arms to keep them dry and warm but still they hurt. As she approached the river she saw Whitley, Spiker and a couple of other slaves she didn't recognize by name. They worked in the pouring rain. Whitley's hat, soggy with rain water, drooped about his face. Spiker worked without benefit of hat or oilskin. They had done a good job on the levee she saw as she drew closer to them. It was three sacks high and as long and wide as two wagons. She had no idea they'd filled that many bags. Pride filled her. The ache in her hands lessened. Whitley's plan just might work.

Phina reached the river's edge and saw how high the water had risen. Her hopes were dashed. The water was much too high. Whitley's plan wasn't going to work. Lightning flashed in the distance and thunder rumbled louder. The storm wasn't over.

"Hey! Get away from the river."

Startled by the shouted command, she turned to see Whitley striding her way.

He waved her away from the water, and shouted again, "Get away from the wa—" He stopped just feet from her. "My God, Phina, it's you!"

She looked up into his eyes, wanting to take the worry and concern away from him but knowing she couldn't. He was breathless and she knew it was from fatigue. "Of course it's me," she answered. "I couldn't let you and the slaves do all this work and not help."

Whitley took hold of her arm and ushered her away from the bank. "Don't stand so close to the water. If you were to fall in you'd be swept downstream before anyone could save you." His voice softened as his gaze swept over her upturned face. "What are you doing down here, and dressed like this?"

Rain fell into her eyes and caused her to blink rapidly. Thunder rumbled loudly and lightning brightened the sky as the storm drew nearer. Even dripping wet, with water running down his face and mud caked on his oilskin Whitley was handsome, attractive and appealing. The rain started falling harder and she had to shout to make him hear her.

"I've been helping tie the bags in the barn."

"You shouldn't be here. You were supposed to help Rubra in the kitchen."

"I couldn't stay there when I knew you—" Phina caught herself. "When Carillon needed my help." She raised her hand to brush rain out of her eyes and Whitley caught her wrist in mid air.

"Phina!" he whispered her name hoarsely as he looked at her swollen fingers, raw with burns from the rope. "Dammit, what did you do to yourself?"

210

The concern she saw in his eyes warmed her even as the rain came harder, colder and chilled her. "I've been working to save my home."

Anger fired in his eyes. His hands tightened on her wrist. "Your home isn't in danger. It's the slaves' homes we're in danger of losing."

"Whatever threatens any part of Carillon threatens me," she said defiantly and pulled her arm away from him.

At the sound of an approaching horse they both turned around and saw Ellison riding up. At the same time Spiker called to Whitley.

"Mr. Whitley! Come quick. The water's rising faster."

Whitley rushed over to Spiker and the other two slaves and Ellison met him there. Phina stayed behind Whitley not wanting to get in their way.

"Damn!" Whitley cursed when he saw that the river had already covered the first row of bags.

"Whitley, we've got to get out of here," Ellison said, rain dripping from his hat. "This isn't holding. We must be getting overflow from the Flint or one of the low-lying creeks upstream."

For a moment Whitley just looked at the levee. Phina knew he was trying to decide whether or not to give up or keep fighting. He looked up at Ellison who sat on his horse. "Round up everyone and get them to the *garconniere*. It'll be safe there." Ellison dug his heels into his horse's flanks and took off. Whitley turned to Spiker. "You and the others get on the wagon and head for higher ground. Make a ride through the quarters and make sure no one has returned for anything. If they have get them and get out fast."

211

"What about you and Miss Phina?" Spiker asked, water running into his mouth as he talked.

"We'll take my horse."

Spiker climbed up on the wagon with the three other men and slapped the reins on the horse's back and took off.

"Come with me," Whitley said, taking hold of her arm again. Whitley didn't try to hide his anger at having to worry about her safety.

"I can walk by myself," she said, struggling to free herself from his grasp. Her feet sank sometimes ankle deep into the soggy ground along the bank. The rain came so hard and fast she could barely see Whitley's back in front of her. She'd never admit it but she was glad Whitley was leading the way. She wasn't sure she could find her way in the downpour.

Whitley took hold of the reins and untied his horse. He reached to help Phina mount when a burst of thunder split the air. The horse reared up and bolted, knocking Whitley into Phina and both of them to the ground. Phina landed hard on a limb and winced as it dug into her side. She realized the river was already overflowing its banks. She lay in two or three inches of water. Torrents of rain slashed her face. She tried to open her eyes and find Whitley, but the water stung. She wanted to lash out at the rain and tell it to stop but she didn't have the breath. Her bruised body cried out as she struggled to stand. From out of nowhere, Whitley grasped her arm and yanked her to her feet.

"Run, Phina! Run!" He grabbed hold of her swollen hand and pulled her behind him.

Water swirled around her feet and ankles as they splashed through it toward higher ground. Her heartbeat increased. She pushed to keep up with Whitley. A

212

drumming started in her ears. Her chest tightened with dread. She felt the water rising past her ankles and tried to pick her feet up higher so it wouldn't slow her down.

"Faster!" Whitley shouted.

Phina forgot the pain in her hands, her chest and in her sides. The water could overtake them and sweep them away. Fear embedded itself deep within her. She couldn't swim. What would she do if the water came higher and she lost her hold on Whitley?

In a flash of lightning she saw the slaves' houses in the distance. Hope surged within her at the thought of finding Spiker and the wagon. All of a sudden Whitley tripped and fell into the swirling muddy water. The force of his fall yanked her into the knee deep water along with him. They both came up spitting, sputtering and coughing. Phina swallowed some of the river water. Her stomach revolted against it, and she thought she was going to retch.

Whitley called her name, grabbed her arm and pulled her to her feet again, not giving her time to think about how she felt. They raced past the first few cabins. Phina knew Whitley was looking for Spiker and the wagon too. Even though they were in the midst of the quarters, they were not safe yet. Right from the beginning she'd known it was the slaves' homes that were in danger.

Stopping in front of a white oak, Whitley told her to climb up. The water was already past her knees so she didn't even take time to look at him, although she knew a tree wasn't the safest place to be when it was lightning. She closed her fingers around the lowest branch and hauled herself up. Her hands cried out in pain from the rough treatment but she ignored it. She

213

felt Whitley's hands on her derriere, forcing her upward as she fought and clawed her way up the tree. All at once a small limb snapped beneath her weight and she lost her footing.

Phina screamed. Her foot hit Whitley's head and glanced off his shoulder. He caught her leg, giving her time to steady herself.

"Don't take time to think, Phina. Go higher," he called to her through the wind and rain. "Hurry! The water hasn't crested."

Phina climbed until she neared the top and could go no farther without swaying the spindly trunk. She looked down and saw Whitley right below her. Phina leaned her head against a solid limb and rested while Whitley pulled himself up beside her.

Rain beat against their heads. Thunder boomed loudly around them shaking the tree. Lightning crashed, blinding Phina and splitting the tree beside them. Branches from the fallen tree scraped, bit and dug into her flesh.

Phina closed her eyes and screamed.

Chapter Fifteen

Phina didn't open her eyes. Whitley's warm arms closed around her and held her tightly to his chest. Somehow, when the storm calmed a little he'd managed to straddle the limb with his back against the trunk. Phina snuggled close to him. He took off his oilskin and covered both their heads and shoulders with it, protecting them from the driving rain.

Twigs snapped, rain fell, thunder crashed, lightning flashed through most of the night. Phina didn't know when she'd ever been so miserable, so achy, so wet. But at the same time she'd never felt so safe, so warm as she did nestled under the oilskin with Whitley.

After assuring her he was firmly planted on the tree and wasn't going to fall into the water, she allowed herself to snuggle her nose into the crook of his neck.

Phina awakened sometime during the night. She wasn't quite sure what had disturbed her. With her cheek pressed next to Whitley's warm chest she listened. All she heard was the steady beating of his heart. She melted against his warmth for a moment, not wanting to disturb the peacefulness of being so close to him. At this moment she wasn't threatened, only protected, and she didn't want to lose that wonderful feeling.

Remaining still and ever so quiet, Phina realized it wasn't raining any more. She heard no thunder, saw no lightning. The storm had passed for now, but would there be another on its way as had been the case the past three days?

Coming fully awake her body cried out for her to find a different position. Her muscles cramped and ached from the inactivity. She hated to disturb Whitley's rest but she was too uncomfortable to stay put any longer. She raised her head and found she had a crick in her neck. She moaned with relief as she stretched out her arms, then Whitley stirred too.

"Phina," he whispered.

It was too dark under the oilcloth. She couldn't see him but she felt his breath on her face.

"I think the rain has stopped." She whispered too but didn't know why. It was as if they were afraid they'd disturb the storm and start the rain again.

"How do you feel?" he asked. "Are you all right?"

She smiled, pleased he was concerned about her.

"I'm wet, hungry, and sore. Other than that I'm fine. How about you?"

"A few scratches, I think, but the only thing bothering me is that I hate to be wet." He shifted, adjusting the position of his legs. "Hold on to my waist. I'm going to remove the poncho and take a look around."

The first thing Phina saw when the poncho lifted was scattered purple clouds sailing across the heavens making way for the stars. Another smile swept across her face. If the clouds were dissipating that meant the rain was over.

"Looks like the water might be three or four feet high," Whitley said, looking down.

Phina followed his gaze to the slightly churning, muddy water below. A heavily shadowed moon gave a little light. "Do you think it's crested?" she asked.

"It's hard to tell. I'd think maybe so if the water was still, but there's still movement in it. I don't think it's risen more than a foot or two since we climbed up." He shifted again, trying to make himself more comfortable against the trunk of the tree.

"Should we try to make it home?"

Whitley shook his head, then combed his hair out of his eyes with his fingers. He tried to straighten his damp, limp shirt about his shoulders. "I don't think that would be a good idea. We'd better wait until Spiker and Ellison come looking for us. We don't know what's happening upstream. A creek could dump more water on top of us all of a sudden and catch us. At least we're safe here."

"You don't think it'll get this high?"

He gave her a hint of a smile. "Well, let's say it's unlikely. I never thought the Chattahoochee would overflow it's banks either, but it did. We usually have more trouble with droughts than flash floods."

Without the warmth of Whitley's body or the protection of the poncho the night wind quickly chilled Phina's skin and she wrapped her arms around herself. She shivered. She didn't know when she'd lost her hat, maybe when the horse bolted and ran away, but her hair was drying and lay in matted clumps down her back. She watched Whitley looking around and knew how close she'd come to losing her life. Phina didn't want to die and leave her mother alone with no one to care for her. A strange feeling struck her. She didn't want to leave Whitley either. Suddenly she became more determined to make Carillon her home and bring her mother to the house to live. She shivered again.

"Come here," Whitley said as clouds swept away from the moon and bathed his face in a soft light. "Lean back against me. I'll keep you warm. It looks like we might be here the rest of the night."

Phina didn't need a second invitation. She leaned forward and settled herself against his chest, immediately finding warmth and safety in his arms.

She sighed contentedly. "I don't suppose your fiancé would be happy to see us like this."

"Probably not. Besides, we're not officially engaged. We have an understanding."

Phina knew she was the reason they weren't officially engaged. She'd interrupted the party. But tonight she felt no guilt for that.

Whitley laid his chin on the top of her head. "What about you, Phina? Do you have someone waiting for you in New Orleans?"

"Not really. Mr. Braxton, an older gentleman who lives at the boardinghouse has called on me, but I've resisted his efforts to make anything between us permanent."

"How old is he?"

"In his fifties, I'm sure."

Whitley chuckled. "You were right to refuse him. He's too old for you. You need a man who will be around to help you raise your children."

She snuggled closer to him. Yes, she needed someone younger, like Whitley. But he was spoken for. And if she planned to move her mother to Carillon she had to get used to the idea of seeing Whitley with the golden-haired Flannery.

"How are your hands?" he asked in a sleepy voice.

"Better," she replied softly. How could anything bother her when she lay with her cheek pressed against Whitley's chest? She closed her eyes.

The sound of voices startled Phina out of sleep. Whitley awakened at the same time. The night was still purple, the moon still high in the sky.

"Listen," he said.

"Whitley! Miss Phina!" Spiker called to them, still some distance away.

"Thank God!" Whitley said.

"They've come for us," Phina whispered joyfully, even though she was going to miss the warmth of Whitley's embrace.

"I was beginning to think they were going to wait until morning."

Little more than an hour later, Phina crawled into bed, dressed in a long-sleeved, cotton nightgown. She'd never been so wet for such a long period of time. She felt chilled to the bone. Nothing would be as warm as Whitley's arms around her but the gown would help ward off chills.

As soon as she'd made it home, she'd washed in a tub of warm water to get the feel of the muddy river water off her skin and out of her hair. Usually she'd linger in the tub, but not this time. She was tired of being wet. The tub was taken out of her room, and Tasma came in carrying a steaming bowl of soup.

"You wants me ta gets some salve for dem hands?" Tasma asked, then clucked her tongue disapprovingly as she looked at them. "Ain't right fo' a perty white woman likes ya to work dat hard."

219

Phina gave her a little smile. "My hands are fine. I just want to eat and sleep." The bowl was filled with thick, sweet corn chowder. Phina's mouth watered. She picked up the spoon and tasted it. Delicious.

"Mr. Whitley's not happy mama let yous go down to de river," Tasma told her as she mopped up water with a towel from where the tub had been. "Mama tole him she can't tells you what ta do you being a white woman and all."

Phina listened and continued to eat. "Whitley has no reason to blame your mother. No one could have stopped me."

Tasma's dark eyes rounded, showing the clear whites of her eyes. "Spiker could. He's stronger than Mr. Whitley. Won't nobody on dis heah plantation mess wid him."

"Maybe so." She paused and ate another mouthful. "But I have a feeling that Spiker wouldn't have tried to stop me. We have an understanding."

"What's dat? What understanding?" Tasma rose from the floor and leaned against the bedpost, her gaze intent on Phina's face.

Phina saw that Tasma's eyes were more than curious. The girl looked almost worried. She decided it was best not to tease Tasma about Spiker. Obviously, Spiker was a sore subject with her. "I only meant that he's very careful around me, and he's very protective of Whitley."

"Yes'um. I thinks Mr. Whitley's de only one he cares 'bout."

Pushing the soup aside, Phina picked up the bowl of figs and ate two or three of them before handing the tray back to Tasma. "Thank you. That was very good and I appreciate you staying up to care for me." Phina looked out her window and saw dawn breaking across the sky. "It looks like the storms have passed. You go get a couple of hours sleep. I think you're going to have a busy day."

Tasma got as far as the door, then turned back to Phina and asked, "Miss Phina, do yous know hows I can gets Spiker ta court me?"

Swallowing hard, Phina studied Tasma a moment. She could have asked Tasma the same question about Whitley. "I'm afraid I've not been very successful in that area myself, Tasma. The only thing I can suggest is for you to smile at him, be very nice to him and do things for him."

"I's nice to him," she defended immediately and threw the wet towel over her shoulder. "And I smile every times I see him. What kinds of things am I suppose ta do fo' him?"

"Well you can make his supper, mend his clothes, or clean his house. Men like for women to do those kind of things for them."

Tasma pursed her lips, hurrumphed, nodded, picked up the tray and walked out, closing the door behind her.

Phina slid down on her pillows and looked out the window at the approaching dawn. She knew how Tasma felt. There were many things to like and admire about Whitley. He was fair in his dealings with the slaves, and his efforts to save their homes proved he respected them and their lives. She also had no reason to believe he hadn't been fair in his treatment of her. He readily gave her an allowance after the sheriff insisted and except for a couple of occasions he'd been nice to her during her stay at Carillon. It would be so easy for her to start doing the things for him that she'd told Tasma to do, but she couldn't. It wouldn't do her any good to foster those soft feelings that were developing for Whitley. He was promised to another.

Dawn lighted her room so she reached over to turn out the lamp as a soft knock sounded on her door. Thinking it was Tasma who'd come back she called, "Come in."

Whitley opened the door and stepped inside. His hair was dry and combed. He wore tan breeches but no shirt and his feet were bare. Her breath quickened and she sat up straighter in the bed. Was he trying to cross the bridge that had been built between them the night she arrived?

"I wanted to check on you before I lay down." Whitley leaned against the wall. He didn't know what in the hell he was doing in her bedroom half-dressed.

"I'm fine. What about you?"

Her voice sounded softly husky to his ears, encouraging him to continue this foolhardy escapade. He *knew* all the reasons he shouldn't be in her room. He *knew* better than to come to her after the experience they'd shared. Their emotions were high. He *knew* that. Still he couldn't deny himself the presence of her company. He *knew* he couldn't rest until he'd checked on her one more time.

"A few bruises, a bit sore. Nothing to worry about."

"Did we do any good?"

"We won't know until the water recedes."

"Will that be today?"

"Maybe. How's your hands?"

Phina held them up. The swelling had gone down but they were red, chafed and raw in places. "They're better."

Her answer was breathless. And why shouldn't it

222

be? She was in bed, in her nightgown. No self-respecting woman let a man into her bedroom after she was dressed for bed. And if all that wasn't enough, Whitley was shirtless. She should tell him to leave. But she didn't want him to.

"Let me see." Whitley pushed away from the door and walked over to her and sat down on the edge of her bed.

She looked up and he looked down. Their gaze met.

Phina felt her breath leap. She'd never been so close to a bare chest before, and Whitley had a beautiful chest. His shoulders were wide and his torso tapered just enough. Firm muscles rippled beneath the skin in his upper arms. The muscles across his chest and down his midriff were full and well-defined. His skin was smooth-looking and the same lightly tanned color of his face, indicating that at times he worked in the sun without a shirt. Phina found herself wanting to reach over and touch him. Could she be that brazen?

Whitley took first one hand and then the other and looked them over carefully. His touch was warm, gentle. "I don't think there'll be any scarring." He didn't let go of her hand and she didn't pull it away.

"No. I actually have very strong hands from pulling and breaking threads in sewing I've done."

She looked up and he looked down. Their gaze met.

"I was very proud of you for all the things you did to save the slaves' homes," he said.

"I didn't do anything that everyone else wasn't already doing."

"But you didn't have to help."

"You're wrong," she whispered earnestly. "I did."

"You put your life in danger for Carillon."

223

"I knew what I was doing. What happens at Caril
lon is important to me."

"You were very brave after my horse ran off."

She shook her head and her hair fell over her shoul
ders and down the front of her nightgown.

"No, listen," he said and cupped the side of her face
with his hand. "You had the forethought to wea
proper clothes. If you'd had on skirts and petticoat
they would have dragged you down into the water
and if by some chance they hadn't, you would have
never made it to climb that tree. And, although, I
knew there were times you wanted to with all the
lightning popping and crackling around us and thun
der shaking the tree you never became hysterical."

His hand was so warm against her cheek, she looked
away before he could see in her eyes what she was
feeling inside. "I know I screamed."

A sincere smile lifted the corners of his lips. "Only
enough to make me feel needed."

His fingers glided down to her chin and he gently
forced her to face him again. *She looked up and he
looked down. Their gaze met.*

Phina had never felt so peaceful as she did at this
moment. Whitley's praise, his presence had her wish
ing she could also have his love. All the fear of what
happened with the flood and all the fear she felt for her
future didn't matter at this moment. Her heart, her
mind, her whole being was so full of yearning for
Whitley all other feelings faded away.

"You're a very beautiful woman, Phina."

"And you are very handsome," she answered.

"The first night you came to Carillon I wondered
how a woman could have such glorious hair. I thought

it an outrage for you to have worn it down in front of everyone."

She smiled. "I lost my combs on the journey and had no pins to hold it up. I was embarrassed later when I realized what you must have thought about me."

He chuckled lightly. "I thought it a bit brazen of you at the time." He reached over and ran his hand down the length of her hair, pausing briefly as his hand skimmed her breast. *Their eyes met.* "I know I shouldn't be here in your room."

She nodded. She was afraid to speak. She wanted to make the magic of this moment last. She wanted to somehow find a way to make Whitley always look at her with the loving expression that was on his face and in his eyes.

He caressed the palm of her hand with the tips of his fingers, moving them in a circular motion. His gaze swept down her face to her breasts where they lay beneath the soft cotton gown. Closing his eyes, he inhaled deeply. "You smell wonderful. Fresh. Your skin is so soft."

Phina's breath came in little gasps. She knew their emotions were running high because of the storm and the flooding and their time together in the tree. But just the storm wouldn't have caused all these feelings boiling inside her. Whitley was the reason.

Did he know he was causing a fire to erupt in the pit of her stomach? Did he know her chest was so tight she could hardly breathe? Did he know she yearned to have him pull her close so she could feel his warm breath on her face as he did when they were stranded in the tree? Did he know she wanted to place her hands

225

on his bare skin and caress him? Did he know that she was contemplating loving him?

Whitley knew he was in danger of doing something stupid, crazy, dangerous. He was damn sure Anchor wouldn't approve of him sitting on Phina's bed, wanting like hell to kiss her until she was breathless. He was supposed to be committed to Flannery. And he had been until Phina came along. He'd been faithful and devoted to her, too. But Flannery had never made him want her like this. Oh, he'd wanted to make love to Flannery, but only because she was a beautiful woman. With Phina, he realized he wanted *her,* not because she was a beautiful woman but because of all the warm feelings she stirred within him.

She looked at him and he looked at her. Their gaze met.

He wanted to touch her.

She wanted to touch him.

He wanted to kiss her.

She wanted to kiss him.

He swallowed hard.

She swallowed hard.

He moved closer.

She moved closer.

He lowered his lids.

She closed her eyes.

Their lips parted, met, pressed, opened and kissed.

Phina had never felt anything so wonderful in her life. Nothing had ever been close. Her hands played across Whitley's broad, naked back. She felt his muscles move beneath her hands.

Whitley was aggressive as his lips moved hungrily against hers, teaching her how to move with him and enjoy the kiss. He pressed her into the pillows, yet with

226

his arms pulled her up against his chest and pinned her tightly to him with his arms.

"I knew your kisses would be sweet," he whispered against her lips.

"I've never been kissed like this before," she said in answer to his statement.

His hands slid around her waist and crept up to her breasts. He palmed them, fondled them beneath the cotton barrier. At first she tensed, but the feeling deep inside her was so wonderful she denied the alarm that told her she was letting Whitley take liberties.

She sighed softly with pleasure as his hands moved gently over her. Her head tilted backward and his lips slipped down her cheek, over her jawline and down her neck. She didn't understand this glorious feeling washing over her, she only knew she didn't want it to end.

Phina sighed as he caressed her breasts beneath her gown. She felt wild. Wicked. Wonderful. She ran her hands up and down the length of his back, making her stomach muscles tighten. She gloried in the feel of him beneath her palms. Her fingers slid into the hair at the back of his head and she played with it. His hair made her palm tingle. How could she not want this man to love her?

Whitley had been hot and hard before but he'd never been as crazy for a woman as he was this one. He couldn't touch her fast enough. He couldn't kiss her hard enough. He couldn't stop the throbbing in his manhood or the rapid beat of his heart. She was soft, responsive, participating in every move he made. He knew he was supposed to stay true to Flannery, but how could he when Phina was near, so willing and he wanted her so desperately?

He knew he was supposed to go slow, but how could

227

he when his whole body told him he wanted this woman quickly, without delay? For the first time in his life he cared who was beneath him. He wanted Phina. He wanted her to want him with the same intensity.

Loud thunder cracked through the air. Phina and Whitley jumped. The magic of the moment was broken.

Phina realized what she was doing and immediately pushed away from Whitley.

Whitley rose from the bed, breathing hard. He ran a shaky hand through his hair. "I thought the storms were over," he said, looking out the window.

Her chest heaved, hurt. "Yes, so did I." How could she have allowed Whitley such freedoms? How could she have been so foolish, so caught up in the glory of Whitley's touch that she forgot her upbringing? How was she going to live with him knowing how much she wanted him?

She looked at him and he looked at her. Their eyes met.

"Look, Phina, I'm—"

"No, don't say it please," she whispered. "The storms, the flooding has us acting crazy. Just go and we'll forget this happened."

"You're right. Now that it's daylight I better go assess the damage to the slaves' homes." He turned and walked out the door without looking back.

Phina fell back against the pillows. She squeezed her eyes shut and clenched her fists. She should have had more control, but she couldn't be sorry for what happened between them, and she didn't want to hear that Whitley was sorry about it. But she couldn't let it happen again.

228

* * *

Thunder rumbled across the sky as Tasma made her way over to the *garconniere*. Rubra had told her the men would be bunking down in the carriage house and the barns. The women and small children were to stay in the small guest house not far from the main house. Her booted feet squashed in the muddy ground as she walked. She was tired. Tired of the rain. Tired of worrying all night about Miss Phina. Tired of worrying about what she'd let Cush do. Tired of worrying whether or not Spiker was ever going to love her.

Dark purple patches of clouds covered the early morning sky. Even though thunder sounded in the distance, Tasma was sure the worst of the storms were over. The wind was still, morning birds chirped and the sky promised sunshine later in the day. As she passed by the carriage house she saw three young boys playing in mud puddles, splashing the dirty water all over one another. She stopped for a minute and watched them, enjoying the freedom from worry she saw in their faces. She remembered when she used to be as carefree as the young boys. But everything had changed for her when she turned twelve and Rubra gave her permission to work in the big house. That's when she first started noticing Spiker and had fallen in love with him.

He'd been distant and cool toward her from the beginning. But she'd thought surely he'd notice her when she turned fourteen and became a woman.

"Tasma!"

Tasma cringed as she looked up to see Cush running toward her. She groaned in earnest. He was the last person she wanted to see.

Cush stopped his lanky frame in front of her, a wide grin on his face. "I's been looking for ya. How's ya doing?"

Tasma frowned, keeping her gaze on the young ones playing in the puddles. She didn't want to look into his eyes. Because of the storms and flooding she had successfully avoided him since she'd left his cabin a few nights ago. She'd wished a thousand times that night had never happened. She didn't know why her anger at Spiker had driven her into Cush's arms.

"I's fine," she answered. "Why you lookin fo' me?"

"I's wanted ta make sure you's all right afta what we did. I's hopin' you gone let me talk ta yore mama 'bout us."

She cut her eyes around to him. "What fo'? My mama don't have time ta talks ta you. And I's don't have time." She started to walk away.

Cush caught her by the arm. "Tasma, where you goin'? I wants ta talk ta ya."

She pulled her arm out of his grasp and glared at him. "I's tired. I's been up all night worryin' 'bout Miss Phina being out in de storm. She tole me ta rest. And I'm gonna rest."

His expression softened. "I'll walks ya." He tried to take hold of her arm again.

"No," she pushed away from him. "I's wants ta be by myself, Cush. You go on and leave me alone."

"Tasma. I'm yore man now. Ya can't tells me whats ta do. I's the one tells you what ta do."

Anger flared inside her. She was Rubra's daughter. She could have any man she wanted. And she didn't want Cush. Tasma lifted her shoulders, then yanked her hands to her hips and outlined her waist. She cocked her head and looked up at him with defiant

230

eyes. "You ain't my man. You never will be. Now gets away from me."

Cush jerked her roughly to him. "What you mean? Afta de other night—"

"It didn't mean nothin'." She was so angry her words were almost spit at him. Just because she let him have his way with her didn't mean she was his woman. She tried to pull away from him. "Let me go!"

He held her up close to his face and spoke lowly. "You my woman now."

Tasma's nostrils flared with each troubled breath. "You weren't the first man fo' me and you won't be de last. Now let go my arms befo' I kicks you in de wee wee."

"You little hell bitch!" Cush raised his hand to strike her. "I'll teach ya—"

"Cush! Cush! Let her go."

Tasma looked around and saw Spiker heading toward them. Her heart soared to her throat and she choked with emotion. Spiker had come to her rescue. She threw off Cush's hold and ran to Spiker, throwing her arms around him. She wanted him to put his arms around her but he didn't. He didn't push her away either so she snuggled herself into his chest and inhaled his warmth, gloried in his strength.

"Yous don't have anythin' to do with dis, white boy. Dis is between me and Tasma."

"What do you have to say about that, Tasma?" Spiker asked. "Do you want him messing with you?"

"Course not! I tole him I's didn't wants ta be his woman." She rolled her eyes upward and looked lovingly at Spiker.

His expression was hard and mean. "Leave her alone," he said to Cush.

Cush looked around nervously. Tasma knew he was looking for some of his friends to back him up. Alone he wouldn't take on Spiker. "We'll settle dis later, white boy."

Spiker didn't blink. "Whenever you're ready."

Cush's gaze darted to Tasma. "I'm not through wid you either. I won't lets you make a fool of me." He turned and sauntered away.

With her arms around his waist Tasma looked up lovingly at her rescuer. "Oh, Spiker, I's so glad you came along. Cush was turning mean."

He took her by the upper arms and set her away from him. "You best be getting on wherever you were going. And, Tasma—don't be eyeing a man if you don't want his attention."

"Yous de only man I wants."

For a moment she thought he was considering her, then abruptly he turned and walked away.

Stars of happiness filled Tasma's eyes. The sun lifted above the horizon. Spiker had taken up for her. The world looked beautiful.

Chapter Sixteen

Whitley sat at his desk and stared at the piece of paper in front of him. He didn't really want to do what he had planned, but he had no choice. Right from the beginning he should have offered Phina money, a lump sum and a monthly allowance in exchange for her leaving Carillon and promising never to return. He'd been over the reasons why he hadn't wanted to do that so many times that he'd grown weary.

He had to find a way to get rid of the burning desire he had for Phina. Getting rid of *her* seemed the simplest way to do that.

He'd allowed her to stay at Carillon too long. It was no longer a matter of her just interfering with his wedding plans. She was interrupting his whole life.

If he allowed her to stay at Carillon he'd remember how she felt in his arms, how she felt lying beneath him on the bed. The truth of the matter was that he didn't trust himself to leave her alone. He'd come too close to making love to her yesterday. She'd been too willing, too responsive, too eager. She'd matched his ardent mood, his aggressiveness, his desire. He had to get her out of Carillon, out of his life.

Maybe he'd wanted her simply because she was forbidden to him. He was engaged to Flannery, even though it wasn't official yet. Whitley leaned back in his chair and closed his eyes. He rubbed his palms together trying to recapture the feel of Phina. His hands were too rough. She was much softer. He parted his lips and he licked them wanting to taste the sweetness inside her mouth again. Damn! It was no use. He opened his eyes and stared at the paper again. What a fool he was to be acting like a schoolboy who was trying to remember his first time with a woman. The problem was that those few minutes with Phina had been so special.

Whitley remembered the first time Anchor took him into town and paid for him to be with a woman. He didn't exactly know what to do and she wasn't much help. She let him kiss her and touch her breasts, but she was cold and unresponsive. Since that day Whitley had learned a lot about pleasing himself and the woman too. Over the years he'd been with a lot of different women and he'd discovered that some of them enjoyed sex and others didn't. But all of them wanted the dollar he laid on their dressers when he left. Most of them were more interested in the money than what he could do for them in the bed.

But Phina had been different. She warmed to his touch with an eagerness that overwhelmed him, left him wanting more—the rest of her. He had to believe Flannery would be more like Phina once they married, once she was free to allow him to touch her, kiss her and make love to her.

Anchor had handpicked Flannery for him because she was not only from one of the most respected families in the county, she was the most beautiful young woman in the area. Many young men had tried to court her, but Anchor and George Matheson had already decided their fate. Flannery and Whitley had willingly let their fathers control their lives. Whitley had never regretted letting Anchor make the decisions. Hadn't Anchor always been right?

Whitley moaned inwardly as his hand made a fist. For the first time in fifteen years he was doubting that Anchor had known what was best for him. And it was all because of a dark-eyed, dark-haired beauty.

Yesterday, after he'd left Phina's bed and made sure the water was receding, he'd ridden into town and talked to Robert. The lawyer reminded him again that Phina could always decide she wanted more money and take him to court at any time. His future would never be certain. Whitley understood all that, still he had to do something now.

"Rubra said you wanted to see me."

Glancing up, Whitley saw Phina standing in the doorway of his office wearing the sage-colored dress she so often wore. He remembered when he thought she wanted an allowance to buy new dresses and jewelry. She hadn't even purchased new combs for her hair. She'd sent the money to her mother and hadn't asked for one penny more for herself. Whitley's chest tightened.

"Yes, come in, Phina. How are your hands?" he asked, finding it hard to look into her eyes. He had to say one thing while feeling something else.

"Better. Thank you for asking. I heard the water has receded this morning and that most of the damage done to the slaves' homes is repairable."

He nodded. "It's more clean up work than anything else. Three of the oldest ones will be torn down and rebuilt. I've put Spiker in charge of seeing that everyone's house gets a new coat of paint inside and out, new beds and other furniture as well as new work boots. Most of them ruined their shoes in the mud and water."

Phina stared at him, willing him to look into her eyes and tell her how he felt about what had happened between them. Had it shaken him like it had her? Had he found it impossible to forget about it even though they had agreed they would? Had he pledged to make sure it would never happen again?

"I'm sure all the slaves are pleased about that. It's generous of you," she finally said.

"They seem to be pleased. I should have taken more of an interest in the slaves since Anchor's death. I can't get over the fact that I own these people and they are looking to me to take care of them the way Anchor did and his father before him."

"I can help," she offered, taking a step forward. "I'll make new curtains for all of their houses. You don't mind, do you?"

"That's not necessary, Phina. Besides, Samella is an excellent seamstress."

"Oh, I know she is. I've seen her work, and she'll help me, of course. We get along very well together. I'll put off my work on the flower garden until we get the curtains finished."

Whitley wondered if Flannery would have so readily wanted to make curtains for his slaves. Somehow he didn't think so. Another reason he had to get rid of Phina. She was making herself too useful, too needed, too indispensable at Carillon. Damn, he didn't want to do it, but it was time to put a stop to this.

236

He swallowed hard and put an edge to his voice as he said, "Sit down, Phina. I want to talk to you."

Phina was surprised and a little hurt by Whitley's abrupt change of attitude but did as she was told. They hadn't had a chance to talk since he went to her bedroom. He'd been so busy checking on the water damage to the slaves' homes and the orchards. She'd worried when Rubra told her he wanted to see her in his office but he'd seemed so friendly she'd decided he'd put the incident in the past where it should be.

Whitley rose from his chair and walked around his desk and handed her a piece of paper. "This is a bank draft in the amount of five thousand dollars. It's for you."

She gasped.

Whitley continued as he reached back onto the desk and picked up another sheet. "And this is a document stating I will send you a monthly allowance of fifty dollars in exchange for you renouncing all claim to Carillon. I want you to take the draft, sign this paper and leave immediately."

Stunned, hurt, devastated Phina could only look at Whitley. What had she done? What had happened? Why was he suddenly willing to give her what she'd asked for when she first came to Carillon. He was even offering her more than she expected, but——. A pain pierced her heart. She didn't want to leave. She had been thinking about the possibility of bringing her mother to Carillon. It was so beautiful, so peaceful. She knew her mother would get better under the constant care of Tasma and Rubra. She wanted to live at Carillon. This was her father's home. And she'd never felt it stronger than she did at this moment.

Phina knew what had happened. They'd been intimate, and he was sorry it had happened. He didn't want her around when he married Flannery. She knew that. She could even understand it. But could she leave? Could she walk away from Carillon and give up being near Whitley, give up this beautiful home and what it offered simply because it would make Whitley and Flannery's life easier?

"Phina." He said her name so softly it might have been a whisper.

"I have to think about it," she said breathlessly.

He stepped back. "Think about it? Why? You asked for the allowance when you came here. I've added five thousand to that. What's there to think about?"

Five thousand dollars up front and fifty a month would surely take care of her mother, but Phina couldn't get past the fact that he was paying to get rid of her. That hurt deeply. She looked at his handsome face set so sternly in a grim expression and just as quickly anger overcame her. He wanted to pay her off and get rid of her so he and Flannery could live happily ever after at Carillon.

She had to ask herself how she could refuse his proposal when money was exactly what she came to Carillon seeking. But that was before she'd spent time here. That was before she worked in the flower garden, made the clothes for the slaves or tied bags of dirt until her fingers bled. That was before Whitley's kisses. How could she leave when she'd just realized how much she wanted to stay?

"No."

"No?" he echoed, clearly shocked by her announcement.

She rose from the chair and laid the papers on his desk. She brushed the wrinkles from her skirt while she calmed her breathing. At last she found the courage to say what had to be said. She turned to him and spoke softly. "I've thought about it, and I've decided not to take your money."

"I'm offering you more than you asked for."

Doing her best to remain calm she answered, "That's very generous of you, however, I find I must refuse." Her words were stilted.

He took a menacing step toward her. "You can't refuse. Even if you won in court all you'd be entitled to is an allowance."

"No, you're wrong. This is my father's home. I can live here."

"Not without my permission."

Her voice remained soft even though she shook with anger. "I don't need your permission. For now, I have it from the sheriff. You can't make me leave."

Whitley sneered and came closer. "So your true motives come out after all. You are a little money grubber."

"How dare you say that!" Her temper flared quick, hot. "I'm refusing your money."

His eyes narrowed and a muscle worked in his jaw. He backed her against the desk. Phina could go no farther. "Only because you hope to get more by staying here. If this goes to court, I won't let you win."

"You can't keep me from it. I have proof."

"I'll have a dozen women lined up to testify and they'll all be wearing a silver bell. Phina, believe me, I won't let you win."

What she saw in his eyes belied his hurtful words. They were scanning her face with passionate desire. She saw that he was still attracted to her. She was still attracted to him. And they both knew it.

"You wouldn't do that," she whispered.

"I will, Phina. You have until the day the new judge arrives to accept my offer."

They remained with their gazes locked together, Phina pressed against the desk, Whitley's knees brushing her skirts.

A light knock sounded on the door. Whitley turned and stepped away from Phina. She straightened.

"What is it, Lon?" he asked.

Lon scratched the back of his head. "Miss Flannery and her mother is here ta see you."

Phina saw the surprise in Whitley's features. "Did you show them into the parlor?"

"Yessir. Rubra said tell ya she's gettin' dem somethin' ta drink."

"Good. Tell them I'll be right there."

Whitley grabbed his jacket off the coat tree and pulled it on over his double-breasted waistcoat. He threw a glance at Phina. "We'll continue this discussion later."

Still feeling the sting of his offer, she said in an overly sweet voice, "Please invite your guests to stay for dinner. I'd like to meet Mrs. Matheson and your intended."

"Like hell," he muttered as he walked out the door.

Phina didn't know why she'd made that last snippy remark. She didn't want to meet Flannery, and she didn't want to give Whitley more cause to hate her. She didn't want to have to look into the eyes of the woman who would be Whitley's wife. She'd heard about Flannery shortly after she arrived. That Whitley wanted her out of the house shouldn't have surprised her. Sighing she sank back into the chair in front of his desk.

240

Why had it hurt her so bad for him to offer her that money she asked herself, but knew the answer? She'd allowed herself to fall in love with Whitley. It hurt because she was jealous. Phina let her forehead drop into her hand. When did it happen? How could she have let it happen? She knew Whitley was bound to another. She'd come to Carillon with the goal of obtaining money from her father for her mother. Now Whitley was offering her exactly that, enough money to live comfortably. Was she stupid to have thrown it back at him? Was she crazy to want to live at Carillon knowing Whitley would be married to another woman?

Whitley swore beneath his breath as he made his way down the long hallway toward the parlor. What in the hell were Flannery and her mother doing at Carillon? He hadn't been over to see them the past couple of Sundays, but he thought they all accepted his excuse of needing to stay on the plantation until all the seed was in the ground. Maybe the Mathesons had heard about the flooding and had come to check on him, he thought as he stopped outside the parlor door and straightened his bow-tied cravat. He looked into the cornice-framed mirror and combed through his hair with his hand. Taking a calming breath, and entered the room.

"Mrs. Matheson, Flannery, how good to see you." He walked over to the settee and took first Mrs. Matheson's hand and kissed it, then Flannery's. Both women were beautifully outfitted in dresses trimmed with lace and bows. Flannery wore a brilliant shade of blue and her mother a dark purple. Their bonnets were trimmed with bows and fancy feathers. As the ladies responded to his greeting he was reminded of how simply Phina dressed. She had very few dresses and only one bonnet, yet she always looked lovely.

"I'm told Rubra is bringing in some tea," he said as he took a chair in front of the settee.

"We really can't stay that long," Mrs. Matheson said. "We promised George we wouldn't tarry, but we didn't want to leave The Pines without saying good-bye."

"Leave The Pines?" Taken completely by surprise, Whitley sat forward in his chair. "I don't understand."

Mrs. Matheson laughed gently and spread her fan. "Oh, not for long, Whitley. George has decided that Flannery and I should go to Mobile and stay at his cousin's plantation for a month or two. Longer if necessary."

"Why?" he asked, realizing his feelings were ambivalent about this news.

"He's worried about those Indians we keep hearing about," she said disdainfully. "Even though, they are still far away from us, he'd rather we leave Georgia until they're caught."

"Has there been recent news?" he asked, noticing that Flannery sat stiffly, quietly, dutifully beside her mother. He looked at her and smiled. She returned it. He watched Flannery as Mrs. Matheson talked and he was struck by the realization that even though Flannery was beautiful he no longer desired her. Afraid she'd see the truth in his eyes he looked away and returned his attention to her mother.

"And just last evening he heard they're burning crops all over the state. Of course, we haven't seen them in our area, but I think George may have cause to worry."

Indians were the last thing on his mind now. The flood and his feelings for Phina had made him forget about any threat from Indians. Whitley looked at the woman Anchor had wanted him to marry and wondered how in the hell he was going to do it? He'd never gone against Anchor's wishes. He owed Anchor his trust, his loyalty, his life. He had to do this for Anchor.

"He's right," Whitley said when he realized she'd spoken again and was expecting an answer. "Leaving for a few weeks is the sensible thing to do. No need to take chances when they can be avoided."

"I'm glad you agree."

"When do you leave?"

"Tomorrow. I know you'll miss her, but hopefully *everything* will be worked out by the time we return." Bertha said as she closed her fan with a snap and patted her daughter's hand. "Flannery asked that I give you two a few minutes alone to say goodbye, and I agreed. I'll go check on our refreshments."

As soon as Whitley saw Mrs. Matheson's skirts clear the doorway he moved over to the settee and took Flannery's hand. This was the woman he was going to marry. Not Phina. This was the woman that was supposed to fill his dreams, his thoughts, his future. This was the woman he had to take and foresake all others. He was bound by his commitment to Anchor. He wouldn't let down the man who'd saved his life.

"It's good to see you again," he said, picking up her warm hand and holding it in both of his. She was so beautiful. He wanted to want her. "You're looking lovely today, Flannery. I've missed you."

"How sweet of you to notice." She smiled coyly and touched the bow of her bonnet.

That coquettish remark wasn't what Whitley wanted to hear. It wasn't what he needed. He needed to know that she loved him in a way she could never love another man. Whitley reached over and kissed her lips. She remained passive so he kissed her again, this time pulling her into his arms and pressing her into the sofa. It wasn't like Flannery to allow him such freedom. He took advantage of it. He forced her lips apart with his tongue and thrust it inside her mouth. He slipped his hand up her midriff and cupped her breast but felt little flesh beneath the layers of material and corset.

Whitley felt no response from her, but worse, he felt no response in himself. Maybe he just needed a little more to get him started. He continued to kiss her and fondle her breasts, hoping for the first stirrings of pleasure. But after a couple of minutes it was clear that neither of them were moved.

Wiping his lips with the back of his hand Whitley leaned back against the settee, trying not to remember how explosive he felt in Phina's arms.

Flannery fussed with the bodice of her gown. "I do hope you enjoyed that, Whitley," she said with a hint of disapproval in her voice.

Confused by his body's lack of reaction, he lied by nodding. It made him feel like a heel but he found he couldn't look her in the eyes and tell her the truth.

"Good. I really shouldn't have let you get so fresh." She looked up at him and smiled. "Mama said I should let you have a few kisses so you'll miss me while I'm gone."

He should have known there was a reason she was

244

letting him be so free with her. Flannery wouldn't do anything without first getting her mother's approval.

"I suppose I'll have to let you do all that touching when we're married. At least for a time."

Whitley drew back. "You'll *have to let me* touch you after we marry? Don't you want to touch me, Flannery?"

"Whitley, please. This is hardly the thing to be discussed now. We'll talk about kissing after we're married."

The only women he'd ever made love to were the ones he'd paid for. Some of the women had begged him to visit them again, but that didn't make up for the fact they wanted their dollar when he walked out the door. They kissed him for money. Flannery had kissed him because it was *expected* of her. Phina had kissed him because she wanted to and had asked nothing from him in return. Whitley wanted to wipe the taste of Flannery off his lips. Even for Anchor, could he marry a woman who didn't want his kisses?

Flannery looked at him with those beautiful blue eyes. "Mama gave us time alone so I could tell you what we've decided." The smile left her face. "We want that dark-haired woman out of your house."

Her words were commanding. Whitley stiffened. He started to tell her that the dark-haired woman had a name and it was Phina.

Flannery continued. "If she's not gone by the time we return, I'll consider our understanding broken, and I'll accept the attentions of other young gentlemen."

Whitley had just offered Phina money to leave, but he damn sure didn't want Flannery telling him he had to make her leave. "I expect a new judge will have been appointed by your return and my—problem will be

245

settled." His words were forced through clenched teeth.

Flannery smiled. "Good. Now, you can go get Mama. I told her I'd let her know when we finished."

Whitley rose from the small sofa, wondering just how close they were to being permanently finished. Flannery knew all the rules of society. She was beautiful to look at. The sad thing was there was no passion in her, and she didn't create any in him.

Phina rose from the chair and stretched her arms over her head. She'd never been one to feel sorry for herself more than a few minutes. She needed to get started on her sewing. She had a lot of curtains to make. Besides, there was no need to worry about Whitley trying to throw her off Carillon. She had right and justice on her side and they always won, didn't they?

She planned to tiptoe past the parlor and take a quick peek inside at Whitley's guests. It caught her completely off guard to see Flannery sitting in the parlor by herself. Phina started to mind her own business and continue on to the sewing room upstairs, but how could she pass up a perfect opportunity to speak to the golden-haired beauty who was to be Whitley's wife?

Lifting her shoulders and her chin, Phina walked into the parlor. Plastering a friendly smile on her face she said, "Oh, hello. You must be Flannery. I don't believe we've met. I'm Phina."

Flannery's mouth gaped in surprise. She remained seated stiffly on the settee. Within a few seconds she'd composed herself. Flannery turned her head away from Phina and tilted her chin upward and said in a snobbish manner, "I'm waiting for my mother and Whitley to return, if you don't mind."

Actually she did, but she wasn't going to say that. Since Flannery was going to be living at Carillon one day they should at least learn how to be nice to each other. It amused her that Flannery refused to look at her. If she were in Flannery's position she would have looked her in the eyes and proudly announced herself as Whitley's fiance.

"Of course I don't mind. I'm happy to have you visit our house."

Flannery snapped her head around and glared as if she'd been caught blaspheming the church. "I don't believe this is *your* house."

Her vehemence shook Phina. She could understand her being cold and unfriendly but not her overt rudeness. Phina walked over to the settee and sat down beside her. Flannery moved the skirt of her dress out of the way so it wouldn't touch any part of Phina's. "Really? You do know that I live here, don't you?"

"Not for long." Flannery turned away from her again, refusing to look at Phina.

It was clear that Flannery wasn't going to be nice. An impish feeling settled over Phina. "It's a shame that both Whitley and your mother left you alone in this house." Phina put an adequately concerned expression on her face. "My goodness, don't they know what it would do to your reputation if word got out that you were left in Whitley's home unchaperoned. I faint to think what would happen."

Flannery lifted her chin higher. "It's perfectly all right. My mother is here with me."

"Of course she is, but you know how gossip is twisted until there is no truth in it. Why, if it were to

247

get out that you were left unattended in Whitley's house the gossip mongers would ruin you. Surely they'd assume you were alone with Whitley. You'd never live it down."

Flannery's eyes grew larger. She rose from the settee. "You wouldn't tell anyone?"

Phina rose too. "Me! Of course not! But it might be best if you waited on the front porch until they return. You know how slaves talk. They pass gossip from one plantation to another. You can't trust them, you know."

"Yes, I believe you're right." Flannery allowed Phina to walk her to the front door.

"I'm sure they'll be along in a minute or two. In the meantime, you'll be safe from gossip out here."

Phina opened the door and Flannery walked through it, then Phina closed it behind the golden-haired snob and threw the lock.

As she turned around she dusted her hands as if it'd been a dirty job. She hadn't exactly thrown Flannery out of her father's house, but the way she'd handled it was close enough to make her feel better. In fact, she felt very pleased with herself.

Phina picked up her skirts and ran up the stairs, smiling.

Chapter Seventeen

Tasma's feet hit the cool wooden floor. She burst out the front door, making it to the side of the house before she started heaving and retching. She held on to the corner of the house and tried not to make too much noise. Trying to be quiet just made her stomach roil and pitch all the more.

This was the fourth morning in a row that she'd awakened sick to her stomach. When she felt certain she was through she leaned against the house and rested. "Oh, lordy, lordy be," she whispered over and over again to herself as she picked up the tail of her nightdress and wiped her mouth. If Cush gave her a child she was going to kill him, she thought.

Maybe it was just the bad water from the flooding making her sick. Mr. Whitley said that's what made some of them sick for a few days after the flood. Even Mr. Ellison had been laid low with dysentery for more than a week. Yes, that had to be it. The water was still bad. After convincing herself of that, she wiped sweat off her forehead and turned to slip back into the house before her mother woke up.

Tasma opened the door gently and stepped inside.

Rubra stood in the middle of the floor, her large frame almost filling the room. Her hands were stuck to her wide hips, hiking her dress up at the hem on each side. Her brows drew together in a frown. Her full lips jutted outward.

"You been lying ta me, girl. Yous ain't got no stomach sickness. You's gots a chile in dat belly of yours."

Tasma leaned back away from her mother. She shook her head, her eyes widening with fear. "No, Mama. Dat ain't true. I's can't have no baby in my belly. I ain't done nothin'," she lied.

"Hush yore mouth, Tasma, if you can't speak de truth." Rubra looked ready to pounce on her. Her dark eyes seemed to spear Tasma with accusations. "You gonna tell me you ain't let no man mess wid you?"

Tasma's eyes blinked wildly. She and Cush only did it one time and it was over so quickly she thought sure no one would ever know it happened. She's been so sure there was no way she could be with child. Rubra stalked over to her and took hold of one of her breasts and gently squeezed. Tasma yelled out in pain.

"Dem sore?" Rubra asked.

"Yeah, Mama." Tasma's eyes filled with tears. "Deys been sore for days now. Why'd ya pinch me like dat?"

"Mmm—humm swollen too, I see." Rubra nodded her head as if assuring herself what she said was true. "Dem breasts weren't be sore if you gots stomach fever. Yous still gone tell me ain't no man messed wid you?"

Tasma brushed her stinging eyes with the back of her hands. She looked down at the floor. Her mother was right. She hadn't wanted to admit it. It'd been almost four weeks since she let Cush take her. She'd missed her monthly curse last week, but she hadn't been regular for more than a few months so she didn't think much about it. Now what was she going to do?

She knew Rubra would make them get married. Tasma cringed inwardly. She couldn't stand the thought of lying in bed beside Cush night after night when she didn't even like to be around him. She'd run away before she'd marry Cush. And since the day Spiker had taken up for her he'd been nicer to her and had just begun to pay her a little attention. She expected any day now he was going to ask her if he could come calling on her.

"I knows you wid chile," Rubra thundered loudly. "I guess it's Cush's chile. He de only one been calling on ya."

Without thinking of the consequences, Tasma said, "No, Mama. It's not Cush's." Tears formed in her eyes and rolled down her dark cheeks. Tasma never cried but she couldn't stop the tears today. "It's Spiker's chile," she whispered, then hung her head downward.

"Spiker!" Rubra covered her face with her hands and shook her head slowly. Her heavy bosom heaved and trembled. "Oh dear Lord, not dat man. Not wid my baby. Not dat man."

"I's didn't means ta do it, Mama," Tasma pleaded. "It was only one time. It was so quick I's didn't think any one would ever know."

A calm came over Rubra. She threw her shoulders back and arched her neck. "I's have him whipped fo' dis. Yessir, I'll fix that high and mighty darkie. He gone marry you, Tasma. I's see ta dat too, but first he'd gone be whipped proper."

251

Tasma's eyes twitched and her whole body trembled. She was frightened about what she'd done, frightened for Spiker. "I—I don't wants Spiker whipped."

"Dat ain't gots nothin' ta do wid you." She grabbed Tasma by the shoulder and spun her around. "Come on we're going ta see Mr. Whitley."

Whitley walked out the double French doors on the side of the house to the veranda where he had breakfast every morning. Today he was up earlier than most mornings. Hetty was spreading a white tablecloth over the breakfast table.

"I's get your coffee right away, Mr. Whitley."

"No rush, Hetty. I'm up early because I couldn't sleep." He walked over to one of the small Corinthian columns that held up the balcony and leaned against it. It was a beautiful morning. Sunshine was on the horizon. A twittery breeze stirred the humid air and birds chirped and called to their mates. Since the flooding the weather had made for a perfect summer, hot sunshiny days with an occasional late afternoon thunder shower to water the gardens. They lost half of the peanut crop and some of the cornstalks had been beaten down by the storms. The only good thing about the rains was that the ground was soft and easy to plow. They should get the rest of the cottonseed planted in record time.

Whitley unbuttoned his shirt and let the breeze cool his heated skin. He hadn't slept well at all since he'd tried to get Phina to leave Carillon. No, he hadn't slept well since the first night he kissed her. He couldn't stop thinking about how good she felt in his arms, how

252

sweet her mouth tasted, how easily she responded to and matched his ardor. It would be so much easier, he was sure, to forget about her if he didn't have to sit at the dinner table with her every night. They were polite to each other in the evenings, but a coolness had settled into their conversations. He wanted their relationship to return to the friendly one they had eased into before the storms. Whitley knew that would never happen. The truth was that deep inside himself at the core of his desire he wanted to be more than friendly with her. He wanted to make love to her.

From behind him, Whitley heard Hetty humming a peaceful tune. Every once in a while she'd sing a few words. He closed his eyes and saw Phina lying in bed, her lustrous dark hair fanning the white pillow. Of all the many different women Whitley had been with over the past fifteen years none of them had touched him like Phina had. His hands ached to caress her smooth skin. They ached to crush her hair beneath his fingers. They ached to caress that soft, womanly part of her he most desired.

But he couldn't. He was committed to Flannery. And he was indebted to Anchor. Anchor had trusted him with Carillon and he had to live up to that trust. If for no other reason, he had to marry Flannery because that was what Anchor had wanted.

Why was Phina the only woman he'd not been able to get out of his mind? Whitley looked out over the lawn and down to the formal garden. She'd done a beautiful job on the grounds, even doing a lot of the work herself. And because of her, all of the slaves had new clothes to wear and new curtains for their windows. She appeared to be getting used to Spiker, and Cass was teaching her how to ride.

253

When Phina had made it clear to him she wasn't leaving, he'd dropped the subject. He wasn't sure he'd make good his threat to have women perjure themselves when they went before the judge, but he knew he had to get her off Carillon.

A bobwhite chirped loudly in a tree and Hetty continued to hum in a low throaty voice. Morning sun broke through the trees and shone upon his face. There was something fresh and inviting about early morning.

"Mr. Whitley?"

He turned around and saw Rubra and Tasma coming out the door. The set expression on the older woman's face told him something was wrong. "Yes, Rubra. What is it?"

She yanked Tasma by the shoulder and placed her in front of her. "Spiker done got my Tasma wid chile."

Hetty stopped humming and the birds stopped chirping. Even the air seemed to go still. "What?" Whitley asked, coming out of the languid mood the peaceful morning had prompted. His gaze darted from Rubra to Tasma. "What are you talking about, Rubra?"

The older woman spoke up strongly. "Tasma been heavin' her guts out every mornin' dis week. She says it's Spiker's chile."

Whitley felt that old protectiveness surge within him. He stared at Tasma. She looked frightened, and she didn't look old enough to get pregnant. He spoke directly to her. "Is this true, Tasma?"

"Yessir," she said in a high-pitched, frail-sounding voice. She scrunched her shoulders up and around her neck, making her appear even younger. "He de one."

"Tasma don't lie," Rubra told him in a matter-of-fact tone.

Damn, he wished this hadn't happened. "I'll have to talk to Spiker."

"Go ahead, but it won't change things none. Spiker gone be whipped fo' dis."

Whitley's lips tightened. "I don't believe in whippings, Rubra. Everyone on this plantation knows that."

"Don't matter none 'bout dat. Mr. Anchor's daddy's set de rules long time ago. Ain't nobody changed 'em fo' as I know. If'n one of de men messes wid a young girl and gets her wid chile, he's ta be whipped, then marry her."

Whitley was trying not to get angry at the slave for being so vocal. "Neither Anchor nor his father is here anymore. You're free to marry and have children whenever you want. You don't have to get my permission."

Rubra reared back and looked at Whitley. "Nobody ever tole us de rules changed. Yous changin' des rule jest cause Spiker is yore favored and everybody knows he is."

The fine hairs on the back of Whitley's neck felt like they were crawling down his spine. He clenched his teeth tighter. "You're speaking out of line, Rubra."

She shook her head slowly. "No sir, I's speaks de truth."

Her insistence irritated him. "I'm not favoring Spiker," his words and expression were cold. "I repeat, I don't believe in whippings, and I don't believe in telling you how to live or who to marry. All I expect from you is that you remain on Carillon and do your job."

Standing her ground, Rubra said, "You lets Spiker gets by wid dis and won't none of us trust you no mo'. Mark my words. You'll lose the respect of all us 'round here."

Whitley tensed. She showed no signs of relenting. Maybe it was best he call the slaves together and settle this in front of all of them. "Rubra, you and Tasma go get everyone together at the meetinghouse. I'll be down there in a few minutes." He turned to Hetty who stood quietly over by the breakfast table. "Get Spiker here immediately."

When they'd all left Whitley hit the heel of his palm against the column. He should have had a talk with the slaves after Anchor's death and established his own set of rules. He knew there were things Anchor did, like whippings that he didn't approve of but he never expected a slave to want one of his own people whipped. It was barbaric. Rubra was just angry because Tasma was her daughter. The other slaves would be reasonable and understand, he was sure.

"You wanted to see me."

Whitley turned around and saw Spiker standing in the doorway. He was dressed in a clean white shirt tightly buttoned at the throat. Whitley was proud of Spiker and with good reason. After he'd befriended him seven years ago, Spiker had been a model slave. From Whitley he'd learned to talk correctly and had learned a lot about managing the plantation.

"Tasma says she's pregnant and it's your baby."

Spiker appeared too startled to say anything at first. His eyes rounded in surprise, his mouth dropped open. "Tasma's pregnant? Nooo—sir. It ain't mine. I've never touched her I swear."

"Why would she say it's yours?"

256

"I don't know, but it ain't. She's been after me since she came to work in the big house more than a year ago. I've talked to her but that's all. It ain't my baby."

"Let's go down to the meetinghouse and see if we can get this straightened out." Whitley walked over to the table Hetty had left set for breakfast. He poured a cup of coffee and handed it to Spiker. "Here drink this. I'm afraid you're going to need it. You're going to have to find a way to prove that baby isn't yours."

It looked as if all of the slaves were waiting in the clearing around the meetinghouse for Whitley when he and Spiker walked up a few minutes later. The men and women parted and let them through to the center where Rubra and Tasma stood. Rubra stood defiantly, looking over the crowd. Tasma hovered close by, frightened. On the walk over Whitley had decided that the only way to handle this was to let Spiker and Tasma confront each other face to face.

"There he is," Rubra said clearly as Spiker walked toward them. "Dat's de man who messed wid Tasma. Now she's carryin' his chile."

Out of the corner of his eye Whitley saw Ellison walking toward him, a coiled whip in his hand. Whitley stiffened. For the first time in his life, Whitley wanted to hit Ellison.

Spiker walked forward. "If Tasma claims her baby is mine she lies. I haven't touched her."

"Don't call my girl a liar. She don't lie."

"I don't either."

"I seen ya wid her down by de river one night," someone called out from the group of men to the left.

"Dat's right. I seen 'em too," another young man acknowledged.

Spiker turned to Whitley and said, "She followed

257

me down to the river. I was taking her home. I didn't touch her."

The crowd mumbled their disapproval of Spiker's statement.

"He almost hit Cush one day jest fo' talkin' ta her," Jasper said.

"Yeah, I wuz there. I seen it too," Deke agreed.

"I watched her go inside his cabin one day," someone else said.

"Is what they say true?" Whitley asked.

Spiker didn't flinch. "I didn't invite her over. She just showed up. And Cush had her by the arm and was trying to force her to go with him. I thought he was going to hit her."

"I ain't gone hit Tasma," Cush spoke up as he walked closer to the center. "I wanted her fo' my woman til Spiker messed wid her. She tole me I weren't de only man fo' her."

Spiker gave Cush a mean look, then snapped his head around to Tasma. "Tell them the truth. Tell them it isn't my baby."

Tasma looked around, her gaze lighting on first one face in the crowd, then another. Whitley wasn't sure who to believe. He wanted to believe Spiker but he wasn't denying any of the accusations against him. And no one knew better than Whitley how easy it was for things to get out of hand. As he thought of Phina he saw her and Chatalene hurrying toward the meetinghouse. Apparently they'd just heard about the meeting. Phina's hair was down and flying out behind her. His stomach quaked, a tightening settled in his groin. Yes, he knew how easily it would have been for Spiker to lose control with Tasma.

"You responsible fo' dis and everybody heah knows it," Rubra said. "No need ta lie no mo'."

"I'm not lying." Spiker's voice remained firm. He looked at the whip as Ellison shifted it from one hand to the other.

"Spiker," Whitley said his name calmly.

The slave swung around to face him. "I didn't do it. I know what her mama wants, and I know the rules. She wants me whipped. But I didn't touch her. I haven't touched a woman since my wife died." He looked around the circle of men, meeting the eyes of his kind. "I take care of myself in private."

Tasma spoke up for the first time. "I don't want him whipped. If'in you'll jest make him marry me, it'll be all right."

Shouts of protest erupted throughout the crowd.

"No!"

"Not fair!"

"It's not right he go unpunished!"

"You'd whip any of de rest of us!"

"Whip him!"

"Prove he's not yore favorite!"

"Whip him fo' messing wid Tasma!"

"Whip him!"

"Don't lets him get away wid it!"

The crowd quickly turned into a mob. For a moment Whitley thought the men were going to turn on him and jump him. He looked at the accused. Spiker shook his head dejectedly.

Ellison walked closer to Whitley and Spiker. "You're going to have an insurrection on your hands if you don't whip him."

Whitley looked at him with cold eyes. "I don't believe in whippings. How many times do I have to say it?"

"It's the rule and it's the middle of the game. Now's not the time to change the rules. You'll lose the respect of all of them if you do." Ellison grinned. "Besides, you didn't mind telling me a few weeks ago that I had to obey the rules. You said they hadn't changed just because Anchor died."

Dammit, Whitley knew Ellison was right. He couldn't have some of the rules applying some of the time. He had to maintain the respect of his slaves.

Whitley's and Spiker's gaze met, both of them knowing what had to be done. Spiker turned toward Tasma, giving her one last chance to take back the lie. She lifted her chin and squared her shoulders. Slowly, as he kept his gaze on Tasma's face Spiker pulled his white shirt out of his breeches and pulled it over his head. He slung the shirt to the ground and proudly walked over to the whipping post and knelt down.

Whitley's stomach knotted. Ellison sniffed and coiled the whip tighter. Silence flooded the crowd.

Phina rushed up to Whitley. "You're not going to let Ellison whip him, are you?" she asked, horror and concern written on her face.

Whitley wanted to tell her it wasn't going to happen but he knew it was. He would lose respect of the slaves if he didn't give into their demands. They considered it his duty to punish Spiker according to what they'd always believed. Anchor had warned him to never lose respect of the slaves or they turn against him. For him it wasn't the right thing to do under any circumstances, but the slaves were following the rules that were set down more than forty years ago. They believed they were right.

260

He looked into Phina's eyes and said, "It has to be."

"No," she pleaded, taking hold of his arm. "It's not right."

"I know," he said softly. "But if these people are to ever trust me again. I have to do this."

Whitley was numb as he moved to the center of the circle. He had to be the one to do this horrible deed. Damn, he wished he'd had a stiff drink. There were a lot of things he wanted to say but he'd have to make it short for Spiker's benefit. He knew he was in hell down on his knees hugging that four foot post.

"Listen to me." He waited until everyone was quiet. "I made my feelings on whippings clear to Anchor and all of you years ago. But I understand you were not informed that anything had changed since Anchor's death. Hear me well, this will be the last whipping on Carillon for *any* reason."

Ellison stepped forward and unfurled the whip.

Phina rushed and stood in front of Spiker. "No, I won't let you do this. This is a stupid reason to whip a man."

The crowd rumbled with disapproval. "Step aside, Phina," he said.

"Whitley, this isn't right," she pleaded.

His eyes turned cold. Every moment he waited was agony for Spiker. "Phina, get out of the way."

Phina's gaze searched the crowd. Whitley reached over and grabbed the whip out of Ellison's hand. "Get her."

Ellison locked his arms around Phina's waist and lifted her off the ground. Whitley drew back and snapped the leather whip against Spiker's back. The slapping sound echoed around them. Spiker grunted. Phina screamed. Tasma started to run to Spiker but

261

Rubra grabbed her. Quickly, Whitley drew back and snapped the whip again, the licks jarring him as it made contact with Spiker's back. Whitley turned sick to his stomach. Sweat broke out on his forehead. He cracked the whip the third time, then threw it to the ground. Phina struggled out of Ellison's arms and rushed to Spiker's side.

"Get to work," Whitley yelled to the onlookers. He trembled with anger. No one in the crowd moved so Whitley issued the order again. "Ellison, see they're married before the day's over. Have some of the men get started today on building them a house of their own."

At last he turned to look at Spiker. Phina was tearing strips off her petticoat to press against the bleeding wounds. The slaves would have seen through it if he'd held back with the lashes. He wanted to walk over to Spiker and tell him how sorry he was that he had to do it, but he had a feeling he was the last person Spiker wanted to see right now.

He turned and headed toward the house. Whitley grabbed his own shoulder and held it. He was taken back in time to when he was lifted onto the back of a horse and a noose tied around his neck. His shoulder had been dislocated, his eyes swollen shut. He'd burned and ached all over. Anchor had been his savior. His mind flashed forward to another time. Spiker was kneeling in front of the whipping post and Ellison's father was ripping Spiker's back with a studded whip. He'd been Spiker's savior that day. He'd put the slave to bed and tended his wounds. Today he'd been the punisher. And he didn't like it.

Chapter Eighteen

"You're drinking."

Whitley held up his glass and looked at the amber liquid sloshing inside it. His gaze darted to Phina. "Is that what I'm doing? Thank God! I thought I was wallowing in self-pity. So good of you to point it out to me."

Phina didn't let his sarcasm bother her as she walked farther into the parlor and set a covered tray on the table in front of the settee. "Rubra said you hadn't eaten all day."

Standing in front of the unlit fireplace, leaning a shoulder against the baroque mantel, he sipped his drink as he watched her in the gilt framed mirror. "I'm not hungry. But thanks for thinking about me. Please go ahead in to dinner without me."

She walked over to stand in front of him, looking pointedly at him. "I had dinner two hours ago."

Whitley's eyebrows arched. "Perhaps it's later than I thought."

"Obviously. I asked Rubra to prepare a tray for you before she retired for the evening."

This time his brows drew together in a frown. "I'm not hungry," he restated.

"You're not a drinker either, but you seem to be putting it down rather fast. You need something to eat."

He whirled, his eyes cold and hard. "Dammit, Phina, I'm somewhere around the age of thirty. I don't think I need a mother in my life."

She flinched. "I'm not trying to be your mother. I'm trying to keep you from being sick in the morning. If you continue drinking without eating anything that is exactly what's going to happen to you."

"Fine. Let it happen," he said crisply. "Now go away and leave me alone."

Whitley had taken off his jacket, waistcoat and cravat and rolled up the sleeves of his white shirt to just below his elbows. His dark gray trousers were held up by a pair of red and gray striped suspenders. The first shadows of beard were showing on his face, and his hair looked as if his hands had combed through it numerous times, but it still fell attractively across his forehead.

Rubra said he'd refused breakfast when he returned from the meetinghouse that morning and that he'd spent the entire day working at his office desk. He'd even refused to meet with the merchant who'd brought supplies up from Bainbridge, letting Ellison take care of the business for him. When Rubra told Phina he declined to dine with her she also told her that he'd started drinking. Phina didn't have to question the older woman to know what was wrong with Whitley.

At first Phina couldn't comprehend why the whipping had to take place and even now that she understood, she still wished it hadn't happened. Looking at

264

Whitley, she knew that he wished it hadn't happened too, but emptying the liquor decanter wasn't going to change anything. Phina hated to see Whitley do this to himself. He was too good a man to berate, abuse or punish himself in such a manner. Chatalene had explained to her that if he'd let Spiker get away with his ill-treatment of Tasma the rest of the slaves would have never forgiven him or trusted him again to do what was right.

Not knowing what else to do to get Whitley's attention, Phina walked over to the side table and poured a small amount of liquor into a glass and took a sip. The fiery stuff burned down her throat and into her stomach. It took all she could do not to cough and fan her mouth with her hand. Somehow, she managed to keep a straight face and look into Whitley's eyes.

"You're not a drinker," Whitley said, watching her carefully.

She held up the glass much in the same way Whitley had earlier and looked at the swirling liquid. "Oh, is that what I'm doing?" she mimicked his words.

Whitley strode over to stand beside her, and to refill his glass. "Don't try my patience tonight, Phina. I'm in no mood for it. Put the drink down and leave me."

Her throat still burned but she sipped the stinging liquid again. Heat rushed to her cheeks and down her neck, making her feel flushed, but to her surprise the liquor didn't leave a bad taste in her mouth.

Keeping her gaze on his face she said, "I heard a man at the boardinghouse say only a fool drinks alone. You're not a fool, Whitley, I don't want you to behave as one. If you're going to drink, I'll drink with you."

"Not true, Phina. Only a foolish master whips his

slaves and only a fool goes against his own vow. I did both today." He turned away from her and walked over to the window. Pushing aside the sheer panel, he looked out into the darkness of evening and propped the toe of his booted foot on the edge of the window-sill.

Phina remained where she stood. The silence between them stretched while she contemplated leaving him alone. She looked at him, his back to her. His hair hung below his collar, a slight upwards curl to the ends. His broad shoulders and slim hips made him especially appealing to her feminine eye. But those same broad shoulders were slightly hunched, indicating how he suffered. At that moment she knew she would do anything to spare him pain. This protectiveness astounded her, disconcerted her, yet assured her Whitley didn't need to be alone tonight.

"You're being too hard on yourself. I don't believe in whippings. I'm not even sure I believe in slavery. But what you did had to be done."

Whitley faced her and laughed out loud, his white teeth gleamed in the soft lamplight. "It had to be done?" He continued to chuckle. "This from the woman who stood in front of Spiker and tried to stop me. Will you never cease to amaze me, Phina?"

His gaze met hers and she knew he was trying hard to be sarcastic, but instead his words sounded lonely, desperate for something she couldn't put her finger on. "I did what I felt I had to do just as you did what you had to do. You had no choice in the matter."

"No, that's where you're wrong," he said. "I did have a choice. I simply chose not to take it. I didn't have to whip Spiker."

She walked closer to him, her red skirts swishing

266

about her legs. "Yes, you did, and Spiker knew you had to do it too. That's why he knelt in front of that post. He wouldn't have shamed you in front of the other slaves. Spiker respected you too much for that to happen. He wouldn't have let you disgrace yourself by pardoning him. If you hadn't given him those lashes you would have lost the respect of your slaves. They have to know they can trust you to be a fair leader."

"No." He shook his head. "Spiker expected better from me. I expected better from myself."

"He expected you to be master of this plantation. Master of all the slaves."

"Master! What a goddammed word that is. I'm master of nothing." His hand tightened around the glass and a faraway look came into his eyes. "Until I met Anchor, I didn't have anything. I knew my name was Whitley and that's all I knew. When Anchor found me he said I looked to be fifteen. But I could have been thirteen or seventeen. I didn't know my letters or my numbers." He looked at her earnestly. "I don't know how I came about living on the streets. I know I traveled with a man at one time, but I don't know what happened to him. He went away one day and never came back. I don't remember if he was my father—" Whitley stopped abruptly. He turned and flung his glass into the unlit fireplace. The fine crystal made a slight tinkling noise as it hit against the fire-bricks and broke into hundreds of pieces before falling soundlessly into the cold ashes.

"Damn it, Phina, don't feel sorry for me."

The brandy tasted strong in her mouth as she lied and said, "I don't."

He inhaled deeply and calmed. "Yes, you do. I see it in your eyes. You've often tried to mother me by doing things like offering to warm a cup of milk for me or to get me dry clothes."

She wanted to look away so he couldn't read her telling eyes, but she couldn't. It was as if she longed for him to know what she was feeling. Maybe she wanted him to know that her words said one thing but her lips another. Maybe she wanted him to know what she was feeling as she gazed into his eyes and said, "I never felt motherly at those times."

The atmosphere in the room changed from being charged to intimate. Without having planned ahead, Phina knew what she was doing. Desire outweighed what she knew to be right and proper. She was setting the course for the evening. She was leading Whitley and it would be up to him if he followed.

Whitley started toward her. "If not motherly, what did you feel at those times, Phina?"

She swallowed hard, weakening under his constant gaze. "I'm not sure. I only know I wasn't trying to be a mother to you."

He raked the backs of his fingers down her cheek as he stopped in front of her. "Any chance you wanted to be a lover?"

Phina wanted his touch. She wanted it, welcomed it, and tried to push aside the little voice that told her the drink was making him do it.

"You shouldn't talk like that," she said, shaking off some of the desirous feelings that had settled over her. Reason and emotion were fighting inside her and she wasn't sure which was going to win. She wasn't sure which she wanted to win. In addition to having had too much to drink he was also committed to another woman. She couldn't overlook that either. "You've had too much to drink and not enough to eat. Come sit down and see what Rubra prepared for you."

On stiff legs, she walked over to the settee and sat down. Much to her surprise, Whitley followed and eased down beside her. She lifted the napkin off the tray. Bite-sized chunks of beef, potatoes and onions filled a small plate. A large slice of buttered bread lay to one side. In separate dishes there were servings of pickled beets and sliced peaches coated in a cinnamon sauce.

Phina picked up the tray and placed it on his lap, then she handed him the fork. "You'll feel better once you have something in your stomach."

He took the fork from her. With a little bit of a smile on his lips he asked, "Do you still want to deny mothering me?"

Relief flooded through Phina when she saw his smile. Whatever she was doing was working. "I won't deny caring about you," she said softly. "Now eat."

He speared a piece of meat, then a potato and put it into his mouth and chewed. "You know, Phina, we actually have a lot in common."

"I suppose in some things we do," she said, watching him eat. "Both of us grew up without a father, but of course, I had my mother to care for me."

"And now you're taking care of your mother."

A sadness washed over Phina. Tears rushed to her eyes. She blinked and held them in. "Yes." Phina knew she needed to go back to New Orleans and check on her mother. But she was afraid if she left she would somehow be giving up possession of Carillon, leaving Whitley free to have it all, to not welcome her back when she returned.

269

"I suppose you trust the woman who's looking after her."

"Yes." Phina folded the napkin she'd taken off the tray, pleased that he'd asked about her mother. "She and her daughter take care of the boardinghouse where we live. They're very fond of my mother."

"Have you no beau waiting impatiently for your return, Phina?"

"Beau?" she said, feeling a bit uncomfortable, knowing that Mr. Braxton was the closest to a beau. He and Whitley weren't all that different in appearance. Both were tall with broad shoulders, but there was several years difference in their ages. But it was the difference in the way she felt when she was with them that let her know she'd never long for Mr. Braxton's touch the way she did for Whitley's. At last she looked away from him. "Only Mr. Braxton," she whispered.

"The older gentleman you told me about."

"Yes."

Whitley never touched the beets but finished the meat and potatoes, and started on the peaches. After a couple of bites he held a forkful up to Phina and she opened her mouth and took it. The cinnamon and sugary taste filled her mouth. She'd already had her dessert with dinner, but found she couldn't resist the chance of having Whitley feed her. It was an intimacy she didn't want to miss.

"Why doesn't a beautiful woman like you have a younger beau?"

She refolded the napkin in her lap for the third time. "I've had callers but no one special."

He gave her another bite of the peaches and she took it. Neither of them spoke again until the bowl

270

was empty and Whitley had set the tray on the table in front of them.

"Do you feel better now?" she asked, her gaze still on his face.

He sat back and put his arm up on the top of the settee, stretching his long legs out in front of him. Again he gave her a bit of a smile. "I feel like I have been properly mothered tonight."

A slice of disappointment slithered down into Phina's breasts. She wasn't sure what kind of relationship she wanted from Whitley, but she didn't want him to think of her as a mother—or a sister.

"You haven't asked about Spiker," she said, changing the subject.

Whitley reached out and tucked a wispy strand of hair behind her ear. A tingling chill ran up her back as his fingers grazed her cheek. "Rubra told me he was all right."

Phina nodded. "He wouldn't speak to anyone, but by late in the afternoon he was helping the other men build the floor to his house." Whitley wasn't looking at her face. He was looking at her ear as he continued to brush her hair with his fingertips while she talked. "Whitley," she said and waited for him to look at her with those piercing blue-green eyes. "He wasn't badly hurt."

"But he *was* hurt." His hand traced down to her ear. When he reached the bottom he caressed the lobe with his thumb and forefinger. "I hated like hell doing it. It'll never happen again while I'm master of this plantation."

"I think you made that clear to the slaves this morning. Now that Anchor is dead you don't have to run

271

things the way he did. You can bring your own ideas and dreams to Carillon."

Whitley had had just enough brandy to make him completely relaxed. When he'd started drinking getting drunk was the only thing on his mind. But now with Phina here so close to him, looking at him with her dark eyes, he found that the incident with Spiker was fading and in its place were feelings he'd managed to suppress the past few weeks. He wanted to love Phina. He wanted to make love to her, knowing good and well he was committed to another. What was he to do? Flannery was cold and indifferent to his kisses, but Phina—Phina was warm and responsive to his touch.

"You have small ears. Soft." His hand left her earlobe and traveled down to her jawline and followed the bone around to her other ear. Again he caressed her lobe between his thumb and forefinger. He knew he shouldn't be touching her but how could he not when it seemed like such an innocent gesture? But even as he thought that he knew it untrue. The way he was touching Phina, what he was thinking was not innocent. It was building a slow heat of desire deep inside him.

Phina wanted to open her arms, her mouth, her heart to Whitley. She had from the moment she'd walked in and seen how badly he hurt. She wasn't sure when it happened that she started wanting Whitley's kisses, his touch. The very thought of it should be a violation of her duty to secure a place for her and her mother from Anchor McCabe's estate, but right now that seemed distant. She loved this man. And if it were true that she loved him, what ever happened between them would be sanctioned.

Whitley let his fingers slip down her neck and she

272

automatically arched her head back. He was touching her as if she were fine silk and she loved every second of it.

"You're much too beautiful tonight, Phina." His voice was husky. "Much too tempting." He cupped her cheek with his palm and leaned very close to her. "Go while I'll allow it," he whispered.

His sweet breath smelled of peaches, cinnamon, and brandy. Phina wanted to taste him. She didn't want to go. Desire and expectation rippled down her back and settled in the pit of her stomach. She wouldn't let him send her away when she was so close to having his lips upon hers once more.

Their gazes met, searched, then stilled. "You shouldn't be alone tonight," she said, not knowing where the words she spoke were coming from but knowing they felt right.

"How is a desperate man to take that statement, Phina?"

Her slow breaths changed to gentle gasps, warning her now was the time to back down or go forward and leave regret behind. Desire for this man overpowered her modesty, her innocence, her duty.

"As an invitation."

Surprise lighted his eyes. His hand cupped the back of her neck and brought her breasts closer to his chest, her face closer to his. "I'm not playing a game, Phina. I'm serious. Go."

Phina didn't flinch. He wasn't telling her anything she didn't already know. In a rush of awareness that made what he was saying to her perfectly clear, Phina made her decision. A roaring filled her ears blocking out everything but Whitley. "I want to stay the night

273

with you." She lowered her lashes and lifted her face to his.

Whitley pressed his lips to hers, kissing her gently at first, but the taste of her, the feel of her in his arms, her breasts clasped against his chest started a fire inside him he knew only sexual release would put out. He kissed her over and over again, knowing he was supposed to be committed to Flannery, knowing that in the morning he'd still fight Phina for every acre of Carillon. But all that didn't keep him from wanting her tonight. It didn't keep him from pushing all those things from his mind and concentrating on the desirable woman in his arms, the woman who wanted him.

In a fluid motion he rose from the sofa, pulling her with him. He slid one arm around her back and fitted his other underneath her buttocks and lifted her into his arms. He carried her through the foyer and up the stairs, telling himself that taking her to his room would give her time to come to her senses and stop him.

The door to his room was ajar so he kicked it open. A lamp burned low, casting a pale yellow light upon the room. Phina knew when his booted feet left the highly polished wood floor and stepped onto the tightly woven wool rug. He carried her over to the Chippendale bed with its canopy of red and green striped satin. The covers had been turned down, exposing gleaming white sheets and fluffy pillows. He laid her down on her back, then straddled her. He held his weight off her by supporting himself with his knees.

Whitley looked down into her eyes and what he saw brought him up short. She wasn't going to push him away. She wasn't going to deny them this night. Their union couldn't be prevented. They'd hungered too much, shared too much, missed too many opportunities.

Anchor had loved Whitley, but he wanted and needed to be loved by a woman. Phina wanted to be that woman.

Phina raised up to meet Whitley. She yearned for his kisses, his touch. His open lips met hers in an impassioned kiss, meant to seduce, to escalate and to satisfy.

"Are you sure about this?" he asked as his lips left hers to travel over her cheeks, her eyes and back to her lips again. He needed to hear her say what he saw in her face.

"I've never been more sure of anything in my life," she answered truthfully.

Whitley worked at opening the small buttons running down the back of her dress. When the bodice slipped off her shoulder, her breath came unevenly. Whitley slid off the bed and pulled Phina with him. He turned her around and with trembling fingers unlaced her corset and untied her petticoats. He helped her shed them all. Next he pulled off his boots and Phina slipped out of her shoes and peeled down her stockings. Whitley yanked his shirt over his head and unbuttoned his breeches and started to push them down when his gaze met Phina's. She stood before him in her thin chemise. The nipples of her breasts showed clearly beneath the sheer fabric. He trembled. He wanted her. He needed her. She was an innocent. He knew that. Could he take what she was willing to give, what he wanted so desperately?

Fear grabbed hold of Phina's heart. She saw doubt in Whitley's eyes. He didn't know how much she wanted him. Phina reached up and placed her hands on Whitley's chest. Her hands traced the line of his shoulders, down his biceps, over his elbows to the soft skin on the underside of his wrist, relishing the feel of his bare skin. She loved the muscular strength of him, the power she felt banked inside him.

"Don't turn away from me, Whitley. Please let us have this night. Love me."

He swallowed hard. She wanted him. Not just any man but *him*. "Yes," he whispered and swept her up to him.

Phina accepted his abundance of kisses while her hands played over his shoulders, up into his hair and down to the small of his back where her fingers stopped at the band of his breeches. She slid her hands underneath the heavy cotton and slipped them down as her palms glanced over his firm buttocks. He moaned his approval. All of Phina's leftover vestiges of shyness disappeared. How could she feel uncomfortable with the man she loved? It would be impossible. She couldn't pass up the glory this night promised.

With the ease of a well-versed man, Whitley grasped the tail of her chemise and pulled it over her head, then stepped out of his trousers. The force and demand of his kisses backed Phina against the bed and she fell backward onto the cool white sheets. The bell she always wore fell to the back of her neck and tangled in her hair.

Whitley came to her side.

She reached for him.

In the pale light, he looked at Phina adoringly, desire showing strongly in his manhood. He supported himself on one elbow while with the other hand he lightly caressed her breasts, first one, then the other. He was filled with passion and desire but also joy that Phina had come to him.

Phina was acutely aware of Whitley's every touch, the slight roughness of his beard as it skimmed across her skin. No one had ever touched her bare breasts. It was frightening, exhilarating. He bent his head and pulled the tip of one breast into his mouth as his hands slowly sculpted them. The muscles in her abdomen contracted and quivered convulsively beneath the flaming heat of his sucking motions. It drove her crazy with wanting, mad with desire.

"Whitley?" she whispered huskily. "What are you doing? I've never felt this way before."

"Nor have I," he mumbled against her breast. "I'm so damn hard for you." He covered her body with his, pressing himself between her legs. His mouth left her breasts and moved up to her lips, over to her earlobe, down her neck and across her shoulder.

All her senses burst to life as she smelled cinnamon, tasted brandy, felt naked skin, saw Whitley's arousal, heard him whispering, "You are so beautiful. You smell wonderful. You feel so good. You're mine."

"Yes," she found herself answering, wanting, begging it to be so.

As they kissed with fervor Whitley's hands molded her shape. His palm caressed her waist, her hip, her inner and outer thigh. He kissed her stomach, burying his face in the hollow of her abdomen. Waves of pleasure radiated through her as she felt strength in his hands, hunger in his kisses, desire in his manhood. She softly moaned her pleasure.

Whitley knew he couldn't hold off much longer. It'd been too long since he'd been with a woman. That made being with Phina all the more special and that made him want her all the more as he nudged her legs farther apart and settled himself at her opening. He'd

277

never made love to a virgin, and he wasn't prepared for the resistance he encountered. He'd never met a barrier before. A feeling Whitley had never experienced before washed over him. He didn't know what it was or how to explain it. Suddenly he became stronger, bigger, fiercer. This woman beneath him was his. She'd never been any other man's woman. He slid his arms under her back and cupped her to his chest in a possessive embrace. From this moment on she would be his and only his. He wanted himself inside her. He wanted her to feel all the glorious sensations he felt.

"Bite my shoulder if it hurts," he whispered as he gently forced his way inside.

A few minutes later Phina lay languid beneath Whitley. She fondled the firm ridged muscles in his back. She stroked up and down the spare line of his hip. The pleasure of his ministrations had ended and a burning had embedded itself between her legs. Whitley had told her the pain wouldn't last long and it hadn't, but now she found that she felt empty inside, as if something was missing. She wondered why there was such a magnificent buildup to such an earth-shattering letdown.

Whitley lay on top of Phina waiting for his breathing to slow. He'd never had an experience like he'd just shared with Phina, and he was eager to see if it could be repeated. It was glorifying. He'd become well acquainted with a woman's body over the past fifteen years, but his time with Phina had surpassed his wildest dreams. He knew he'd taken her to the brink of satisfaction and then, because she was a virgin she'd lost it in the pain of penetration. This time he'd make sure she was satisfied before he allowed himself release.

Lifting his head, he looked down into her eyes. She was confused. He understood. "I'm sorry it had to be that way the first time for you. It will be better the next time, I promise."

She nodded.

He brushed her damp hair back and kissed her forehead, her eyes, her nose. "Did I ever tell you how attractive you are when fine strands of your hair falls to frame your face?"

She shook her head.

"It's true." He smiled and kissed her lips briefly. "You're beautiful, Phina. Not just in your looks but in your response to me. Do you believe me?"

"Yes," she whispered.

He kissed her lips, her cheek, and down her neck, letting his tongue taste her skin. His hand made a leisurely sweep over her waist and down her hip. He felt her shudder.

"Has the pain gone away?" he asked, his lips pressed against the soft skin below her ear.

"Yes," she said, coming alive again under his touch.

"Let me show you how good it can be, Phina."

Whitley lowered his head to her breasts and sucked a pink-tipped nipple into his mouth. His hand planed down her hip and over her thigh to find that point between her legs he sought. He moved the tips of his fingers tantalizingly slow against her. Within seconds Whitley felt her hips begin to move to his motion. She was ready for him again. And he was ready for her.

A long time later Whitley lay with Phina cuddled tightly in his arms. He had some serious thinking to do. By Phina's breathing he knew she wasn't sleeping either.

Phina had given him what should have only been

taken in her marriage bed. He was honored. He would accept the responsibility of it. He'd known better than to make love to Phina yet he'd been unable to stop himself.

The only women he'd ever made love to were the ones he'd paid for. Flannery allowed him to kiss her because it was expected of her and she never returned his ardor. Phina had kissed him, touched him, loved him because she wanted to. And she'd asked nothing in return.

But what about Anchor? Whitley had never gone against him. He owed Anchor everything, his life. How could he go against the last wish of the man who'd taken him into his home, fed him, educated him, loved him and given him his home?

Whitley ran his hand up and down Phina's arm. But after tonight, how could he give up Phina? The answer came to him. He couldn't. He loved her.

Phina wanted to sleep but couldn't. Her mind was too full of all the things she and Whitley had shared. Even now, she wanted to start all over again and enjoy every kiss, every caress. But as the glow ebbed and reality returned Phina's thoughts turned to other things.

She didn't understand why she hadn't wanted to stop the mounting feelings that were developing for Whitley. She didn't know why those feelings were stronger than the common sense that was telling her to stay away from Whitley and continue to pursue a place at Carillon for her and her mother. Her love for him was so strong it caused her to deny common sense and what she knew to be right.

Whitley would never allow her to live at Carillon now. He wouldn't do that to Flannery. She knew that.

Yet, she'd let her passion and desire for him, her love for him govern her behavior. Now she'd have to accept the responsibility for her actions. And now she better understood her mother's relationship with Anchor. Diana had known Anchor was married, yet she'd let him into her bed. Phina knew Whitley was promised to Flannery, but she wasn't sorry she'd had tonight.

Phina closed her eyes and pushed her backside up against Whitley's warm belly. Even if she received nothing from Carillon now, she wouldn't go back empty-handed. She had the memory of tonight.

Chapter Nineteen

"Lord have mercy, Miss Phina! Whats you doing in Mr. Whitley's bed wid out yore clothes on!"

Phina's eyes popped open and she saw Tasma standing over her, shaking her head. Shock showed in the slave's dark brown eyes. Coming instantly awake, Phina quickly pulled the sheet under her neck and held it tightly. Her gaze darted to the doorway, fearful someone else might walk by and see her.

"I's afraid you done gots yoreself in more trouble dan I's got into." She shook her head slowly. "Mr. Whitley can't marry you. He's done promised hisself ta Miss Flannery from de Pines. What you gone do wid dat baby he put inside you?"

Phina blinked nervously, stunned by Tasma's words. A baby? She hadn't thought about that possibility. She cleared her throat. "He didn't give me a baby." Her voice was raspy. She cleared her throat again. "I'm sure of it. Besides, last night was the only time we—uh—we—"

"Dat don't matter to dem chillens. Dey's got minds of their own. I gots me a baby wid only doin' it one time." Tasma patted her stomach.

Phina cringed inside. This wasn't the sort of thing she wanted to discuss with Tasma. She rubbed her forehead trying to think. She never had been one to have headaches but she had one now.

"Mama won'ts believe dis. No one else will neither." Tasma clucked her tongue disapprovingly as she continued to stand over Phina.

Phina sat up straighter in bed and looked around the room. How was she going to get out of this? Suddenly she was furious with Whitley. Why hadn't he awakened her? How dare he leave her to be caught sleeping in his bed? It was almost as if he'd planned for this to happen. Surely he knew Tasma would come looking for her when she found her bed empty and undisturbed.

She brushed her hair back and thought about what she needed to say. "Tasma, I don't want Rubra or anyone else on the plantation to know about this."

Tasma placed her hands on her hips and laughed, a deep husky sound that let Phina know her words were falling on deaf ears. "I's can't keep dis to myself, Miss Phina. Mama has ta know what goes on in dis house. It's her job. And I's have ta tell Spiker. He's my man now."

Phina bristled. "It's not your mother's or Spiker's job to know my business. And, I might add, it's your job to do what I tell you to do. Now, I want your promise that you'll keep this to yourself and tell no one."

Tasma cupped her mouth with both hands and chuckled behind them, showing how seriously she took Phina's threat. "I promise. I's won't tell nobody I found you in Mr. Whitley's bed, naked as da day you were born."

Shaking her head in frustration, Phina wrapped the top sheet around her body and eased off the bed. "Just gather my clothes and let's get out of here before someone else comes in," Phina said, knowing this would be all over the plantation by noon.

While Phina washed and dressed she tried to decide what she needed to say to Whitley. She had known what she was doing last night and why she was doing it. Whitley was in pain and needing comfort over the incident with Spiker, and she didn't want to pass up the chance to spend the night with the man she loved. And now, as much as she hated to do it, she would have to leave Carillon. She would go back to New Orleans to care for her mother. Whitley wouldn't want her around Flannery any more than Anchor would have wanted her mother around his wife.

Phina had never realized she was so much like her mother. Now she understood some of the things her mother must have felt, some of the things she must have gone through so many years ago when she was involved with Anchor. Phina knew that if she were to conceive a child because of last night, she wouldn't upset Whitley's life any more than her mother had upset Anchor's life nineteen years ago.

For a moment Phina's stomach muscles tightened as she thought about the possibility of Whitley wanting to marry her, but she quickly discounted that notion as foolish.

Even though it tore at her heart to do it she would find Whitley and tell him that she would take his bank draft and sign the paper giving up all rights to Carillon.

In between her own musing as she dressed, she listened to Tasma tell her that Spiker was stiff and sore

284

but up at dawn working on their house. He still hadn't spoken to her. The two men who'd roomed with Spiker had been given other accommodations until their house was finished. Tasma told her she'd spent the night on the bed but she couldn't convince Spiker to share it with her. He had thrown a blanket on the floor.

While she had a cup of tea and a hot biscuit coated with butter and sugar, Phina took a few minutes to parley with Tasma over her fears that it might take Spiker a long time to come around and accept her as his wife.

Then after a few minutes of fussing with her hair, Phina knew she couldn't delay the inevitable any longer. She went downstairs to find Whitley. The sooner she got this over with the better for her. She didn't want to leave Whitley, she didn't want to leave Carillon. She loved him and his home. But how could she stay and watch him with Flannery? Keeping her courage intact she forced herself to walk into his office.

Whitley rose from his desk as she came into the room. He looked so handsome in his white shirt and gray striped cravat and double-breasted waistcoat. His eyes lighted with pleasure and he smiled, erasing some of the anxiety she felt at confronting him. It didn't appear he was upset with her for what happened between them last night. That made her feel a little better. She'd known he was engaged, that he belonged to another, still she wasn't sorry they'd spent the night together. His hair looked as if he'd run his hands through it a few times. For a moment she thought she would stay and fight for him. But almost as quickly she knew she had to be as strong as her mother was

285

and realize his life had been planned long before she came into it.

"Phina. You look lovely this morning."

"Thank you," she said, denying the feelings that made her heart leap for joy at his praise, the feelings that made her want to forget the reason she came into his office and rush into his arms and tell him how much she loved him. Instead she kept her chin high and walked farther into the room. "I wish you'd awakened me. I'm—I'm afraid Tasma saw me in your bed. I made her promise not to tell anyone, but I fear she'll let it slip. It wasn't my intention to embarrass you in front of the slaves. I hope Flannery never hears of this."

"Phina, it's all right." He walked around the desk to stand before her. "I've already made up my mind. Flannery will have to know about us."

Her eyes widened. "No, Whitley! I didn't want—"

He placed the tips of his fingers on her lips coaxing her to silence. The scent of shaving soap wafted underneath her nose as she allowed him to outline her lips. His gaze never left her face. Phina thrilled to the sweetness of his touch.

"I've been thinking about this all morning. It hasn't been an easy decision for me to make." He paused and moistened his lips. "I've never gone against anything Anchor wanted me to do. From the day he found me to this day whenever I started to do anything I asked myself, 'Would this please Anchor?' My feelings for you have helped me to realize that Anchor is gone and it's time I learned to make decisions based on what I want to do, on what I believe is right. I'm going to withdraw my intent of marriage to Flannery as soon as she returns." He paused. "I'm going to marry you, Phina."

Stunned, Phina couldn't speak. She couldn't move. His fingertips still lay warm upon her lips. She never expected this, never planned on it. Marry Whitley? The thought was too good to be true. But if she let him break his promise to Flannery would he end up hating her? It made her love him all the more to know he was willing to give up the woman he loved, the woman he was promised to in order to marry her simply because it was the right thing to do. But she couldn't let him do it.

"No, I—I don't want that," she said, moving quickly away from his touch before she allowed it to persuade her otherwise. "I can't let you do that to Flannery simply because we—because I—because of last night. That's not fair to her. It's not fair of me to put you in that position."

"It is fair, Phina. I wanted to marry Flannery for all the wrong reasons." He reached and took hold of her hand and held it in both of his. "I want to marry you because I—"

"Whitley." Ellison walked through the open door of Whitley's office at a fast pace, but he stopped abruptly when he saw that Whitley wasn't alone. "Oh, Phina." His gaze caught sight of Whitley holding her hand. Her name softly died on his lips. His gaze met Whitley's. "The door wasn't closed. I didn't know you were busy. I'm sorry I interrupted." His gaze swept over Phina's face. "How are you, Phina? I haven't seen much of you recently. There's been so much to do since the flood, I haven't had time to stop by and say hello."

"I'm very well, thank you." She pulled her hand

287

away from Whitley's and stepped away from him. "I know you had a lot of things to take care of after the water receded. Whitley kept me informed of all the work going on in the slaves' quarters and with the fields. He told me that we're now planting the cotton." Phina knew she was babbling nervously but couldn't seem to stop. She wasn't happy that Ellison caught Whitley holding her hand.

Ellison walked a little farther into the room. "Yes. The corn was tall enough that the rain didn't wash them away or beat them into the ground. We weren't so lucky with the peanuts."

"Good," she said with a nervous smile on her lips. It didn't appear he was going to leave so she decided to. She could continue this conversation with Whitley after he'd concluded his business with Ellison. "Well, if you'll excuse me, I have something I need to attend to."

"Wait, Phina," Ellison said, holding out his arm to stop her. "While I have the two of you together, I'd like to discuss something. Whitley, since Phina is staying in your house, I'd like to ask for permission and blessings to court her."

Phina gasped.

"No," Whitley said without the least bit of hesitation.

Ellison cleared his throat. His gaze darted from Whitley to Phina. Clearly uncomfortable, but not willing to give up, he continued. "I realize you're not her father, Whitley, but I don't want to—"

"I said no, Ellison." His eyes didn't waver from his overseer's face. Whitley turned and walked behind his desk, then looked back at him. "I've just told Phina she's going to marry me."

"What?" Ellison's face flamed red.

"Whitley!" Phina said, recovering from the shock of Ellison's question. She didn't like Whitley's bold announcement, especially when she'd already told him she couldn't marry him.

Ellison's eyes registered his disbelief. "You're engaged to Flannery! What kind of game are you playing?"

Whitley remained calm even though it was clear Ellison was extremely upset. "This is no game. The engagement was never formally announced. We have an understanding, and I plan to withdraw my proposal when Flannery returns."

Phina didn't like the direction this conversation was going. These two men were trying to decide her future without even talking to her. She had to put a stop to this before it caused the two friends to say things they didn't mean. She didn't plan to let Ellison court her.

She faced Ellison, directing her attention to him. She'd talk to Whitley later. "Whitley has asked me to marry him, but I haven't accepted."

Ellison turned away from Whitley and almost pounced on Phina. "May I ask the reason he gave for wanting to marry you? Did he claim undying love for you?" He paused only a second. "I thought not." Ellison sneered his words.

Whitley's eyes narrowed, his lips formed a tight line. "Drop it, Ellison."

"Not now that I know what you're up to."

"Let it go," Whitley said in a low voice that warned Ellison he was serious. "This has nothing to do with you."

"The hell it doesn't," Ellison replied sharply. He pushed the sides of his dark brown jacket away from his hips and rested the heels of his palms against the waistband of his breeches. "I know why you decided to marry Phina. I planned to court her and marry her for the same reason." He stepped closer to Whitley even though the desk was still between them. "My only mistake was in thinking you too honest to do it."

Phina looked from one man to the other. The vehemence she heard in Ellison's voice and the danger she heard in Whitley's frightened her. What was wrong with these two men? What were they talking about? She'd never considered marrying either of them.

Whitley's features hardened. He glowered at Ellison. "It's time for you to excuse yourself."

"Not yet. You and I both know why you want to marry her, and I think it's time for Phina to know."

Whitley's jaw tensed measurably. "Why I'm marrying her is none of your business."

"Want to bet?" He jerked a pointing finger at Whitley. "If I can't marry her you won't either." He whipped his head around to Phina. "Anchor never signed the adoption papers making Whitley his son."

"Ellison!" Whitley turned white with rage. "Damn it! Shut up!"

"Hell no! Whitley is not Anchor's legal son, furthermore he never signed his will leaving Carillon to Whitley."

"Dammit! Ellison!" Whitley hurried from around the desk. Ellison put up both fists and jumped into a fighting stance. "Come on, Whitley. This fight has been coming since the day you got here."

Phina couldn't believe what she was hearing and for a moment she was too stunned to move. Her gaze flew to Whitley. She saw by his face that Ellison was telling the truth. But she didn't have time to think about the implications. She had to stop them from fighting. "No!" She rushed to stand between the two men, pushing at Ellison's chest. "Stop acting like immature school boys!"

Ellison's expression was deadly. "Step aside, Phina."

Whitley stood poised for fight. He clenched and unclenched his fists, working his fingers slowly.

"Wait a minute!" Phina said, finally putting the pieces together. "I'm not going to marry anyone." She looked at Whitley, unable to keep the hurt and disappointment out of her face. "Are you Anchor's legal son?" she asked, seeking proof of his deception.

"Of course I'm his legal son. I—"

"He's a bastard," Ellison said calmly, his fist still raised. "And that's all he'll ever be because Anchor never signed the damn papers."

The full impact of what Ellison was saying suddenly registered on Phina. Confusion settled. Anger hit her sharply. Anchor had never made Whitley his son officially. He had no legal claim to Carillon. She on the other hand had her mother's sworn statement, the bell that hung around her neck, and the journal confirming Anchor was in New Orleans when she was conceived. And now, after all this time, she hears that Whitley has nothing. She had gone to him last night because she loved him and wanted to give him love and comfort. No wonder he was so willing to take her to bed. He had planned it! Shame and hurt buried themselves deep within her.

"You made love to me last night so I would feel obligated to marry you. There'd be no way you could lose. You'd get Carillon either way."

"You're lovers?" Ellison asked, an incredulous expression lighting on his face.

"I get Carillon period," Whitley said tightly, ignoring Ellison. "Whether I marry you or I don't. Anchor told me fifteen years ago that if I worked hard he'd give me Carillon one day. End of subject."

"No!" Phina whispered. "That is not the end of it."

"Phina," Whitley said her name softly. "I didn't have time to explain everything before Ellison came in today. I realized last night that I loved you and—"

Ellison laughed loudly. "You love her. What a nice touch. I've got to hand it to you, Whitley. You're a sly one. You fooled me. I thought I had plenty of time to court Phina and win her hand because you had your prim and proper Flannery waiting for you. And all the time you were thinking the same damn thing I was thinking. Bed Phina and marry her to get Carillon. But dammit, you beat me to it."

Within the blink of an eye, Whitley pushed Phina aside. His tight fist landed underneath Ellison's left eye, his knuckles scraped upward. Ellison's head snapped backward as Whitley's other fist came hard into his midsection.

Astonished, Phina cried out, "Stop!"

Ellison came back with a punch of his own. His fist glanced off Whitley's chin, but the force of the blow smashed Whitley's lip against his teeth. Blood oozed from the cut. Whitley swung at Ellison again, striking his midsection. Ellison staggered and stumbled backward toppling a chair as he fell to the floor.

"Whitley, stop this!" Phina pleaded, grabbing his arm and holding on to him with both her hands.

His gaze bored fiercely into hers. "I want to explain," he said breathlessly, "But, Phina, I've got to settle this with Ellison first."

"I won't let you fight anymore."

He shook his head. "Fighting is over." He pulled his arm and reluctantly Phina let go. He threw a glance to Ellison who was slowly rising from the floor. "I want you off Carillon by the end of the day."

"You can't force me off Carillon. Anchor deeded that five acres and the house to me. It's mine."

Whitley wiped blood from the corner of his mouth as he walked over to his desk. He jerked open a drawer and took out a tin box. "I'll buy it from you. How much do you want?"

Ellison tried to laugh but winced instead and held his stomach. "I'm not giving up my home. You can't get rid of me that easily."

"Then stay on your parcel of the land. You're services at Carillon are no longer needed. You're relieved of your duties immediately. I'll settle your pay and have Lon take it to you later today."

"Who will you get to oversee the slaves? Qualified overseers are hard to come by. Slaves don't like new masters."

"That's not your problem. It's mine. Now leave. I'm going to tell Spiker if he sees you on the grounds he's to throw you in the smokehouse like a common criminal."

"Oh, I'll leave, but I'll be back. Right between you and Phina. When the new judge is appointed I'll be there wanting my share of Carillon, too."

Ellison touched the broken puffy swell underneath his eye as he started toward the door. He turned back to Phina. "Just remember he's lying. If the judge asks

293

him, he doesn't have one damn piece of paper to prove anything he claims."

"Dammit, Ellison!" Whitley slammed the desk drawer shut. "The whole county knows Anchor intended to make me his son and legal heir. The papers were drawn up. He just died before he signed them."

Ellison leaned against the doorjamb and winced, holding his side. "The fact remains that he *never* legally made you his son. He could have signed those papers, but he never did."

"I am his son. He called me son."

"That doesn't mean a damn thing. He called me son at one time too, and told me the same thing when I was younger. And I can prove that in court. I won't let you and Phina cheat me out of my share of Carillon. Part of this place is mine." He turned and walked away.

Whitley heard the back door slam and knew that Ellison had left the house. He felt sick inside. Damn it, why had he waited so long to tell Phina he loved her? Why hadn't he told her last night when he realized it? How could he make her believe him now that Ellison had betrayed him?

He swallowed hard. Self-condemnation wouldn't ease Phina's doubts about his integrity, his love for her or his reasons for allowing her to believe he'd been adopted. Still he had to try to make her understand. He couldn't forget that Anchor took a street urchin and made a respectable man out of him. He had to do what he thought was best for Anchor's legacy. And as far as he was concerned he *was* the only heir to Carillon.

"Phina." He said her name softly as he walked from behind the desk. "When I started making love to you last night I wanted to because you were a warm responsive woman. I've wanted to take you to my bed for weeks now. But as I kissed you and touched you, as you returned my kisses and caresses, I realized I was making love to you because I loved you and for no other reason."

Slowly she turned to look at him. He breathed easier when he saw that she didn't have a reproachful expression on her face. That gave him hope.

"I think it's time for me to consult a lawyer."

That would be the smart thing for her to do he knew, but he didn't want her to. He wanted to convince her that Carillon was his and that it would belong to her by virtue of the fact she was his wife, not because she was Anchor's daughter.

"Phina, I'll admit that I haven't handled things the way they should have been handled, but what happened between us last night didn't have, it doesn't have anything to do with Carillon."

"Right from the beginning you told me you'd do anything to keep Carillon, including lying about my mother. I have no reason to believe you didn't plan what happened between us."

"I tried to stop what was happening between us, Phina," he insisted.

She remained calm. "That was just part of your seduction of me. When you realized you couldn't buy me out of Carillon you decided to prey on my affection for you and later force me to marry you."

He looked deeply into her eyes. "That's not true, Phina."

She gave him a disappointed look. "I almost fell for your plan." Phina picked up her skirts and ran out.

"Phina!" Whitley called to her but she didn't stop. He rushed after her and ran into Lon, almost knocking him to the floor. "Damn," he muttered angrily as he helped the old man regain his balance.

"I'm sorry, Mr. Whitley, but I's trying ta gets outta Miss Phina's way and got in yores."

Whitley ran his hand through his hair. "It's all right. What do you need?"

"De boat wid dat new motor machine on it is down at de dock. Deys waitin' fo' ya."

That must have been what Ellison had come to tell him. He knew Ellison had changed after Anchor's death, but he had no idea how embittered he'd become.

He'd planned on following Phina and making her see that he wanted to marry her because he loved her not because he thought she was his link to keeping Carillon. But maybe he should give her some time to herself. He could speak to her when they met for dinner.

Whitley followed Lon out the back door. "Tell them I'm on my way. I have one stop to make before I go to the river."

Chapter Twenty

Whitley had to push aside all thoughts of Phina and Ellison and concentrate on what he had to do. He should have gone down to see Spiker last night instead of wallowing in his drink. Ellison should have taught him what too much drink could do for a man. He was sure Ellison wouldn't have had the nerve to send for Chatalene if he hadn't started drinking too much.

He slowed when the house came into view. The flat wooden floor had been built and the framing for the walls was up. Whitley saw Spiker off to the side sawing a board. He tensed. Whitley had no idea how Spiker was going to react to him, but he knew this had to be done. "Spiker," he called and started toward him.

Spiker looked up from his cutting. The buck's firmly shaped muscles showed beneath his shirt. He'd be one hell of a man to fight. Spiker straightened, still holding the saw in one hand. The other three men working on the house stopped and watched as he made his way toward Spiker.

He stopped just a few feet from him and asked, "How are you?"

Spiker gave him one slight nod as his eyes held a

steady gaze on Whitley's face. Whitley noticed he had a death grip on the saw.

"I'm not good at this—" Whitley paused and raked the back of his palm across his lips. "What I did yesterday was wrong. But the reason I did it was right. I was afraid I'd have an insurrection on my hands if I didn't follow the rules. I don't expect you to understand, but I want—"

"I understand." Spiker barely moved his lips as he spoke.

Whitley looked into the eyes of the brave man and wondered if he truly did. If it had happened to him, he wouldn't understand. "All the other slaves think I favor you. Has that ever caused you problems with anyone?"

"Nothing I couldn't handle."

"Good," Whitley said. "Put that saw down. I have another job for you."

Spiker looked at the saw, then at his master and slowly, without taking his eyes off Whitley, laid the saw on the ground at his feet.

Whitley breathed easier. "I need an overseer, and I want you." He spoke loud enough for the other men standing around the house to hear. Whitley heard the gasps. Spiker's stunned expression made him want to smile.

"You want me to do what?"

"I had to let Ellison go. You're the new overseer. Starting right now." Whitley turned away.

"Wait just a minute." Spiker followed Whitley saying, "I can't be an overseer. I don't know what to do. Besides it isn't right."

Whitley stopped. "Yes, it is. I'm doing the right thing for the right reasons." A peace settled over Whitley. For so many years he'd lived only to please Anchor, to do what Anchor expected. He'd owed it to the man, but now he realized the debt had been paid. It felt good to be free to make the decisions he wanted to make. And he was going to marry Phina.

Spiker's face hardened "You're just trying to make up for yesterday."

"I'm not trying to make up for anything. What happened yesterday is over and done with and can't be changed. You're the best man for the job. I realized just how much you'd learned from me when you showed Phina around the plantation. Nobody knows more about the managing of this place than you and me. I expect you to take your new job seriously."

Spiker hesitated. "Yes, sir." Spiker threw his shoulders back and asked, "What happened to Mr. Ellison?"

"He's gone and that's all you need to know."

Whitley turned toward the three men who stood, watched and listened. "I want you men to spread the word. Ellison is no longer a part of this plantation. If you see him on Carillon you're to notify me immediately. Spiker is the new overseer. You're to follow his instructions the same way you would any other man. If anyone has a problem with that tell them they're free to speak to me about it, but I don't intend to change my mind. Now get that house built for Spiker and Tasma."

Tasma was beside herself with joy when Miss Phina told her she didn't want dinner. Rubra prepared a hot toddy for Phina and put her to bed after she drank it. As soon as she was sure Phina was asleep, Tasma hurried out of the big house and headed for home. She'd heard Mr. Ellison was gone and that Spiker had been given the job of overseer.

Dusk had given way to the early shades of night. The slither of moonlight that fell from the dark sky did little to light her way. The air was hot and humid.

As soon as Tasma passed the formal garden she lifted the tail of her skirt and started running as fast as she could. She couldn't wait to see her man. Her legs pumped and her arms swished back and forth, racing her forward. Sweat beaded on her upper lip and under her arms. Suddenly a cramping feeling attacked her lower abdomen and brought her up short, almost taking her breath away. Tasma grabbed her stomach and winced as she doubled over and panted for breath. She was so excited about Spiker she'd forgotten she was pregnant. She had no business running like a ghost was after her. Besides, her stomach had been hurting most of the day. With the baby inside her she needed to be more careful.

Taking a deep breath, Tasma proceeded slower toward the cabin she was sharing with Spiker. She knew she'd been right in picking Spiker for her man. No one could be any happier than she was right now. She'd always known Mr. Whitley liked Spiker the best and this proved it. Spiker would come around and love her now that he was her man. She was sure of it.

After standing still for a couple of minutes and breathing deeply, the contractions in her stomach muscles had all but disappeared. They should be completely gone by the time she reached the house. Still, she decided, she'd rest after she talked to Spiker and told him how proud she was of him. He probably wouldn't answer her, but he'd know how she felt just the same.

When she reached the quarters she decided to take the long way around the other cabins to get to hers and Spiker's at the other end. She didn't want to be held up by anyone who might want to stop her and talk about Spiker or what happened with the whipping yesterday. She could do that tomorrow after she'd seen him. Now that he'd been whipped and forced to marry her daughter even Rubra was singing his praises late in the afternoon when the news hit the big house. That had Tasma grinning from ear to ear.

Spiker was sitting in the chair taking his boots off when Tasma stepped inside the dimly lit cabin. The oil lamp which sat in the middle of the table burned low, throwing shiny splotches of light on Spiker's bare chest and arms. It was hot in the one-room house. Spiker looked up at her grudgingly for only a second, then went back to his task. He could be surly if he wanted, Tasma thought. She wasn't going to be. Happiness burst forth from inside her. How could she contain her joy when she had this man, a baby and they were building her a house as big as her mother's?

Tasma ran over to Spiker and threw her arms around his neck and hugged him. She clasped her hands to the sides of his head and pressed his face into her bosom. "I's so happy fo' you, Spiker. I knowed Mr. Whitley loved you de best."

"Take your hands off me!" he said as he grabbed her wrists and slung her away from him. "I don't want you touching me. I thought I made that clear when you tried to see to my back."

Tasma stumbled backward, catching herself with the table to keep from falling. "Whys you do dat?"

301

Her eyes were wide with confusion. There was a slight tremble to her voice. "I jest wanted ya ta know how proud of you I is. We gots a new house being built, a new baby and yous got de best job on de plantation Why shouldn't I be proud?"

"Because you lied. Nobody likes a liar."

His words hit her hard. It wasn't a lie—not exactly. It couldn't be. She'd pretended it was Spiker doing all those things to her that Cush had done.

"You know I haven't touched you," he continued.

"Dat ain't my fault. I's tried ta get ye ta mess wid me," she said honestly.

"So you found somebody else and blamed it on me."

Tasma just looked at him for a moment and fought the tears that threatened. Spiker was mad but at least he was talking to her. He wasn't ignoring her as he had last night when he grabbed a blanket and slept on the floor, refusing to look at her or speak to her.

"It's your fault I's got dis baby. If'in you'd loved me I wouldn't never let Cush touch me."

"So it is Cush's baby." Spiker picked up one of his boots and threw it against the wall. It hit with a hard thud and fell noisily to the floor as he rose to his feet. His nostrils flared as he looked at her. "He had the fun with you, and I got the whipping."

Tasma didn't remember it as fun. In fact, all that poking he did hurt. An idea caught like a light. If Spiker thought it was fun, then after that whipping fun was what he needed.

She took a couple of steps toward him, not really knowing how to go about what she needed to do. "Cush never made me feel da way ya do, Spiker," she said softly. She looked up at him with her big brown

302

eyes. "I gets all warm inside when you looks at me."

When he didn't move away. She inched closer, keeping her eyes on his face. She moistened her lips with her tongue. "I promise I's gone make you happy. Dats why a strong, 'mportant man likes you needs a woman." She reached out and laid her hand gently on his chest. His eyes were fierce as he looked down at her, but he didn't push her away. It was working. She placed her other hand on his chest and rubbed them up and down his bare skin, all the way down to his breeches.

Spiker stood still. His breathing was labored. "It sho' been a long time since you been wid a woman. I's can tell." Tasma let her hand slide lower. She remembered Cush kept telling her to touch him there. She didn't want to touch Cush but she wanted to touch Spiker. When her hand ran over the hard bulge underneath his breeches she felt him shudder. Her own stomach muscles started contracting again, but she wasn't going to stop. Not with Spiker this close to her. She'd rest when Spiker pushed her away.

She worried with the hard shaft beneath her hand trying to find its beginning or its end. Spiker stood still as a soft moan escaped past his lips. She kissed his chest and whispered. "I'll make you happy, Spiker. Let's have some fun." She opened her mouth and ran her tongue over his nipple.

All of a sudden Spiker grabbed each side of her head and pulled her up close to his face. "I might as well get me some of what I've already been whipped for." He covered her lips with his in a hard, bruising kiss. He shoved his tongue into her mouth as he crushed her against his chest, causing her to gasp for breath.

"All right, you little piece of hell," he muttered

against her lips. "I'm going to give you what you've been asking for. And I'm not going to be gentle with you. I'm going to punish you the same way I was punished."

He picked her up in his arms and carried her over to the cot and laid her down. With his boots already off his breeches slid easily to the floor. He took hold of the tail of her dress and shoved it up past her waist, past her breasts and gathered it around the base of her neck.

Tasma was frightened but she didn't want Spiker to know. He was right. He deserved his fun for the whipping. His manhood was hard and pulsating as he shoved into her.

Tasma groaned softly, but didn't try to stop Spiker as he worked up and down, pressing deeply into her and out again. Her stomach hurt but she didn't say anything. She remembered that it hadn't taken Cush very long so it probably wouldn't take Spiker long either.

But it did. Once wasn't enough for Spiker. He had to have more. The second time he was gentle, caressing her breasts, kissing her softly. Tasma wanted to enjoy it, but her stomach hurt too badly. She'd known that after Spiker got over his anger he'd be a tender, loving man and he was.

When he finally slumped against her for the last time Tasma pushed against his chest and cried out, "Go get Mama, Spiker, my stomach is killin' me."

Spiker jumped off the cot and looked down at her. "What's wrong?" he asked in a concerned voice.

"I's don't know," she mumbled. "It jest hurts me real bad." Tasma pulled her knees up to her chest and rocked to her side.

Falling to his knees beside the cot Spiker said, "Tasma, did I hurt you?" His hand trembled as he touched her forehead. "Why didn't you tell me I was hurting you?" he asked in a desperate voice.

"It wasn't you, Spiker. My stomach's hurt me off and on all de day."

He jerked to his feet and hurriedly crammed his legs into his breeches. "Stay on the bed and don't move. I'll be right back with Rubra."

Spiker's hands made fists as he stood in the quiet darkness outside his cabin, chewing on a twig, still shirtless and barefoot. He wasn't alone. Several men and women stood around with him waiting for Rubra to come out and let them know what was happening. Cush was one of the men. He'd given Spiker several sneering looks. Spiker had stayed away from him.

Damn, he knew better than to be rough with a pregnant woman. He knew women could die having a baby. His first wife had died that way. But Tasma had been so seductive he'd forgotten she was pregnant once he kissed her. It had been so long since he'd been with a woman that he'd just plowed right into her with no thought of her condition.

He wouldn't be whipped for this, though. Mr. Whitley said there would be no more whippings on Carillon. He was happy about that. And until Rubra came out and said otherwise there was hope Tasma and her baby would be all right.

The night dragged on until more than two hours had passed before Rubra came out shaking her head. "Po' shame. Po', po' shame," she said as she walked down the two steps, her bulk causing the steps to creak under her weight. "My po' chile done lost her baby."

She walked over to Spiker and said, "She be better in a day or two. Won't take her long. She a fine healthy girl, that one."

Spiker nodded.

"It's his fault she lost de baby," Cush said, coming up to stand beside Rubra. "What we goin' ta do 'bout it?"

Spiker wanted to take his fist and smash it into Cush's face. He'd never liked him and now that he knew he was the one who got Tasma pregnant he liked him less. If Cush knew what was good for him he'd stay away from Spiker.

"Ain't nobody's fault," Rubra said, defending Spiker. "Dis kinda thin' happens. 'Specially wid de first chile. Don't be blaming Spiker fo' dis."

"Go on home, Cush," Rubra said, brushing him away with her hands. "All de rest of ya, too. Nothing else ta be done here tonight. Dat girl needs rest is all. Go on in and sit wid her, Spiker. I's be back later ta check on her."

After a last hard look at Spiker, Cush spun on one heel and stomped away. Jasper, Deke, Chatalene and the others followed. Spiker didn't speak or move until everyone was gone. Then he walked over to the stoop and sat down. He wasn't ready to go back into that hot room. Besides, if Tasma was awake she'd want to talk. She always wanted to talk. He smiled when he thought of how young she was. There was a lot he could teach her. He'd make it up to Tasma for losing the baby. Starting tomorrow he'd be nicer to her. He'd do a good job for Mr. Whitley, too. Spiker let his mind drift away from Tasma and concentrated on his new job.

He was so deep in thought he didn't hear anyone creep up behind him, but all of a sudden a rope was wrapped tightly around his neck, cutting off his air, pulling him backward. Spiker gasped and gagged. He clawed at the thin roping that burned into his windpipe. The rope was too tight. He couldn't get his fingers underneath it. He slid his hands to the back of his neck. The fists that held the weapon were closed tight. Spiker tried to muscle the hands open but without air in his lungs he was losing strength fast. Gasping for air that wouldn't come, he grabbed for his attacker's arms hoping to throw him over his head. He couldn't get a firm grip.

Death was imminent. Fear gripped him. With strength he didn't know he possessed Spiker twisted his torso around. The rope sawed into his neck. Ignoring the searing pain, he struck out at his attacker with all his might and rammed his fist into his assailant's face. He heard a cracking of bone, a grunt and the rope slacked on his neck. Air rushed into his lungs. He dug his heels into the soft earth and grabbed the elbows of the man behind him and threw him over his shoulders. The man landed on his back with a thud. Spiker fell on top of him, slamming his weight into his attacker's neck with his knee. He heard a crunch as the throat collapsed, crushing the windpipe.

Sweat rolled into Spiker's eyes. His neck was wet with blood. He coughed, gasped, trying to get his breath. He looked down at the man who'd tried to murder him and saw it was Cush. Cush! Why was Cush trying to kill him? Then he knew. It was because of Tasma. A sob of lamentation forced its way past Spiker's swollen throat. Cush lay with his head at an odd angle, his eyes open but not seeing. There was no movement in his still body. Cush was dead. He'd crushed the life out of him. Another sob broke from him. He hadn't wanted to kill Cush. What was he going to do? He couldn't stay on Carillon now.

He heard a scream and looked up to see Rubra. She dropped the pot of soup she was carrying, splattering it all over her dress.

Spiker looked around wildly. Darkness and the cover of night welcomed him. Rubra continued to scream. Fear took hold of his heart, common sense left him. Spiker rose to his feet and ran.

Chapter Twenty-one

Whitley sat in the parlor slouched in a chair holding an untouched drink in his hand. He now knew how easy it must have been for Ellison to start relying on the drink. So far he hadn't allowed himself to touch it. He was just holding it. If he concentrated on not drinking the brandy it helped him to not dwell on Phina and his conversation with her earlier that morning. He'd knocked on her door twice since dinner but both times she refused to open it and talk to him. He'd stopped trying when Rubra told him she'd prepared her a toddy of lemon, laudanum and tea early in the evening.

All the windows in the house were open but it was still hot as a December fire. There wasn't even a hint of a breeze stirring the sheers that hung in front of the windows. Whitley had taken off his cravat and waistcoat and unbuttoned his shirt to his waist.

A lot of things had happened over the past two days. The most important was the realization that he loved Phina, and there was no way he could marry Flannery. The second had been that he'd paid his debt to Anchor and there was no reason to feel guilt for not marrying Flannery. But considering the debt paid didn't mean he wouldn't continue to see that Carillon prospered the way Anchor had intended. No matter what anyone said. He was Anchor's son and legal heir. Somehow, he had to make Phina understand that.

A distant scream pealed through the air raising the hair on the back of Whitley's neck. Jumping from his chair, Whitley dropped the glass on the table in front of him. Something had happened in the slave quarters. He ran to his office and took his pistol out of his desk drawer and stuffed it down the waistband of his trousers. Scooping extra bullets from the drawer, he stuck them into his pocket and headed for the hallway.

Whitley bumped into Phina as she hurried down the long foyer, tying the sash of her robe.

"What's wrong?" she asked fearfully.

He took hold of her arms to steady them both. He looked into her eyes and squeezed her gently before letting her go and turning away. "I don't know. Stay here and lock the door behind me."

"No. I'm going," she said, keeping up with his long stride as they headed for the back door. "That was a cry of pain not of fright. Someone's hurt."

"Phina, listen to me. I don't know who or what's out there. Just stay here until I find out. I'll send for you if you can help."

"I'm going," she said firmly.

Knowing he didn't have the time to argue he said, "All right, but stay close to me."

Phina lifted the skirts of her gown and robe and followed Whitley out into the darkness and down the path leading to the slaves quarters. Her skin quickly dampened with sweat as she ran to keep up with him. Her long hair clung to the back of her neck and her

310

clothes flattened against her skin but she didn't slow her pace.

They ran past the meetinghouse. Other slaves just getting their clothes on picked up the pace beside them. Whitley's heart beat faster when he realized the crowd of mumbling and mourning slaves stood in front of Spiker's and Tasma's cabin. He was afraid that making Spiker overseer had caused problems.

Whitley took hold of Phina's hand bringing her with him as he pushed his way through the crowd. Someone was laying on the ground. He knew immediately the frame was too thin to be Spiker but not slight enough to be Tasma.

"Get a lantern," he called out as he knelt beside the dark figure lying so still. It was Cush. By the odd angle of his head Whitley knew his neck was broken.

"What happened?" he asked, looking back into the crowd of faces behind him.

"Maybe Rubra knows," someone said. "She de one who found him."

"Get her."

"She wid Tasma. She's cryin' cause she done lost her baby tanight and deys don't know where Spiker is."

"Tasma lost her baby?" Phina asked in a concerned voice. "Where is she?"

"In de house," someone else answered.

Phina looked down at Whitley and placed her hand on his shoulder. "I'll go stay with Tasma and send Rubra out to talk to you."

He reached up and took hold of her hand and squeezed it softly. "Thanks." He let her go and took the lantern Lon was holding out to him.

Whitley listened to the murmurings behind him as he held the lantern over Cush's face and head, looking

311

him over good. It was apparent everyone thought Spiker was behind this. Cush's body wasn't cold or stiff. He hadn't been dead long. A close inspection showed blood coming from Cush's nose. He'd been hit before he was killed. Whitley continued his search of Cush's body feeling for broken bones or stab wounds. There were none. He picked up Cush's hand hoping to find some sign that there'd been a struggle and that Cush wasn't caught off guard. There were no scrapes on the first hand but when Whitley picked up the second he found a short length of rope wound around his palm.

"Hold the light," he said to Lon.

Carefully Whitley unwound the rope and saw where the rope had cut into his hand so deeply it bled. Whatever he'd been holding with the rope, he'd applied all his strength.

"I's found de other men down at de river," Deke said as he came running up to the group. "Spiker's de only one we can't find."

Whitley rose and looked around the crowd. There was no doubt they thought Spiker had killed Cush. He held up the length of rope. "This was wrapped around Cush's hand. Anybody know how it got there?" There were mumblings but no answers as the men and women pushed back away from Whitley and made room for Rubra.

Rubra mumbled and sniffed behind a white handkerchief she held over her face as she was led to Whitley. "I's don't know what happened ta Spiker," she said, taking the handkerchief down. Her lips trembled and her features were contorted with pain. "I don'ts know where he is."

"It's all right, Rubra," he spoke softly. "Settle down and tell me what you saw."

"I's bringin' my girl some broth cause she done lost her baby tonight. When I came 'round dat corner." She pointed in the direction she was indicating. "I's saw Spiker. He's down on his knees on top of Cush. But Cush—he ain't moving. Spiker looks at me and he runs." She sniffed again. "He didn't say nothin'. Jest took off t'ward de river."

Damn, it was a hot night. Whitley wiped sweat from his forehead with the back of his hand. He had to be careful. He knew that even though he'd whipped Spiker just yesterday, all of the slaves still assumed he favored him, especially since he'd just made Spiker overseer.

Sorry that Cush was dead, he took a deep breath and asked again, "Does anyone know why this piece of rope was wrapped around Cush's hand?" He held it up in front of the lantern for all to see.

"He ain't never liked Spiker," a woman said.

"Does anyone know why Cush and Spiker would be fighting?"

"Cush was real sweet on Tasma," someone called out.

"Theys had words tonight afta Tasma's sickness," another man said. "Ask Rubra."

Whitley turned to her. "Is that true?"

"Yessir," she said, wiping her swollen eyes. "Cush wanted Tasma fo' his woman. I knowed dat."

"Was Cush still here when you went to get the broth?"

She sniffed, then blew her nose. "I's tole him ta go home and he left."

"It appears that Cush came back here looking for

313

trouble and found it." He turned to the now silent crowd. "We won't know for sure what happened until we talk to Spiker. Let's spread out into pairs and see if we can find him."

"Won't never find him. He don't want ta be hanged," Deke offered as fact.

The mumblings started among the slaves.

Whitley bristled. It bothered him that the slaves always assumed the worst. "Listen to me," he said, looking around at all of them. "Cush is laying here beside Spiker's cabin. That tells me he came looking for Spiker. Spiker didn't go looking for him. Cush had a rope in his hand and it's apparent to me he used it on someone or something. It's my guess he was trying to strangle Spiker and didn't realize he was no match for Spiker's strength. If Spiker killed Cush in self-defense there will be no punishment. Is that understood?"

"Will he still be overseer?" someone asked.

"Yes," Whitley said firmly. "If you'll give him a chance he'll be a good one. He knows this plantation as good as I do and he knows you better than Ellison. He'll be fair." He waited for questions but everyone remained quiet. "Deke you and Jasper take care of Cush, then join us. All right. Let's find him."

Phina stood on the front porch of the meetinghouse in the slave quarters where the men were to return after searching for Spiker. So far he hadn't been found. Tasma had wailed and cried until Phina insisted Rubra give her enough laudanum to put her to sleep. The slaves weren't allowed to keep the drug in their possession so Phina had gone to the house to get it.

314

While there, Phina had changed into the breeches and shirt Rubra had cut off for her during the storms and flooding. If they didn't find Spiker by the time Whitley returned she planned to go out with him to look for the slave.

After having been gone for about two hours Whitley came riding up. "Has there been any word?" he asked, not bothering to dismount.

"No sir," Lon answered, stepping down off the porch. "Can't find a thing. It's still too dark. Maybe in an hour at daybreak we'll find him or pick up a trail."

Whitley turned to Phina. His horse snorted and jerked his head as if he were ready to go again. "Do you want to tell me why you're dressed in those clothes?" he asked, his voice less than friendly.

"I had Lon saddle the horse I've been learning to ride. I want to help you look for Spiker. I—"

"No."

"Wait. Listen to me. I—"

"No," he said again. "We have enough men out looking. How's Tasma?"

Phina grabbed hold of Whitley's reins. "She's fine. Now listen to me."

Startled that she'd been so bold, Whitley remained quiet and peered down into her eyes. When he looked at her she wanted to remember each one of his kisses, each caress, the loving way he taught her how to enjoy the pleasures he could give her, but now wasn't the time. And it wasn't the time to remember how he'd deceived her and tricked her into his bed. All those feelings had to be put aside.

Whitley's shirt and hair were damp from sweat. He looked tired. Still, she wished she could put her arms around him and hold him. Even his deception couldn't

315

keep her from loving him. She'd known from the beginning that Whitley would do anything to keep Carillon. And now, she would too. Although she never knew the man, she believed Anchor McCabe to be her father. Carillon belonged to her. She wouldn't let Whitley have it without a fight.

"I know we have some problems we need to talk about, and we will. But what's best for Carillon comes first. I remember Spiker telling me about some caves on the other side of the river when he was showing me around the plantation. Do you know where I'm talking about? Do you think he may be hiding there?"

Whitley nodded. "There are some caverns on this side of the river about three miles down. We've already searched them because that's where he hid six years ago when he ran away. He knew that'd be the first place we looked."

She placed a finger against her lips and thought. "No. I'm sure he said they were on the other side and it wasn't the Chattahoochee River it was—" She couldn't remember the name. "Another river."

"The Apalachicola?"

"No, but that's close."

"The Chipola?"

"Yes, that's it," she said, letting go of the rein. "Maybe he's gone there."

"I don't think so. That's more than thirty miles away. I don't know if Spiker would go that far away from Carillon."

"He's running away. He'll go as far away as he can." Whitley seemed to pause and think about what she said, so Phina headed for her horse. She wasn't going to give him time to ride away without her. "By

316

the time we get over there maybe it will be light enough we can see his tracks."

By the time she mounted, Whitley had walked his horse over to hers. "Phina, I know—"

"Whitley." She settled herself in the saddle and looked directly into his eyes. "It's time you learned that I plan to be a part of Carillon, a part of *whatever* goes on here. You're not getting rid of me."

Thunder rumbled in the distance. Whitley nodded. "Does that mean you're going to marry me?"

"No. It means I'm going to take you to court and win Carillon."

Much to her surprise he gave her a smile of admiration. "We better get started and see if we can pick up a trail. It sounds like rain."

Phina didn't return his smile. "You're the one who doesn't like to get wet." She pulled on the reins and the horse took off.

Darkness had given way to gray as thunder continued to burst through the quietness of dawn and lightning spiraled across pewter-colored sky. Whitley reined in his horse and Phina followed along the banks of the Chattahoochee River.

"We might as well go back. That storm looks like it's moving in fast and carrying a lot of rain. Besides we've gone about as far south as Spiker could have gotten on foot."

"But the rain will wash away Spiker's tracks. We need to keep looking," she argued. "He won't come back on his own, especially if he thinks he may be punished."

"I agree with that, Phina, but you know how fierce

317

storms can be in this area. If that storm is packing rain like the last one we had it won't do us any good to be out here looking. We wouldn't be able to see two feet in front of us."

Even though she hated to admit it, she knew he was right. She was about to turn her horse around and head back when she realized the dark cloud she was looking at over Whitley's shoulder was a smoke cloud not a rain cloud. She swung around in the saddle and looked at the surrounding sky to make sure she wasn't imagining the difference. Surely, what Phina was seeing was a charcoal black thunder cloud lurking between them and Carillon. She popped back around to look at the smoky sky. Her eyes widened and she pointed. "Whitley, look behind you. I think that's a cloud of smoke."

Whitley twisted around in the saddle. "Damn! It is fire and it's coming from the east cornfield."

"Maybe someone is burning the stalks of corn that were ruined by the flooding."

"Not in June when the wind could whip up and carry the flame to the cotton and peanuts. Fields are burned in the winter. Let's go."

Without further words Whitley dug his heels into the horse's flanks and took off. Being a new rider Phina knew she couldn't go at the breakneck speed Whitley pushed his horse so she followed him as closely as she could and still remain on her horse. She had to hold her horse back. The mare wanted to keep up with Whitley's stallion.

As they neared the flaming field the smoke darkened and widened. It appeared several acres had been set on fire. Phina saw Whitley pull his horse up short so she slowed her mount. She watched him jerk in the saddle

318

as if he'd been hit by something. He quickly yanked his horse around and started waving wildly with one arm as he yelled, "Indians! Go back!"

Phina saw the butt of the arrow protruding from the upper part of Whitley's arm. Fear shocked her into action. In a split second she wrenched the horse up short and turned him around. Shots from a pistol peeled through the air, mixing with the inhuman sounds of whooping and hooting. They were being attacked. Whitley had been shot! She dug the heels of her boots deeper into her mount. Whitley was on Carillon's best horse. He would catch her. But that thought also reminded her that the Indians might catch her too. Her heart pounded in her chest. The wind caught her breath and snatched it away.

The horse increased his speed quickly. Phina bounced and rocked in the saddle. Panic threatened to take control. Her life depended on her staying on the horse. She labored for breath, remembering what Deke had told her when he was teaching her to ride. She hugged her knees to the horse's sides and bent low over his neck while she made a conscious effort to feel the horse's movement beneath her and ride with him. Her bouncing stopped. The horse reached its top speed.

She heard Whitley's horse pounding the ground behind her, but she was too afraid of losing control to look back.

"Faster!" he yelled.

From the corner of her eye she saw Whitley's horse nosing up even with hers. The first drops of rain hit her face. "Faster!" he yelled again.

Horses hooves beating and whooping and hollering sounded behind Phina, making her weak with fear. An

319

arrow plowed into the dirt in front of her. She bit back a scream. She couldn't break her concentration. Hers and Whitley's life depended on it. She lay lower in the saddle and clung to the horse.

The rain came hard and fast, stinging her face and her eyes. Within moments they had ridden into an early morning fog and drenching rain. Phina couldn't see anything but gray clouds in front of her. Her horse slowed. She barely saw Whitley's hand as he reached out to grab hold of her rein so they wouldn't get separated in the fog. She could only hope the Indians were having the same trouble seeing what was ahead of them. Lightning split the air, thunder crashed around them and the Indians whooped behind them.

With control of the reins Whitley led her horse at an angle to the right, toward the river. She wanted to know how badly he was hurt but knew he couldn't hear her over the driving wind and rain.

A short time later, she was convinced that Whitley knew what he was doing and when they entered the cover of trees. Their pace slowed. She worried about him, knowing an arrow lodged in his upper arm. He didn't slow down but forged onward. She intended to do the same.

Phina dodged branches, and brushed wet leaves away from her face as they plowed through thick brush. The rain continued to pelt them with stinging fierceness, but she realized with relief that she no longer heard the Indians' strange sounds of the hunt or the pounding of their horses' hooves.

Within a couple of minutes of entering the woods, Whitley stopped the horses and dismounted.

"Get down," he whispered.

"How's your arm?" she asked, dismounting as quickly as she could.

"Don't worry about that now."

Holding his left arm close to his side Whitley handed her his saddlebag, then gave his horse a swift slap on the rump. The stallion took off. Just as quickly he slapped the mare.

"The horses!" she cried into the rain. "We need them!"

"No! I want the Indians to follow the horses. Not us. Let's go." Whitley took hold of her hand and led her through the thick forest, keeping his injured arm held against his chest.

Afraid at any moment she was going to hear those horrible Indian whoops again Phina pushed to keep up with Whitley. They had to find shelter and safety so she could look after his arm. She trembled, not knowing if the Indians were right behind them. She saw rain and green leaves as she held tightly to Whitley's hand. Limbs and leaves slapped her in the face, her boots sunk deep into the soggy earth, but she didn't let anything slow her down.

Whitley stopped in the middle of thick underbrush and held back a leafy limb of a large bush. "Get in."

Not knowing what was in front of her, she followed his order and bent her head. She was immediately thrust into total darkness but out of the rain. She fell to her knees and whipped around in time to see Whitley stumbling in behind her. The branch of the tree snapped back into place, shutting out all but the faintest of daylight coming from the opening of the cave.

Phina didn't have time to rest, or worry about the Indians. She had to see to Whitley's wound. She

321

crawled over to him, touching first his knee, letting her hands feel their way up his wet clothes to his chest. In the darkness she couldn't tell how badly he was bleeding.

"Do you know—how bad—it is?" she asked in spurts, realizing she hadn't yet caught her breath. It didn't appear Whitley had either because it took him a couple of moments to answer.

"I'm—damn lucky. I'm sure—he was aiming for my heart."

At that moment Phina could have given over to wracking sobs of fear, of relief, but she had to be strong for Whitley. He had led them to safety, now she would take over from here. Outside the cave the rain beat wildly, thunder rumbled heavily and lightning brightened the cave long enough for her to see the protrusion of the arrow butt jutting out of his upper arm near his shoulder. For a moment she thought she might faint. Courage took over and she fortified herself for what she knew must be done.

"Do you think the Indians will find us?"

Whitley winced. "Not unless someone told them about this cave. That's unlikely. Don't worry. We're safe here."

Phina took hold of his hand and pressed it to her lips. She wanted to whisper, "I love you," but was afraid he wouldn't understand why she was telling him now. She wished they hadn't argued about Carillon. She wished Flannery wasn't between them.

"Do you think we've lost them?"

His breathing was labored. "I think so."

"I've got to go for help," she said, laying his hand in his lap.

"You're talking crazy. Neither of us are going back out there until I know it's safe."

"No, you're crazy if you think I'm going to let you stay here with that arrow in you and bleed to death without trying to get help."

He chuckled uncomfortably. "I don't think I will." He reached over and felt of his arm. "I don't feel anything warm running down my arm."

"That's because of the wet clothes."

"Well, I don't plan to sit here with this souvenir in me. We're going to take it out."

Phina gasped. "We?"

He winced again as he tried to move. "Everything we need should be in the saddlebag."

"Is there a doctor in there?" Phina asked, trying to calm her runaway pulse as she reached for the leather bag at her feet.

Whitley chuckled again, a nervous laugh. "No, but you should find a skinning knife, matches, a poultice to draw out any poison, and a bottle of whiskey."

Phina swallowed hard. The wet leather was cold in her hands. Was she really going to take the arrow out of Whitley's arm? God help them both. She'd nursed her mother, but she'd never faced anything like this. She moved to the other side of Whitley, closer to the opening of the cave where there was more light.

"I didn't know you kept saddlebags so well stocked."

"On a plantation you never know how far you might be from the main house and supplies when an accident could happen. Men cut themselves with hoes, wild dogs or mountain lions attack, or a man could be snakebit. Sometimes you can't always ride back for help. Like now."

323

"Thank God, you had this," she said, checking to make sure the bag held the things he said. She also found strips of cloth tied into a small bundle.

"Feel around inside the cave and see if you can find any twigs or dry leaves. Anything that will burn. We need to get a fire going."

"A fire in here? Won't the Indians smell the smoke."

"Not in this downpour with the wind whipping in every direction. Besides, I'd like to think they're miles away by now, looking for their own safety. I hope we drew their attention away from the plantation and that all the others are safe."

"So do I."

"Just do what I say, Phina and everything will be fine."

She did. Within a couple of minutes they had a small pile of twigs with dry and wet leaves heaped together. Whenever lightning flashed she saw the butt of the arrow protruding from Whitley's arm. A row of small feathers lined each side of the end of the shaft.

Between the two of them they fanned, blew and pampered the kindling until the glowing embers turned into small flames. Phina welcomed the faint light, the bit of warmth the fire provided. The smoke wasn't as heavy as she expected it to be. It didn't take long for her to get used to the smell of the wood and leaves burning and the sting of the smoke in her eyes.

"Phina, I want you to listen to me and do everything I say. Don't take time to question me, just do it. All right?"

Firelight shone in his eyes and it was a welcome sight. Strands of his hair showed drying while others held water on their tips. His lips paled and showed strain of the pain in his arm. Phina knew it would be worse when they started removal of the arrow.

As if the storm knew the seriousness of what was about to take place, fog dissipated, rain slacked to a mist, the thunder quieted and the lightning disappeared.

"The first thing you need to do is cut the shirt away from my arm. I'm going to turn around so you can see better. Then I want you to cut the arrowhead off as close to the skin as you can get it. The less we have to pull out the better."

Phina moistened her lips and nodded. Smoke caused tears to collect in her eyes and she wiped them away. She wouldn't allow herself to be nervous or to question him. She had to block out everything and do as she was told. With steady hands she cut the shirt away, then sawed the arrow with the knife close to his skin as she could get it.

"I ran up on the Indians before I knew it because of the smoke," Whitley said in a strained voice. "One of them was less than twenty yards from me. I guess that was lucky in a way. At such close range the arrowhead was forced on through my arm rather than lodging in muscle or bone."

Phina didn't answer but continued her work. The rain beat a steady pitter-patter against the leaves outside the cave. A hallow pop reverberated loudly in the cave when Whitley took the cork out of the whiskey bottle. Phina heard each swallow as Whitley drank the liquid. After a couple of minutes she could have snapped the arrow in two but continued to saw in order to keep the edge as smooth as possible. When it broke away, she sighed with relief. The first half was accomplished.

Whitley turned around and faced her. He took the arrowhead from her hand and looked at it. "It's small, thank God. No wonder it didn't do too much damage. This is an arrow they would have used to shoot squirrel or large birds." He put the bottle to his lips and drank from it. "I guess he didn't take time to look at which arrow he pulled from his quiver." Whitley threw the small arrow onto the fire and drank from the bottle again.

When he took the bottle down he saw that Phina was watching him. He coughed and winced, holding his injured arm close to his chest. "I'd offer you some, Phina but take my word you wouldn't like it. This is cheap, hellfire burning whiskey."

Phina smiled, hoping to ease the pain etched in his face. "I'd join you but I have to keep a steady hand. After all, I'm the doctor."

Whitley took a deep breath. "Let's get this bastard out of me before I drink so much I won't be any help." He corked the bottle and laid it between his legs. "I'm going to tell you what to do in case I pass out. When the arrow comes out you need to heat the blade of the knife again and press it to the wound. Front and back."

"No, Whitley, I—"

"Damn it, Phina, don't get weak on me now. There may be a lot of blood but don't let that frighten you. Blood always makes a wound look worse than it is. After you've cauterized it with the knife pour some of this whiskey on it." He coughed again. "Apply the poultice then wrap my arm as best you can with those strips of cloth."

The cave brightened as the storm passed and daylight chased the last vestige of twilight away. Phina

326

shivered. The rain had stopped and the sun was burning through the clouds. She was thankful for the extra light. She brushed her wet stringing hair to her back. She looked into Whitley's eyes and said, "I'm ready."

His Adam's apple moved up and down convulsively. Sweat dotted his forehead and upper lip. "This won't be easy, Phina. Swelling has started around the shaft. It's going to take both our strengths to pull it out. If I pass out from the pain, you keep pulling and twisting until it's out." He wiped his lips with the back of his hand. "Then do what I told you."

Without taking her eyes off his face she rose up on her knees in front of him. Whitley took a deep breath and placed her hands where he wanted them on the arrow, leaving space in between them for his hand. Phina had the physical strength to help get the arrow out. What she needed was the inner strength. When Whitley placed his hands beside hers, from deep inside herself, Phina found the courage to tighten her fingers around the small shaft.

His eyes looking into hers he said, "On the count of three. One. Two. Three."

Phina pulled with all her strength. It didn't appear the arrow was moving until Whitley started twisting it back and forth. His face contorted with pain as he squeezed his eyes shut. She felt the arrow moving, little by little, ripping through raw muscle and flesh.

Whitley's face paled, his lips lost their color. He was weakening. "Don't pass out on me now, Whitley. Wake up! Keep pulling. It's almost out." In a burst of strength she didn't know she possessed Phina pulled with all her might. The arrow came flying out. She fell backward. Whitley slumped against the cave wall, his

327

strength spent. Phina immediately rose to her knees and tended his wounds just as he instructed.

The fire had died down while she worked so she broke more leaves and twigs from the tree and bushes covering the opening of the cave and brought the fire to life again. She didn't want Whitley to catch a chill. They had a long day ahead of them. She would rest while Whitley slept, then when darkness fell she would slip out and find the house and help. She leaned her back against the cold rock of the cave and spread her legs. Her bruised shoulder cried out when she lifted Whitley under his arms and dragged him to her. She rested his back against her chest and laid his head on her shoulder. His weight was heavy upon her but comforting.

Together they slept.

Whitley stirred and groaned, knowing only that there was a burning in his shoulder and something soft beneath his head.

A cool palm was pressed against his forehead. "You're waking up. That's good. Thank God you don't feel feverish."

Whitley realized he was half laying in Phina's arms. He was reluctant to move but knew he was heavy. "I think you're mothering me again," he murmured.

"After what you've been through, I think you need a little, don't you?"

He tried to rise, but fell back holding his shoulder. "Damn! That hurts like hell. I feel like a horse stepped on my arm." He wished he had some water.

"You have some whiskey left. Do you want some?"

He grunted. "I'll see if I can make it without it. I don't want to get drunk."

"As soon as it gets dark I'll go for help."

Whitley tried to chuckle but ended up coughing. Phina patted him lightly on the back. "You're one brave woman, Phina."

"I'm not brave," she said, hugging him to her again. "I want to take care of you and get you home where a doctor can look after you."

Whitley's heart filled with love for Phina. Her words comforted him. No woman had ever wanted to take care of him until this woman. He wanted to curl up in her arms and let her do just that but he couldn't. "We've already done what a doctor could do for me. Getting that arrow out as quickly as we did just may have saved me from blood poisoning. If we're lucky and the Indians didn't attack the house or the slave quarters, Lon, Deke and the others should be already looking for us."

"If that's the case, I hope they find us soon. Your wounds need to be thoroughly cleaned and smothered in a healing salve."

Whitley snuggled his face against Phina's breasts. Phina was warm, loving and caring. He shuddered to think that he had almost married Flannery, a cold woman who was more interested in what her parents and friends thought of her than how her fiancé felt about her.

He admired Phina's strength and courage to come to Carillon seeking a better life for her and her mother. He admired the way she'd taken the time to learn about the plantation, the slaves and their lives. She worked well with them, treating them kindly. Oh yes, there was much to love and admire about Phina.

"Phina," he said softly.

"Yes," she answered quietly.

"I didn't get a chance to tell you before Ellison came

329

in the other morning, but I want to tell you now." She looked down into his eyes and he looked up at her. Smoke drifted between them. All was still. "I made love to you for one reason and one reason only. And for that same reason I'm not going to marry Flannery. I love you, Phina. I want to marry you."

Her eyes widened and her lips parted as she leaned forward. "Whitley—what about Carillon?"

"Carillon has nothing to do with the way I feel about you. Just like you haven't let it stop you from loving me."

"I—I haven't said—"

"You haven't had to. I know you wouldn't have let me make love to you if you didn't love me, Phina. I know that. You may not have admitted it to yourself yet, but—"

"I do love you," she finished for him. She smiled. Whitley smiled. She leaned down and kissed his lips lightly. "I love you. And I want to live with you at Carillon."

He kissed her again. "It took me a long time to admit to myself that I loved you. Even though Anchor's dead, I didn't want to betray his trust in me. He wanted me to marry Flannery and I owed it to him to do what he expected."

"Is it because he saved your life?"

He twisted in her arms so he could take some of his weight off her. "He did more than that, Phina. He could have sent me on my merry way after he ran off the two men, but he didn't. He welcomed me into his home, his life and his heart.

She wanted to get his mind off his wound and on to something else. "What happened?"

"Two men found me walking a horse to town and

assumed I had stolen it. I hadn't. I stole food and clothes on a regular basis, but I knew they'd hang me for stealing a horse. I was sitting on the horse they accused me of stealing, the rope around my neck when Anchor rode up and stopped them. They'd beat me so badly I wasn't thinking clearly, but I remember at first I thought Anchor was an angel. I'd slept in a few churches and had heard more than one sermon about guardian angels. I would have done anything for Anchor McCabe. Anything. I've lived my life just the way he expected me to. I learned the plantation, made the best grades in school, and planned to marry the woman he picked out for me. Then you came along and upset everything."

She moistened her lips. "I guess a lot of things changed after I came to Carillon."

"Yes. And Phina, even if you won't marry me, I still won't marry Flannery. I don't love her. I never loved her. As long as Anchor was alive I was content to let him tell me what to do."

"And now?" she asked expectantly.

"Now I'm making my own decisions. I love you, Phina. I want to marry you." He placed his fingertips under her chin and lifted her face to his. "Say yes."

"Yes," she whispered and lowered her mouth to his and kissed him tenderly.

"It's true Anchor never legally gave me his last name. But I know he planned to sign the papers the night of the party. Robert will testify to that. Phina, when we marry, I want to use Anchor's last name. We'll both take his name. There'll no longer be a question as to who owns Carillon. We both will."

A smile spread across Phina's face. "Yes, Whitley. I like the sound of that."

331

Whitley started to kiss her again but a sharp pain in his arm took his breath.

"What's wrong?" she asked.

"Don't worry, Phina. This thing is going to give me hell for a couple of days." He pushed the tree and bushes away from the cave opening. "The rain has stopped. I think it's time we tried to get out of here."

"What about the Indians? What if they see us?"

"If it's one of the bands we've been hearing about for the last two months we don't have anything to worry about. They always strike at daybreak and go into hiding by the time it's full daylight. They don't want to be caught. I don't think they'll be around again until daybreak tomorrow morning."

"How far are we from the house?"

"Five miles or so. We're closer to Ellison's house. We'll head over there. Even though he's angry with me I'm sure he'll let us have a horse to get back to Carillon."

Whitley groaned as Phina helped him to stand and linked his good arm over her shoulder.

Chapter Twenty-two

Phina sat in the parlor with a loaded single-shot pistol laying in her lap. Rubra, Tasma and Chatalene were with her. The rest of the darkies, those who weren't out with Whitley protecting the fields and main house, were in their meetinghouse. No one could sleep. They all waited for dawn to see if the Indians would return.

She and Whitley had made it to Ellison's house without incident. Samson had told them that Ellison had gone away for a few days. The old man had already heard about the Indian attack from his cronies at Carillon. He said he'd send Ellison over to help if he returned. After taking time for coffee and bread, Samson saddled a horse for them and they rode on to Carillon.

With Spiker still missing it was clear that Deke had taken charge of the darkies. As soon as they arrived at the main house, he apprised Whitley of the damage to the fields and told him there had been no sign of Spiker or the Indians. No work had been done. Most of the slaves were too afraid to go into the fields to work since the attack.

Phina laid the pistol on top of a small table and rose from her chair. She couldn't sit still. Cramps from her monthly flow had bothered her most of the evening, making her irritable and restless.

She wished Whitley had rested more before he went out into the night. She'd cleaned and dressed his wound again, using some of Rubra's medicines, but still she worried that he'd keep the wound open by working his arm. He'd slept for a short time during the afternoon, rest that she knew his injured body needed. He had been more interested in being prepared in case the Indians decided to attack again. If they didn't show up by daybreak, Whitley was going to take the men who were the best shots and go out looking for them. He'd been told the government officials were looking for the Indians, but they didn't know the area. Whitley did. He meant to find the renegades and stop them before they burned any more crops or killed someone.

"Fire! Fire!" Someone shouted from outside the house.

Phina tensed. "Fire! Where?" she asked, looking back at the other three women as if they had the answer.

They all ran to the window and looked out. Phina couldn't see anything. All looked quiet. "Let's go see," she said.

"Mr. Whitley said fo' us ta stay in dis house no matter what goed on out dere," Rubra said.

"I don't care. I'm going to find out what's burning. Someone may need our help. Rubra, you and Chatalene check the back and see if you can see the smoke. Tasma, you stay here on that sofa. You're not well enough to go out."

334

Phina didn't wait to see if any of them obeyed her. She rushed out the front door and down the steps, looking in both directions. From the north side of the house she saw a thin trail of smoke snaking up the sky. She had to look twice to find it because the sky was still so dark. It looked like the smoke was coming from the *garconniere*. The Indians could have thought the guest house was the main house and set it on fire.

Chatalene came up beside her. "Rubra said ain't no smoke out back and fo' ya ta come back inside de house."

"Look." Phina pointed down the tree-lined drive to the pink-tinted sky. "I think the *garconniere* must be on fire. Let's go."

Phina and Chatalene picked up their skirts and ran down the road. The ground felt squashy and muddy from the storm but the two women didn't let that stop them. As they rounded the corner they saw flames leaping from two of the bottom windows. Phina hoped most of the fire was fueled by the drapes and rugs. If they could get those put out before the wood caught most of the house could be saved.

Several of the slaves had already arrived and were starting a water line from the well to the house. When they drew closer she felt heat from the fire as it lay in the humid air. She started to join the water line when she saw Whitley ride up and dismount in front of the house. She ran over to him.

"I's shot one of 'em, Mr. Whitley," Jasper was saying. "He laying over there. But he shot that flaming arrow into de house befo' he fell."

"Is he dead?" Whitley asked as shouts from the slaves and crackling from the fire sounded around him.

"Yessir, I's made sure of dat befo' I ran fo' help."

"Was he alone?"

"Only one I saw."

"Damn! That means they fanned out. They could be burning something else right now. Get up to the house now and check—" he stopped when he spun around and saw Phina standing behind him. "What in the hell are you doing here? I told you to stay in the house."

She flinched at his tone but easily forgave him. She knew he was worried. "I heard the call of fire. I came to help."

"Mr. Whitley! Mr. Whitley!"

Phina and Whitley turned to see Deke riding hard and fast toward them. "They torched the west field!" he said, stopping the horse in front of them.

"How many?"

"Five. Maybe six." Deke's chest heaved with heavy breathing from the hard ride, his dark eyes were round with excitement. Sweat dotted his face.

"Did you kill any of them?"

"No sir. Deys too far away, but dey skedaddled when dey saw us coming."

"We needs help!" someone called from the water line.

"Maybe they're finished for the day. Deke, forget about the field for now, help get this fire out." Whitley turned back to Phina, his eyes looking into hers. "I want you back in the house where you'll be safe. Chatalene, go with her."

"I want to stay and help. This is my home. I—"

"Please, Phina." He took hold of her arms and pulled her close. The heat of his touch warmed her more than the fire. "I have too much to take care of to worry about your safety right now. We've got enough

336

men here to put out this fire, then we'll go straight to the field and see what we can do there. As soon as the fires are under control we're going to go out and find those bastards. You can help me by taking care of yourself."

She gave him a reassuring smile. Maybe her most important job was saving Whitley from added worry. "All right. I can see that Hetty and Rubra have something ready for you and the others to eat before you go." She didn't want him to know that she'd give anything if he didn't have to go after those Indians.

"Good. I've got to go take a look at the one Jasper killed. I'll be back to the house as soon as I can. Tell Rubra to have the coffee ready." He squeezed her arms gently, then turned her loose.

Touching his shoulder Phina stopped him. "How's your arm?"

He smiled down at her. "It hurts like hell but don't worry about me, Phina. I'm all right." He turned and hurried away.

Phina surveyed the scene before her in the breaking light of day. Flames continued to leap from the small guest house but they didn't seem as large. The men were doing a good job of keeping the water flowing.

She turned to Chatalene who still stood quietly beside her. "We best get back and get Hetty into the cook house. The men will need a hearty meal when this is over."

The two women started down the lane at a fast walk. Shortly after they rounded the curve away from the *garconniere,* Phina heard the sound of a horse coming up behind them. Thinking it must be Whitley, she stopped and turned to see what he needed. Fear washed through her as she saw an Indian swoop down

337

and hit Chatalene across the face with a club. She opened her mouth to scream but only a small grunt came out as the horse bore down on her, forcing her to stumble backward. Catching her footing, she looked up in time to see the club coming toward her. Pain spiraled through her head as the stone at the end of the club struck high on her forehead. She felt herself falling backward but couldn't manage to stop herself. She hit the ground hard, wrenching her back and her already bruised shoulder.

Phina was trying desperately to regain her wits and scream when someone grabbed her arm. Her eyes flew open and she saw a naked brown chest with a blue beaded necklace and shiny long hair as black as her own. She opened her mouth to scream but a stinging slap across the face snapped her head back, making her scream a mere whimper.

Dazed, she was lifted and thrown over the back of the horse. The hard backbone of the animal bruised her chest and midriff as she hit the horse with enough force to knock the wind from her lungs. Fear mobilized her. She tried to catch her breath and worm her body off the animal. She felt someone crawl up behind her. She saw a buckskin covered leg drape over the horse beside her face. Planting her hands firmly on the horse's shoulder she tried to plummet herself forward to the ground away from the warm body and smelly horse. A hand caught and tangled in her hair and pushed her face down into the horse's shoulder. The leg kicked and the horse took off, eating up the ground below her. Phina tried to scream but found she had no breath.

Darkness claimed her.

Whitley had looked the Indian over good and couldn't say he'd learned a damn thing. He was shirtless but a wide beaded necklace hung around his neck. A colorfully beaded belt circled his waist and held a large knife. There were no pockets on his buckskins. The pony he'd ridden didn't even have a saddle for him to search.

The Indian looked to be around Whitley's age and judging from the scars on his chest he'd been in a few knife fights. He didn't know if the brave was from the tribe of Cherokee, Creek, or Seminole. They'd all had trouble with the white man at one time or another.

Whitley wished he could have told him that Carillon hadn't been built on Cherokee land. There was no reason for them to want to destroy it, but just as quickly he realized it wouldn't have mattered. They didn't care which white man bore the brunt of their revenge.

"Why dese Injuns wanta bother us, Mr. Whitley?" Deke asked.

Whitley rose and looked at him. "They're not after any of us in particular. They're just on a killing and burning rampage. From what I've heard, they're not picky about who they attack." He pressed a hand to his aching arm and looked past the slave to the burning house. "The posses who are out looking for them probably drove them this far south. I aim to stop them here." He turned to Jasper. "Throw a blanket over him for now. Have someone bury him when the fire's out. Deke, you come with me. We'll ride out to the burned-out fields and see if we can pick up their trail.

339

With the ground still soft from the rain we shouldn't have any problem."

Two hours later Whitley and Deke were on their way back to Carillon for more men and food. They'd found where the Indians rode into the Chattahoochee but not where they exited. He and Deke would get more men and fan out along the bank up and down river. As best he could tell from the horse tracks there were only seven of them. Jasper had already taken care of number eight. They rode past the burned cotton field. The fires had been put out except for a small section and four or five men were working on that. He hoped the slaves had gotten enough water to the *garconniere* soon enough to keep it from burning to the ground.

As they rode up to the front of Carillon Rubra came rushing out of the house to meet them, moving fast for her large frame. "Mr. Whitley! Mr. Whitley, we can't find Miss Phina."

Whitley tried to keep alarm out of his voice as he stopped his horse and looked down at Rubra and asked, "What do you mean, Rubra? You can't find her in the house?"

"Nah sir." Rubra sniffed. "She gone wid dem Indians."

Frightened for Phina's safety, Whitley jumped down from the horse. He moved so quickly he jerked his shoulder and pain shot through his arm. "What are you talking about, Rubra? Stop sniffling and tell me what made you say such a thing."

"We found Chatalene layin' on de ground. She'd been knocked senseless. Blood all over her face. We washed her face an—"

"What about Phina, dammit!" Fear for Phina's safety jumped on him so quickly he trembled.

Rubra flinched at Whitley's tone. "She don't know what happened ta Miss Phina. She say theys walking when she heard a hoss. She turned around and dis big Injun slapped her upside de head wid a stone club."

Whitley's hands made fists. The pain in his arm sharpened, his breath shortened.

"We's looked everywhere. She ain't nowhere 'round heah." Rubra picked up the tail of her apron and wiped her eyes. "I knows dem Indians done kilt her. I knows it."

"Stop that kind of talk, Rubra." Whitley's voice was raspy with fear. Rubra had to be wrong. "Are you sure you've looked everywhere?"

"We's been lookin' an callin' mo' an hour now." She looked up at him with big tears in her dark eyes. Anguish showed in her face. "She ain't here."

Whitley's blood ran cold. He had to face the fact that Phina had been captured. He wouldn't allow himself to think further than that.

The jarring of her body being pummeled against the firm muscled back of the horse awakened Phina. She moaned and tried to raise her head. Dizziness forced her to lower it again. She opened her eyes and saw the ground rushing by beneath. It felt as if she were falling. Wildly, she tried to grab for something to hold on to. A fist came down on the back of her head with bruising force.

Phina groaned from the pain and shut her eyes tightly to keep the dizziness at bay. She didn't know what hurt worse, her head or her stomach and chest

341

from the constant beating of the horse. Slung over the animal in such a manner made it difficult for her to breathe. She didn't know how long they'd been riding, but it was well past daybreak.

As time dragged by she opened her eyes and focused with some clarity. Another horse galloped beside her. She saw its legs. The full realization that she'd been captured by Indians hit Phina. For a fleeting moment she wanted to scream with all the torment she was feeling, but just as quickly she knew that would only gain her another rap on the head. But what could she do? What was going to happen to her? Her head bobbed up and down from the galloping horse. Tears of pain and frustration over her predicament fell onto the rapidly passing ground.

She had enough wits about her to know that she needed to start making some plans, storing up strength. When the horse finally stopped she'd have to fight for her life.

After close to an hour of consciousness Phina was ready to scream just so the Indian would knock her out again so she wouldn't have to endure the pain of the ride or the fear of the unknown. But a few minutes later the animal slowed and they left the rocky ground to travel into the woods. Her hope that Whitley might find her dimmed. How would he keep up with their trail in the thickly-grown woods?

She ventured to raise her head a little to ease the stiffness and saw the buckskinned-covered leg and moccasin-covered foot of one of the other Indians riding along side her. Phina squeezed her eyes shut and tried to prepare herself for whatever might happen once the horse stopped.

As if she'd summoned it by her thoughts the horse

stopped and the Indian threw his leg over her and jumped off. She started to rise but someone grabbed her legs without care and yanked her off the horse, leaving her to fall to the ground. She screamed and caught herself as best she could with her hands, the weight of her body wrenching her wrist painfully.

Without prelude strong arms whipped her over on her back and a man threw his body on top of her. Phina kicked, screamed, scratched and hit at the three Indians who tried to subdue her. Too late she realized they were only playing with her so she would use up her strength, making it easy for them to rape her.

Phina lay panting for breath. One man held her arms above her head, another held her legs apart while the third straddled her stomach. Four other red men, all shirtless with long black hair, watched and laughed from the sidelines.

The one straddling her leaned forward and said, "White woman."

He smiled at her and Phina wanted to scream but she had no more voice. He pressed a darkly-tanned hand to his bare chest and said, "Me get white woman."

"No!" she screamed. "Leave me alone!"

A hand struck her hard across the face, darkness threatened to consume her. Terrified and unable to do more Phina closed her eyes until she felt him pulling down her drawers. Humiliation summoned strength she didn't know she had and she started kicking and fighting again, screaming for the hands to stop pawing and groping at her. Suddenly guttural sounds flew from the Indian's mouth and he slapped her across the face twice, snapping her head from side to side.

"Bloody white woman! Bloody white woman!" She

343

understood him to say as he jumped off her. He must have realized she had her monthly flow. He spoke angrily to the others in their language. Phina feared for her life.

A moccasined foot landed in her ribs, lifting her off the ground. Another came right behind it catching her in the back of the head, then another and another. Phina screamed. Feet pounded her hands and arms as she tried to protect her head. She cried out in pain. Blow after blow struck her as she curled into a little ball, until blessedly she passed out.

Chapter Twenty-three

Phina awakened to pain. It throbbed in her chest, her face and one leg. She awakened to fear robbing her of breath. She'd been captured by Indians and beaten unconscious because they didn't want to rape her while she had her monthly flow. Never before had she been happy to have the curse, but she was at this moment.

Lying prone with her cheek resting on cold, wet ground, she gathered her thoughts and her senses. Her eyes felt dry and swollen. Afraid of what she might see, she had to open them. Her lashes fluttered upward. There was no light. She blinked several times to make sure her eyes had opened. There was no light. Denying the pain that made her want to cry out Phina lifted her head and looked up at where the sky was supposed to be. There was no light. No stars. No moon. She tried to call out but she made no sound. She opened her eyes wider, searching for even the merest hint of shadowy light to appear out of the complete darkness that surrounded her. None did. Her breaths became shallow gasps. She had to be alive. There was too much pain in her body for her to be dead. Fear shocked through her. The Indians must have blinded her. She tried again to scream but made only a slight whimper as intense pain shot up her leg when she tried to move it.

Sounds—talking—laughter—mumblings disturbed Phina's sleep. She wanted to call out for Tasma to be quiet. She had a headache. Her chest hurt every time she breathed in and there was something wrong with her leg. It hurt so badly she wanted to cry. She was stiff, damp and cold. Tasma continued to mumble. Phina couldn't understand what she was saying and she was too tired to tell her to be quiet.

A man's loud laughter made Phina's eyes pop open. In front of her she saw bare-chested men with long black hair seated around a campfire. Memory came rushing back. Indians! Her first thought was that she had to run. She had to get away. But staying perfectly still her gaze searched her surroundings. The firelight cast shadows of the Indians against the walls and after blinking several times Phina realized she wasn't out-side. She lay face down in a cave, and the Indians were between her and the door. Smoke from their campfire hung in the air above their heads and the smell of wood smoke mixed with burned meat. Her stomach recoiled from the noxious odors.

She continued her visual inspection of her captivity. Formations on the cave's ceiling hung eerily above her like swords—like horns—like snakes—like knives ready to fall into her body and cut off her life.

With clarity she remembered being struck on the head with a club, the wild ride over the back of a horse and feet kicking her as she lay upon the ground. No wonder she hurt in so many places. Her eyes open to mere slits, she watched the Indians. They were eating, talking in their strange language, and occasionally laughing. Her stomach contracted as she watched them enjoying their meal. Her tongue was thick and her mouth dry. If she asked for water would they give it to her?

No, she decided after a few moments. They had wanted only one thing from her and when they realized it was her time of the month, they had kicked her until she passed out. Better to remain quiet, she thought.

Maybe they thought her dead. Maybe they intended to keep her until her monthly was over, then rape her. She squeezed her eyes shut at that thought. What was she to do? She hurt so badly she couldn't move an inch without wanting to cry out in pain. How could she defend herself if they tried to rape her again?

When she was bouncing on that horse, she remembered thinking Whitley would find her. Now she knew he wouldn't. They had traveled too far, hidden too well in the depth of the cave. At the realization that Whitley wouldn't find her, she was too overwhelmed to live through the pain, through whatever fate the Indians had in store for her. If she could manage to reach up and break off one of the hanging formations that spread over her like a blanket ready to cover her, she could end her pain, her consuming fear.

But Phina thought of Whitley again. She saw his smiling face telling her he loved her. She saw her mother's pale face as she kissed her goodbye when she'd left for Georgia. She saw the gardens she'd brought back to life at Carillon. The glory of all she held dear flashed across her mind. She turned her head and looked at the Indians, eating, talking, laughing enjoying life. No, she wouldn't give up without a fight. She had too much to live for.

For now she'd remain still and quiet, hoping they would think her dead or unconscious. Whitley had said Indians always make their raids at daybreak. If that were the case they should be leaving soon. She had no fear they'd take her with them. She'd only be in their way. Once they left, she'd crawl over to the campfire and look for any food or water they might have left. If she were going to have any strength to fight them she had to have nourishment.

She needed to check her leg, too. She didn't know if it was broken or badly bruised. She only knew it hurt intensely. Phina was stiff, sore and in pain, but she played it safe and didn't move. If the Indians knew she was awake, they might attack her again before she could get away. She closed her eyes and rested.

Phina awakened to a large hand covering her mouth. She grabbed for the hand and tried to scream.

"Shh. It's me, Spiker."

Earlier she thought she'd heard Tasma and now she thought she heard Spiker. Phina clawed at the hand covering her mouth and tried to kick but the pain in one of her legs was so great she felt like retching.

"Miss Phina! It's me. Spiker!"

Phina opened her eyes and saw the white of Spiker's eyes. She stopped fighting. Spiker? "Spiker!" she managed to say in a hoarse whisper.

"Yes, Miss Phina, it's me."

She tried to rise but her body was so badly bruised she only managed to whimper.

"What's wrong? Where do you hurt? How did the Indians get you?" he asked.

It was so dark in the cave she could only make out his eyes. She heard his friendly voice and warm hand on her shoulder. Suddenly she wanted to grab hold to both and not let go. "H-hold me, Spiker," she whispered.

"I—I—don't know if it's right that I do that, Miss Phina. You don't like for me to touch you."

Phina understood his reluctance. Many times over the last few months she'd told him not to touch her. "Please, Spiker. Hold me. I'm c—cold and frightened."

Spiker settled on his knees and carefully slipped his hands under her arms, lifted her by the shoulders, and pressed her against his chest. He was warm, strong. She wanted to cry with joy, with relief, with pain. But instead she managed to simply relish the immediate safety of his arms.

"What happened? How did the Indians get you?" he asked again.

"They attacked Carillon." She felt him tense.

"Did they hurt anybody else? Where's Mr. Whitley?"

"I'm not sure. Fire. I remember there was fire." She didn't want to whimper but the pain in her leg and chest consumed her. "Do you have water?"

"No, Miss Phina, not with me, but the river is right outside. I'll go get you some."

"No!" She clung to him, shivering at the thought of him leaving her.

"It's all right, Miss Phina. I watched the Indians ride away just a few minutes ago. I was hiding in another cave when I heard them ride up. I looked out and saw them throw you on the ground, then start kicking you. I knew I couldn't take them all on so I decided to stay in hiding and try to get them one at a time. I watched them hide their horses in the big cave. I came running as soon as they left."

"They're gone?"

"They are right now. That's why I have to get you out of here before they come back. It'll be daylight soon. Come on. I'll help you up."

Phina tried to rise but cried out in pain and fell back into Spiker's arms, panting for a pain-free breath. She lay her cheek against his chest and rested. He held her firmly but without no pressure, giving her the reassurance she needed. "I think my leg is broken," she whispered between gasps. "Maybe some ribs, too. I don't know. It hurts too bad to move, Spiker."

"That's all right, Miss Phina. I'll carry you back to Carillon."

Phina tried to laugh but only a funny sounding grunt came out of her mouth. She didn't know how far they were from Carillon, but she remembered riding on that horse for what seemed like hours. "How far are we from Carillon?" she asked.

"Twenty or twenty-five miles the way I know. Longer by horse."

Despair settled over her. "You can't carry me that far."

"I'm strong. I'll make it." He shifted her in his arms. "Lean against this wall while I get you some water. I promise I'll be right back."

Phina wanted to cling to him. It was ironic that three months ago she told him if he touched her again she'd scratch his eyes out and now she didn't want him to let her go. But she needed water so she allowed him to help her lean against the cave wall. The cold dampness of the stone penetrated her dress. The river that ran just below the caverns must be the reason they were so wet. Even though it hurt to move, she felt better now that she wasn't lying with her ribs on the hard ground. She could see the opening of the cave spilling the first shreds of light into the mouth. This cave looked to be much larger than the one she'd shared with Whitley just a few days ago.

A thorough examination of her body told her that she was bruised and swollen in several places from her forehead to her feet. There was damage to her ribs and one of her hands and one of the bones in her left leg was broken above the ankle. She still wore her dress and drawers but her shoes were missing. She didn't know when they were taken off or what had happened to her leg. She wouldn't be running or walking away from this cave. "Oh, Spiker," she whispered desperately, letting her head roll back and forth across the cold, hard limestone of the cave walls. "How are we going to get out of here?"

A shadow appeared in front of the opening. She tensed. Spiker bent over and walked through. He carried the water in a deeply cupped piece of bark from a tree. Spiker helped her to drink. At first she sipped the water, but it went down so easily she greedily finished it off.

"You want some more?"

She wiped her lips with her tongue and shook her head. "That was enough for now." She tried to take a deep breath but it hurt too badly. "Spiker, you're going to have to go for help. You've got to go find Whitley and bring him back to get me."

The whites of Spiker's eyes became clearer. "I'm not leaving you here. Mr. Whitley—"

"Spiker, I can't walk. I would only slow you down so that the Indians could overtake us. They have horses and would look for us. Are you hurt anywhere? Can you run?"

"I'm fine, Miss Phina. And I can run fast, but I can't leave you in this cave for the Indians to come back and get."

"How long will it take you to run the twenty-five miles back to Carillon?"

"Four or five hours maybe. That's about how long it took me to get here, but I wasn't running all the way."

"Then you should have time to make it to Carillon and get back here before dark."

"I can get back with help before dark, but I don't think we can make it back here before the Indians return. Miss Phina I can't leave you here."

Phina swallowed hard and said, "I don't think the Indians will bother me for a couple of more days. They'll wait until—well," she paused and reached out into the darkness and found his hand, holding it between hers. "Spiker, I can't walk. You'd have to carry me every step of the way. You can run to Carillon and the trip back will be twice or three times as fast because you'll be on horseback. Now, we're wasting time talking."

"I can't go back to Carillon without you, Miss Phina. Mr. Whitley might not shoot me if I have you in my arms, but he's sure to kill me on the spot because I killed Cush. He might not give me time to tell him about you."

"That's fear talking, Spiker, and I won't have it. You know Whitley's not going to kill you. Nobody blames you for Cush's death. Everyone knows it was self-defense. They found the piece of rope he was trying to strangle you with still in his hand." She pulled up her dress, showing her dirty blood-stained petticoat. "Here, tear off a piece of this and no one will doubt that you know where I am."

He procrastinated. "Mr. Whitley won't like me leaving you here for the Indians to come back and find. I'm going to take you to another cave."

"You said they put their horses in. How many caves are there?"

"At least ten that I know of, but some of the others aren't as big. I'll hide you in one of those. There are a lot of chambers in all the caves."

Phina took a deep breath. "All right, let's go." She reached up and grabbed hold of the sharpest formation. Spiker helped her pull and twist until the stalactite broke away. She hid the weapon in the folds of her skirt.

"I won't let you down," he promised, then reached down and picked her up and hurried out of the cave.

Phina's chest heaved, tightened, hurt as she held the sobs at bay. She hated to see Spiker go. His presence made her feel safer. But she knew they'd never make it to Carillon alive if Spiker tried to carry her. The Indians would hunt them down and kill them.

"Hurry, Spiker," she whispered. "Hurry!"

Sun beat hotly on his back. He craved a drop of water. Spiker had stopped running more than an hour ago when he'd pushed himself beyond his endurance and had fallen to the ground. As soon as he was able to put one foot in front of the other he was on his way again. He'd hoped for a traveler to pass by so he could send word on to Whitley but the news of the Indian attack must have warned everyone off the roads.

Spiker didn't know how much time had passed but

353

the sun was well on its way to noon when he crested a rise and saw the valley leading to the slaves quarters nestled below. His heart lifted. Suddenly he felt stronger. His pace picked up and he ran to the bottom of the hill. He knew Miss Phina said Mr. Whitley didn't want to hang him. Mr. Whitley hadn't wanted to whip him either, but he had to in order to keep the respect of the slaves. Still he took the piece of petticoat out of his pocket and let it wave from his hand.

The quarters were quiet as he entered from the south section. At first it didn't bother him. He assumed everyone was out in the fields or tending their chores, or looking for Miss Phina. The stillness gripped him with fear as he ran down the main road in front of the cabins. Tired and thirsty, he couldn't think clearly. Maybe the Indians had captured them all. What if they'd done to Tasma what they'd wanted to do to Miss Phina? What if they'd kicked her after she'd just lost her baby? He'd kill every one of them if they'd touched her.

He ran faster and called, "Tasma! Tasma!"

As he rounded the corner Tasma, Rubra and some of the other women came rushing out of the meeting-house. Relief surged within him when he saw Tasma was unharmed. He grabbed her by the shoulders as he came to a halt and pulled her to him, hassling for breath. "I—I thought the I—Indians had gotten you." His mouth was so dry he could hardly speak. He wrapped his arms around Tasma, letting her absorb some of his weight. Her slim arms circled his back, reassuring him, comforting him. He pulled her closer, gaining strength from her.

"Spiker, you came back to me. Yous home," Tasma

354

cried. "I's so worried 'bout you. Why you run away like dat?"

Spiker knew he didn't have time to talk to Tasma. He didn't even have time to rest. He had to find Mr. Whitley and get back to Miss Phina.

"Yous came back jest in time, Spiker," Rubra said. "We all needs you here ta look afta us."

Spiker wasn't sure he believed what he just heard. Surely Rubra didn't mean the slaves needed him. Taking a deep breath he set Tasma away from him. "Where's Mr. Whitley?"

Rubra's eyes rounded in outrage. "He's out looking fo' dem Injuns. Dey hit Chatalene over de head and took Miss Phina wid 'em. All de men out lookin'. Ain't no one here but us womenfolk."

"I need some water," he said, still trying to get his breathing calmed.

Tasma turned to one of the other women who'd followed them out of the meetinghouse. "Get him some water. Bread too. He looks half starved."

Spiker had to think. What was he to do? He couldn't wait until Mr. Whitley came home. He had to get Miss Phina away from those Indians. "Didn't Mr. Whitley leave anyone here to help protect you?" Spiker asked, looking from Rubra to Tasma.

"He left us a gun. Tole us ta shoot dem Injuns if dey came back," Tasma told him.

"Mr. Whitley even took all dey boys dat was big enough ta ride. Ain't nobody heah but us and a few chilens. Deys all out lookin' fo' her."

"I know where she is."

Gasps sounded from the women gathered outside the meetinghouse.

"I've got to get a wagon and go after her. She's hurt too bad to walk."

"Oh, holy saints," Rubra wailed. "What's we gone do?"

"Send one of de boys to ring da bell on de front lawn," Tasma spoke up immediately, taking charge. "Maybe Mr. Whitley's close 'nuff to hear it. I'll go wid Spiker ta get Miss Phina."

Spiker was proud of Tasma's courage but he couldn't let her go. "No," he said, taking her by the shoulders. "The Indians are too dangerous. Besides, I know you're still weak from losing your baby."

"I's fine," she said firmly. "Tell him, Mama. I'm goin'."

Rubra's eyes widened. "I's don't wants you goin' where those Injuns are!"

One of the younger girls handed Spiker a cup of water and a piece of bread. He drained the cup in a couple of seconds and asked for more. As he ate the bread he said, "We're wasting time. Rubra, if any of the men come back you tell them to find Mr. Whitley and tell him that Miss Phina is in one of the big caves down by the Chipola River and that I've gone after her. I'm going to take a wagon."

"I's tell de first rider who comes in ta go find Mr. Whitley and get him ta dat cave."

"I'm goin' up to de big house and get de medicines fo' Miss Phina. I's meet you at de top of de hill," Tasma said.

Spiker grabbed her arm. "I said you weren't going. I don't want you to get hurt. I can't look after you and Miss Phina too."

"It's my job ta look afta Miss Phina." She yanked her arm away and took off. Calling back over her shoulder she said, "Get dat wagon ready. I's be waitin' at de hill."

Rubra shook her head. "I's never could control dat girl." A low moan issued from Rubra as she looked at Spiker. "Take care of my girl."

Spiker nodded. "Get some blankets for Miss Phina while I harness the horses."

The sun was hanging midway down the western sky by the time Tasma and Spiker pulled the wagon to a stop about half a mile from the cave where he'd left Phina. Spiker had pushed the horses as hard as he dared. Tasma had told him to go faster but he knew he had to reserve some of the team's strength or they'd never make it back to Carillon.

Tasma clutched her bag of medicines as Spiker helped her down from the wagon. "Leave that here," he said. "We're not going to be in that cave long enough for you to tend her there. You can do that on the way back. Just stay quiet and stay behind me and walk as quietly as possible."

Tasma nodded silently.

Spiker didn't see any sign that the Indians had returned as he peered over a vine-covered boulder, looking at the entrance to the cave where he'd left Phina. He waited and listened. All was quiet.

"Where is she? I can't see anything," Tasma whispered, looking over Spiker's shoulder.

"There," he spoke softly as he pointed with his finger. "Between those two yellow pines is an opening that leads into the cave. It's a big cave."

Tasma sighed. "You de smartest man in de world, Spiker. Nobody else coulda found Miss Phina like you did. Mr. Whitley gone be so proud of you."

Her words made him feel good, but still he said, "Not since I killed Cush."

"Hush yore mouth. Dat man tried ta kill you, Spiker. Everybody knows dat. Mr. Whitley done said there won't be no punishment."

Spiker looked over his shoulder and smiled at her. He just might enjoy having Tasma for his woman if Mr. Whitley decided not to punish him for killing Cush. "You stay here. I'll go get her."

Tasma's eyes rounded in horror. "I's not staying heah by myself where de Injuns can get me. I's goin' wid you."

"All right. Let's go."

As they approached the cave, Tasma darted ahead of Spiker and rushed into the cave entrance. "Tasma!" he called softly and hurried in behind her just in time to see an arrow as it was released from a bow, landing in Tasma's side just above her waist. Tasma never made a sound as she fell wide-eyed to the ground.

"No!" Spiker yelled.

The Indian reached over his shoulder for another arrow. Spiker saw Phina raise up behind the renegade and hit him on the back with a large piece of rock formation. Dazed, the Indian knocked her away with the back of his hand, giving Spiker enough time to reach him. He grabbed the Indian by the neck and lifted him off the ground. Even though Spiker was much larger than the renegade, the Indian fought hard. In the end he was no match for Spiker's strength. Spiker's thumbs squeezed into the hollow of the Indian's throat until he stopped struggling, until he stopped kicking, until he stopped breathing, then Spiker let him drop to the ground.

Phina had managed to crawl to where Tasma lay by the time Spiker got to her.

"I'm gone die. I knows I'm gone die," she was saying to Phina as Spiker knelt beside her.

Seeing the arrow protruding from Tasma's side renewed Spiker's anger. He wanted to kill the Indian again.

"You're not going to die," Phina whispered softly. "Whitley showed me how to take arrows out, remember. But we have to get out of here first. The rest of the Indians will be back soon."

"Am I gone die, Spiker?" she asked, looking at him with fearful eyes and trembling lips.

He looked down and brushed a shaky hand across her forehead. "Not as long as I'm alive, sweet honey. I'm going to take care of you."

"Where's Whitley?" Phina asked, glancing up at him.

"I didn't see him. He was out looking for you. I told Rubra where to find us. She'll tell him."

"Did you bring horses?"

"I've got a wagon hidden about a half a mile from here. We brought medicine."

"Good. She's going to need it. Take Tasma to the wagon first. Try not to jar her too much. We don't want her losing any more blood."

Spiker looked around the cave. "Where are the rest of the Indians?"

"I—I don't know. I guess they're searching all the caves, trying to find me. Get Tasma to the wagon and hurry back to get me before the others show up."

Phina watched as Spiker gently lifted Tasma from the ground, talking softly to her as he hurried out of the cave. She was afraid the others would return at any moment. Phina looked back at the dead Indian. She couldn't walk, but she could crawl and follow Spiker. She couldn't wait for him to come back into the cave to get her. Every inch of ground she covered would put them that much closer to getting away before the others returned and found their comrade.

With small pebbles and twigs scratching her palms, feet and legs, Phina started crawling out of the cave. The bright sunlight hurt her eyes as she emerged from the semidarkness. She looked around at the lush under growth of shrubs and bushes and trees. She had no idea which direction Spiker had taken. If she crawled the wrong way he might not find her. Her spirits sagged and she rested her face on her arms, praying the Indians wouldn't return before they could get away.

The rustling sounds of leaves and footsteps alerted Phina that someone was approaching. She raised her head and held her breath until Spiker appeared. Relief made her weak. It looked as if they were going to get away before the Indians returned.

"Miss Phina, what are you doing out here in the open?"

"I was going to follow you but I didn't know which way you went."

"It's just as well. You're already hurt bad enough." He fell to his knees beside her and reached to scoop her up in his arms as the sound of galloping horses sounded in the distance. Phina and Spiker looked at each other.

"Hurry!" she said.

Spiker rose with her in his arms and took only a couple of steps before his foot caught in a vine and he stumbled, sending them both crashing to the ground. Phina tried not to cry out from the spiraling burning

360

pain that shot through her as she landed shoulders first onto the ground. Within seconds Spiker was beside her, lifting her into his arms once again. "No!" she cried. "Leave me and get back to Tasma. You can't save all of us."

His eyes were wild with determination, his words breathless as he said, "I'm not leaving you, Miss Phina."

He rose to his feet as the first of the Indians came into view, not fifty yards from them. Spiker turned to run. But the sound of horses coming toward them stopped him.

"It's too late. We're surrounded," Spiker said in a tired voice. "I'm sorry, Miss Phina."

"Drop me! If you run fast maybe you can save Tasma and yourself."

"I'm not leaving," he said resolutely. Phina was going to throw herself out of his arms and force him to go when she saw men on the horses coming toward them. It was Whitley!

Crying out with joy she said, "Look!" Whitley and about twenty slaves were galloping toward them. Gunfire rang out. Spiker held tightly to Phina and moved toward the safety of a tree. After shooting off a few arrows, the Indians saw they were outnumbered. Whooping and hollering, they retreated.

The renegades disappeared into the thick forest surrounding the caves, Whitley and the slaves chasing them. Spiker didn't wait for instructions. He took off running toward the wagon.

Chapter Twenty-four

His hat and oilskin didn't keep Whitley from feeling damp as he rode in the drizzling rain to The Pines. As soon as word was out that the Indians had been captured and turned over to government officials by Sheriff Abe Pelham, George Matheson had sent for his wife and daughter. Yesterday, Flannery had sent word she was home. Whitley didn't want to wait to see her. The sooner he told her he couldn't marry her the better.

He pulled his hat down lower over his face, content to let his horse pick his way over the muddy ground. It had been more than a week since they'd found Phina and caught the Indians. Whitley and the slaves had chased them into a ravine. Whitley's first shot had apparently killed their leader because the others had thrown down their bows and arrows. Jasper, Spiker and Whitley had each killed one of the renegades before the rest were captured.

In time, Phina was going to be all right, but the doctor still wasn't sure about Tasma. The arrow had embedded itself deep in thick muscles and tissue of her side. The doctor had a hell of a time removing it. She lost a lot of blood, and now she'd had fever the last three days. The wound was inflamed and festering.

Whitley had made sure the doctor gave Phina something to make her sleep most of the time. When she was awake she was in pain. Not only had she been severely beaten, the Indians had broken her leg and cracked a couple of her ribs, and sprained her wrist.

His hands tightened on the reins as he thought about how they'd treated her. If Abe hadn't been riding with them and stopped him he would have killed them all.

When he'd caught up with the wagon he rode in it with Phina and Tasma all the way back to Carillon, encouraging Spiker to go faster. Phina had insisted they hadn't raped her. At first he didn't believe her, thinking she was too distraught and humiliated to admit it, but when she explained he was overcome with relief. The wounds she had now would heal. If they'd raped her she might have been lost to him forever.

He'd spent every night in a chair beside Phina's bed. Now he had to tell Flannery that's where he belonged. Beside Phina. When he'd heard the Indians had captured her one thing had become very clear to him. Nothing was more important to him than Phina. Not even Carillon. Now he knew what he had to do. And it all started right here at The Pines. After he settled this, he'd ride into town.

Whitley dismounted in front of the stately four-pillared home of the Mathesons. He handed the reins over to the darkie who ran up to meet him.

"Good afta'noon, Mr. Whitley," he said, rain running down his face.

"Afternoon, Hirsh."

363

"We's heard 'bout you killing dem Injuns. We's all proud as we can be of dat."

"Killing a man isn't anything to be proud of. You remember that." What Whitley told the young man and what he felt were two different things. After he'd seen what the Indians had done to Phina he'd wanted to kill them all.

He took the six steps up to the porch of the grand home, two at a time, then removed his oilskin, hat and gloves and laid them in a chair before knocking. Moses met him at the door and asked him to wait in the gallery while he went to tell the Mathesons Whitley was there. After the usual ten minute wait Moses came back and Whitley followed him into the parlor. Some things never changed. Bertha and Flannery sat in their appointed places but George was missing.

"Whitley, how good to see you," Bertha said, smiling. "We didn't expect you to call this soon. We only sent word we were back yesterday. Do sit down."

"I know." He settled himself in the wing back chair. "And I'm sorry I didn't give you longer to rest from your trip." He turned to Flannery. Obviously, the trip away from The Pines had been good for her. She was more beautiful than ever. And he was more convinced than ever before that she was not the woman he wanted to spend the rest of his life with. Not for Anchor. Not for anyone. "Flannery, you're looking very beautiful today."

She smiled and batted her fan. "Thank you, Whitley. Mama and I had a wonderful time. We heard of your heroic escapades. We were so pleased you weren't harmed. Isn't that right, Mama."

"Oh my, yes. And Flannery's right. We had a wonderful time. We picked out some of the most beautiful fabrics for her new dresses and gowns."

They hadn't said very many words but Whitley had already heard enough. It angered him that they didn't ask about Phina or Tasma. Surely they'd heard that both the women had been hurt. He turned to Bertha, eager to get this visit over with. "Mrs. Matheson, I know it's highly irregular but might I please have a few minutes alone with Flannery."

"Oh, dear." She clasped her hand to her breasts.

"Please. I assure you I only want to talk to her. I promise I'll not move from this chair."

She smiled and rose from the sofa. "Very well, but only for a minute or two. I'll go see about getting you something to drink."

As soon as she was out the door Flannery said coyly, "Whitley, I do believe you intend to ruin my reputation in spite of everything I do to keep you from it."

He leaned forward. "No, Flannery. I know how important your reputation is to you. That's why I'm here to withdraw my offer of your hand in marriage. I'll pay whatever your father deems acceptable for breaking our engagement." Much to his surprise there was no shock in her expression, only irritated resignation.

"I assume you haven't settled things with that dreadful woman in your house. Papa told me he thought as much."

Whitley bristled but was determined not to let it show. "I've settled some things. I now believe she's Anchor's daughter, although I haven't told her that yet."

She threw her fan onto the settee and rose. "Then

365

don't. She doesn't have to know. I'm sure you can talk the judge into seeing things your way. It's acceptable behavior from someone of your position in the community."

He stood and faced her. "It's not acceptable to me. I want her to know. Flannery." He waited for her to look at him. "I love her. I want to marry her."

She gasped. Stunned, she blinked rapidly. "You're not serious."

"I'm very serious. I wanted to marry you for all the wrong reasons. I wanted to—"

Flannery spun away from his penetrating gaze and Whitley stopped. He knew she didn't love him. He hadn't expected this to hurt her.

After a moment she turned back to face him. "Well, no matter. There are other men in the county as wealthy as you and with considerably fewer problems. I have to maintain a certain position in life, you know."

Whitley almost smiled. He knew. "I understand completely. You're place in society has always been your top priority."

"What else is there?"

He could have said love and caring for others. The kinds of things he found in Phina, but he knew she'd scoff at those. "Should we wait until your father returns to tell your parents we won't be getting married?"

"No." Her full lips pouted. "I'd rather tell them in my own way. You don't mind, do you? I won't say anything bad about you, but I must tell them that I'm the one who rejected you because of all your problems at Carillon."

"For you're reputation?"

366

She nodded.

"I'm sure you'll say the perfect things, and I'll never contradict you, Flannery."

She smiled. "Thank you."

Whitley nodded and turned away. He picked up his pace as he walked down the gallery to the front door. His next stop was town.

It was late in the evening when Whitley made it back to Carillon. He was wet and tired, but he'd never felt better. No one could have loved and respected Anchor more than he had. And if he was to stay true to what was best for Carillon, doing what Anchor would have wanted he knew he had to renounce all claim to Carillon and agree that Phina was Anchor's daughter. He'd told Robert to draw up the papers stating just that. He planned to go back into town in a couple of days and pick up the papers and give them to Phina when she was feeling better.

Chatalene was sitting by Phina's bed when he walked into her room. A lamp burned low, casting dark shadows around the room. She rose from the chair when Whitley entered.

"How is she?" he whispered, looking down at Phina lying peacefully on white sheets. The swelling in her face had gone down but the bruises were still a dark purple.

"Much better. I's washed her and helped her into a clean gown, then she ate all her soup and drank two cups of tea."

"Good. Any word on Tasma?"

"Rubra said her fever's down ta'day. Spiker, he still wid her."

He nodded. "I'm glad. You go home. I'll stay with Phina tonight."

Chatalene turned away and Whitley walked closer to Phina's bed. Her coloring was better, her lips not so pale. He bent down and softly kissed her cheek. She stirred.

Phina's eyes fluttered open. "Whitley."

"Shh—" he said, caressing her forehead. "I didn't mean to wake you."

"I'm glad you're home." She took hold of his hand, carried it to her lips and kissed it.

"I had some business to take care of."

"Chatalene told me. I've been waiting for you to return. I couldn't remember if I'd thanked you for saving my life."

He smiled. "About a dozen times since you got home. And I keep telling you. Spiker saved your life. He found you."

"But the Indians had surrounded us and you came riding up just in time."

He smiled. "I want you to get some sleep."

Phina raised up on her elbows. Her long dark hair cascaded over her pillow. "I've been doing nothing but sleeping for over a week now. I don't want to sleep any more. I told Chatalene not to give me any more of that stuff the doctor left. It makes me sleep too much."

"That's what you're supposed to do. It takes the pain away."

"I'm feeling better. My ribs aren't as sore and my leg doesn't hurt continuously anymore."

He knelt down beside her. "I'm glad. I wish I could have stopped the Indians from hurting you." He swallowed hard. "I have something for you." He reached

368

into his shirt and pulled out a small package. "Want me to open it for you?"

She nodded.

Whitley carefully unwrapped the gift he'd picked up at the mercantile when he was in town and showed her the four combs carved out of ivory.

"Oh, Whitley, thank you!" Her eyes lighted with glee. "They're the most beautiful combs I've ever seen." She fingered them lovingly. "I saw them the day Spiker took me to town, but I didn't have enough money to buy them. I wanted them so badly. The lady in the mercantile must have told you."

He shook his head. "No. I went in to buy you some rose water and saw these behind the counter. I knew they would look beautiful in your hair."

Phina laid the combs on the night table and reached up and touched his cheek. "Come lie with me," she whispered.

"I'm wet. It's been raining most of the day. Let me change and I'll be back."

"No." She gripped his hand and looked into his eyes. "Don't go. Just take your wet clothes off and join me." She turned him loose and held back the sheet.

His eyes searched her face. "Phina, I don't think that's a good idea."

"It's what I want. Join me."

Not wanting to disappoint her, Whitley shrugged out of his wet clothes. She watched him. He watched her. When he was completely naked he slipped into bed beside her, careful not to touch her leg. She was warm and soft as he snuggled up against her. "I don't want to hurt your ribs or bump your leg," he whispered as he kissed the soft skin of her neck, just below her ear.

369

She slipped her arms around him. "I need you to hold me. I need to know that everything is all right between us."

"Yes, Phina. I love you and as soon as you're well enough I want to marry you. That hasn't changed. It's not going to change."

"I love you, too," she whispered against his lips as her hands ran up and down his back.

Whitley's arousal showed in the tremble in his hand and by his hardness lying between them. "I was so frightened when I thought I'd lost you, Phina. I went through hell trying to find you." He kissed her mouth, her cheeks, her forehead, her neck, loving her with his lips and his tongue.

"Do my kisses hurt?"

"No, they feel wonderful. I don't want you to stop." She wrapped her arms around his neck. "I was so afraid you wouldn't find me. I thought I was going to die. I didn't want to die."

"Don't think about that now. It's over." His hands pressed her close, running up and down her arms, over her back. "Just think about my hands on you. Think about my lips on yours." He kissed her deeply, probing her mouth with his tongue. "Does that take away all your fears?"

"Mmm—that's wonderful," she answered dreamily. "I want you to love me, Whitley."

"Oh, Phina, I want to love you, believe me. But I don't want to hurt you. You're not well enough."

Phina slipped her hands down between them and cupped his penis in her hands. Whitley gasped with pleasure. "I'll let you know if you hurt me."

* * *

370

The next day Phina and Whitley were married by the preacher from the church on the outskirts of town. Whitley tried to get her to wait until she was feeling better but she insisted. At the end of the ceremony the preacher pronounced them Mr. and Mrs. Whitley McCabe. They took the name with pride and felt confident that Anchor would have approved of the man he treated like a son marrying the daughter he never knew he had.

Three days later, Phina was sitting on the front porch with her leg propped up enjoying the midafternoon sunshine when she saw a rider coming up the tree-lined lane. For a moment she tensed, remembering the incident with the Indians. She didn't know when she would feel completely safe again. As the rider approached she realized it was Ellison.

She assumed he'd heard about the Indian attacks and about their marriage and had come as a neighborly gesture.

He dismounted and confidently walked up the steps to the porch, stopping in front of her. Her ready smile and friendly greeting died on her lips when the first words out of his mouth were, "You fell for all his lies, didn't you?"

Phina gasped loudly. "What?" she asked, startled by his accusation and the vehemence she heard in his voice.

He took his hat off and glared at her. "I tried to tell you he only wanted to marry you so that Carillon would be his, but you wouldn't listen to me, would you? You had to marry him."

His tone and his words let her know this wasn't a

visit to try and make amends like she hoped. "I love Whitley and he loves me," she said.

"Oh, I'll agree that you love him, but he doesn't love you, Phina."

Phina felt shaky. "I think you better go."

Ellison laughed. "You swallowed it all, didn't you? All his sweet kisses and words of love. Hell, I was planning to tell you all those things myself. Whitley wanted Carillon. He's always wanted it, and his only sure way of getting it was to marry you."

"I want you to leave," Phina said, stronger than her last plea for him to go. "I don't believe a word you're saying."

"You don't have to believe me." He smiled confidently. "Time will prove me right. Before you married Whitley, the judge would have listened to your claim and would have given you Carillon and Whitley knew it. But now that you're married to him anything that you own belongs to Whitley, including all of Carillon."

"Whitley loves me!" she said, almost rising out of her chair.

"Every man in the county would have loved you for a chance to own Carillon. You've been duped, Phina."

"Stop it! You're only saying these things to get me to doubt my husband."

"I think not." Ellison remained calm, collected. "I've just returned from talking with a lawyer over in Atlanta. Something you should have done a long time ago. Surely before rushing into marriage. According to him, of the three of us, you were the only one who had a real chance at claiming Carillon. Whitley would have lost it all. Robert Higgins would have told Whitley that he didn't have a chance in hell without those signed documents."

"Go away!" she pleaded. "I know my husband loves me."

"He makes love to you. There's a difference, Phina. Most any man who knows how to please a woman can make her think he loves her. Shall I kiss you and caress you to prove it?"

Her throat hurt from holding back tears, holding back all the things she wanted to scream at him. "You're lying. If you don't leave I'm going to call Lon to go get Whitley."

Ellison calmly combed his hair back with his hands. "I'll leave. But don't take my word for anything. I wouldn't want you to do that. Ask Whitley what Robert told him about his chances of winning Carillon in court. If you want to know the truth ask him." Ellison settled his hat on his head and turned away.

Phina trembled as she watched Ellison ride away. Did Whitley marry her only so that he could keep control of Carillon? She had to know for sure. Tears stung her eyes but she wouldn't let them fall.

After a few minutes Lon and Rubra came out and tried to get her to go in and rest but she refused. She wanted to wait for Whitley to come home. At last, by early afternoon, he had returned.

"Rubra told me I'd find you out here. It's good to see you sitting outside," he said as he knelt in front of her. "I checked on Tasma before I came up to the house. She's feeling better. She says Spiker's love brought her through and kept her from dying."

"Knowing Tasma, I'm sure that's true." Her words were stiff, forced. She couldn't make polite conversation when so much more was on her mind.

"Naturally, she wants to come see you, but I told her she'd have to wait until she's better. Her wound is healing, but she's weak from the fever."

Phina nodded automatically, and swallowed hard. Her mind wasn't on Tasma. Looking at her husband's face, she couldn't believe all the things Ellison said. She knew men could make love to women they didn't love. New Orleans had plenty of women for just that purpose.

She moistened her lips. "Whitley, I want to ask you something."

He took hold of her hands and laid them in her lap, but she pulled away from his touch. "What's wrong?" he asked.

It still hurt if she tried to breathe too deeply, especially at times like now. "Did your lawyer, Robert tell you that I would probably win Carillon in court? That you, in fact, had only a slim chance of winning any part of this plantation?"

"Yes, that's true," he agreed easily, and shifted his weight to his other foot. "But, Phina, none of that matters now because we're married. Carillon belongs to both of us."

Phina squeezed her eyes shut for a moment. It mattered to her. Ellison was right. Whitley married her for Carillon, not because he loved her. But deep inside she must have known that. He'd told her many times that he'd do anything to keep Carillon, and that included telling her he loved her. She hadn't wanted to listen to him. She opened her eyes. Tears collected on her lashes.

"Phina, love, what's wrong?" He tried to touch her cheek. She turned away.

"I want you to leave."

374

"What?"

"I want you to leave my presence, my bed, my life." Her voice was husky with emotion.

He rose and looked down at her, an incredulous expression on his face. "What are you talking about? Phina, I love you. You love me. We've already talked this out. I didn't marry you in order to get Carillon."

"Many times, you told me you'd do anything to get this plantation. You can be happy now. You have Carillon but you won't have me." Her words were forced past tightly clenched teeth.

"What caused you to bring this up again? Surely, you're not doubting my love again."

"No," she said earnestly. "You don't love me. You've never loved me. You only married me to get Carillon. I won't let you have it. I won't."

"Phina, you're tired. You've been up too long today. You don't know what you're saying."

"Rubra! Lon!" she called, her voice trembling.

"Phina, stop this and listen to me." He tried to take hold of her hands but she dodged him.

"Don't touch me," she cried. "Please, don't touch me. Live here if you must but don't touch me."

Stunned with disbelief, Whitley backed away from her.

"Miss Phina? Mr. Whitley, what's goin' on out heah?"

Phina wiped her eyes. "Get Lon and help me upstairs. I don't feel very well."

"Mr. Whitley's standin' rights dere. He'll takes you up de stairs."

Phina refused to look at Whitley again. His betrayal hurt too bad. Why hadn't he just asked for a marriage of convenience rather than pretend to love her?

"No. Mr. Whitley was just leaving. Please go get Lon immediately."

Phina lay in her bed all afternoon, miserable, her heart broken. Whitley obviously felt guilty. Rubra told her that he'd ridden off toward town shortly after she came upstairs. She was ready to sink into her pillows and allow herself a good cry when Rubra came bustling into her bedroom.

"Miss Phina, there's a lady here ta see you. She say it's mighty important."

Phina turned her face away from Rubra. "No, I'm not up to seeing anyone. Send her away."

"I's thinks you wants ta see dis one." Rubra pulled back the drapes and late afternoon sunshine filled the room with a warm glow.

"Rubra, please, don't. I don't want all that light in here. I don't want to see anyone."

"Hello, darling."

Phina's gaze flew to the door. Diana Groutas stood in the doorway looking healthier, prettier than Phina had seen her in years.

"Oh, Mama!" She held out her arms, wishing she could jump off the bed and run to the beloved woman. "Mama, how did you get here? How did you know I needed you?" Diana rushed to her daughter's bedside. They hugged and kissed and laughed for several long minutes.

"You're looking wonderful, Mama," Phina said, when she'd wiped away the last joyful tear from her eyes and sent Rubra for tea.

"I'm feeling wonderful. When I got the message from Whitley that you'd been hurt and needed me, I decided it was time to get myself out of that bed. I hadn't been coughing or having fever all summer, but I didn't have the energy to get out of bed and do anything."

"Whitley wrote you and told you I needed you?"

"He sure did." She smiled and fluffed the lace collar of her dress. "I guess he wanted to surprise you. He had one of his darkies deliver the letter straight to me."

"Yes, it is a surprise. That was very kind of him," Phina said softly. He must have sent that letter as soon as she arrived at Carillon after the Indian attack. He should have told her he'd sent for her mother.

"It was more than kind, Phina. I guess you told him I'd just about spent all the money you sent me three months ago. He had a darkie deliver a letter to me that said you'd been in an accident and needed me if I could possibly make the trip. He even sent extra money so I could hire a companion to come with me in case I was too weak to travel on my own."

The pit of Phina's stomach felt empty. Had she really listened to Ellison? Did she really doubt her husband's love? Suddenly she wasn't clear about anything except her love for Whitley. That hadn't changed. But did he love her or did he marry her just to keep control of Carillon?

"Anyway," her mother continued. "I decided to see if another doctor could help me feel better. Irene and Sally asked a doctor from the other side of town to come see me. He said the only thing wrong with me was that I was taking so much laudanum that I didn't have the energy to even get out of bed. He said I should have stopped taking the medication when my fever and cough went away. Naturally, I thought he was just trying to kill me by taking my medicine away. But I knew Whitley wouldn't have sent for me if you hadn't needed me so I took a chance on the new doctor. The old one hadn't done anything for me. The first three or four days I thought I was going to die without that medication, Phina. I was sick. But by the fifth day I was feeling stronger and stronger. That stuff was poisoning me, and I didn't know it. I took the money Whitley sent me, bought a new traveling dress and boarded the stagecoach. Here I am. And just in time it appears. You don't look too good."

Her mother talked fast, but Phina understood and was dazed by her mother's story. It never occurred to her that mother didn't need the medication.

"Now enough about me. I want to know what happened to you. Start at the beginning."

Phina rubbed her forehead and settled against her pillows as Rubra came in with a pot of steaming tea. "Mama, I've got so much to tell you."

Diana took her hands. "I've got plenty of time, Phina. I'm here to stay."

A warm glow spread over Phina. Her spirits lifted, and she smiled. Because of Whitley, her mother was where she'd always belonged—at Carillon.

Phina and her mother had talked into the night. It was clear Diana felt Whitley loved her daughter and that Ellison was simply trying to cause trouble between them. After Diana went to bed and Phina had time to think, she was convinced of the same thing. She'd let a troublemaker turn her against her husband. Why would he have sent for her mother if he didn't love her? He didn't have to do that to get Carillon. He did it because he loved her. Why had she listened to Ellison? Why had she sent Whitley away?

378

When it was clear she couldn't sleep she decided to get out of bed and go to Whitley's room. If she were close to his things maybe she would feel better. He'd been sleeping with her since they married. She'd planned to move into his room when she was able to walk. It was difficult for her to get off the bed with the splint holding her leg straight, but she managed. She hopped over to the chair where the cane Whitley brought her lay. Her leg hurt dreadfully but she would rest better if she was in Whitley's room.

She took the cane and slowly limped her way down to Whitley's room. She opened the door and was startled to see Whitley pop up in bed, his naked chest shining in the moonlight.

"Phina! What the hell are you doing trying to walk on that leg?"

He rushed to her and picked her up and laid her on his bed.

"I didn't know you were home. Rubra told me you'd left, but no one told me you came back."

"I didn't tell anyone. I slipped into the house a few minutes ago. Now what are you doing out of bed and on that leg? Do you want to limp the rest of your life?"

He did care for her. He did love her. She saw it in his eyes, heard it in his voice. How could she have doubted him and believed Ellison? "I couldn't sleep. I thought maybe if I was in your room close to you I could sleep."

"What are you saying, Phina?"

"Forgive me. Forgive me for doubting your love."

Whitley walked over to the dresser and picked up some papers. He struck a match and lit the lamp. "I was going to show you this tomorrow." He handed her the papers. "I asked Robert to draw up this paper

379

renouncing all claim to Carillon before we were married, Phina. I didn't want you to think I was marrying you for this plantation."

"Why didn't you tell me that this afternoon?"

"I thought you needed proof so I rode into town to get it."

"I'm sorry I let Ellison influence me."

"Ellison! Dammit, was he over here bothering you? I should have known he was behind your reaction."

"It wasn't hard for him to convince me. I've always known how much you love this plantation."

Whitley slid into the bed beside her and looked deeply into her eyes. "I do. I'll never deny that, Phina. But I love you more. I'd rather have your love than Carillon."

Phina smiled. "You have us both."

Their lips met and kissed tenderly.

"I think it's time I gave you this." Whitley let a gold chain drop from his hand. A gold bell dangled on the end of it. "This belongs to the mistress of Carillon."

"You had a gold bell made for me," she whispered in surprise.

"No. Anchor gave it to me. The night he told me he was going to make me his son. I wish you could have known him. He was a fine man. Here, let me put it on you."

"I'm pleased to have it. I must have lost the silver one when the Indians attacked—"

"Shh—don't think about that." He fastened the clasp and let the bell drop to her chest. "You look beautiful wearing it." He kissed her again.

"Thank you for the bell." She looked into his eyes, wondering again how she could have allowed Ellison

380

to make her doubt her husband. "And thank you for bringing my mother to Carillon."

He brushed her hair away from her shoulder and reached over and kissed her neck. "She belongs here. I want it to be her home."

Phina's heart swelled with love for her husband.

"I'm afraid we haven't heard the last of Ellison," he said as he stroked her arm affectionately. "He may make good on his threat and take us to court for a share of Carillon."

"I don't think so. He's already seen a lawyer in Atlanta who told him he doesn't have a chance at winning. I think this was his last attempt to break us up."

"He almost did."

"I know and I'm sorry." She looked lovingly into his eyes. "I love you, Whitley McCabe."

"I love you, Phina McCabe."

He pulled her into his arms and kissed her, then made love to her until sunrise.

Author's Note

Twenty-three caves have been mapped at Florida Caverns State Park in Marianna. Northwest Florida is honeycombed with caverns but most of the passages remain underwater because the water table is so high.

Indians are believed to have hidden in these caves on the banks of the Chipola River when General Andrew Jackson explored Spanish Florida in 1818 and later when President Andrew Jackson forced the removal of the Cherokees from Georgia.

PINNACLE BOOKS HAS
SOMETHING FOR EVERYONE —

MAGICIANS, EXPLORERS, WITCHES AND CATS

THE HANDYMAN   (377-3, $3.95/$4.95)
He is a magician who likes hands. He likes their comfortable
shape and weight and size. He likes the portability of the hands
once they are severed from the rest of the ponderous body. Detec-
tive Lanark must discover who The Handyman is before more
handless bodies appear.

PASSAGE TO EDEN   (538-5, $4.95/$5.95)
Set in a world of prehistoric beauty, here is the epic story of a
courageous seafarer whose wanderings lead him to the ends of
the old world — and to the discovery of a new world in the rugged,
untamed wilderness of northwestern America.

BLACK BODY   (505-9, $5.95/$6.95)
An extraordinary chronicle, this is the diary of a witch, a journal
of the secrets of her race kept in return for not being burned for
her "sin." It is the story of Alba, that rarest of creatures, a white
witch: beautiful and able to walk in the human world undetected.

THE WHITE PUMA   (532-6, $4.95/NCR)
The white puma has recognized the men who deprived him of his
family. Now, like other predators before him, he has become a
man-hater. This story is a fitting tribute to this magnificent animal that stands for all living creatures that have become, through
man's carelessness, close to disappearing forever from the face of
the earth.